© Joyce Ravid

Jonathan Rabb is the author of three previous novels: *Rosa*, *The Overseer*, and *The Book of Q*. He lives with his wife, Andra, and two children in Savannah, Georgia.

SHADOW AND LIGHT

LIGHT

JONATHAN RABB

Picador

———

Sarah Crichton Books
Farrar, Straus and Giroux
New York

www.picadorusa.com

Picador® is a U.S. registered trademark and is used by Farrar, Straus and Giroux under license from Pan Books Limited.

For information on Picador Reading Group Guides, please contact Picador.
E-mail: readinggroupguides@picadorusa.com

Designed by Ralph Fowler/rlf design

ISBN 978-0-312-42941-6

First published in the United States by Sarah Crichton Books, an imprint of Farrar, Straus and Giroux

First Picador Edition: April 2010

10 9 8 7 6 5 4 3 2 1

FOR SUSANNAH AND JEREMY

SHADOW AND LIGHT

CHAPTER ONE

1927

THEY SAY IT IS RARE to have good reason to leave Berlin. In the summer you have Wannsee, where the beaches are powdered and cool, and where for a few pfennigs even a clerk and his girl can manage a cabana for the day. The cold months bring the Ice Palast up near the Oranienburger Gate, or a quick trip out to Luna Park for the rides and amusements, where a bit of cocoa and schnapps can keep a family warm for the duration. And always there is that thickness of life in the east, where whiskey (if you're lucky) and flesh (if not too old) play back and forth in a careless game of half-conscious decay. No reason, then, to leave the city with so much to keep a hand occupied.

And yet she was empty—not truly empty, of course, but thin to the point of concern. A phenomenon had descended on Berlin in early February, something no one could control or predict. Naturally they could explain it, but only in the language of high science and complexity. For the rest, it was simply *Weisserhimmel*—white sky—days on end of a too-bright sun without the sense to generate a trace of heat. Every forty years or so, it came as a faint reminder of the city's Nordic past, but history was not what Berliners chose to see. They were unnerved, their world made too clear, and so they left: businesses took unexpected holidays, schools indefinite recesses. It would all pass in a few days' time, but in the meanwhile, only the stalwarts were keeping the city alive.

Still, a few hours on the outskirts of town could do wonders. The sun might have been no less forgiving, but at least the surroundings were unfamiliar for a reason. Nonetheless, Nikolai Hoffner continued to glance into his rearview mirror as he drove. The Berlin he saw seemed compressed, small, her reflection strangely misleading. Even distance was doing little to help. He knew it best not to stare.

Instead, he opened his mouth wide and chanced a look at his teeth; they seemed to shake with the car's motion. The tooth, he had been told, would have to come out. Funny, but it didn't look all that different from the others, a bit thick, crooked, yellowed by tobacco. Hoffner had little faith in doctors, but he believed in pain, and that was enough. He was meant to rub some sort of ointment on his gums every few hours, at least until he could make time for an appointment. He was finding a brandy worked just as well.

The road to Neubabelsberg—the new road to Neubabelsberg—was straight and smooth, and for the price of a few pfennigs had you out to the film studios in less than half an hour. Someone had had the brilliant idea that Berlin needed a racing circuit, an asphalt totem to Mercedes and Daimler and Cadillac—although no one spoke of Cadillac—that ripped through the satiny pine needles and heavenly green leaves of the Grunwald. There had always been something of an escape when it came to the woods and lakes and beaches of the great, untamed forest. Now even that was gone, or going, eighteen kilometers uninterrupted. It seemed to dull everything.

With a quick press of the accelerator, Hoffner decided to test the old car. The exhaust roared and a hum rose as the rubber tires heated on the road. That was always the trick: to smell when they had reached their limit. These had the tang of disarmament surplus, the good military stuff that appeared now and then from some unknown warehouse. Everyone knew not to ask.

A big Buick hooted angrily from behind, and Hoffner checked his mirror again: the car had come from nowhere. He waved the driver on and watched as first the radiator, then the cabin, raced by. The Kriminalpolizei had yet to invest in speed. It would take something else to catch the criminals.

There was a sudden thud to his undercarriage—a parting gift from the Buick—and Hoffner waited for the agonizing scrape of metal on asphalt, but none came. Still, there might have been a puncture, or something wedged in where it wasn't meant to be. Not that Hoffner knew anything about a car's tending-to, but he reckoned he should take a look. After all, he would need a bit of grease on his face and hands to show at least some effort to the boy they would be sending out to tow him.

He brought the car down onto the grass and reached over for the two yellow flags he kept in the glove compartment. It was a pointless exercise—six meters in front, six meters behind—but someone had taken great pains to devise *die Verkehrsnotverfahren* (emergency traffic procedures), the totality of which filled a full eight pages in the bureau's slender handbook on automobile operation: Who was he to question their essentialness? The flags blew aimless warning to the deserted road as Hoffner lay on his back and pulled himself under.

Surprisingly, everything looked to be in working order. Various metal shafts stretched across at odd angles. Metal boxes to hold other metal things were bolted to iron casings, and while there were two or three wires hanging down from their protective covers—each wrapped in some sort of black adhesive—nothing appeared to be torn or strained or even mildly put out. The wood above was worn but whole, and the tires looked somehow thicker from this vantage point. Hoffner imagined much the same might have been said of his own fifty-three-year-old frame: shoulders still wide even if the barrel chest was relocating south with ever-increasing speed. He caught sight of a line of blurred handwriting on one of the tires and slowly inched his way over. Closer in, the scrawl became *Frankreich, Süd, 26117-7-6, Vichy.*

Hoffner smiled. These had been slated for reparations, not surplus, and yet somehow—just somehow—they had failed to make it across the border. In fact, very little these days was making it to the French or English or Belgians or Italians—how the Italians had managed to get in on the spoils, having sided with the Kaiser up through 1915, still puzzled him—except, of course, for the great waves of money. There, things were decidedly different. The French might have been willing to turn a blind eye to a few tires ending up in the service of Berlin's police corps, but if so much as a single pfennig of repayments, or interest on repayments, or interest on the loans taken out to pay for the interest on those repayments went missing, then came the cries from Paris for the occupation of the Rhine and beyond. It was a constant plea in the papers from the ever-teetering Social Democrats to keep our new allies happy, keep the payments flowing out, no matter how many times the mark had to be revalued or devalued or carted around like so many reams of waste tissue just to pay for a bit of bread. Luckily, the worst of it was behind them now, or so said those same papers: who cared if Versailles and its treaty were beginning to prompt some rather unpleasant responses from points far right? Odd, but Hoffner had always thought Vichy in the north.

He slid out, planted himself on the running board, and flipped open his flask. The Hungarians, thank God, had remained loyal to the Kaiser up to the bitter end: little chance, then, of a shortage on slivovitz anytime soon. He took a swig of the brandy and stared out into the green wood as a familiar burning settled in at the back of his throat. A trio of wild boar was digging up the ground no more than twenty meters off. They were a dark brown, and their haunches looked fat and muscular. These had done well to keep the meat on during the winter. The smallest turned and cocked its head as it stared back. No hint of fear, it stood unwavering. Clearly, it knew it was not its place to cede ground. Hoffner marveled at the misguided certainty.

He tossed back a second drink just as a goose-squawk horn rang out from the road. Hoffner turned to see a prewar delivery truck pulling up, its open back packed with small glass canisters, each filled with some sort of blue liquid. Hoffner wondered if perhaps he might have failed to hear about an imminent hair tonic shortage, but the man who stepped from the cab quickly put all such concerns to rest. He was perfectly bald, with a few stray wisps of black matted down above the ears. Hoffner stood as he approached.

"'Twenty-two Opel?" The man spoke with an easy authority. "They'll give you a bit of trouble on a road like this."

Hoffner nodded, although he couldn't remember whether the car was a '21 or a '22. "I thought I'd caught something underneath," he said. "Didn't see anything."

"High frame," said the man. "Not meant for these speeds."

"You know your cars, then?"

"I take an interest. So nothing up in the housing?"

Hoffner motioned to the car. "You're welcome to take a look."

The man stepped over, released the catch on the metal bonnet, and raised it. "You keep it well." He leaned in and jiggled a few bits and pieces.

"Yes," said Hoffner, never having once opened the thing up himself. He noticed the baby boar still watching them. "Cigarette?"

The man stood upright and refastened the bonnet. "Very kind."

"I'm the one who should be thanking you."

"For what? Your car is in perfect order." They both lit up and leaned back against the bonnet. "Unless it's for the company?" Hoffner held out the flask. "No," said the man. "I'm not much good with that."

Hoffner nodded over to the truck. "You've an interesting load."

"Toilet-washing liquid," said the man. "Very glamorous. I'm heading out to the studios. Same as you." It was an obvious point: Who else would be taking this road? "I shouldn't, of course. Slows everyone down, but then, why not? I choose my times well enough. Eleven on a Monday. Very little traffic either way. If you'd really been unlucky, you'd have been here for quite some time."

"Depends on what you mean by luck."

The man smiled absently. "Fair enough."

"And here I thought the studios would have had—"

"A bigger outfit running their toilet-washing-liquid interests?" The man had evidently run through this before. There was an odd charm to it all. "Of course, but then I'm an inside man. I was owed. Favors and so forth. Highly confidential stuff."

"The intricate world of toilet-liquid syndicates."

"Exactly." The man nodded over at the boars. "They'll make someone a nice bit of eating."

"That would be a shame."

"You don't like eating?"

Hoffner took a pull on his cigarette. "So how does one become an 'inside man'?"

"The usual course. A producer, director—I don't remember which—one of them had an eye for my daughter. Got me the contract. On a limited basis, of course. One man, one truck. Enough liquid for the small buildings. More if she spread her legs."

"Imagine if she marries him?"

"I don't. She ran off to Darmstadt with a butcher's apprentice two years ago. I think the studio felt sorry. Old widower abandoned by his only daughter."

"That's a bit rough."

"Not really. They let me keep the contract. Don't know why. I never liked her much. She's probably fat now. Fat like that big one there. With a child. A fat little boy. He probably beats her. The butcher, not the child."

Here it was, thought Hoffner. The man had lived through the Kaiser, the war, unemployment, a daughter, and none of it mattered, not so much at its heart as in its passing. Berlin's saving grace had always been her incessant movement forward. Only a real Berliner understood that.

"Quite a sky," said the man. Even the briefest of conversations had to make mention of it. "It'll pass."

"I imagine it will."

The man took a last pull, then flicked his cigarette to the ground. "Bit early for a cop to be heading out to the studios."

All this certainty in the Grunwald this morning, thought Hoffner. "Highly confidential stuff."

The man exhaled as he pushed himself up. "Yah. I'm sure it is." Inside the cab, he leaned out the window. "Watch where you piss out there. Make my life a little easier." He put the truck in gear and headed off.

Hoffner crushed out his cigarette and noticed all three of the boars now looking back. For some reason, he bent over and picked up the man's cigarette; it was still moist. He then opened the door, tossed the butts onto the passenger-side floor, and pressed the starter. The sound sent the boars darting into the wood, and Hoffner turned to see them disappear. This they were afraid of.

Settling in, he pulled the door shut and headed up onto the road.

. . .

THE FIRST OF THE STUDIO buildings emerged on the horizon like a caravan of turtles. The film men had bought the land before the war, an abandoned factory stuck out in the middle of nowhere. Safer that way, they reasoned: no apartment complexes nearby to go up in flames should the reels catch fire. The place had grown in the intervening years. Under a vacant sky, the sprawl seemed even more desolate.

Hoffner pulled up to the gate and waited, a walled fence stretching off in either direction. The Ufa emblem dangled precariously above. To the side, a large billboard advertised the most recent studio triumphs: posters of Emil Jannings and Asta Nielsen, Conrad Veidt in some menacing pose, along with the warnings APPALLING! DANGEROUS! DAUGHTERS BEWARE! Veidt's shadow was especially well placed—obscuring the crucial E and W in BEWARE!—and informing the casual reader that, perhaps, the daughters might be nude in this particular film. Hoffner appreciated the designer's ingenuity.

He reached for his badge as the guard approached.

"No need for that, Herr Kriminal-Oberkommissar." The man's easy grin seemed at odds with the long coat, braiding at the shoulders, and equally impressive hat. He might have been a doorman at the Adlon or Esplanade if not for the Ufa logo on his lapel. "Bauer," he continued. "Oberwachtmeister Anders Bauer, retired. I was at the Alex with you, last posting before my thirty-five came up."

"Bauer." Hoffner nodded as if he recalled the man. "Of course." It was nothing new for an old Schutzi sergeant to find himself a night watchman or gatekeeper around town, especially when everyone's pension had blown up with the inflation. Why not out at the film studios: more exotic, Hoffner imagined. "You've landed yourself a nice bit of work."

"Can't complain, Herr Kriminal-Oberkommissar." He handed Hoffner a yellow card that read "Day Pass—Grosse Halle." "Hot meals at the commissary. Good uniform." Bauer's expression hardened. "Naturally you've come about that business with Thyssen, Herr Kriminal-Oberkommissar." He brought a clipboard up and pointed to where Hoffner was meant to sign.

Hoffner enjoyed the dedication: it was still in the old dog's blood. "Business," he said as he scrawled his name. "I was told suicide."

"You hear things, Herr Kriminal-Oberkommissar. That's all." Bauer gave an unconvinced nod. "But if they say suicide, then it must be suicide."

Hoffner placed the card in his coat pocket. "Well then, you hear anything else, you let me know. Just between the two of us—Herr Oberwachtmeister."

The man's eyes flashed momentarily. "Absolutely, Herr Kriminal-Oberkommissar." And with a sudden Teutonic precision, Bauer returned to the gate, pulled up the barrier, and motioned Hoffner through. Not wanting to spoil the man's performance, Hoffner took the car in without the slightest idea where he was going.

As it turned out, every road seemed to lead to the Grosse Halle. Hoffner followed the signs past a series of bungalows and out into an open area where a stone wall with turrets rose in the distance. At its side, a dragon's head peeked out from behind a bush. For anyone who had stepped inside a movie palace in the last two years, this would have been exhilarating: images meant to be seen only in flickering light now made real, if perhaps less epic. Hoffner's son Georgi had explained it all to him, angles and lenses and lighting, but what was the point in knowing when it reduced it to this? Even so, Hoffner barely noticed them as he turned down a narrow lane, past a row of flat, soulless buildings and up toward the Great Studio.

The papers had been full of it last year when the massive thing had gone up, this many meters long, that many meters wide, "as tall as ten men to the catwalks!" and with an entire wall made of glass for natural light. Had the sky shown even the slightest hint of color there might have been something ominous in its stare. Instead, the place simply looked brown.

A young man in a bow tie and plain shirt was waiting in front of a line of entrance doors. He was conspicuous for his lack of movement among the others of his breed, darting about with their clipboards and papers and tidy vitality. The boy began to jog over the moment he saw Hoffner pull in between two Daimlers.

"Herr Chief Inspector," he said. Hoffner stepped out of the car. "Eggermann, Rudi Eggermann. Everyone calls me Rudi." The boy had been trained on how to present himself. "We have the Herr Direktor waiting upstairs for you."

Hoffner's suit drew several glances as he and the boy made their way up toward the main entrance. Stylish for 1923, it seemed to match the color of the brick.

"Very impressive," Hoffner said as he peered up at the building and its myriad doors. He pulled a cigarette from his pocket.

"Yes. Thank you, Herr Chief Inspector."

Hoffner nodded vaguely in the direction of the doors as he lit up. "How do you know which one?"

Confusion cut across the boy's face. "Which one what, Herr Chief Inspector?"

"Which one to use. The doors. Where they go."

"Oh." The boy nodded eagerly. "How do we know. Of course. Actually, it's not all that difficult—"

"I'm joking with you, Herr Rudi." Hoffner let out a long stream of smoke. "You managed to pick me out among the Mercedes and Daimlers. I'm assuming you know your way around."

Inside, the foyer housed a small office, a row of telephone booths, and a single wide corridor that led deeper into the building. Halfway down the hall, the boy was forced to slow for a train of women who looked as if they had each come second to the winner of a Marie Antoinette dress-up contest. Each held a fashion magazine or cheap little novel in her grasp as they all shuttled down the hall and into a large room where an entire legion of French aristocrats were either sitting or reading or dozing. A dice game among a few comtes and peasants had drawn a crowd in a corner. Nice to see the Weimar democratic spirit alive and well, thought Hoffner.

He followed the boy into a waiting elevator, and they headed up.

THE PENTHOUSE FLOOR was an open-air atrium, with a carpeted balcony that extended around all four sides in pristine white. Hoffner peered over the edge to the little chessboard of activity eight stories down as he followed the boy past the offices and dressing suites reserved for Ufa's executives and major stars.

The design was really quite ingenious, the whole thing subdivided by movable bricked-in walls so that the big films and little ones could all be shot at the same time. Great sand deserts butted up against French palaces, a section of Friedrichstrasse seemed to end on a mountaintop, and the most curious was a casino that looked on the verge of an elephant stampede. Hovering above it all were the tall cranes with cameras and lights attached, distant figures perched on poles or hanging from wires. The rising chatter would have been deafening if not for the glass dome that extended across the atrium from the floor below. Up in the heavens, however, all was serene. Hoffner wondered if the designers realized how clever they had been to choose Babelsberg for their tower.

"My younger boy is very interested in all of this," Hoffner said as he continued to gaze over.

"It's an exciting industry, Herr Chief Inspector." Hoffner wondered if young Rudi carried the brochure with him at all times. "May I ask how old?"

"Third year, Friedrichs-Werdersches Gymnasium." A great torrent of water was now making its way down the mountain. "A fencer. Sixteen."

"You should have him get in touch with us. We could find something for him—running scripts, filing film. On the weekends, of course."

"No," Hoffner said easily as he watched the water disappear as quickly as it had come. "This isn't the sort of place for a boy of sixteen."

There was an awkward nod before Rudi motioned to the corner office. "Here we are," he said, rather too relieved.

Hoffner looked up to see a heavyset man standing outside the door. His suit was a recent purchase, though he had yet to learn how to wear it. The man nodded with an unwarranted familiarity as Hoffner approached.

"Hoffner, Kern," Kern said, ignoring Rudi entirely. "You're free to do whatever it is you do, Eggermann. We'll be taking it from here."

Hoffner waited a moment, then turned to his young guide. "You've been very kind, Herr Rudi. Please inform your studio security man I won't be needing him." And without so much as a nod, Hoffner took hold of the handle and started in.

Kern's thick hand quickly held the door in place. "What the hell do you think you're doing, Kripo?"

Again Hoffner waited before turning. "Well, I could waste my time on your notebook full of scribblings or your ideas about when and how all this happened. Or you could tell me how you chose to make private security your calling, the freedom and glamour and so forth, when we both know there are three, more likely four, failed Kripo entrance examinations in your not-too-distinguished past. I was hoping to save you all of that in front of Herr Rudi here, but it seems that's not meant to be. My guess is that the two or three very powerful men inside this office are waiting to tell me just exactly what they think I need to know without any help from you. So thank you for standing guard until I arrived, but I think we're done." Hoffner pointed to Kern's shirt. "And you might want to take care of that. Jam tart can leave a stain."

Hoffner knew it was poor form to enjoy the look on Kern's face as much as he did, but then they had brought him all the way out here on a Monday morning for what was probably nothing more than another aimless tryst gone wrong, all of which would be conveniently brushed aside by some well-placed cash or favors for men too far above him at the Alex for any of it to trickle down his way. He would still have to go through the paperwork for the extra petrol allotment when he got back. Kern seemed the appropriate repository for such frustrations.

Kern, his suit even more apish, continued to hold the door: it was impressive to see that much rage contained. He seemed on the verge of saying something, when instead, he took a quick, defiant glance at Eggermann and then headed down the hall. Loud enough for Hoffner to hear, he muttered "Ass," then disappeared through the stairwell door.

Hoffner had hoped to see a bit of victory in Rudi's face, but the boy simply stared uncomfortably. He was out of his depth. Shame. Evidently out here they were trained to cede ground. Hoffner nodded again and stepped inside the office.

He found himself in a quite lovely and quite empty anteroom: sofa, two chairs, and a secretary's desk with a large Ufa emblem emblazoned on the front. Everything was bright, too bright, from the pale yellow color of the walls, to the beige carpet, to the white satin pillows lazing along the armrests. Jannings and Nielsen once again dominated the walls, while various film magazines stretched across a low Chinoise coffee table. The final touch was a potted palm tree in the corner. Hoffner wondered if it was possible to appear more ludicrous: there was a desperation to it that cried out, "Look at us, America! We make films, too!"

He stepped over to a second door, knocked, and pushed through.

The larger office, by contrast, was stark to the point of sterility. A long, flat desk stared out from the one corner that seemed to defy the light streaming in from the wall-to-wall window. A designer's metal chair stood sentry behind. The only nods to comfort were two low, overstuffed chairs in front of the window, but then they were denied the remarkable view of the Grunwald and beyond. One man stood staring out. Another sat in one of the chairs. The third, and oldest, was making his way across to Hoffner.

"Ah, Herr Chief Inspector. Hoffner, is it?" He extended his hand. He was in a perfectly cut gray suit. "You've dispensed with Herr Kern, I see. My congratulations."

This was the new affectation. Weimar had brought democracy and prosperity and nude dancing and cocaine and the handshake. The clipped nod was a thing of the past. He took the man's hand. "Nikolai Hoffner. Yes, *mein Herr.*"

"Joachim Ritter. Counsel for the studio. We finally sent Kern out. Bit of an oaf, wouldn't you say?" Hoffner said nothing. Ritter turned to the man in the chair, who was clutching a tall glass of whiskey. "This is one of our screenwriters, Paul Metzner. Still a bit shaken up. He's the one who found the body."

"I'm fine, really," Metzner said as he placed the whiskey on the desk. "Anything I can help with."

The third man now turned from the window. "And this is Herr Major Alexander Grau," Ritter continued as Grau stepped over. "The studio's director."

Grau was tall, slim, and, even without the title, undeniably Prussian. He looked much younger than Hoffner would have imagined for the head of Europe's largest studio—midforties at most—but with none of the self-conscious arrogance that comes with early success. Grau was a man certain of his place and unimpressed by his own power. In the wrong hands, it was a dangerous combination.

"Herr Chief Inspector." Grau was not a man for handshakes. He offered a clipped nod. "I can't say we have much to tell you."

"Just a few questions, then, *mein Herr*." Hoffner pulled a notebook from his coat pocket. "When did you find the body, Herr Metzner?"

Ritter answered: "Eight-thirty this morning. They had a meeting to discuss a script."

Hoffner asked, "And this meeting was planned well in advance?"

Ritter continued: "A day or two. It's the usual course. Thyssen was producing the film."

"He's produced several of my scripts," Metzner piped in from his chair. The glance from Ritter made it clear that Metzner had been told to sit quietly. Grau looked almost indifferent.

Hoffner jotted down a few lines to make it look official. "Was there a secretary outside when you arrived, Herr Metzner?"

"Yes," Ritter answered. "She heard and saw nothing. We have her in an office down the hall. She was feeling a bit faint."

"Anyone else?"

Ritter looked momentarily puzzled.

"Anyone else waiting in the room with her?" Hoffner clarified. "Others who would have had appointments— I'll need to speak with them as well."

"Oh, I see. Yes." Ritter glanced over at Grau, who nodded. "We can have that arranged."

"Good." Hoffner dispensed with the usual questions of pressure and lovers and gambling. Ritter would have chosen one, an offhand remark, a lowering of the eyes, poor old Thyssen; Grau would simply have looked inconvenienced by it all: it was pointless to play out the charade. Instead, Hoffner placed the notebook in his pocket and said, "So, the body, *meine Herren*?" Ritter began to move toward the private bathroom, but Hoffner stopped him. "If Herr Metzner could show me how he found it, *mein Herr*. Procedure. You understand."

"Of course." Ritter turned to Metzner. "Paul?"

Metzner stood, but Grau interrupted: "Unfortunately, I have a meeting, Herr Chief Inspector. Is there anything else you need from me?"

So much easier, thought Hoffner, when things were made this transparent: Grau was here simply to make sure Hoffner understood the hierarchy in play.

"Not at all, Herr Direktor. Thank you for your time." Hoffner extended his hand and enjoyed the slight tightening in Grau's cheeks.

Grau took it and said, "Herr Chief Inspector. Gentlemen."

He was gone by the time Metzner drew up to Hoffner's side. "I've written several murder films myself," Metzner said.

"Really?" Hoffner walked with him across the room. "And here I thought this was a suicide."

"Herr Metzner is very enthusiastic," Ritter cut in. "We pay him for his imagination."

Metzner pushed open the door to the bathroom and waited for Hoffner to move past him. Instead, Hoffner stopped. "Were any of your detectives ever the hero, Herr Metzner?"

Metzner needed a moment. "No, I don't think so."

"Then I doubt you'll be of much use to me," Hoffner said, and stepped through.

The room was almost half the size of the office, its floor in black-and-white marble, the wallpaper a deep maroon. Just in case the walk from the desk had been too taxing, there was a divan at the side of a pedestal sink, both in reach of a telephone that sat atop an iron-and-glass side table. The toilet, as far as Hoffner could tell, required its own little cabin, which was at the far end and up a few steps: the image of the mysterious blue liquid fixed in his mind before Hoffner turned to the centerpiece of the room. It was a long steel massage table that stood directly across from a sunken bathtub. And it was there, in the tub, that Hoffner found Herr Thyssen.

The water had gone pinkish, with strings of deep red floating throughout. Thyssen's head was resting against a porthole window, his eyes staring out unmoving. He was young and fit, and had rough calluses at the tips of his fingers. The hand with the Browning revolver rose awkwardly over the edge; in such cases, more often than not, the recoil from the shot caused the elbow bone to snap against the porcelain. Thyssen had been lucky. His arm had flown free. The single bullet hole was just below his left nipple.

"And this is the way you found him?" Hoffner crouched down and placed two fingers on the chest: the flesh was hard, like cold rubber. The water was ice-cold.

"Exactly," said Metzner, peering over as best he could. "Nothing's been touched."

Hoffner glanced over at the towel rack. Everything was perfectly in place. He looked for a robe. There was none. "Looks standard enough," he said, even if he didn't believe a word of it. The body angle and water temperature were wrong. And the blood made no sense. There was something else, but Hoffner couldn't quite place it.

He stood and reached for a towel.

"That's all you're going to do?" said Metzner, almost disappointed.

"Is there something else you want me to do?"

"Well—you hardly touched the body."

"Oh, the body." Hoffner nodded. "You want me to look for marks or gashes or fingerprints. That sort of thing."

"Well—yes. Isn't that part of the procedure?"

Again Hoffner nodded. "I'll leave that to your film detectives." He finished with the towel. Ritter was standing in the doorway. "You said there were people for me to see. Why don't we do that."

AGAINST HIS PROTESTATIONS, Metzner was sent down to his office, while Hoffner called into the Alex for someone to come out and pick up the body.

"You're sure it's absolutely necessary?" Ritter spoke casually as the two men made their way to an office at the far side of the atrium. "You can't just let us have the family make the arrangements?"

"Standard procedure," Hoffner lied. "We need an examination, an official record." He wanted someone to take a look at the late Herr Thyssen. "The family will have him by the end of the week."

Ritter knew not to press it. "You Kripo men usually come in twos," he said.

"You've had a lot of experience with us, then, *mein Herr*?"

"It's a film studio, Herr Chief Inspector. There's always someone's hand to hold."

"Or pull from a tub."

"That, too."

Hoffner found the man surprisingly likable. "I had a tendency to lose mine."

"Your hands?"

"My partners."

"Ah." They reached the door, and Ritter stopped. "I've started with any staff who might have had even passing contact with Thyssen in the last twenty-four hours. Script runners, copyists, that sort of thing. You understand I can't pull executives out of meetings at a moment's notice. I could set up a few interviews for you back in town. At our Potsdamer offices, tomorrow morning, say."

"That would be fine."

"Good. Not that I think any of them would have much to tell you."

"The Herr Major mentioned that, yes."

"Even so, we want the studio to be as helpful as we can. I suspect we can have all this sorted out in the next day or two. After all, suicide's no crime."

Lawyers brought pressure to bear in such delicate ways, thought Hoffner.

Ritter reached for the handle, but for some reason stopped himself. "Hoffner," he said, as if the name had suddenly taken on new meaning. He turned. "Of course. The 'chisel murders.' Grizzly stuff after the war, wasn't it?"

This was a badge Hoffner reluctantly carried. "A long time ago. Yes."

"All those women killed. And Feld, or Filder? Your young partner, always in the papers."

"Fichte," Hoffner corrected.

"That's right. You couldn't open one without seeing his face. You know, we thought about making a film. He was rather charismatic. Too gruesome, though, even for us. Might work now, though."

"It might," Hoffner said blandly.

"No doubt your Fichte's a Kriminaldirektor by now."

"No doubt."

Fichte had been dead for eight years. As had Martha. As had Sascha, all but for the dying.

It was odd to think of Sascha now, easier not to. At least the dead remained as they were, with no questions to be answered. Fichte's death had been unfortunate but no real surprise: his kind of ambition always fell prey to the corrupt. That the boy had been unable to see how deep the corruption ran at the Alex was hardly tragic, more a lesson in misguided arrogance. Hoffner's last image of him—lying on a slab, his lungs filled with poison—was enough to give Fichte's death its meaning, and why look beyond that?

For Martha there had been no hope of meaning. She had been killed for Hoffner's own arrogance—and naïveté and stupidity and recklessness—and any thought of understanding it, or seeing beyond it, was pointless. He had let them murder his wife. To ask why—to waken the dead—would have required a self-damning too exhausting to bear.

Only the very young had the resilience to sustain that kind of loathing. His son Sascha had been sixteen at the time. Hoffner hadn't seen him since.

"Winter of '20?" said Ritter.

"Nineteen," corrected Hoffner. "It was during the revolution."

"That's right." Ritter's smile returned. "Did we have a revolution? I'll have to check the film archives."

Ritter opened the door to a group of eight or nine studio employees sitting in a small anteroom. They turned as one as Hoffner stepped inside.

Ritter said, "Thank you, ladies and gentlemen. This won't take long. The chief inspector has a few questions for each of you." He turned to Hoffner. "You can take them individually through to the office. Give me a ring when you've finished. Dial 9. They'll find me."

Hoffner studied the faces, all young, all with something and nothing to hide. It would be a waste of time. There was a boy in the corner, clearly intent on the girl next to him. The Kriminalpolizei had just interrupted his best efforts. It was laced across his face.

"That one there," said Hoffner as Ritter turned to go. Hoffner was pointing to the boy. "He's not involved in this."

Ritter turned back. "And why is that?"

"Because he's my son."

LISL

THE SECOND OFFICE was no more comfortable than the first, not that Hoffner or the boy was in any mood to sit.

"What do you want me to say, Georgi?" Hoffner was onto his second cigarette. "I'm surprised. That's all."

"I thought you knew." It was a hollow answer. Georg had been doing his best to keep things light, but even he had his doubts about this last one. "Either way, it's where we are now."

Hoffner nodded once, twice. He had always liked Georg's candor. Now it just seemed grating. "You've left school, then?"

"For the time being." Georg was taller than his father. He seemed to grow taller still with this admission. "The last two months."

"And the money I've been sending you for tuition and rooms?"

"Very helpful, thank you. I share a flat with a friend just south of Friedenau."

"How artistic of you. And this friend—also a filmmaker in the making?"

"He's a writer."

"That's unfortunate." An ugly thought entered Hoffner's mind. "Your brother wouldn't have had anything to do with this, would he?" Georg's eyes grew momentarily sharper. Hoffner had never seen it in the boy before, that severity that invades the face and leaves no trace of childhood. Georg had found it at only sixteen. Hoffner crushed out his cigarette. "A stupid question. I apologize."

Georg let it pass. "I haven't spoken with Sascha in months. I'm not even sure he's in Berlin."

These were the tidbits Hoffner was allowed from time to time. He saw Georg only on weekends: Who had time for anything more? The boy's aunts were no doubt still keeping a close watch. Naturally, they had decided not to tell him about this recent gambit.

"And you make a bit of money running from office to office?" It was the best Hoffner could come up with to sound conciliatory.

"A bit. It helps to be on tuition."

"Yes, I'm sure it does." There was always an immense charm with this one. Martha had seen it from the start. "So no fencing."

"Once in a while. My flatmate's good with a foil."

"You're better with a saber."

"True. But he's not." Georg nodded toward the door. "So what's this all about?"

"A police matter."

"And?"

Ever the eager one. Hoffner had always thought it would send the boy into the Kripo, maybe a directorship. The imagination was obviously taking him elsewhere. "One of your executives put a bullet in his chest."

"Suicide?"

"So they tell me."

"It's a high-risk venture, Papi."

Hoffner was looking for another cigarette; his pockets were empty. "You're quite familiar with all this, then?" He found a box on the table and pulled one out: they were Luckys, not the easiest brand to find in

Berlin. "Tell me, is anything in here not Americano?" He lit up and pocketed two more.

"It depends on the office."

"Grau?"

"The Herr Major? Strictly a Bergmann smoker. Maybe a few stubs from a Monopol MR in the ashtray, now and then."

"All this in two months? I'm impressed, Georgi."

The boy's face grew more serious. "Was it Thyssen?"

Hoffner was too good to give anything away. Even so, he knew the boy would be told soon enough. "Why do you ask?"

"A lot of late-night meetings. Unfamiliar faces."

Hoffner weighed his words carefully. "Faces you were meant to see?" Georg said nothing. "Not something you want to play at, Georgi. Leave it alone."

"I thought it was just a suicide?"

"Good. Then you can put your imagination to rest."

"It would make for a nice bit of script."

"I'll talk to Herr Ritter. See if he's interested." Hoffner nodded at the door. "I'll need forty minutes with that lot. Then I'll give you a ride back into town. Size up your flat."

Georg did his best to speak with authority. "I'm on until five-thirty."

"Not today you're not." Hoffner took a pull on the cigarette. "Herr Ritter and I are quite chummy. I'm sure they can do without you for one afternoon."

NO ONE HAD ANYTHING TO SAY. A trio of teary-eyed young secretaries and copyists spoke through handkerchiefs about the late, and quite marvelous, Herr Thyssen. More restrained, though no less captivated, were a messenger and a mailroom boy. Hoffner counted four crushes among them. "I've done a bit of mountain climbing myself," the fatter of the two boys volunteered. "Herr Thyssen was very accomplished, you know." At least now Hoffner had an explanation for the calloused fingertips. It was the only information worth jotting down.

Downstairs, Georg was waiting when he stepped from the elevator.

"You'll have someone keeping an eye out for you now," Hoffner said as he patted his pockets for a cigarette; the Luckys were long gone. "Good man, Ritter."

Georg showed only a moment's irritation as they moved down the hall. "I'll be fine on my own, Father."

It was the "Father" that gave it away. Georg rarely felt the need for it. Sascha, on the other hand, had taken it as his stock-in-trade. Funny how contempt could linger in the ears after eight years of silence.

"No reason not to have a few friends," said Hoffner.

Outside, the old Opel seemed somehow more lumbering squeezed in among the top-flight roadsters and saloons. Even they, however, looked almost brittle under the pale sun, as if the slightest touch might shatter their perfectly sculpted bodies. Hoffner brought his hand up to shade his eyes. "Quite a collection," he said. He pulled open the door.

Georg pointed to a red Brenabor sports coupe. "Jenny Jugo drives that one. She says she can get it up over a hundred on the circuit back to town."

"You've spoken with Jenny Jugo?"

"Sure."

Hoffner was beginning to see his son in an entirely new light. "Lovely shoulders on that girl." Hoffner got in behind the wheel. "And lips."

"You should see her in the buff," said Georg as he pulled the passenger door shut.

Hoffner put the car in gear. "Quite a life, your filmmaking."

. . .

THE FLAT WAS TWO ROOMS, hardly furnished, and with a single-flame stove for meals that were never cooked. Hoffner noticed a few knickknacks from the old place on Friesenstrasse, the most prominent a Japanese fan Martha had kept on the wall by her bed. It stood open on a small side table, with an oval picture of her at its side. Hoffner recalled having the same photo somewhere.

The flatmate had staked out the other table, a large-frame picture of a plump family seated and standing in a garden. The man at center clutched at his lapel with wide little butcher's fingers, the small black, red, and gold Social Democrat pin proudly on display.

"So, how old does the landlord think you are?" Hoffner glanced through the few books the boys had stacked by the window: a volume of Möricke, another by Lorca, a few potboilers by Karl May, and of course something thick from Döblin. Georg was in the other room, out of sight, rummaging through something.

"Twenty," said Georg. "He was very impressed with the letter you wrote, especially with the Kripo seal at the top."

"Did I vouch for your butcher's son as well?"

"Sewage inspector, Papi. Albert's father is a sewage inspector. So you see, you're both inspectors."

Hoffner leafed through the Möricke. "And where is the young Herr Sewage now? I was hoping to meet him."

"His father couldn't get him out of work." Georg reappeared at the door with several glossy photos and a few envelopes in hand. "He sets copy at the *Nacht-Ausgabe*."

"A Scherl paper?" Hoffner replaced the book. "Bit right-wing. That must be something of a disappointment for Herr Sewage Senior."

"It's a job, Papi, not his politics. And it's Lettinger. Albert's father is Herr Bernard Lettinger. You might actually have to meet him one day."

"What a pleasure that would be."

Georg handed Hoffner the various photos, each with a personal note to Georg. All were convinced of his bright future.

"Very nice," said Hoffner. "You haven't seen Veidt naked, have you? That would be distressing."

Georg ignored him and held out the envelopes. "These came a few months back." His expression was focused. "You're welcome to read through them, if you want."

Hoffner recognized Sascha's handwriting, the return address Munich. He hesitated, then held up the photos. "I think I'll take a closer look at these." He turned, trying to remember where the chair was. There it was. By the window. Hoffner moved to it and sat.

Georg was still by the door. "He mentions you."

Hoffner peered intently at one of the pictures. "I told you lovely shoulders." He flipped through a few more, trying to find his own focus. At some point Georg tossed the letters onto the table, headed to the stove, and said, "I can make a coffee, if you like."

Hoffner heard the muted resignation in the boy's voice; he continued to glance at the faces as he nodded.

Georg said, "Some of those are up-and-comers. You won't recognize them. Still, good to have friends, as you say."

Hoffner wondered when the boy had become this young man. In a single afternoon, it seemed. He continued to leaf through the pictures, mostly unfamiliar, until he came to a monocled figure glaring up from the stack. The thick script was in keeping with the expression:

You have promise, young Hoffner. Learn to be inspired. Fritz
Lang.

From the look in Lang's good eye, the inspiration was clearly meant to be Fritz Lang. Hoffner was about to say something when the late Herr Thyssen's body suddenly came to mind.

Georg glanced over. "So you found that one." He was adjusting the flame under the coffeepot. "Not sure what it means, but if the great Herr Direktor chose to say it, then it must mean something, don't you think?"

Hoffner continued to stare at the picture. "Naturally." He hadn't heard a word. "You wouldn't have any idea where Lang might be right now, would you?" This is what had struck him out at the studio. He had seen it all before in a file: the angle of the head, the arms, the temperature of the water. "Babelsberg? In town?"

Georg knew the look in his father's eyes: always best to give the simplest answer. "He's editing. At the studio. Making a recut of *Metropolis*. Why?"

"You know this for certain?"

Georg nodded.

Hoffner stood and pulled his coat and hat from the rack. "I'm afraid I'm going to have to miss out on your coffee."

Georg turned off the flame. He hadn't wanted any to begin with. "Thyssen?"

Hoffner peered over at the boy. Perhaps Lang had hit on it: promise was so right with this one. "Something to clear up." He fished through his pockets for his notebook. "I can give you a lift back out. You were planning on taking a tram and who knows how many buses back when I left. This would be a bit easier."

Georg was two steps behind his father as Hoffner started down the stairs.

THE ALEX—Berlin's Polizei Presidium—is a mass of red-brown brick and stone on the southern edge of Alexanderplatz, a fifteen-minute ride farther into town from the flat, traffic permitting. A product of the Kaiser's civic expansion days—those heady times before war and defeat and democracy sent the old man off to the Nether-lands—the Alex had once been the third-largest building in the city. The police president had even lived inside, on the first floor at the top of an imposing marble staircase. It might have been a bit awk-ward having to share his official residence with upward of seven hun-dred criminals on any given day, but then, the address was probably worth it.

Hoffner slowed for an oncoming livery truck before heading into the square. The newspaper kiosk and soup cart were doing a nice business at the front of the building, taking full advantage of the con-struction workers, who seemed to be in constant demand at the old place. Today, the green-putty-and-hobnail-boot crew was working on one of the fourth-floor windows, the domain of the Polpo, Berlin's political police. Hoffner had the image of an interrogation gone terri-bly wrong, shattered glass, a body flying out and then down, down, down. Then again, maybe that was too much even for the Polpo.

He found a spot at the far end of the square and handed Georg a few pfennigs for a magazine. "Get what you like, then wait in the car."

Hoffner headed across the cobblestone, glancing up at the few untended nicks high on the building's façade—half the department had them as remnants of left-wing bullets from '19, the other of right-wing Kappist grenades from '20—but either way it was a long time since the Alex had come under attack. Much relieved, the line of entrance archways peered out with neutral sobriety.

Hoffner passed through the central gate and into the entrance atrium, which was part of a cavernous corridor that ran all four sides of the building. It ringed the glassed-over courtyard, where a line of armored trucks—each with a machine-gun turret at top—stood in a neat clump at center. Except for an occasional dustup at one of the slaughterhouse factories, the trucks stood idle. This, so Hoffner had been told, was progress. He cut past them and headed up the stairs.

It was somewhere between the second and third floors that the stink kicked in. At first he thought it was an overcooked egg, but the closer he got, the more chemical it became.

A young detective sergeant appeared at the top of the steps, a bowl of something yellow in his outstretched hands as he made his way down.

"It's clogged the sink," the boy said.

Hoffner flattened himself against the wall and brought his handkerchief to his nose. "Egg yolk?" he said.

The boy nearly missed a step. "How did you . . . ?"

"Mix some cream with whiskey and pour it into the sink. That should take care of the stench. And don't just toss it out. Take it down to the morgue and spill it into the slop drain."

The boy nodded as he continued to move past Hoffner. "Scheringer was trying to do mildewed clothes."

"Next time, tell him he'd do better to take a whiff of his own flat on a Friday night."

The boy laughed as he reached the landing. "You're the expert."

It was a fair point. Hoffner had been known to add to the general pong over the years—a few experiments of his own to approximate the smell of a decomposing corpse (sulfur and rotten fruit), or gunfire residue on a man's suit (damp cigar ash, dog hair, and chicory), or, his most recent, skin scrubbed clean of human blood (an old rag saturated in iodine and dark chocolate). More than a few of the junior detectives had broken cases based on their intimacy with Hoffner's concoctions, the best a young Kriminal-Assistent named Dönicker, who had cracked a particularly baffling murder case simply by smelling a woman's panties. The woman, a Molly Dimp, had seemed the perfect innocent—grieving sister and partner in a not terribly promising music-hall act—except for a slight burn mark on her upper thigh, which no one had been able to explain or fully identify. She had claimed to have received it from a man trying to recover payments on her brother's gambling debts, but it had seemed an odd spot for intimidation. K.A. Dönicker, with nothing much to lose, had asked to sift through the young lady's laundry, whereupon sifting had become sniffing and the incriminating pair of silk blues had quickly been discovered. The scent of tobacco, Schnauzer, and chicory—so Dönicker described it—had sent Fräulein Dimp to the gallows, her burn mark later identified as the nub end of a Luger pistol placed too soon against the skin after firing. Evidently, she, too, had had enough of her brother's indiscretions. Dönicker had won promotion and, as thanks, had sent Hoffner a fresh pair of silk blues. Hoffner had had the panties bronzed and now used them as a paperweight.

Chancing the worst, he pocketed his handkerchief and stepped up to the third floor. This was the sole domain of the Kripo—Department IV within police circles—offices, archives, and interrogation rooms where the standard crimes of the republic were investigated: swindlers and drug syndicates, burglars and murderers, and, on occasion, even the most charming of suicides. Anything that hinted at deeper threats went upstairs to the Polpo—the boys of 1A—anything less spectacular to the drones of the Schutzpolizei. Turning toward his office, Hoffner suddenly recalled an image of Bauer sitting at the security desk. He did remember him. There was something comforting in that.

He made his way to the back of the building and to the cramped space that was his office. As always, it was littered with paper: open files covered the desk; casebooks, statutes, and codes—the new SPD editions, of course—lay open across the bookshelves that ran along the far wall; and bits and pieces of old case evidence were shoved in here and there—plaster casts of skulls and the like—giving the whole thing a somewhat macabre feel. The only recent additions were the *F*, *T*, and *B* volumes of Brockhaus's *Konversations-Lexikon*. Hoffner had survived for years on the *E* and *S* installments of the encyclopedia. For some reason, the new volumes had seemed the logical progression.

Other things had evolved as well. A wide, empty space dominated the wall across from his desk. There had been a time when he had kept a map of Berlin there, a new one for each case. For years, Hoffner had trusted in the city's moods as the surest clues to any crime: watch the map and eventually Berlin would assert herself in the temper and personality of her districts. It had always been just a matter of seeing the variations, finding what didn't belong, and allowing those idiosyncrasies to guide him. Berlin called for deviation, not patterning. That was what made her unique and knowable.

Now, however, nothing belonged: Where were the deviations when there was nothing genuine to deviate from? He might have blamed the war, or Weimar, or even the whim of democracy itself, but Hoffner knew better. Berlin was simply aging too quickly. She was now grasping at a misspent youth she had never lived. Life was gay and reckless and fully abandoned, and the city looked foolish trying so desperately to please. Crime was merely one more wild escapade on a night that was stretching on for far too long. Hoffner did not want a map. He had no need to be reminded of the city's pitiableness.

He tossed his coat and hat onto the desk and opened the filing cabinet. He was trying to remember the year as he leafed through—'23, '22. He stopped as he ran across the second folder in February 1921: *L. Rosenthal, F. Lang*. He pulled it out and sat at his desk.

There was a picture of Frau Rosenthal a few pages in, her ashen face and small breasts peeking up through the water. It was all identical, from the position of the body in the tub, to the angle of the arm and the Browning revolver, to the placement of the bullet hole. Even the hollow gaze of the eyes seemed intent on the same distant point. It was as if Herr Thyssen had taken this as his guide.

Hoffner closed the file and grabbed his coat and hat. Out of habit, he shot a parting glance at the mapless wall. There was nothing to see. All that the faded plaster managed now was a matting of lifeless shadows.

BAUER REQUIRED only another signature before letting them through the gate. Hoffner dropped Georg at the Great Studio, where they made arrangements to meet each other midweek, but both knew it was pointless.

Ten minutes on, Hoffner found himself in the foyer of Die Abteilung Redigierungen Meisterstücken—Department of Editorial Masterworks—far grander in name than in person. Its foyer reminded him of a dentist's surgery, with its long glass partition and single door leading off somewhere into the dull rectangularity of the building. Waiting for the girl behind the desk to slide back the glass, Hoffner felt a tedium that seemed to penetrate the wallpaper.

"Yes?" she said, and pointed to yet one more sign-in sheet.

Hoffner had rarely heard a more dismissive invitation. He scribbled his name and said, "I'm looking for Herr Lang, Fräulein."

"Herr Lang is not available, *mein Herr*."

Hoffner produced his badge. "Yes, Fräulein, he is." Her eyes widened and she reached for the telephone. "No, no, Fräulein. You'll just tell me where I can find him. All right?"

The building was one narrow corridor, with doors in perfect intervals along either side. Room 17 merited a double space. Hoffner turned the handle and slowly stepped in.

Except for a sputtering of white light from a projector's lens—focused through the central of three small openings in the far wall—the half-room was covered in red haze. To the right was a long table with various contraptions for cutting and splicing film, viewers of different sizes, and tall stacks of canisters. There were also several cups of half-finished coffee, bits and pieces of sandwich and pastry on various trays. A single operator stood under the red bulb manning the projector: clearly, he had been here for some time. He turned and waved a hand for Hoffner to close the door and keep quiet. Hoffner did as he was told before pulling his badge from his coat pocket. He mouthed the word "Lang."

The man stared at the badge for what seemed an inordinately long time. He then looked up at Hoffner's face, as if to see if metal and flesh somehow matched. Hoffner noticed a set of stairs to the left. He pointed over to them, but the man continued to stare.

A single crackling "Focus!" barked from an intercom somewhere on the wall. The man turned at once to the projector, and Hoffner took that as his cue to head for the steps.

The viewing room was insulated by a second door, which Hoffner now opened with great care. At once, a brightness from the screen forced his hand to his face. As his eyes adjusted, Hoffner saw a single figure sitting amid the four or five rows of plush chairs. Even from the back and in half-shadow, Lang had the look of authority. Hoffner closed the door and waited silently.

He watched as the screen filled with a mass of people in the shape of an ever-widening triangle. Ahead of them lay the steps to a grand building, pale, flat, and endless. The whole thing seemed to dull as they moved, humanity lost in the thickening wave of gray. Its oppression was strangely hypnotic.

"It's much better from up here." Lang kept his eyes on the screen: he spoke with the deep resonant roll of Austrian German. "Or you can continue to stand."

Hoffner obliged and took a seat in the last row.

Still gazing up, Lang said, "Coward." He then leaned forward, flipped a switch on some unseen gadget, and shouted, "Take it off!"

The screen went black, and a wash of golden light settled on the small room.

Lang turned, his arm held casually over the back of the chair. He stared at Hoffner for only a moment and then said, "A policeman. Of course you'd have sat in the back. I love policemen."

Crisp would have been the best word to describe Lang in person. He wore a riding jacket and tie, and his hair was slick above a workable forehead. He had high cheeks and a full, long nose. Most compelling, though, was the effortless smile. He looked as if he was expecting someone to take a magazine photograph.

"You're surprised?" Lang said no less easily. "That I should spot you like that. I'm right, aren't I?"

Hoffner remained where he was. "You are, *mein Herr*. No one called, then?"

The nonmonocled eye narrowed. The other seemed to grow wider by comparison, lending his confusion a hint of lunacy. "I don't permit calls while I'm viewing my films." He turned his head to the back wall and raised his voice. "I don't permit *any* interruptions." He turned back to Hoffner, his eyes once again in their normal contrapuntal state. "And who would have called, Herr—?"

"Hoffner." He stood. "Chief Inspector Nikolai Hoffner."

The smile returned. "*Chief* Inspector. I didn't have you so advanced."

"You wouldn't be the first."

Lang seemed to like the candor. He nodded to the screen. "You've seen my latest effort, then?"

Hoffner nodded. "Of course." He hadn't.

"It's a lie," said Lang as he pulled a cigarette from a silver case. "No one has. I haven't finished it myself." He tapped the cigarette on the case. "It should never have gone out, but then there's always some marketing genius to bring up distribution cycles or advertising schedules, or whatever it is that runs their tiny lives, and out it goes." He lit up. "And then they're all shocked when it isn't what they thought it should be. Still, it's making them money hand over fist."

He looked at Hoffner as if the two had had this conversation a thousand times: the intimacy was oddly engaging.

"I've spent a good deal of time at Alexanderplatz," Lang continued, his eyes fixed on Hoffner. "At the Alex." He was pleased with his familiarity. "There has to be an authenticity to film, an honesty of purpose." The cigarette dabbed at the air like a baton. "You can't make a *Mabuse* or a *Destiny* without it. You have to be inspired by truth and then find the reality beyond it. You see what I'm saying?"

Hoffner had never considered a reality beyond truth, but in this little room it might have made sense. He nodded over to Lang's silver case. "You have another, *mein Herr?*"

Lang measured Hoffner, then stood. "Of course." He held out the case. "My apologies. You smoke American?"

Hoffner stepped over and took one. "When I have to." He lit up. "So—how many cases did our First Sergeant Bauer let you take a look at over the years, Herr Lang?" Hoffner picked at a stray piece of tobacco on his tongue while Lang smiled with that same, odd intimacy.

"Very good, Herr Chief Inspector. Too many to count. I miss him there."

"I'm sure there's someone new."

"There always is, isn't there?" Lang took another pull on the cigarette. This time it was too self-conscious. "And now, Herr Chief Inspector, what is it I've done?"

"There's been a suicide." Hoffner opted for the direct approach. "One of your executives in the new studio building."

Lang seemed mildly intrigued. "How unfortunate."

"Sometime last night. A single bullet to the chest. From a Browning. In a bathtub."

Lang's gaze grew colder. "As I said, unfortunate."

"You were here from—"

"All night, Herr Chief Inspector. Since eight. You can ask Karl in the booth." Lang leaned over for the intercom.

"That won't be necessary, Herr Lang. I'm sure you were here."

For the first time, Lang seemed on uneven ground. "What has this to do with me?"

"Your wife. Frau Rosenthal—"

"My *first* wife. And how do you have any of that information?"

"They also let me leaf through the files at the Alex, from time to time."

"They had those files sealed or destroyed."

"I'm sure that's what they told you."

Lang was now almost aggressive. "And?"

"The decision came down that it was suicide."

"The 'decision.' You don't sound convinced."

"It didn't matter then."

"And now?"

Hoffner had taken him far enough. A man like Lang could be helpful, if kept willing. Baiting him for too long would only cause problems down the line. Hoffner took another pull and then held out the cigarette. "It's quite good. A little mild, but good."

Lang seemed momentarily put off. Just as quickly, the smile returned. "You like something a bit tougher, Herr Chief Inspector?"

"With a bit more bite, perhaps."

Lang nodded and headed for a small table at the end of the row. He picked up a decanter. "Would a brandy do?" He poured out two glasses.

"Very kind."

Lang returned and handed Hoffner a glass. They drank. "My Lisl was an unstable woman," he said, again on intimate terms. "We'd seen several specialists, but there was a deep sadness there. It was only a matter of time. I told all of this to the detectives six years ago."

Hoffner took another sip. "You remarried quite quickly." Hoffner had followed Lang's goings-on for several months after the suicide: it was all in the file. The woman whom the unstable Frau Lisl had caught Lang with on that deeply sad night had become the second Mrs. Lang in a matter of weeks. To his credit, Lang was still married to this one.

"A very difficult time for me," Lang said with almost too much rec- ollection. "Thea—Fräulein von Harbou—was a great friend and com- fort." Hoffner finished off his glass. He said nothing. "You think I'm somehow involved with this?" said Lang. "Because a man chooses to take his life with a gun in a bathtub? I don't imagine it's the first time for either, Herr Chief Inspector."

"No, I don't imagine it is." Hoffner placed his glass on a nearby armrest. "You've no interest in who's dead this time, *mein Herr*?"

"Are you accusing me of something, Herr Chief Inspector?"

It was a fair point. "Someone goes to great lengths to make sure that a death looks identical to a suicide—"

"A death?" Lang perked up. "Are you implying something other than suicide?"

Hoffner ignored the obvious point. "Whatever questions may still be lingering from that earlier case, *mein Herr*, there seems to be only one possible conclusion. Who would want to lead me directly to you?"

This had not been so obvious. Lang stood silently for a moment. He then placed his glass next to Hoffner's and asked, "Who was in the bathtub?"

"Gerhard Thyssen."

Lang nodded as he thought. "Thyssen. Clever man." He spoke with genuine appreciation.

"Was he bringing any pressure to bear on the release date?"

"I'm sure he was. They all were. He was probably one of the few who knew it was a mistake. But no one—" Lang stopped himself. For a man who trafficked in the illusion of murder, deception, and betrayal, he seemed curiously squeamish when faced with its reality. It made him almost human.

Hoffner said, "You have no enemies, *mein Herr?*"

"Of course I have enemies, Herr Chief Inspector. It's the friends one would be hard-pressed to find. But this seems—clumsy. Obvious."

"Agreed."

Lang took a moment, then retrieved his glass and headed to the table. "Another?"

It was an odd reaction, somehow too easy. Hoffner watched as Lang lifted the decanter. "Thank you, no," said Hoffner. He then took a last pull on his cigarette and crushed it into the ashtray. Lang knew something; Hoffner could see it. The man just didn't realize it yet.

Lang was placing the decanter back on the tray when Hoffner caught the instant of recognition in his eyes. It was as if Lang was searching for something in the pale crystal. When he found it, he turned to Hoffner. "The Volker girl," he said. "An actress. She was sleeping with Thyssen."

Hoffner had expected something more convincing. "And this makes her unusual?"

Lang's smile returned. "Fair enough. We'd all slept with her. Thyssen's turn, I suppose. She'd been on a picture of mine. Meant to do a few scenes a week ago or so. She never made it to the set."

"Again, this makes her unusual?"

Lang seemed surprised by the question. "A nineteen-year-old starlet in a Fritz Lang production? A girl like that doesn't miss a moment of shooting."

It was the first bit of perfect truth Lang had given up. "And someone tried to contact her?"

"I'm sure."

"And she hasn't been back?"

"Not that I'm aware of, no."

Hoffner knew there was nothing more Lang could give him. "I'll
need her information."

"I'll make a call."

Twenty minutes on, Hoffner watched as the studio gate slipped
from sight in his rearview mirror, the afternoon glare forcing a momentary wince. As if on cue, his tooth began to throb.

Passing on the second brandy, he thought. That was a mistake.

LENI

IT WAS ODD finding himself back in this part of town.
Hoffner had stayed away ever since Georg had gone off to
Gymnasium, the old flat now lost to memory. Even toward the end,
though, the place had been little more than a string of darkened
rooms, only his own, the boy's, and the kitchen showing any willingness to life. The rental agent had commented on the strange patterns
of dust; he had also pointed out the lone cup of something once-
liquid brown on a side table in the living room. Hoffner had felt an
instant of purpose at its discovery, as if this had been Martha's last,
and he was somehow meant to remember it. He had thrown it away
with the rest of the china.

Truth to tell, a two-room walk-up near the Alex was hardly the
place to transplant twenty years of accrued furnishings, even those
bits and pieces accustomed to living in empty silhouette. He had
tossed it all.

Fräulein Volker's flat was a few blocks farther south from the old place, in that part of Kreuzberg that believed it had outrun its seaminess. There were no flophouses this far out, and the smell of boiling cabbage and root stock took on a tanginess that might even have passed for a bit of flavor.

The building was exactly what he imagined, five or six stories nestled in and among more of the same on a pleasant little square: just the place for a budding starlet, especially one who might be finding herself back behind a shop counter within the month. It had that freshly scrubbed air of assistant salesclerk or legal secretary evident in the well-kept flower boxes atop each stoop. Promise and hope hung in the air like the smell of diluted ammonia.

Naturally, Fräulein Volker's name appeared next to the bell for the top-floor flat. Wonderful. There was no point in ringing: Hoffner knew he would find no one there. That left the porter, who was less than delighted to be summoned, even more impatient at the sight of the badge.

"Not for me to know, Herr Detective." The man spoke with a dry certainty. His leather suspenders were speckled with crumbs from something flaky and green. In a strange twist, the pieces in his mustache were a cottony red. "I don't keep track of them." He combed a few fingers through the mustache. "They pay once a month, keep things clean, it's their business."

"No one's asked after her, or come by?"

"No." Still more certainty. "There was a telephone call, yesterday, the day before. Where she works. I don't know." An overly eager voice called from behind him. The man turned and shouted, "A minute!" He looked back at Hoffner with a smile meant to convey some unspoken bond between men. "A friend," he said, the yellow teeth rounding out the color scheme. He reached into his pocket and pulled out a set of keys. "Take it." He handed Hoffner a small silver one. "Look around. Just slide it under my door when you're done."

Hoffner heard a woman's cackling laughter through the wall as he headed up the stairs, followed by what sounded like "Then put your knickers back on the phonograph," but it was only a guess. Maybe, then, the flower boxes were meant merely as a distraction?

The flat was at least three rooms, with a long corridor stretching to the back and a separate kitchen tucked in up at the front. The size notwithstanding, Hoffner had expected something more modest. Instead, the decor was a collision of that stark, metallic aggression so popular nowadays—low, boxy bookcases and reedy, narrow tables. He always thought that this particular trend had everything looking like a letter of the alphabet: the L-shaped sofa, the S-shaped chairs, the V-shaped lamps with their two-headed bulbs. Somehow it was all meant to suggest a kind of coherence. The only thing that made any real sense was how well Herr Thyssen had been keeping his little friend.

It was hardly a surprise, then, to find her hanging nude above the sofa: these wall-sized photographs were all the rage now. Hoffner stared up at the daring Fräulein Volker, sitting with her back to the camera, her shoulders turned, her eyes gazing out through a wave of flaxen hair. She held a flimsy piece of cloth in her hands to cover the breasts, but the rest draped over her upper thighs with just enough of a droop to bring full attention to the pale swellings of her perfectly formed rump. O-shaped, thought Hoffner. Two lovely half-Os.

He was inclined to take a closer look, when he heard something moving from one of the back rooms. He waited through several seconds of silence until it came again. It was the sound of a drawer being opened and closed. Luckily, Hoffner never felt uneasy in moments like these; he never let surprise create what wasn't there. Instead, he quietly made his way down the corridor and stopped at the doorway to the bedroom.

A woman—tall and slim—was leaning over one of the side tables, a stack of papers held in one hand. The other was sifting through the drawer's contents. From the dark coloring of her hair, Hoffner knew this was not Ingrid Volker. The well-fitted green skirt and white blouse—neither German-made—were also not in keeping with the Fräulein's sophistication: they showed a bit of taste. The woman turned to see Hoffner staring across at her.

She stood there, not as if she had been caught out, which she had, but as if she had already accepted the challenge: any accusation now would seem foolish. The strength was less in her gaze or the way she stood—although both conveyed an unrelenting certainty—as in the easy grasp of her fingers. They were long and thin and perfectly delicate, and it was their indifference that gave them their power: she might just as well have been holding the stack out to him. Her face had that same quality, fine and pale and seemingly inviting, but perhaps just too inviting to take the risk. She would have called herself beautiful, and Hoffner would have agreed.

"Coyle," she said. "Helen Coyle." Hoffner had her in her early thirties. "And you must be a policeman."

That was the third time today someone had stated the obvious. Maybe it was time for a new suit? "An American who can spot a German detective," he said. "Impressive." Hoffner saw the first crack in her otherwise flawless stare.

"I thought my accent was better," she said.

"It is. Quite excellent. It's the watch. Not the kind a European would wear."

She glanced down for a moment, then back. "You're a very good policeman. You don't wear one."

"No, I don't." Hoffner was no less affable. "How did you get in here, Fräulein?"

"The door was open."

"That's probably not the case."

"True. It probably wasn't." She reached over to the bed and picked up her coat. "Should we get a coffee—or a brandy? That would be more European, wouldn't it?"

"Fräulein Coyle—"

"Helen. Leni, if you prefer."

The world was now filled with such familiarity. "Fräulein," Hoffner said patiently, "I'm really going to need to know how you got inside this flat. Then we can move on to the why and the who. All right?"

"So you don't drink brandy?"

Hoffner stifled the urge to smile. "I've a bottle back in my office at the Alex. I'd be more than happy to discuss it there."

"Subtle but to the point. A very, very good policeman." She pulled a pack of cigarettes from her coat. "Rothmans. I know. English. But at least I'm getting closer to the Continent." She tossed the coat onto the bed and tapped one out. "You have a light?" Hoffner obliged, and two spears of smoke streamed from her nose. "Thyssen," she said casually. "But you probably knew that. He had a set of keys. At his flat. So that makes two doors that were left open."

She knew why he had come and showed no hesitation at throwing it back in his face. Hoffner had to applaud the bravura. "And you knew they were for this particular flat," he said. "These keys you just happened to find lying about?"

This time, the dip in her stare brought a playful smile to the eyes. "Are you going to pick up on every little detail from now on?"

"There've been so few of them, Fräulein, you leave me little choice." He nodded at the papers. "Anything of interest?"

She thought a moment, then extended the stack to him as she spoke: "A few letters to and from Thyssen. Bills. Cards from the night-clubs they must have been to." Hoffner began to glance through. "Each of them has a little note on the back—what she drank, what they danced to. Pretty soppy stuff. I would have killed myself, too."

Hoffner continued to read. "Then it's lucky you weren't involved with her, Fräulein." He looked up. "So who are you involved with?"

She seemed oddly naked without the papers and coat, only the cig-arette at her chest to lend the pose a hint of modesty. Again she waited before answering. "Now that would require a brandy, don't you think, Herr Detective?"

ROLLO'S WAS A FEW BLOCKS north and deeper into the real Kreuzberg: with character, she said.

Hoffner had been happy enough to leave the flat. No doubt Fräulein Coyle had found the most interesting papers; anything more significant would require a much closer look, and that was something he would need to go back for on his own.

He ordered two brandies.

It was a cramped little bar, a few tables in the back, where the light seemed to dim as the smell of vinegar potatoes grew more pungent. She had picked a spot somewhere in the middle, although they could have sat anywhere. Aside from the barman, the only other person in the place was a young woman dozing at the back, her head tilted against the wall, her mouth gaped open in sleep. The ringlets in her hair had begun to droop as well, joining her lips in a chorus of silent *oohs*. But it was the faded ruffles on the collar and cuffs that made it clear where she had spent the afternoon: business at the nearby hotels always slowed around five. The slab of cheese and bread, along with a half-glass of slivovitz, were all that stood between her and the long night ahead.

"Throw some paint on that face," said Coyle, "a long satin number on that figure, and I'd have her working for Sam Goldwyn in a week."

The American was not shy about talking. In fact, she had spent the better part of the walk over regaling him with tales of her past: Ziegfeld girl (always down front), promise of a small film role, Hollywood, too many wayward nights stretching into weeks, name after name after name (most of which Hoffner had never heard), a month drying out, two months (all right, a year), film role gone, a few well-heeled keepers (more meaningless names), a flat of her own, bootstraps, and finally the kindness of Sam Goldwyn himself. As far as Hoffner could make out, Leni—she was now insisting on Leni—was what her associates called a talent agent, in the pay of Metro-Goldwyn-Mayer, and in Berlin trying to find Ingrid Volker. It was as simple as that, and that, of course, made it anything but simple.

"She's a prostitute," said Hoffner.

The brandies arrived. "Of course she is. What difference does that make?"

"You don't think much of your business, do you?"

"What a ridiculous thing to say." She pulled out a cigarette. "Give Sleeping Beauty over there another choice and she might just surprise you."

Hoffner lit hers. "The whore with the golden heart. I think I've seen that film."

"The cop without one. Less popular, but just as gripping."

Hoffner marveled at the way she let nothing slip by. There was a rawness to it that made her almost brittle. He lit his own, then took a drink. "Your German is quite excellent. I would say flawless."

"My mother was Austrian, although I think the town is somewhere in Hungary now. I can never follow any of that. She met my father in a Viennese brothel—and no, she was a nurse. The place caught fire. He was an artist—Paris, Prague, Vienna. Wherever young Americans were supposed to go to figure it all out. He'd convinced one of the girls to pose for him—"

"I'm sure he had."

"Dad lost two fingers from the burns and never picked up a brush again. So he picked up my mother and took her back to Pennsylvania."

Hoffner knew he was not the first to hear this rendition of the story. Still, it had all the necessary elements: artists and nurses, Vienna and fingers. He tapped out a bit of ash, keeping his eyes on the cigarette. "And a few years later—you."

"So there is a heart in there somewhere?"

"Unlikely."

"I'm sure Frau Hoffner would disagree."

Hoffner knew she wouldn't have. He finished his drink and said, "Another?" Before Coyle could answer, he called over to the barman. "Two more." He then looked across at her. "Someone at Ufa gave you the keys to Thyssen's, Fräulein."

It was the first time this afternoon that anything had caught her by surprise. In fact, Hoffner wondered if it might have been the first time altogether. The barman drew up and waited while she tossed back what was left in her glass. She then placed it on the table and watched as the man spilled out two more before heading back to the bar.

"If we had a napkin," she said, "we could squeeze out another half-glass between us."

Hoffner took a last pull on his cigarette. "I need to know who it was at Ufa, Fräulein."

"Leni, please."

He crushed the stub into the ashtray and said nothing.

For a moment she looked as if she might be calculating odds. When she finally spoke, her tone was flat and distant. "You've met Joachim Ritter?" Hoffner nodded. "Goldwyn's very interested in Fräulein Volker. One of his directors saw her in a cabaret, thinks he can be her Stiller." When Hoffner began to ask, she explained, "Mauritz Stiller. Discovered Garbo. They say she was a pudgy little thing. Now look at her. At least this Volker girl is meant to be skinny. Goldwyn wants to steal her before the Germans discover her. Or at least before Ufa does. He'll pay a great deal for her contract."

"And Ufa is happy to sell off a potential star?"

"For what Goldwyn is offering? She'd have to be the biggest box-office draw Ufa has ever seen—and she'd have to do it for the next ten years. Ritter's too smart not to take the money up front and let the Americans see if she's worth it. So, given what's on the table, Ritter thought I should have as much access to her as I could."

"And he knew Thyssen would have the keys to her place?"

"Yes."

"Meaning Ritter had no trouble sending you to a dead man's flat to find those keys?"

Her stare was now impenetrable. "I was improvising."

"You've a reputation, then, for tracking down missing girls, no matter where it takes you?"

"Girls, boys. Whatever's in demand."

Hoffner now realized he had underestimated her. There was a hollowness there, one that gave her an almost cruel precision. What he had yet to determine was how effortless that precision might be. "You'll want to do a little less improvising, Fräulein."

"But this would seem the best time for it, don't you think, Detective?"

"In Los Angeles, perhaps. Not here."

A faint light of mockery played in her eyes. "Am I being told to stay away?" Before he could answer, she said, "Hoffner." She was studying him, the cigarette just out of lips' reach. "That's very German. It's the Nikolai that's not right."

He still had half a glass; he could afford the time. At least that was the reason he gave himself for answering. "Really?"

"Of course. Douglas Fairbanks makes you swoon. Doug Fairbanks sells you ladies' shoes."

"So you'd want a Nicki—"

"That's horrible."

Martha had thought otherwise. "Nick, then."

"Too much. I'd go in a completely different direction. Unless you're directing. Then the Russian thing works just fine."

"And Fräulein Volker?" Clearly, this was where she wanted him to go: no reason not to follow.

"Same problem," she said. "It fights against itself. Ingrid Volker. Swedish, German—which is it?"

"Maybe that's what makes it interesting?"

"No. It's the wrong kind of interesting." There was nothing aggressive in the tone, just the truth. "Why try and make sense of it? Berlin, Los Angeles. That's never the point. It's always about the studio. If you don't understand that, you have no idea what you're getting yourself into."

This morning's escapade had made that clearer than Hoffner wanted to admit. He took his billfold out and, along with a few marks, pulled his card. "In case Berlin proves to be more than it seems." He placed the card by her glass, then set the bills by his own.

"A free pass, Herr Detective?" She was looking directly at him. "I'm touched." She took the card and, reading, feigned surprise. "Only your office number and address?" She slid it back toward him. "I don't trust police stations. You'll have to do better than that if you want my help."

He really had underestimated her. He pulled a pen from his pocket and wrote his information on the back of the card.

" 'Göhrener Strasse,' " she read. "That's a bit dicey, isn't it?"

"You know Berlin?"

"Not really." She placed the card in her purse. "I'm at the Adlon. Room 427." She stood. "Just in case Berlin proves to be more than it seems."

She was already heading for the girl at the back before Hoffner could answer. He watched as she scribbled a note on a napkin, then placed it under the girl's glass, all the while making sure not to wake her. Hoffner was still sitting when she came back to retrieve her things. He stood and helped her into her coat.

"Two weeks," she said. "You won't even recognize her." She let his hands rest for just too long on her shoulders before turning to him. "Happy hunting, Detective."

She was through the door just as the girl began coughing herself awake.

THE SIGHT OF THE CYRILLIC SCRIPT—cut deep into the stone—meant that there was no turning back. Hoffner had made the promise to himself years ago: retreat was always possible from the gravel foreyard; it was even advisable when wending his way through the small, unkempt garden where the building's four un-washed floors remained far enough removed to seem almost impar-tial. But not now. The place held him in its grasp.

He rang the bell and continued to stare up at the lettering. Remark-able how the shape could make even the words "Château Russe" seem unforgiving.

A wraith of an attendant opened the door and recognized him at once, her disapproval marred only by her resignation. "You've half an hour," she said in Russian. "The doors lock at seven. Not a minute later." She pulled back the door and waited for him to pass.

Durable and cold was how the place always presented itself, walls of scarred wood climbing to an imagined ceiling: the sound of his own footfalls only added to the empty desperation. Mother Russia was calling her own home with a futility each of them evidently craved.

He stepped into a large hall, tables and chairs scattered about under the glow of lamps outmanned by the shadows. Three large chandeliers hung from the ceiling, but they, too, were pitifully overwhelmed. Each had lost several bulbs to neglect, leaving a pattern of lights that seemed to be sending out some kind of coded plea of contrition. There were moments of life here and there—a game of cards, chess— but most of the occupants sat silently by themselves. One man had clearly been the recipient of recent guests. He slouched courageously in a tunic and cap, a few medals pinned at his chest. Even so, the eyes stared out vacantly. If he had seen kindness, he had forgotten it. More likely, he had learned not to expect it.

In all the years Hoffner had been coming, he had never once met any of these others, no gentle "Good evening, Colonel" as he passed by. Their isolation was complete, a place where death stood as a bright beacon to those who had grown too sensitive to the light. They remained alive only because they refused to look forward.

Her chair was off by the far wall and empty, which meant Hoffner had a nice climb ahead of him. He was still catching his breath as he stepped through the doorway to Dormitory 3, the two rows of beds jutting out from the wall, barracks-style. All but two were empty, hers about halfway down. Had this been a German institution, each bed would have come with a chair at its side, a neat little dresser with room for some well-tended treasures on top—pictures, comb, brush, a favorite glass or vase—but this was not German. She had insisted on a kind of comfort that came only from memory, no matter how distant or revised. Cossacks and rifles and burning villages were conveniently erased. She belonged with Russians, with Jews. He had found her the only place in Berlin to accommodate both.

He spoke in Russian. "Hello, Mama."

She was propped up on a pillow in a pose of sitting sleep. She opened her eyes. She, too, had long given up on kindness.

"Is it Thursday?"

He knew she knew otherwise. "Monday. I always come Mondays."

"True, but you don't come, so it might as well be Thursday."

Hoffner saw a chair a few beds down. He stepped over and placed it just out of arm's reach of her bed. Sitting, he pulled a small bag of chocolates from his pocket. "Hirschorn's," he said as he leaned forward to place it on her stomach. "The ones with the nuts."

"How many have you had?"

"None."

"So you don't like them?"

This, in some form or other, was always the opening act: chocolates, flowers, a book. It never mattered which. Hoffner reached over again, tore off the string, and took a piece. He put it in his mouth. "Delicious."

For some reason, his mother still had remarkably fine-looking hands. She slid one into the bag, felt around for the appropriate piece, and then brought it to her mouth. Her face, in strict contrast, had aged in deep, mottled lines, as if to offset the litheness of the fingers. "You've only made it worse for me," she said. "They'll all want a bit of chocolate now, and the two of us will be through this by the time you go. They'll smell it on me, and they'll know." She took a bite.

Hoffner reached into his other pocket and pulled out a second bag. He placed it at the foot of the bed. "You can dole it out to the most deserving."

She took a second bite and nodded distantly.

"You're not feeling well?" he said. He only now noticed the short table at the other side of the bed. It was littered with a few vials, each half-filled with a deep red liquid.

"That's what they say."

"You've no opinion on the matter?"

She managed a moment without self-pity. "Something in my chest." She then plucked out a second piece of chocolate. "They'd tell me not to have this." She took a healthy bite and, for the first time, showed a trace of pleasure.

"Then maybe you shouldn't."

Pulling the bag up close to her face, she began to scrutinize the contents. "Maybe." Her eyes remained fixed as she lowered her voice. "They're giving me trouble again."

"Who? The director? Tell him we've been through this."

"Not the director. He understands the situation. He's only too happy to let me know how well he understands the situation."

"Then who?"

"The doctors. The women. Everyone. They treat me as if I don't belong."

"It's all in your head."

That, of course, was not entirely true. Most of the residents of the Château—a French name for a Russian home; Hoffner had never understood it—had arrived just after the war, fleeing either the Bolsheviks or the Whites or whatever else Jews flee from. It was a place where those too old to make a new start in a new world were set aside by a government still trying to find its way. The onetime Reichs President Ebert, with some sympathy for his own, had done what he could. Evidently it had not been much.

It was, however, exactly what Frau Hoffner had been longing for, even if Russia had last seen her in the summer of 1871. In fact, she had been a German citizen since 1873, and had converted two years later to some form of Christianity—Hoffner had never been told which—so as not to be an impediment to her husband's career. Even then, Walther Hoffner had managed to rise only so far as the noble, if bitter, rank of Kripo detective sergeant, on a pension half as large as the one his son was due to make. Dead nine years, Walther had left his wife seeking her past. She had gone to an official on Münzstrasse for the paperwork, whereupon Rokel Hoffner had, once again, become a Jew.

The director had promised to keep the particulars of her history discreet. Such men lived on empty promises.

"I can take you out of here," Hoffner said. They were now on to the second act. "You only pretend to be weak and disagreeable. You could have a room of your own, maybe two, closer into town. I've got the money."

"Then why don't you do it?"

This was where he had learned to appreciate the stamina of self-pity. "Because you don't want me to."

"Why should that stop you?"

He smiled with a recollected warmth. "It shouldn't, but it does. Are you going to leave me a few pieces?"

She handed him the bag. "I wasn't always like this."

"You aren't like this now. It's just for me. As punishment. We both know I deserve it."

"Yes, but you don't let it sink in. You've never let things sink in. It makes it all a waste."

She was never shy with the truth. He took a chocolate. "I saw Georgi today." This brought a spark of life to her eyes. "He's out at one of the film studios. Running errands for very important people."

The moment of joy slipped away. "He doesn't know about any of this? You haven't told him?"

"Why would I tell him?"

"Because you can be overly sentimental."

She had always confused sentiment with duty, he thought. "And who would that help?"

"I don't want him to see this place, or me in it."

"It's been seven years. If he doesn't know by now, he won't. He's a boy of sixteen with a dying grandmother. He'll see you at the funeral."

This seemed to quiet any concern. Funny how she never asked about Sascha anymore. A bell rang in the corridor and Hoffner hoisted himself up.

She said, "Always so relieved when you hear it."

He leaned over and kissed her on the forehead. "I count the minutes."

She waited until he had his hat in hand to say, "It doesn't make you a better man that you come."

If that were all it took, thought Hoffner, how easy a thing it would be to unburden himself of all manner of self-delusion. He buttoned his coat. "I'll try to come by next Monday. I'll bring a book, a novel. We'll read a bit together."

Her eyes were already shut. Even then, she was no closer to peace than when he had first arrived, and it was that, and that alone, that always cut him. Not for the sadness or loneliness or desperation that breathed in every corner of the place, but for his own failure. Hoffner carried it like an added weight to his own isolation, out into the street, and imagined that this was what shame must have felt like.

IT HAD BEEN A DAY OF FLATS, Georg's, the Volker girl's, and now his own. The lamplight beyond the shades spilled into the room and brought what few pieces of furniture he had into partial relief. Hoffner tossed his hat onto a chair, and set the small plate of cheese and dumplings on the table. He had picked up the food at the bar around the corner; it was still relatively warm. The plate would go back tomorrow morning.

He turned on the light by the stove and opened the icebox. He remembered having boiled a few eggs two, three days ago, and leaned down to retrieve them. Instead, he found a plate of beef, noodles, and peas, with a note at its side: *The eggs spoiled and you would have eaten them. I'll be by later. M.*

Schiller, his landlord, must have let her up, thought Hoffner. Schiller liked big-breasted women. Hoffner's involvement with Maria had raised him threefold in Schiller's eyes. "A nice healthy girl," Schiller had said that first time he saw Hoffner send her out into the night. "Well done, Kripo." Schiller had no respect for the police. Not that he was a socialist or Communist, or whatever "ist" was now most despising of authority. He just thought he could take care of himself.

Hoffner preferred small breasts. They were never the prize and therefore required no special expertise. Women like Maria expected a bit of fanfare, even a delight and gratitude that Hoffner lacked the will to pretend. He recalled the disappointment in her eyes that first time she had unveiled them, certainly well kept for a woman somewhere past forty, but he had known to set the tone even then. There would be nothing between them to hint at anticipation, let alone happiness. Only a plate of beef and a sometime comfort.

He picked up the food, turned out the light, and stepped over to the window. He took solace in seeing Berlin under darkness. The days of unwavering sun were beginning to dull the city's angularity: patterns were still there, but the details were being washed away. Berlin reemerged at night, but only in her backstreets. Elsewhere, she was giving in to the erosion. Constant light, natural or otherwise, had a fondness for decay.

He heard the knock at the door and thought she might have given him at least time to finish the meal. Letting go the shade, he placed the plate on the table as the knocking became more insistent. "All right, all right," he said. "You know I haven't room to hide a girl."

He pulled open the door and found Leni standing in front of him. Her face was paler than he remembered.

From the corridor's far end, Schiller's voice rose with winded insistence. "Look here," he said, hulking his large frame toward them. "You don't just push your way through—"

"It's all right, Schiller." Hoffner continued to stare at her. "I know the lady." He was waiting to see something in the eyes.

"And you think that settles it?" Schiller wanted more for his efforts. "Me having to run after her? This isn't some cheap house up in Prenzlauer where jilted girls go running after—"

"I've been attacked, *mein Herr*." Leni spoke with the same quiet authority that had been so convincing this afternoon. This time, however, she had left a small wedge open for sympathy. "Herr Hoffner is the only friend I have in Berlin. You'll forgive my indiscretion."

Hoffner noticed the rips along her coat sleeve and the small welt under her chin. How he had missed them only moments ago puzzled him.

Schiller saw them now as well. "Well, I—" He seemed to fold in on himself. "Attacked, was it?" He fumbled for another moment, then looked at Hoffner. "That's serious business, then. Nothing to do with me." He nodded as if to reassure himself and began to back his way down the corridor. "I'll say good luck to you, then, Fräulein." He bounced a nod Hoffner's way. "Kripo." And, realizing this was his best opportunity, quickly turned and headed to the stairs.

For an instant Hoffner felt something strangely familiar, a tightening in his chest he hadn't known in years. It was the need to protect. Just as quickly it was gone. With no other choice, he pulled back the door and invited her in.

INGRID

"VERY NICE," she said, giving the place the once-over before settling into the sofa. "I didn't realize chief inspectors lived so high on the hog."

Hoffner pulled two glasses and a bottle from a shelf and placed them on the table in front of her. Without asking, he poured out two brandies. "High on the what?" he asked.

"The hog. The good life. Top of the line." The window for sympathy had evidently closed. She took her glass. "I don't suppose it translates."

"I don't suppose it does," he said, and pulled over a chair.

"I might have been laying it on a bit thick, but you really are the only person I know in town. The boys out at the studio don't count."

"Or volunteer their home addresses." Hoffner took a drink.

She tried a smile, but the welt won out. "That, too."

"You'll want something for that." He went to the icebox, and she said, "And about this afternoon. If anything I said—" She stopped herself.

Hoffner pulled some ice from the bucket and reached over for a rag by the sink. "Said about what?"

"At the bar. Your wife. I didn't know." He could feel her watching him as he folded the rag over the ice. "I did a little poking around," she continued. "It's something I do. Habit, I suppose."

He tied a small knot and started back to her. "It's a long time ago," he said, and handed her the ice.

"Still, pretty horrible. A victim in one of your own murder cases. How do you get past that?"

No room for sympathy at all, he thought. He waited until she had the ice under her chin before saying, "So where was this attack?" He sat.

"I do that sometimes. I don't know why." There was a surprising vulnerability in her face, not for any lingering fear, but for the sudden recognition of her own callousness. "Keep on pressing at something. It's stupid. And it's none of my business. I'm sorry."

Hoffner noticed the empty glass and poured her another. "As I said, a long time ago."

"That's just to be kind."

He topped off his own. "Maybe it is." He placed the bottle on the table and tapped at his pockets for a cigarette. She quickly pulled out her case.

"If you're willing to slum it," she said. He took one and she explained, "It was a spot near the Hallesches Gate." She snapped her purse shut and exhaled: the sound and smoke seemed to focus her. "It was one of the names in the Volker girl's cards. Lots of lederhosen and sunburnt thighs."

The Hallesches Gate, thought Hoffner. Just the place for an American. Hoffner narrowed it down to the Cozy Corner or The Trap. "For the tourists," he said. "You enjoyed it?"

"As far as it went."

What a perfect answer: enough to show him how little would shock her, still more to let him know how far she might take things. Hoffner said, "The real sex clubs don't advertise in the same way."

"Must have been a laugh for Thyssen and the girl. A trip to the zoo to gawk at the animals."

"Or a safe way to dabble."

This brought a moment's surprise. "You don't think he was homosexual?"

Hoffner hadn't thought about it one way or the other. Still, it was nice to see her caught unawares. "Him, her, too soon to tell, although I don't think either would be a first in your line of work."

"And you don't approve."

"Of your line of work?" He allowed himself a half-smile. "I don't think my approval is much of an issue. What a man does or doesn't do—he'll do it anyway. All that matters is if he gets killed for it and a girl goes missing. That's when my opinion matters."

She stared across at him, the smoke from her cigarette curling between them. "You didn't answer my question."

"I don't believe you asked a question."

"The brandy's not terribly good."

"It goes with the furnishings."

"You could do better."

"That would require a bit of effort."

"Still, it might be worthwhile."

"It might."

Hoffner hadn't played at this in years. The transparency of the thing made it all the more daring: he could almost feel the excitement in her breath. From somewhere deep within him, his isolation seemed to take on a voice all its own. It said, This isn't the way out for you, and you know it. Then again, it might just have been a plea for its own self-preservation, and why let it damn him for that?

"Let me take a look," he said, and reached across for the ice. She handed him the rag, then tilted her head. The neck was lithe and smooth, the tiny blue-red bumps of the welt only drawing out its fineness. He placed his fingers against her skin. She breathed in deeply and he released.

"You'll have that for a day or two," he said.

"I don't usually bruise so easily." She had a compact out and was doing what she could with a bit of powder.

"Back of the hand?"

"The man was a brute. I don't think he meant to hit me. There was a lot of pushing. He might even have slipped."

"Any idea why?"

"Wet floor?" It was the only false note she had struck. She knew it instantly. "I asked to have a look at one of the private rooms." She seemed to take her misstep out on the butt of her cigarette, crushing it into the ashtray. "Someone remembered seeing the Volker girl and a man heading up to one a week or so ago. My friend with the knuckles didn't think I needed a viewing." She brushed the ash from her fingers.

"So you became an added sideshow for the tourists."

"Something like that."

Hoffner didn't believe it. The clubs around the Hallesches Gate thrived on a kind of wholesome depravity: what corruption there was never ventured beyond the safe. How else could they keep the tourists coming in? He tossed back his glass and said, "Well then, we should have another chat with him."

The chance to gauge her reaction was lost to the sound of a key in the lock. Hoffner turned to see Maria, packages in hand, moving toward the icebox. Unaware of her audience, she placed a few bottles of beer, some day-old bread, and a slab of butter on the counter. When she turned, her surprise quickly gave way to a bare silence.

It was nearly half a minute before she spoke. "Schiller said you weren't back." Again she waited. "He gave me the key."

What a bastard Schiller was, thought Hoffner. He stood. "Must not have seen me come in." He motioned to Leni. "This is Fräulein Coyle. She's involved with a case. An American. Fräulein Coyle, Fräulein Gerber."

Leni nodded from her seat with that vacant smile the beautiful reserve for the plain. "Delighted."

Maria had evidently seen it before; her gaze was all the more unkind. "An American? How exotic a case for you, Nikolai." She reached for the chair, expecting to find her coat, when she realized she was still wearing it. "I'll go, then. Let you work it through."

"Actually," Leni broke in as she stood, "we were just going our-selves, Fräulein. I've made a mess of things, and the chief inspector has been kind enough to come to my rescue."

Hoffner had no idea whether Leni was trying to help him or hurt him; either way, she was doing her very best. "The Fräulein was attacked," he said, and, not knowing why, "You should stay. I won't be long." The words "Let me pity you" might just as well have been ring-ing in the room.

"There's beer and bread and butter," Maria said. "I don't think you have coffee." She placed the key by the sink. "You'll see Herr Schiller gets it back." Hoffner took a step toward her, but it was an empty ges-ture. "Fräulein," she said as she moved to the door. Her "Nikolai" lin-gered in the corridor like the stench of a wet dog.

Hoffner had long ago dispensed with remorse for these moments of relief. There would be something unpleasant in the next day or two, recriminations, a list of offenses, and he would submit to them all before watching her try to bring him back. But there would be no going back this time. Instead, he would suffer through the sudden sur-prise in her face at his acceptance of it all, the chance lost, the truth in her appraisal, on and on. Her eyes would grow impossibly warm—"No, no, it's not what I meant"—then equally cold at his firmness. It would all fall away, and he could already feel the weight lifting.

"Shall we, Fräulein?" he said, as if the last few minutes had played out only for him.

Sensible enough to let it pass, Leni headed for the door.

THERE ARE THOSE PARTS OF TOWN that mock at their own seediness, garish light, music trailing out into the streets, with a bit of good humor that insists that, even if the stink lies just beneath the sur-face, why let it spoil the fun. None is more accomplished than the

Hallesches Gate, towering above the proceedings with an elbow to the ribs, goading the half-conscious boozer to gawk at the excess.

It is a cheap little show, and not worth the ticket for those who know Berlin. There might have been a time when the sex halls and whiskey parlors served an honest purpose as counterweights to a scorched life of middle-class unemployment, inflation, and malnutrition. Hoffner had even seen something noble in a city that knew how to tend to its own with the promise of temporary oblivion—but not now. The laughter had turned in on itself, skewering the very people who were keeping the places alive: the half-naked Negress, the cocaine-needled arm of the man dressed as a woman dressed as a man dressed as . . . The uniforms were as clear as day, giving it all a kind of manageable vice. Hoffner imagined that these were the boys and girls shunned by the private clubs and secret societies of schooldays, now triumphant in an unintended conformity. Staring into one such pack, he found it difficult to know who was sneering at whom.

Monday was African Night at The Trap, where the two or three Negroes on staff were joined by the rest in blackface. A tiny blonde, who had gone to great lengths to tar the backs of her hands, took Hoffner's coat and hat and handed him a ticket. A genuine African in loincloth delicately pulled Leni's from her shoulders and retreated with the girl.

"She wouldn't know what to do with him if she got the chance." Leni spoke over the noise as a fat, very German little man led them through the crowd. "We've got better in the States."

Hoffner followed her. "You spent a good deal of time breeding them, if I remember."

"Not fair bringing up past indiscretions."

"I wasn't trying to be fair."

They arrived at the table and he ordered them two brandies.

"I'm impressed," she said as she glanced through the menu. "You didn't pull out your badge, race to get to the bottom of things. You're playing this very well."

Truth to tell, Hoffner wasn't exactly sure what he was playing at. "You're too kind."

"And no—I don't see him, if that's what you're wondering." She had yet to take her eyes from the menu.

The band was thumping away with something American—lots of horns and drums—as Hoffner scanned above the faces. The private rooms were a floor up, along an exposed balcony that ran the length of each wall. Sexual romps, with perhaps just a hint of professional pleasure tossed in, were paid for on the sly, a passed note to the maître d', a few marks exchanged, followed by some token gift placed on the table—a white rose, a pouch of tobacco—to inform the large men at the foot of the stairs that access had been granted. From the look of things, tonight's choice was a yellow glove.

"They don't allow prostitutes," she said, her eyes still fixed on the menu. "I asked." She seemed momentarily confused. "What exactly is a 'Nubian Moon'?"

Hoffner continued to track the balcony. "Something chocolate, I imagine. In the shape of a woman's ass."

She looked up with a surprised admiration. "You've eaten here before?"

"No." He looked across at her. "Odd that he's not here."

"Maybe someone didn't like the way he was treating the guests?"

"Maybe someone didn't want one of those guests coming back and finding him." Hoffner called over a waiter. "We'll have a Nubian Moon and two spoons."

Hoffner watched as the couples, trios, and quartets made their way up the stairs, arms around waists, stolen gropes and playful slaps, the carpet stained with too many liters of spilled whiskey to count. This was how the self-parody played itself out, up to the narrow stage, where the shrieked laughter of false vulgarity served as the last desperate plea for attention. The large men who escorted these bands to their appointed doors seemed almost inhuman by comparison, their stony faces and measured steps the stuff of a Fritz Lang imagination. And as with Lang, there was something hypnotic to the movement. Hoffner watched as the doors opened and closed, as the eager slipped in and the sated out. It was several minutes before he realized that none of the escorts was stopping at a door about halfway down the back wall. There was nothing to it other than its absence from the ritual.

"You were right," Leni said, licking at her spoonful. "It's very nice chocolate. We don't get this kind of stuff in the States."

Hoffner turned to see two round mounds of dark pudding sitting in a raised cup. He had no idea when it had arrived. "Which room did they say Thyssen and the girl used?"

She dipped in for a second helping. "So the trance is broken."

"Sorry."

"No, it was fun to watch. You lick your lips every so often." She set her spoon by the cup. "They didn't say which room."

He pulled a few marks from his pocket and placed them on the table. "Have a bit more. We won't be coming back. Things might get unpleasant."

There was a studied calm in her expression, as if such warnings carried no weight. He might have mistaken it for arrogance, but he knew better. This was control, and willingly or not, Hoffner could feel its pull from across the table. "I've had my fill," she said, pushing back her chair. He stood and followed her through the crowd to the stairs.

She was reaching for the banister when a powerful hand rose up to stop her. Its owner was equally dense. "No, no, Fräulein. Private rooms."

Leni nodded to a group wending its way up. "They don't look that private."

The shrug seemed to swallow the boy's neck completely. "What can I say? Private."

Hoffner stepped forward while reaching into his pocket. Almost at once, the boy was on him, the smirk gone, the hands moving with unexpected speed. He seemed to have Hoffner's arm in his grasp when just as quickly his expression turned to shock, then pain. Hoffner held the boy's wrist, twisting and pinning it up against the chest: it was remarkable to see that much size incapable of movement. "Don't" was all Hoffner said. The boy nodded once. With his free hand, Hoffner again reached into his pocket and pulled out his badge. "You see what I was trying to find? You know what it is?" Again the boy nodded. "There's a room upstairs I'd like to see. You'll be taking me to it." The final nod was little more than a spasm of pain. "Good." Hoffner released and the boy instantly brought his hand up to his shoulder.

His words were sweaty with justification. "I thought you had—"

"I know what you thought I had. Just take us up."

Hoffner expected the signal to be a little less obvious than a stumble on the stairs, but subtlety was not really The Trap's selling point. Evidently neither was subterfuge: waiting outside the door was a small, pasty man buffered by a trio of interchangeably large thugs. Hoffner had never mentioned which room he wanted to see.

"Detective." The man spoke through a practiced smile. "We've never met, have we?"

The none-too-veiled reference to the Kripo men on his payroll made the man at least something of a challenge. Hoffner said, "I'm sure you pay them very well, *mein Herr*."

"I'm sure I have no idea what you mean, Detective."

"Yes, I'm sure you don't. But we both know I'm not here about what goes on inside the rest of these rooms. Just this one."

"Same as the others, Detective. And we'd be delighted to open one up to you—and your lady friend, of course—along with any guests you require. Unfortunately, this one is being remodeled."

"But then you see that's my particular fetish, *mein Herr*. The smell of paint, the ripped fabric."

For just an instant, the man's eyes narrowed. "You'd be wise to let this go, Detective." It was as if the man was speaking on orders.

"Was that the same message you had for the lady earlier tonight?" said Hoffner. "When one of your boys smacked her around?"

The man seemed momentarily at a loss. He turned his eyes to the thug nearest him, who quietly shook his head. It was the first unrehearsed moment Hoffner had seen. "Perhaps the lady is mistaken."

"She's not," Leni cut in.

Hoffner said, "The door, *mein Herr*." This time the man's eyes darted to the entrance below. "Whoever it is," Hoffner countered, "they won't get here in time. The door. I won't ask again."

There comes a moment when a man gives in to the futility of his situation. Some falter under the weight; others feel the release. Luckily for Hoffner, Herr TrapTrap was one of the latter. He pulled a key from his pocket and, with a sudden sense of purpose, unlocked the door. He stood aside.

Hoffner said, "You'll wait here, Fräulein."

The room was all mirrors and draped fabric, with an oversized bed against the far wall. Aside from that, the place was empty. Hoffner started for the bed when Leni brushed past him. "There's a door back here," she said. "Behind the curtains." She tried to open it.

The man had been cleverer than Hoffner realized. This was all taking time. "It looks like we'll be needing another key, *mein Herr*." He would deal with Leni later.

The man waited until he had the second lock open before saying, "You're making a mistake, Detective." The uncertainty now had a hint of self-preservation.

"Well, then I imagine we both are." Hoffner pushed open the door and, in mock surrender, turned to Leni. "Fräulein?"

He followed her down a short corridor—more mirrors and fabric—and through to a second door. And it was there that everything became strangely familiar: the half-room, the narrow openings in the far wall, the projector, the red haze. Even the canisters of film, though smaller, were stacked in much the same way as were those out at Ufa.

"Don't touch anything," Hoffner said as he stepped over to one of the slits and peered down at the rows of plush chairs.

"It gets better," Leni said from behind him. She was holding back a curtain beyond the canisters to reveal yet one more room. This one, however, was pure artifice. The walls were lined with set pieces—a woman's boudoir, a saloon from the American West, a forest glade—while above, filming lights hung along several iron poles. A camera stood off to the side, wedged in among a low bed, a chair, and something that resembled a rock. "A studio and screening room all in one," she said. "I wonder what's on the bill for tonight."

A reel was slotted into the projector. Hoffner found the most obvious switch, turned it, and watched as the thing instantly clicked into motion. Again he peered through one of the openings.

It took him a moment to understand what he was seeing. When he did, he nearly blanched. A girl in a flimsy nightdress was being taken by two men, the terror in her screams no less deafening for their silence. If there was an eroticism to it, Hoffner couldn't see it. This was a brutality even he had rarely met.

Without warning, the girl's voice suddenly erupted in the room and Hoffner felt it like the snapping of a rib, its raw anguish echoing with the same guttural cries of the insane.

"Is that an animal?" Leni said. Hoffner turned to see her standing across from him. Hers was more confusion than shock, as she had yet to look through to the screen. She stepped toward one of the openings, and Hoffner immediately turned off the projector.

It was several seconds before he spoke. "Where did that voice come from?"

"What was on the screen?" she asked.

"Nothing. How did they do that—the voice?"

"I don't know, and don't tell me it was nothing."

The last minute had taken something from him, and while there might have been a measure of hope in Leni's instance of compassion, he knew that it—like the images—would fade. It was the voice, and the voice alone, that would remain.

"Was it the Volker girl?" she said, almost in a whisper. She had heard something human in it, something to shake her.

The gasping mouth, the fingers tearing at the cloth, the inescapable sound: he held it for a moment, then stepped over to the table. He needed the distance.

"No," he said, and began to look through the canisters. Each had a strip of adhesive along the rim: Geli T., Louisa F., Hans P. He found Ingrid V. in the second pile just as he heard the click of Leni's lighter. She had found her way to the door.

"You shouldn't smoke," he said. "Not with all the open reels."

"I don't care. Did you find her?" He turned and nodded. "Then let's get out of here."

The sound of footsteps from the corridor told him that was no longer a possibility.

Two men bulled their way into the room, each in a brown coat, brown suit, brown, brown, brown. Maybe everyone was right: the outfit was so obvious. "Detectives," Hoffner said, not waiting for the badges to come out.

"And what do we have here?" the older of the two began.

Hoffner's voice was low, controlled. "Something rather unpleasant."

The man nodded to Leni. "Who's she?"

"None of your concern, Detective Sergeant." It was a reasonable guess. Even the hierarchy of corruption had its protocol: inspectors stayed in on rainy nights; sergeants and the like were left to handle the mop-up work.

The man let out a long breath. "And you'd be—?"

"Chief Inspector Nikolai Hoffner. Alexanderplatz. That's a few bump-ups for you, just yet."

The Alex always carried a nice weight when it came to the precinct boys. Internal investigations had a nasty habit of emanating from within its walls.

The Herr Detective Sergeant opted for feigned ignorance. "Well, you lot at the Alex obviously know more than we do, Herr Chief Inspector. We had Herr Lüben here running an honest business."

It was odd giving TrapTrap a name, thought Hoffner. "Sex and dope," he said. "What could be more honest than that?"

The detective sergeant smiled, ignorance bleeding into sham camaraderie. "Pretty harmless stuff, Herr Chief Inspector. People need a bit of fun now and then. Who's to judge, really?"

Hoffner mirrored the smile. "Who, indeed?" The response confused the man: Where was the usual dressing-down to draw focus away from the real issue? Hoffner spoke no less easily: "But this has nothing to do with that, does it, Herr Detective Sergeant? Not that you have any idea what's in these films—I'm right in assuming that, aren't I?" The man said nothing. "No, of course not."

Herr Lüben cut in: "Whatever you think you saw, Herr Chief Inspector, don't for a minute think it wasn't of the girl's choosing. No one goes on film without a bit of a past. We invite only the most enthusiastic."

Hoffner always found it curious the moment a man rediscovers his courage, as if genuine backbone could be misplaced. "I'd hardly describe what was there as enthusiasm, *mein Herr*."

"The camera can be very deceptive, Herr Chief Inspector. It shows you what you want to see. Obviously, your tastes stray to the more vicious."

Hoffner let the word settle before saying, "I don't believe I mentioned what I saw, Herr Lüben." And without waiting: "It all comes down. Poles, scenery, camera, projector. The detective sergeant will be spending the rest of the evening dismantling this little enterprise. And he's going to make absolutely certain that every one of those reels finds its way to my office." Hoffner turned to see just how impressive Leni was: she was writing in a small notebook. "You have the list, Fräulein?" She nodded as she finished with the names.

The detective sergeant made one last effort: "This isn't really your jurisdiction, Herr Chief Inspector."

"I'll keep that in mind." ·

Placing the Volker girl's canister in his pocket, Hoffner turned and escorted Leni to the door.

"YOU DIDN'T EVEN TAKE HIS NAME," Leni said. She had waited until they were in the cab to make clear just how much she still had to learn.

"That would have pushed it too far," said Hoffner. "Given him something to lose." He cracked the window and tapped out the ash from his cigarette. "I don't need his name."

"And you trust him?"

"To do this? Yes."

"You know they'll just set it up somewhere else."

"I imagine that's true."

"And that doesn't trouble you?"

The buildings began to grow taller, whiter. Even the lamplight seemed cleaner. They were moving north. "Of course it troubles me, but removing a few lights, a camera, and plasterboard isn't going to do much to stop that." He took a last pull and flicked the cigarette out the window.

"And the voice?" she said more quietly.

He waited before answering. "What about it?"

"It was—I don't know." She seemed to lose herself. She then looked at him. "Is it possible to do that?"

"Evidently."

"How? And why? There has to be more to it. You know there is."

She was right, but Hoffner had no intention of taking things any further tonight. "We'll see."

He sat back as the driver turned onto Unter den Linden. The dual column of trees at the center stretched out like a pair of protective arms, but only for those who could afford its comfort: this was the way west. Hoffner had always marveled at how deceptive the avenue was, the promise of it all just out of reach, imagined from the top of a tram or a bus—or the back of a cab—but never met. Even the buildings goaded with false hope.

The best and worst of them was the Adlon, its awnings draped in endless flags, the majesty of the place concentrated in the detail of its stonework and glass, all of which seemed to grow more immense as it rose. It was a massive thing that gave Hoffner the impression of a fat man puffing out his chest.

The cab drew up to the curb, and Hoffner leaned over for the door. Leni pulled him back. "So that's how you're going to leave me? Out in the cold."

Hoffner stared at her, then past her to the hotel. "It looks warm enough."

"You're not even going to ask, are you?"

"Ask what?"

"If you can come up, have a drink." A smile inched its way down to her mouth.

This might have been a possibility from the start, but still, it managed to catch Hoffner by surprise. Instinct answered, "I don't suppose I am."

The answer seemed to delight her. "You're playing it all very well."

If there was hope in her eyes, Hoffner knew not to find it. "I'll say good night, then, Fräulein."

Effortlessly, she placed her hand on his. "Yes," she said. "You will." And with that, she opened the door and stepped out. He watched her under the awning and through the revolving doors. "Friedrichstrasse, number 71," he said as he settled back into the seat.

There was always one more stop before sleep.

THE ELEVATOR ATTENDANT stared up at the brass panel of lighted numbers, the lever in his hand clasped like a cudgel. "Bit late for you, isn't it, Herr Detective?" He continued to look up.

"He's in, then?" Hoffner watched along with him—seven, eight, nine . . .

"Quarter to eleven, like clockwork, *mein Herr.*"

Hoffner nodded as the man gently brought the lever up, then placed his other hand on the metalwork gate. With a subtle bump, the car came to a stop. "Second salon tonight, *mein Herr.* The one with the Greek statues. He's expecting you."

The Admiral's Gate was a recent addition—or renovation—among the Friedrichstrasse gentlemen's clubs. A onetime casino serving the likes of the Kaiser, it had fallen on rough times after the abdication and the arrival of the Social Democrats, who, though keen to reshape

German society in the mold of the new workingman, had failed to provide that man with any work. Such shortsightedness might not have been a concern to the Gate's usual clientele, but they were the ones being forced to gamble on foreign investments and overseas bonds to keep the new society afloat: days filled with high-stakes wagers left little taste for such things at night. Then again, it might simply have been that the place reminded everyone of the good old times, and why wallow in what was gone?

The casino's doors had closed in December of '24, and Alby Pimm, the man Hoffner had come to see, had bought the space the following spring, making it the property of the Little Alderman Company. To those in the know, it was a clever name, cleverer if you were speaking directly to Pimm. A little alderman—the familiar term for a picklock—was the preferred choice for the city's more accomplished second-story men, and as Pimm had begun his career in petty theft, he felt a certain fondness for the tools of his trade. Added to that, Pimm himself was small, at just over a meter and a half tall. His pale skin and shock of curly jet-black hair had, over the years, given him an almost boyish quality. Recently, however, the hair had turned gray overnight, aging the face and lending it a look more suited to the leader of one of Berlin's more notorious syndicates.

Pimm was reading a paper at the back, easy in a plush leather chair under the watchful eye of a none-too-dreadful reproduction of Michelangelo's *David*, when Hoffner stepped into the room. A series of Persian rugs dotted the floor, while various busts and torsos lined the walls, which were a dark mahogany, ostensibly to bring out the fleece-white brightness of the marble. Hoffner always imagined that Pimm chose this contrast to set his own sallow face as the perfect balance between the two. A few society toffs were lounging in equally comfortable chairs, little clumps of twos and threes, snifters of brandy or the day's papers strewn across the short tables littered about. Naturally, these men belonged to other, more serious clubs, but there was always something thrilling in spending a few hours in close proximity to the likes of Pimm and his boys. There might even be a bit of cards or a conversation about "the rackets" to give it all a real-life jolt.

"You've ruined a fine woman," Pimm said, still reading as Hoffner drew up. "You should know she's shattered."

Hoffner was never surprised by what information Pimm had at his disposal. "Maria's not the shattering type," he said as he sat.

"True." Pimm folded the paper and held it out to one of his men. "I suppose she'll recover. They all have. Drink?"

"Whiskey."

Pimm seemed mildly surprised. "Rough night, then." He nodded to a second man, who was standing by the wall. "So, what is it I can do for you, Nikolai?"

Hoffner glanced at the men still seated. "I think I'll wait for that whiskey."

They had known each other too long for Pimm not to understand. With a nod, the rest of his crew moved off. "You know you can trust them," Pimm said once his men were out of earshot. "Radek might even feel a bit hurt after everything he's done for you."

"I'll have Maria get in touch with him."

Pimm smiled. "Not all that hurt." The whiskey arrived, and Hoffner took a drink. "So," Pimm continued. "Now that you have my whiskey and my undivided attention—"

"What's the market like for sex films, Alby?"

Pimm's eyes widened in mock astonishment. "We're wasting no time tonight, are we? Sex films. I didn't know there was a market."

"Neither did I, but there seems to be something of a business in it upstairs at The Trap. Pretty brutal stuff."

"The Trap?" Pimm shook his head. "That's a bit edgy for them. What do you mean by brutal?"

"Not the usual ten-pfennig romp out at Luna Park on a Saturday night. This was a girl getting raped, sodomized."

Pimm's face darkened. "You're sure this was The Trap?"

"With studio and screening room, all in one."

Pimm was clearly on new ground as well. "You saw this?" Hoffner nodded, and Pimm shook his head trying to find an answer. "That I haven't heard of."

"And the other?"

"The romp? Purely nickelodeon. Maybe a midnight showing at some tiny cinema up in the north. But even then, there's really no point. You can't make any money in it."

"Why?"

"Oh, it's cheap enough to slap a bit of scenery together and put something on film, but where do you show it? I doubt the Ufa–Palast am Zoo is waiting for ten minutes of some prostitute sucking down a trio of schoolboys to fill its thousand seats."

"So a different kind of night out for your salesclerk and his young lady friend?"

"Exactly. Not that everyone hasn't thought about it, but the resources are just too much of a tangle. Projection machines, screens. It's not like a book or a magazine that a man can pick up and work with at home. It's not even like a crank machine out at a park. An entire film of sex requires a certain public commitment that, unless it's in a club like this, no one would ever admit to."

"But you could have it here."

"Of course. And bring it out every so often for a bit of fun, but not on a regular basis, and certainly not the sort of thing you're talking about. Honestly, I can see needing four, maybe five films at most, and I'd be getting them for free. And if I want that few—" Again he shook his head. "As far as I know, Nikolai, there is no market."

It was at moments like these that Hoffner remembered why he

always came to Pimm: men who dictated the paths of extortion, death, and violence saw nothing shameful in the truth. In fact, it was the certainty of truth that made conscience irrelevant. "And, I suppose, even less of a market for a girl getting terrorized on the screen."

"Well," said Pimm, "there's no accounting for taste."

"I'd hardly call this a matter of taste, Alby."

"Don't fool yourself, Nikolai. You'd be surprised by what people want—and how many of them would want it. Still something like that—"

"What about sound?" said Hoffner.

Pimm cocked his head as if he hadn't heard. "What?"

"Sound," said Hoffner. "The girl's screams. The men. I could hear them."

"I don't understand."

"In the film. There was sound in the film."

Pimm hesitated. "You mean there was a phonograph—"

"No. Voices. Sounds. In the film."

Pimm said nothing. He then slowly shook his head, and Hoffner said, "So what the hell are they doing at The Trap?"

Pimm's mind was circling for an answer when he turned and raised his hand to one of his men. He touched his ear and said, "Let's see if we can find out."

Half a minute later, the man approached with a telephone. He placed it on the table, drew the long wire behind the chair, and stepped away. Pimm picked up and dialed. The line engaged. "Maurice? It's Alby."

Pimm had a talent for giving up nothing while finding out exactly what he needed. From the little Hoffner could gather, Pimm was on the line with the Sass brothers. Their territory was more south and west. Still, the Hallesches Gate cut across lines.

"Good, good," said Pimm. "And mine to Eva and Renée." He hung up. "They know nothing."

"Which means?"

"They're the only ones who'd try something like this." Pimm was still thinking things through. "Unless . . ." There was no reason to finish the thought.

"Unless someone new is getting a foot in."

Pimm dismissed the idea out of hand. "There isn't someone new, Nikolai. Trust me. I'd be the first to know."

Pimm was right, of course: no one would be stupid enough to deny the head of the Immertreu a taste on any new ventures. What little money there might be, Pimm would be seeing his share of it.

Pimm continued: "Just putting together the machinery would be too much of an outlay for an upstart mob. They'd have had to come to me for the loan."

It was the word "machinery" that triggered something for Hoffner. He spoke even as he tried to piece it together: "Unless they didn't need the cash and already had everything in place."

Pimm was shaking his head even before Hoffner had finished. "Not a chance, Nikolai. It's not possible."

"Why not? I'm not saying it's all of Ufa. I'm not even saying that the studio is branching out, but someone there is thinking about it." There was no reason to confuse Pimm with talk of Thyssen and the Volker girl, but Hoffner sensed it was the only way to explain the connection.

Pimm was no more convinced. "It still doesn't answer the question of distribution. Where do they show it?"

"They haven't gotten there yet."

"Why? They don't need it. Aside from the Americans, it's the top studio in the world. Why put any of that at risk?"

Hoffner had no answer. He finished his whiskey.

Pimm said, "You're going to have to let me see it."

Hoffner placed his glass on the table. "See what?"

"The reel, Nikolai. The girl. You have the film. I know you too well. And yes, I do have a projection machine."

"I thought there was no market in it?"

"For the sex, no. But you don't think I'm going to wait in a line to see a proper film. I have a friend. He gets me the reels before they get to the theaters. You'll come by one night. We'll see the next Pabst before everyone else."

"I'm not such a fan."

Pimm smiled. "The reel, Nikolai. So we can see if it's Ufa quality."

Pimm had managed it well, the seats, the curtains, the tracer lights along the carpeting: it actually had the feel of a small theater. Hoffner watched as Pimm worked the levers on the projector, slotting the reel onto the large arm before checking the lens. He then began to thread the film in, but stopped, pulling it out and blowing into the opening. He tried again, and again he stopped.

"Something the matter?" said Hoffner.

"The film." Pimm was eyeing it closely. He tried it one last time. "It's not standard. It doesn't thread properly."

Hoffner stepped over. Not that he knew what he was looking for, but he took hold of the reel and held it up to the light.

Pimm said, "It's too wide. For the slot. Two or three centimeters at least. It's not going to work in any projection machine I know of."

The girl's screams suddenly seemed to fill the room. The projector, thought Hoffner. Of course. That had been the key. This had been about sound. Why had he let himself get so distracted?

Almost to himself, he said, "Herr TrapTrap was cleverer than I thought."

CHAPTER TWO

THE BANKER

HOFFNER SETTLED on a cup of hot water. The coffee grounds from yesterday were too many days removed from flavor to warrant the effort. Still, the cup retained a distant taste of something dark.

He had thought about a bath, but the steam room at Pimm's club—after two hours of meaningless racing about last night—had managed things well enough, its remnants still visible in the puckered smoothness of his fingers and toes. Even so, it was making this morning's shave a bit easier under a cold tap.

She had woken him with the promise of a hotel breakfast. It was a rare thing, the sound of his telephone. Hoffner never used it himself and had felt foolish at its installation—the only private line in the building—but Kriminaldirektor Präger had insisted on it, and if the Herr Direktor wanted instant access to his chief inspectors, so be it. Hoffner couldn't recall having given Leni the number.

The razor tore at his neck, and he dabbed at the skin with a bit of paper before rinsing off. There had been no projector, no lights, no camera. The Herr Detective Sergeant had been meticulous in his dismantling: "Destroyed, Herr Chief Inspector. As you instructed." It was a lie, but even Pimm's presence had done nothing to alter the man's story. Hoffner had expected, even hoped, for a little more from Pimm, a quiet threat, a broken jaw. Strange to think he knew him that well, but it had been too many years stepping into each other's business—the old bull cop and the little crime boss—and always with one thing in mind: Berlin. She needed them both, and Hoffner had learned to forgive Pimm almost anything when it came to protecting her. Pimm, to his credit, had learned to keep his other affairs to himself. Still, it would have done Hoffner a world of good to see Pimm shatter the man's kneecap.

The film canisters were now neatly stacked on Hoffner's office floor—no way to take a look at them, of course, but there nonetheless. The air of victory in the Herr Detective Sergeant's departing nod had been almost too much. Even the steam had been no match for its contempt.

By seven-thirty, the Adlon was already bristling with activity, guests and business associates swelling the breakfast salon like so many pieces of swallowed meat: the conversation hummed with the sound of digestion. Leni was at a back table, nestled under a richly draped window, no hint of sun breaking through to challenge the white, white light of the chandeliers. It might have been in aid of keeping out the glare, but Hoffner guessed that the drapes remained closed no matter what the season. How the well-off ate was, after all, a private matter.

She was reading through the *Berliner Tageblatt*—the right paper for the right crowd—although he did notice a corner of the *Lokalanzeiger* peeking out from the bottom of the stack.

"You're letting a little bit too much show," he said as he waited for her to look up. She glanced at him, then discreetly checked her blouse. "The *Anzeiger*," he added, nodding at the paper. "They'll burn your toast if they see it."

Her finger lingered a moment before she found a smile. "I should be more careful." She placed the stack of papers on an empty seat and said, "There's nothing worth reading in this one, anyway."

"Just the news?" Hoffner sat across from her and unrolled his napkin.

"Exactly." There was a pot of coffee and he poured himself a cup. "Get what you like," she said. "The studio's paying. I had the duck omelet with caviar. Should have had the rabbit crepes, but they were less expensive."

Hoffner placed a piece of black bread on a plate and smeared it with butter. "I'm fine with this."

Leni raised her hand and a waiter appeared. "The gentleman will have the rabbit crepes and a glass of champagne. And I'll take another orange."

Hoffner blinked and the man was gone. "I won't eat it," he said.

"You'll have a bite just to say you've had it, and I'll have the cham-pagne."

"I didn't say I wouldn't drink it."

Her hand went up and the man reappeared. "Two glasses of cham-pagne."

"It's a neat trick," Hoffner said once the man had disappeared again. "The vanishing act."

"I'm sure he's well trained."

"He's nothing if not well trained."

"I'm surprised you came."

He knew she wasn't. "I was out of coffee."

"Oh, that's right." And, reaching for her glass: "You've got a son out at the studio, don't you?"

If she had meant to shock him, she had done a poor job of it. Per-sonal swipes never struck Hoffner with any force. It was something she could never have known, but still, it seemed slightly amateurish given last night. "As I discovered yesterday. Yes."

"He was working with Thyssen."

Hoffner reapplied the butter. "He was delivering him scripts and coffee. Terribly sensitive stuff. But you knew that."

"I suppose I did."

"So there's a piece of information we both already had." He set the knife down. "Or was there another reason you felt the need to tell me?"

The champagne arrived, and she said, "I'm wondering if you understand how delicate things might become."

The words had all the trappings of intimidation, but none of the tone. Both were puzzling. Hoffner waited until the man was gone. "Is that meant as some sort of threat?"

"That's an unkind thing to say. Of course not. I just know the way the studio boys work. What leverage they find, they use."

"Oh, I see. So it'll be the studio that threatens my son. Or rather, threatens me through my son. Or threatens us both. It all gets rather involved."

She picked up her glass. "You really can be very dense. They won't threaten you. They'll use him to mislead you. It's much simpler and much more effective." She took a drink.

That was twice he had failed to see the obvious when with her: first with the projector, now this. It was unsettling to think of himself as this easily distracted. Hoffner nodded and took a drink.

She reached for her purse. "I brought you this." She placed the small notebook from last night on the table. He had completely forgotten it.

"I'll just need the page with the names," he said. "You can tear it out, if you want."

"That's the trouble," she said. "It's not mine to be tearing pages from." And, with no time for him to ask, "It was there last night, in the back room when we arrived. I thought it was the only way they'd let me take it out, if they thought I'd brought it in." She slid the book across to him. "I think it's some sort of ledger. It might be nothing."

Hoffner wondered if anything was ever as straightforward as she made it appear. "You decided to take it," he said.

"Yes."

"So why not give it to me last night in the cab?"

"I forgot."

He might have pressed, but he knew she would only enjoy it. Instead, he took hold of the book and flipped through the pages.

She was right. It was a ledger: the classic accountant's book with a thin red stripe down the left side of the cover. Inside, there was little else by way of detail. The columns were a list of initials—*L.F., H.P.*— the rows headed by abbreviated phrases—*Cam. Tr., Loc. R.* Hoffner assumed the initials stood for the names on the film canisters, the rest for terms obvious to those in the industry. More than that was pure guesswork.

The only thing he was absolutely certain of was that it was German. Who else could so easily dismiss content in favor of strict accounting: so much paid, so much received, so many hours? It reminded him of those volumes he had once seen at the General Staff, endless sheets of boys' names—14th Bavarian, 11th Jäger, Leibregiment—ranks and dates and death all laid out in perfect lines: a different sort of brutality and humiliation, to be sure, but no less sanitized on an ordered page.

It was all undeniably German, except for the numbers themselves, and it was there that Hoffner found his deviations. A German 7 would have been far more rigid, the 1's without so much business at the top. But it was the 4's that gave it away. Each had a little foot sticking out at the bottom as if to keep the top-heavy digit from tipping over. Hoffner had actually spent a good deal of time studying different styles of numbers during the Taparan craze, a game that had been everywhere just after the war. The papers had claimed it had come from Japan or China, but everyone knew it was the editors at the *BZ* who had come up with the brainteaser simply to sell more issues. The gist of the thing was really quite basic: take a random series of twenty numbers in a five-by-five grid, and then eliminate them—one by one—by jumping smaller numbers over larger ones into the empty spaces. The object was to have a single number left at the end, although that rarely happened. Naturally, an entire culture of Taparan sprouted up, drawing enthusiasts from across Europe. There were even tournaments where speed and fewest numbers on the end board determined winners—one Italian actually making it down to a "perfect singleton" a remarkable three times in one six-week period. Hoffner had thought it all rather silly until he found himself one morning staring over the shoulder of a not-terribly-adept Taparanist on the tram. Unable to hold back a few simple suggestions, Hoffner had quickly become as addicted as everyone else. Of the fourteen tournaments he entered, he came in first or second in six of them, the third-highest result in Berlin. He was even invited by the *BZ* to pose with several other "champions," but passed on the opportunity, although he might simply have forgotten the appointment.

It was at the tournaments that he discovered the variations in style. The ornate 1 and the footed 4 were a particular idiosyncrasy of the Danes and the Dutch. And as foreign firms were rare in the world of Berlin accountants, Hoffner now had somewhere to go with the little book. He closed it and placed it in his pocket.

"Probably right," he said. "Doesn't look like much of anything."

Leni was still with her glass. "That's a quick assessment."

"It is what it is." Hoffner's indifference never assumed a practiced tone. It seemed to satisfy.

She took a drink. "So where are we off to today?"

She had a talent for making the obvious seem spontaneous. "There's a man meant to hang at four. I put him there. I should probably put in an appearance. You?"

She smiled behind her glass. "You won't admit how helpful I am, will you?"

"You're very helpful."

The smile rose. "I might head out to the studio. Have a chat with Lang."

Hoffner nodded casually. Her subtlety had a distinctly American leadenness. "I hear he's a rather odd character."

"I'll be sure to bring my monocle."

She finished her glass as a series of plates swept onto the table, elegant folds of something white in a cream sauce, along with a peeled orange in the shape of a star. For some reason there was a dollop of raspberry jam situated above it like a floating Mars. Hoffner waited until she had smeared one of her wedges in the red paste before taking his fork to the crepes. They had the consistency of thick butter and uncooked dough, with just the slightest hint of rancid lamb. It was enough just to keep the thing in his mouth.

"The duck was no better," she said, reaching for a second wedge. "I wanted to make sure we were on an even footing."

Hoffner swallowed, then tossed back his glass before raising it. "Another," he said as a passing waiter emerged from nowhere.

TODAY IT WAS GAS. As ever, the stink at the Alex was growing stronger as Hoffner reached the third floor.

"It's the back stairwell lamps," came a voice from one of the offices. It happened to belong to Kriminaldirektor Präger and was therefore enough to stop Hoffner at the door. Hoffner popped his head through as Präger continued to read whatever it was he was pretending to read.

"They leak," Präger continued. "The lamps." Präger's was the largest office on the floor, although it might have been an illusion given the sparseness of the place—desk, chair, telephone, two filing cabinets. It had been this way for fifteen years, and Präger—slim, tall, and fine-boned—looked like one more perfectly positioned piece of furniture.

"Might be a kettle on one of the stoves," said Hoffner.

"Different taste in the mouth. This is sweeter."

"You've become something of a connoisseur?" Hoffner thought he saw the hint of a grin as Präger continued to read.

"You've got company at your desk," Präger said as he flipped the page.

"You've been at my desk. Should I be concerned?"

"Depends on what you've done." Präger looked up. "Any news on the Burstein case?"

"He'll hang. He's confessed."

"Of his own will?"

"Close enough."

Präger went back to his papers. "Let's remember we're not the Polpo, Nikolai."

"I'll try to keep that in mind, Herr Kriminaldirektor. My company—nice long legs?"

Präger's grin reappeared as he read. "I wouldn't know."

"Shame." Hoffner started out the door.

"Oh." Präger looked up again. "And why do I have a suicide in my morgue?"

Here, at last, was the point of this little exchange. Präger was never one to come across as aggressive, let alone intrusive. He might have had his moments, but odd bodies in the morgue never provoked them. Hoffner turned back. "Someone gave you a call?"

"A lawyer. From Ufa. He wanted to know if examining suicides was standard procedure."

"And?"

"I told him of course it was. You'll let me know if I shouldn't have." Not expecting an answer, Präger picked up his pen and began scribbling something on one of the sheets. Hoffner took that as his cue to move out into the corridor.

Evidently Ritter had wasted no time in going over his head: at least now Hoffner knew what to expect with Ufa.

As it turned out, it was Georg who was waiting for him when he stepped into his office. The boy was seated across from the desk, his nose in a book, as Hoffner tossed his coat and hat onto the rack.

"At least I was right on the legs," he said.

"Pardon?" Georg said, looking up.

"Nothing." Hoffner headed over. "So—what is it we're reading?"

Georg flipped to the front cover and stared down at the title. "It's good. Everyone's got it. You wouldn't like it."

Hoffner angled his head and made out the title *Steppenwolf*. He had seen it in every bookshop in Berlin, not that he knew anything about it. "Bit arty, is it?"

"No, just young and earnest." Georg placed the book on the desk. "Look, Papi, I'm as unhappy about this as you are."

Hoffner was shuffling through the mail on his desk. "If I knew what this was, Georgi, I'd commiserate."

"You didn't get a call?"

"Obviously, Ufa's sent you."

The need to explain only heightened Georg's frustration. "You're meeting with some of the bigwigs at Potsdamer Platz. At eleven. They wanted to make sure you kept the appointment."

"And they couldn't do this with a telephone call?"

"Obviously not."

Things were becoming clearer by the minute. Ufa wasn't satisfied merely going over his head: they wanted to kick his feet out from under him as well. "It can't be much past eight-thirty."

"Eight-eighteen," Georg corrected.

"So what am I supposed to do with you for two and a half hours?"

"Funny, Papi, but I was thinking the same thing myself."

THERE ARE ANY NUMBER OF THINGS Berliners choose to forget: the best time to arrive at Schuckert's in the morning for the fresh fig tarts—seven-twenty, but then who doesn't love waiting in that line with all those aromas and free little cups of coffee; or the fastest way at lunch to get from City Hall back to an office on Spandau Strasse for forgotten papers—you cut through the Alexanderplatz U-Bahn station, but then you miss out on all the salesgirls from Tietz and Aschinger's darting out for a smoke or a sandwich up on the square; or that Brecht is a Jew and a Communist, and so is Weill, and maybe even Klemperer—but then who needs to be reminded of such things when all those people are so interesting.

In the case of Französische Strasse, it is their current loathing of the French that Berliners put aside, not all that difficult to do, as the street is a lovely walk, with the dome of St. Hedwig peeking out from over the trees and L'Église Française nestled back within its own garden. And, of course, there are all those marvelous buildings in between, modeled on the Parisian style, although most Berliners would raise an eyebrow these days at the mention of it.

No one, however, could accuse the Dresdener Bank of approaching anything French. A late arrival on the street, it casts a sour glare through three stories of lifeless windows cut from a palatial slab of gray stone. More off-putting—though so very popular in all those prewar academic and financial institutions—is its ersatz Greek front of four columns and pediment that looks tacked onto the façade like an afterthought: someone's staggeringly clever idea to transform the place into the high temple of Berlin capitalism. Given the city's recent fiscal insecurities, the artifice comes across as more apt than ever.

Heavy, however, was all that came to mind as Georg pushed open the door. He let his father step past him and into the cathedral vastness of the bank's public hall. This was not a place for the irresolute. If the windows outside conveyed a dull vacancy, here they shone with a precision that seemed to bend the light to their will. Beams of focused white cut through the air and made the chandeliers above almost redundant. The marble floors demanded an equal resolve, a kind of clipped march from those who were moving toward the line of tellers that stood a short tram ride farther in. And beyond them, a legion of desks—each manned by a crisply etched young clerk in a gray suit and black tie—led up to the mezzanine offices, where, behind a series of glass walls, older, even crisper men totted up accounts or filed papers: these were the gray-suited pupils within the six barren eyes peering out.

"You'd never manage this with a set," Georg said as he gazed up along the walls and ceiling: the place seemed to swallow his voice. "It's all too—solid."

They drew up to a solitary desk, and Hoffner said, "I think that's the point, Georgi." The man behind showed no reaction as Hoffner continued, "Herr Leber, please. You can tell him Herr Kriminal-Oberkommissar Hoffner is here to see him."

Several hushed "ja jas" later, Hoffner and Georg were pointed in the direction of a row of chairs along the far wall. It was another half-minute before they settled into a particularly uncomfortable pair.

"Should have brought your book," Hoffner whispered as they both stared out at the muted give-and-take along the tellers' windows.

"I don't think you're meant to read in here, Papi. Bit too frivolous for this crew."

Hoffner smiled to himself. It was good to have the boy next to him again. He had begun to forget all this.

A fat girl appeared at the top of the mezzanine steps and made her way down, past the clerks and tellers, across the expanse, and toward them. She seemed to grow wider with each step. Hoffner and Georg stood.

"Herr Kriminal-Oberkommissar." She spoke in statements. "Herr Zweiter-Direktions-Assistent Leber will see you. Please follow me."

Leber's office was somewhere beyond and above the central hall, difficult to pinpoint given the stairways and whitewashed corridors Hoffner and Georg were now led through. The fat girl knocked once, waited for the barked "One moment," then nodded to Hoffner. She was gone by the time Leber opened the door.

"Nikolai!"

Leber was tall, wiry, and in possession of a set of oddly large teeth: even with the lips closed, the teeth never seemed completely hidden. He wore the same thin mustache from university days, although the rest of his hair had abandoned him. His suit, on so thin a frame, gave the impression of having been bought half a size too large.

"What a long time," he said, his smile presenting the entire collection. "And this must be . . . little Sascha? Come in, come in." Leber ushered the two into his office.

"It's good to see you, Jürgen," Hoffner said as he glanced around. "Very impressive." It wasn't. The room had a desk, filing cabinet, and several stacks of account books spread out across the floor. There were no windows.

"Well, you know—thirty-some-odd years with a bank and they give you your own office, a secretary. I can't complain."

That was the wonderful thing about Leber. He never saw how

dreadful his little life really was—no wife, no children, no standing at his beloved bank. Still, he could always be counted on to send a letter out once a year summoning the fencing club back to Heidelberg, a chance to parade around the old stamping grounds, share a few buckets of beer. Hoffner imagined Leber arriving at the station, racing past the old digs, then on to the beer hall to find perhaps two or three equally desperate lives trying to rekindle something from a forgotten past, except Leber's desperation was never filled with despair. He had found some kind of contentment—perhaps he had been born with it—that allowed him moments of genuine joy.

Hoffner's arrival, so it seemed, was one of them. Leber pulled a bottle from the bottom drawer, along with three glasses, and began to pour out what smelled like peach schnapps.

"Little Sascha," he said. "Hard to believe it. A young man."

"Actually, it's Georg," said Hoffner.

Leber stopped, his teeth more suited to a look of surprise. "Georg?" He passed out the glasses. "I can't believe it. How time goes." He lifted his glass in a quick toast, then took the smallest sip possible. Hoffner had to remind himself of this little nugget: with all the reasons in the world to drink to excess, Leber never managed more than half a glass of anything. It made him all the more pathetic, even if Hoffner sometimes wondered if it was possible to envy such a man.

"So what are you, Georg?" Leber motioned to the chairs in front of his desk as he sat. "Twenty, twenty-one?"

"Sixteen," Georg said as he and Hoffner sat.

"Sixteen!" Leber leaned back and rolled his eyes with a smile. "Do you remember sixteen, Nikolai? And Sascha—he must be—"

"Twenty-four."

"Twenty-four." Leber lingered on the words as if they carried some hidden message. He then turned to Hoffner. "So. What brings you to the bank?"

Hoffner set his glass on the desk. "Georg claims to have a tremendous interest in finance. Accounting, to be specific. He's asked if I knew anyone."

"Really?" Leber straightened up with an air of unwarranted authority. "Interested in accounting." A sleeve had begun to swallow his hand as he continued to stare across at the boy.

Georg, to his credit, simply stared back. When Hoffner prodded with a gentle "Georg?" the boy affected a smile and said, "Accounting. Yes. I find it—very exciting."

"How marvelous. Finally a Hoffner with some sense."

"He met someone," said Hoffner. "At one of his fencing tournaments."

Leber's eagerness drew him closer in. "You're a fencer as well? Really. Foil, saber, épée . . . ?" It was all too easy, thought Hoffner.

"Saber," Georg answered. He seemed perfectly content to play along.

"Oh." For just a moment Leber seemed to deflate. "I was foil. Saber was a bit too . . . unwieldy. I liked foil, though. But I remember your father with a saber—" Leber cut himself off. "So this fellow, at the tournament?"

Hoffner said, "He's doing some sort of apprenticing with one of the larger firms. Talks about it all the time."

"Which firm?"

Hoffner turned. "Which one is it, Georg?" Hoffner marveled at the boy's composure. Really very gifted, this one.

Georg broke into a shy smile. "I'm afraid I don't know. I should have asked, I suppose."

"No, no," said Leber. "Not much to distinguish them."

"Why don't you show him the book?" said Hoffner.

This one, however, was beyond the boy's talents. Georg sat frozen as he tried to find an answer until Hoffner said, "Oh no, wait."

Hoffner reached into his coat pocket. "I have it here." He slid the small ledger across the desk. "You might be able to tell from this."

Leber stared down at the book, then at Hoffner. His expression had lost its enthusiasm.

Hoffner said affably, "He let Georg borrow it. Just to have a look. You know boys."

"No," said Leber coldly. "I don't." Even sternness seemed to hang awkwardly on him. He looked across at Georg. "You'll bring it back to him and tell him not to do that sort of thing again." Georg nodded sheepishly, and Leber turned to Hoffner. "I can't look at that ledger, Nikolai. It wouldn't be right. Ethically."

"No, no, of course not," said Hoffner. "I think it's some sort of foreign firm, anyway. The boy's parents are Danes."

Leber nodded vaguely. He was leaning back, mulling over the indiscretion. "These apprentices. Think it's a game. Showing off to their friends or some girl with something that could be quite sensitive."

Hoffner smiled dryly. "The adolescent treats to be found in an accounting ledger." Leber ignored the comment, and Hoffner said, "You're sure you won't take a look?"

It was the tone that brought Leber back. He was perfectly still for several moments before he said, "You want me to take a look." The voice held a newfound distance. Hoffner remained quiet as Leber continued to stare. "Georg doesn't have an interest in accounting, does he, Nikolai?"

Hoffner let the silence settle. "No."

"It's about this little book."

"Yes."

Leber nodded slowly to himself. "Of course it is." He waited, then said, "You've always thought me a silly man, haven't you?" It was strange to hear no malice in the voice. "A little story. Something about fencing—always a nice touch—and then on to what you need. And so clever. Truth is, you've always been clever, at least cleverer than I am." For some reason, Leber glanced around the office. "Not impressive in the slightest, is it? I know it. You know it. The boy knows it. In fact, it's all rather horrible. But the one thing it is, Nikolai, is earned, whatever that might mean. I'll take the stares of pity, the indifference, even the little comments. You'd be surprised how quickly one gets used to them. What I won't be is ridiculous, especially in front of an audience."

Hoffner felt a prick of shame; he knew it would have to wait. "Any idea who might have put this together, Jürgen?"

"Ethics be damned?"

"The man who wrote it didn't have any, if that makes it any easier."

"That's never the point."

"A man's dead."

"One always is."

Hoffner had forgotten this piece to Leber, the strength—erratic as it might be—yet somehow always there. It was what had made him so unpredictable on the strip. Hoffner matched Leber's gaze and said, "He won't tell you this, Georg, but Herr Leber had no time for the saber because he was too busy defending his German national foil championship three years running."

Georg nodded appreciatively, but knew to keep quiet.

Hoffner said, "You'd be doing me a tremendous good turn."

"Would I?"

Both men knew this was as close to an apology as Hoffner was likely to get. For several seconds, Leber said nothing. He then slowly leaned back.

When he finally spoke, there was no trace of emotion. "It's a Kapel binding, which means you were right, foreign. Not that a few Berlin firms aren't still using them, but most have moved on to the Parmanian. Funny, really. Berliners using the Hungarian books, while foreigners use the German. The irony of it." Leber waited again and then reached over and took the ledger. His expression was stone as he scanned the pages. "Parents as Danes. Clever. You probably thought Dutch as well. The 4's and the 1's." He placed the book back on the desk. "You'd have been wrong on both counts. It's Swiss. The 8's are too wide to be anything else, and he's put a double line at every third of a page instead of at every quarter. Something the Swiss like to do. I don't know why. I've never asked." This was the way Leber had been on the strip, relentless, focused, detached. "There are three firms I would suggest, but I don't know if any of them specializes in film industry accounting. It's a rather specific skill." Leber clearly enjoyed the look of surprise in Hoffner's eyes. "We've done a bit of work with Decla, a few projects out at Ufa. The industry abbreviations are standard." He took a sheet of paper, scribbled three names on it, and slid it across to Hoffner.

Hoffner quietly retrieved both the page and the book, and said, "You wouldn't have told me if I'd asked you directly." He folded the paper and slipped it into his pocket.

"No, you're right, I wouldn't have. But then Georg here would have missed out on his father having to ask for help." With anyone else, this might have seemed cruel. With Leber, it was simply where the point had been aiming all along.

Hoffner stood, and Georg followed. "It's good seeing you, Jürgen."

Leber stood. "You'll come up to Heidelberg this year. Renner always asks about you."

"He's in Köln?"

"Stuttgart."

"That's right." Hoffner extended his hand and the two shook. A nod for Georg sufficed.

Leber waited until father and son were at the door before saying, "You weren't always this much of a shit, were you?"

Hoffner took hold of the handle. He could feel Georg staring at him from the corridor. "No," said Hoffner. "I think I was."

OUT ON THE STREET, the sun had perched above the bank, turning the pavement to glass: there was nowhere to look without squinting.

Georg was the first to break the silence. "He takes things very seriously, doesn't he?"

Hoffner nodded distractedly as they passed a bus stop with an advertising poster for tooth cream. A bob-haired young woman sat wearily peering into a mirror, her long fingers pulling down on her lower lip, her gums somehow never more sensuous. If not for the brush in her hand and the large-print mandate DON'T STAY BEHIND THE TOOTH CREAM TIMES! USE CHLORODONT AND GUARD AGAINST PINK TOOTHBRUSH! Hoffner might have taken it for a teaser—albeit an odd one—for a Tiller Girls review. After all, wasn't their draw "Things You've Never Dreamed of Seeing!"? Hoffner imagined Leber, a kindred spirit, standing first in line, brush in hand. It was enough to provoke another twinge of conscience.

"He's got the right body for a champion," Georg tried again. "I envy him those arms."

Again Hoffner nodded as he took them past the Metropol—some Lehár operetta in the offing—and up toward Unter den Linden. A cab raced by, and Hoffner said, "That was my fault." His eyes were focused in front of him. "Putting you in that position. I'm sorry for that."

The sound of his father's voice was less shocking than the apology. Georg nodded awkwardly.

Hoffner said, "He deserved better as well, I suppose." The Brandenburg Gate came into view. "You remember·that carousel off the

Siegesallee?" Again Georg nodded, relieved to be on to something new. Hoffner headed them across the street and said, "Good. We've got over an hour. We'll have a bit of fun."

THE PARK WAS MORE WIDE OPEN here than Hoffner remembered. A boy of about nine was racing about with a stick, scratching jagged lines into the graveled dirt as a clutch of nannies looked on from chairs and benches at the rim of the trees. Four or five older children were playing at some sort of game, disappearing and reappearing from behind the carousel, which spun slowly to accommodate the youngest riders. Off to the side, a man with a cane tapped at the brim of his hat each time a little boy passed by: "Opa! Opa!" and another mock salute. Beyond them, the park was deserted, only the very young, the very old, and the well paid willing to suffer through this uncompromising sky. Hoffner and Georg settled in at the last of the benches.

"You liked that one, I think," said Hoffner, nodding at an old blue on the inner row. "You had a name for it."

Georg watched as the horse slipped by. "Did I?"

"Bompo or . . . Bommio?"

"Ponky Bo," Georg said as the horse reappeared.

"That's right." Hoffner pulled a cigarette from his pocket and lit up. "Odd name." He let out a strain of smoke. "You're much too old for this now, aren't you?" It was as if this had just occurred to him.

Georg said nothing as the boy with the stick fell, his chin slapping at the dirt. A moment later the air filled with screams, and one of the women raced over.

Georg said, "They're all very little, aren't they?"

"You never cried out like that," said Hoffner. "I always appreciated that."

"I wouldn't have with you."

Hoffner watched as the little boy got to his feet, his chin bloodied, the nanny dabbing at it with a cloth. Within half a minute, he was back with his stick. "Don't know why I thought this was where to take you," Hoffner said. "Bit ridiculous."

Georg nodded as he stood. "Probably." He reached into his pocket and pulled out a few coins. "I've got four pfennigs. Good for two rides."

Hoffner looked up. "Well, you give my best to Ponky Bo."

"I don't ride alone, Papi."

Hoffner snorted a laugh. It was his own fault, anyway. Why not? He took a last draw, stood, and flicked the cigarette to the ground.

Up on the carousel, he found a stationary banc between two poles and settled in behind Georg. A man—somewhere in his midtwenties—emerged from the central booth. He was tall, thin, and missing an arm.

"He says it can manage your weight," Georg said, already on top of his horse.

The man said, "More fun up than down."

"I'm fine here," said Hoffner.

Georg gathered the reins and said, "So where did you lose it?"

The boy's candor caught Hoffner momentarily off guard. He might have said something had the man not chimed in no less easily.

"Isonzo."

Hoffner chalked it up to that feeling of immortality in the young and the lame. Berlin seemed to be breeding it just now.

The man added, "July of '17."

Georg nodded, and the man stepped down to the booth. He pulled a lever and the carousel began to move. Waiting for them to pass by, he hopped back up.

"Shouldn't have lost it at all," he said as he leaned against a pole. "Caught something in the shoulder. Ran out of petrol getting me back, at least that's what they said. Medic had to tie it off. I suppose he saved my life."

Hoffner gripped at the bench. Even at this speed, the motion was making him queasy.

"Nannies don't like it much," the man continued. "Except for the ones who've been intrigued, if you know what I mean." Hoffner had no interest in knowing what he meant. "Doesn't seem to bother the little ones, though, so I suppose that's good."

Hoffner felt himself going green. "A bit young to have been at Isonzo."

"Yah." The man managed to pull a cigarette from his shirt pocket and light it without the least difficulty. "Told them I was twenty. We all lied, at least the ones I was with. I was fifteen." A little girl vomited, and the man stepped back down and pulled the lever. The carousel slowed and Hoffner immediately felt better. They swung around and he hopped up again.

"You don't want to go over?" said Hoffner.

"She's not done," said the man. "Besides"—he nodded at the benches—"the pretty one on the end might be hers." A crate of a woman rose and began to make her way over. "Oh well," he said, and flicked his cigarette to the edge. "It wasn't a secret. They all knew. Generals, colonels, whoever was running the thing. They needed bodies. We wanted to go. It was good to be tall. Not too many questions."

Georg said, "You ever think—"

"No." The answer came too quickly. "I went. I came back. Besides, they give you a good extra pension if you lose an arm."

The girl was on solid ground now, crying, the large woman doing what she could to remove the remains of breakfast from her smock.

"My brother joined when he was sixteen," said Georg. Georg might have been looking at the man, but Hoffner knew this had been meant for him.

The man nodded indifferently. "He make it back?"

"He never went," Hoffner said. "He joined in '19, during the revolution. Freikorps."

For the first time the man showed an emotion: something between distaste and bitterness. "Freikorps. Right-wing pricks. Sorry." He wasn't.

"You'll get no argument from me," said Hoffner.

The girl was now trying to break free: tears and vomiting had turned to defiance. Georg dismounted. "Well, good luck to you, then."

The man pushed himself up from the pole. "You as well." He bobbed a nod to Hoffner and stepped down to the booth. Hoffner followed Georg to the edge, and the two hopped off and headed for the trees.

"He's in town," Georg said. The gravel muffled their voices.

"What?"

"Sascha. He's in town."

Hoffner stopped. It was another few strides before Georg turned to him. Hoffner said, "I thought you said you hadn't heard from him in months?"

"I lied."

Hoffner stifled the urge to reach over and slap the boy across the face.

"He's doing well, Papi. He's not what you think." Georg spoke with a remarkable calm. "He's invited me to something tonight."

"Tonight," Hoffner said quietly.

"A get-together. He asked for you to come."

"Really?"

Georg held his ground.

"Where?" said Hoffner.

"Up in Wedding. The Pharus Hall."

That hardly made sense. Wedding was a workers' district. The Pharus Hall was for gatherings of the Communist variety. "So your brother's a Red now?"

"Do you want to see him?"

It was a question Hoffner had never fully been able to answer. "How long?"

"How long what?"

"How long has he been in town?"

Georg knew not to go down this path. "You should see him. It's tonight. At eight."

The music from the carousel started up again, and Hoffner said, "There's an appointment I need to get to." He saw a slight clenching in Georg's jaw. "We don't want to be late."

A numbness glazed over the boy's eyes. He waited and then said, "We? You've always been better on your own."

They stood like this, with nothing between them, until Georg finally turned and headed off. Hoffner watched the boy go, his son lost in the stride of this young man. It would always be like this, he thought, the current too swift for either of them.

He turned to the carousel and saw the girl retching again. This time she had managed to include her shoes.

THE ACCOUNTANT

HOFFNER NEVER MADE IT to Potsdamer Platz.

Had he been at all aware of why Ufa deserved his contempt—they had sent Georg to him; they had made this morning an inevitability; they had brought Sascha back from the dead—he might have acted differently. After all, it was dangerous to let such things affect a case. But Hoffner was not aware. He never troubled himself with personal motivations: only criminals merited that kind of digging. His sins were of a different order and thus lived free of any deeper origin. To him, the missed appointment was simply a flexing of muscles: they had told him when to come, and he had told them no.

By noon, he was finished with the first firm on Leber's list and was enjoying a bit of minced pork, onions, and peppers on a roll—a nice *Hackepeterbrötchen* with a few gherkins on the side—helped down by a pale ale and corn-schnapps chaser: even a cop could pretend to have a Berlin morning now and then.

Standing at one of the café's pillar tables, he read through the sporting pages of the BZ (WHEEL JAMS: RIDER LOSES EAR), and tried to forget the chief accountant and his smell of talcum and lavender: "A Kapel binding?" The man's disdain had bordered on the personal. "We don't use those sorts of bindings anymore, Herr Kriminal-Oberkommissar." Hoffner wondered if perhaps poor old Kapel had been caught in some sort of erotic intrigue, something to do with red ink and sheets of lined paper, a nice full girl with bits and pieces of leather binding squeezed in where they weren't meant to be. Or maybe that was just the way accountants were taught to answer. He finished with the cycling results and bought another roll for later.

It was gone by the time he reached the fourth floor of the second firm, its accounting hall a study in efficiency and regret. A stiff, sallow man appeared from around the side of a long wooden counter where three rows of perfectly aligned desks stretched to a distant wall. Trunks, arms, and hands manned each station as fingers scribbled quietly in ledgers the size of a woman's torso. Had some of these living husks not been wearing eyeglasses, the heads would have been indistinguishable from one another.

"Herr Kriminal-Oberkommissar." The man managed just enough voice to be heard over the scribbling. He seemed genuinely eager to help. "Yes, we use them." The appearance of Hoffner's little book prompted a simple nod. Good old Kapel. Maybe the girl had refused to press charges? "No, I'm afraid I can't examine the contents. The ethical question. You understand." Hoffner wondered if this might be the only phrase to be found in the accountant's training manual. "But," the man continued, "should the Herr Kriminal-Oberkommissar wish to describe these contents, perhaps I might be able to determine whether we are working with such a firm." Evidently ethics came in any number of varieties.

Unfortunately, none of them turned out to be of any help. "No, I'm quite certain, Herr Kriminal-Oberkommissar. No clients within the film industry." The moment of hope slipped back into Hoffner's pocket along with the book, leaving him with only the routine, useless questions: Anything untoward in the last few weeks? Ledgers gone missing? Odd behavior from any of the staff? How one might be able to determine behavior odder than what was already on display, however, was beyond Hoffner's grasp.

"Nothing missing, no." The man thought a moment. "A bit of rough news last week, but I wouldn't say odd. I suppose one might have seen it coming." Hoffner waited. "One of our juniors," said the man. "Something to do with drink or gambling. Seems it was a bit too much. And then, of course, he'd fought in the war. Battle fatigue, that sort of thing, although he was a top-rate accountant. Very talented. Wrapped a rope around his neck. There was mention of a girl, but I don't involve myself with personal matters."

An accountant killing himself, thought Hoffner: what startling news. He nodded and placed his card on the counter. "Well, if you think of anything else . . ." He was about to head out when he noticed a single pair of eyes peering up at him from the third row. If not for the sameness everywhere else, he might have missed them, but the man seemed to know that a glance would be enough. The eyes went back to their ledger, and Hoffner said to the chief accountant, "You wouldn't have a recommendation for lunch, would you, *mein Herr?*" He spoke just loudly enough to be heard beyond the counter.

"Lunch?" It was clear the man had never considered anything other than the wax-papered sandwiches and pieces of fruit his wife sent along with him every day. "I suppose one could eat at one of the cafés, Herr Kriminal-Oberkommissar. I think there's one across the street."

"Across the street," Hoffner said with a little more volume. "Thank you, *mein Herr.*"

Five minutes later, Hoffner watched from his table as Glancing Eyes emerged from the firm. The man darted across the street, made his way inside and over to the counter. Pulling a brown paper bag from his pocket, he ordered a schnapps.

"The same," said Hoffner as he drew up. The barman poured out a second while the man reached into the bag and removed a banana. Two cigarettes followed, placed neatly on the counter.

"Not much of a lunch," said Hoffner.

"It manages." The man lit the first.

"Bit hard to find—bananas."

"Used to be, but the Americans love them. Can't seem to go any-where without them. Berlin's a regular jungle now." The man took a wedge into his mouth. "He wouldn't have killed himself." He was no less direct.

"Drink and girls and gambling notwithstanding."

The man was oddly intent on his chewing. "No girls, trust me."

Hoffner heard the faint strains of disdain. "That might have been reason enough."

The disdain now surfaced in a single nod and snort. "Maybe before the war," he said. "But not now. Why do you think so many Americans are here?"

Hoffner watched as the man swallowed and took a second bite. "So your friend had no reason to kill himself?"

"My friend," the man echoed. "Yes, Grauer was happy, homosexual, and very talented with a ledger. He was making senior before thirty, and no one makes senior before thirty."

"Then why is he dead?"

"That's your job, isn't it?"

Hoffner never imagined an accountant with so much life—with any life, for that matter. Still, the banana was odd. He pulled the ledger from his pocket, opened it, and placed it on the bar. The man needed only a glance.

"It's his," he said as he took a last bite.

"But he wasn't working with any film companies."

"Gramophones." The man produced a card and placed it on top of the ledger. The word "Tri-Ergon" and an address were written in red ink. "It was in his file. He was working with them for the past six weeks." The man used the last of his cigarette to light the second and then tossed back his schnapps. He stared a moment too long at the empty glass: it was the only gesture to betray him. "You might want to ask them why he had to die."

Not waiting for an answer, the man grabbed his paper bag and headed for the door.

FORTY MINUTES LATER, Hoffner stepped from a tram and into the faint aroma of hacked flesh. The card had sent him east to the edge of the slaughterhouse district, not so far in as to taste the blood in the air, but close enough to recognize its acrid sweetness. White-aproned men—clothes and skin stained a pale pink—stood outside the few remaining factory-like halls, sucking on cigarettes and talking to one another about knives and bones and girls and money. Hoffner remembered having come here as a boy—SPÄTZEL UND SONNE, now long gone—a paper package strangled with rope and stuffed with fat sausage and chops, every Thursday with his father when the meat had been at its cheapest. Spätzel had been an old Jew—not the religious kind, but enough of one to speak a German Hoffner had never fully understood. The place retained a distant sense of that unknown, though not enough to save it. Now it was just a few buildings lost to the rising wave that was the new Berlin. In a few years' time it would be gone, and even its smell would be washed away.

He found the address. Soot covered the brass lettering, common enough this close to the rail yards, but even then, the place had the look of a building not meant to be found.

He rang the bell, and a minute later, a woman appeared, her hair pulled back in a taut bun, her stare no less severe: remarkable how quickly the sourness of schooldays could settle in one's throat.

"Yes?" she said.

Hoffner produced his badge.

The woman grew sharper. "About time, isn't it?" She stepped back and ushered him through. Hoffner knew not to ask and followed her into a large workroom that was empty save for perhaps a dozen long tables with tools spread across.

A stairway and narrow corridor later, he stepped into an office overwhelmed by floor-to-ceiling shelves. Each was crammed with electrical detritus that defied organization, although there seemed to be some kind of symmetry to it all. Hoffner imagined there was a code somewhere, the man kneeling at the center of the floor no doubt its sole proprietor. His back to them, the man was intent on a collection of tubes and wiring, muttering something that sounded like "loose potatoes."

The woman cleared her throat, and the man let out a frustrated groan. "Yes, Fräulein Edelbaum?" He spoke without turning.

"A policeman, Herr Vogt, is here to see you."

The man turned, his face wider than Hoffner expected. The high forehead and sunken eyes nested above a neatly cropped mustache and beard. It was always small men who stumped Hoffner when it came to age.

Vogt looked pained, then quickly recovered. "I thought I made it clear, Fräulein." He turned his attention to Hoffner. "A misunderstanding, *mein Herr*. Totally unnecessary. We . . ." He suddenly realized he was still on his knees. He placed a hand on the desk and hoisted himself up. "Herr . . . ?"

"Hoffner." Hoffner's tone was steady, reassuring. "Chief Inspector Nikolai Hoffner."

"Yes." Herr Vogt was no more reassured. "Herr Chief Inspector. It's just some foolishness. I'm sure it'll pass."

The Fräulein was not so convinced. "They come almost every week, Herr Chief Inspector. Always the same place. It shouldn't be allowed."

Hoffner nodded even if he had no idea what she was talking about.

"I can show you the area." She started for the door.

"No, no." Vogt jumped in. "You have your work to get to, Fräulein. I can show the Herr Chief Inspector."

"Make sure he sees—"

"Yes, Fräulein. The bit by the fence. I won't forget."

She did her best with a smile. "Very good, *mein Herr*."

Vogt motioned Hoffner to the door, and four minutes later, they stood outside the building in a wide alleyway. The words JEWS OUT! were painted in white across the brick.

"The building there," Vogt said, pointing to the next door down. "They make skullcaps and little boxes for prayers." He seemed uneasy out-of-doors.

"Phylacteries," Hoffner said.

"Yes." Vogt lacked the depth in his face to hide his surprise.

Hoffner said, "And the boys who do this don't realize your building ends here and theirs begins there."

"I suppose not. How does a police inspector know to call them phylacteries?"

"So what do you want me to do, Herr Vogt? Send the boys a copy of the city building plans so they can paint on the right side?"

Vogt's expression hardened. "I'm also a Jew, Herr Chief Inspector."

"Yes," said Hoffner easily. "I know. As is your Fräulein Edelbaum, I imagine." Hoffner let Vogt's confusion take hold. "I didn't come about the boys. The same reason you didn't want the police coming at all, even for this. I came about a dead accountant."

Vogt's eyes widened. He began to shake his head nervously. "I don't know what you're talking about."

"Something to do with sound. For film. Rather unpleasant films at that. Does that jar the memory, Herr Vogt?"

The shaking turned to blinking. It was as if Hoffner were watching a bell slot machine ticking toward payout. Without warning, Vogt turned and headed for the door.

UPSTAIRS, VOGT LOCKED THE OFFICE and found two chairs in and among the electrics. Rummaging through the desk, he unearthed a bottle of something brown, two glasses—a quick blow into each—and handed one to Hoffner. They sat.

Vogt seemed to find comfort in the pouring. "He kept a file on us?" It was the first time he had spoken since the alleyway.

"There was a ledger."

Vogt topped up Hoffner's. "Of course there was. Typical Ufa lunacy."

Vogt placed the bottle on the desk and settled into his chair. The two men sat silently, glasses in hand, as Vogt rubbed the back of his hand against his beard. He seemed to be debating whether to take a drink: maybe he hadn't earned it just yet, thought Hoffner.

"The audion tube," Vogt finally said. "You've never heard of it, but that's why you're here."

"It's a triode vacuum for sound amplification." Hoffner gave him no time to ask. "They're using them in the latest riot wagons. We had a training. I'm told the speakers can be heard for miles. Quite remarkable. You were saying?"

Vogt seemed less impressed than slightly bruised. "Oh. Yes. Well . . . the audion. Since you're familiar with it." He took a drink and placed the glass on the desk. "About twenty years ago an American—a man named De Forest—invented the thing. Very important in the development of sound. Ten years later—1919 or so—he went one better and came up with something truly astounding. He called it Phonofilm. Not just amplification, but a system that could record sound directly onto film as a parallel line. An optical sound-on-film process."

"Fascinating, *mein Herr*. And this is leading me to the accountant how?"

Vogt seemed to lose his place. "The accountant . . . ? Oh yes. The accountant." He nodded and pressed on. "Sound on film. Rather stunning if you think about it. The basics of the thing were that these parallel lines could photographically record electrical waveforms from a microphone, which were then translated back into sound waves when the film was projected. Imagine that—photographically recording from a microphone. Remarkable." Hoffner now realized he was in for the duration. There was nothing to do but nod.

"You see where we're going?" Vogt said eagerly. "To play it back, the film simply had to pass across a sensor inside the film projector, which then translated the sound-wave images into electrical impulses that came out through the loudspeaker, like a phonograph." Vogt didn't seem to care that this was now flying right by his guest. "The beauty of the thing was that it could do both image and sound simultaneously. Brilliant. Except it couldn't. Synchronization was the key, and De Forest couldn't find it."

Hoffner saw Vogt waiting for some kind of response. "How sad for him."

"Yes. But there were these three very clever Germans—exceptionally clever—who came up with a way to find absolute synchronization." Vogt reached over to the desk, sifted through a few piles, and tossed over a little gadget. "A 'glow lamp light modulator for variable density sound.' " Vogt arched his eyebrows as if to say, "Impressive." "That little flywheel mechanism you're holding—that was the key. Film has a tendency to speed up or slow down when it's feeding through a projector, and when it does, the sound gets garbled, or even slips a cell. That little piece prevents variations in film speed and therefore eliminates any possibility in the distortion of sound. Faultless synchronization."

"Thank goodness for those Germans."

"Yes."

"And how long did it take you to come up with it?"

Vogt gave in to a meek smile. "About two years. But then, we'd already been in the business of sound-on-film for quite some time. Since 1919, to be exact, when we developed our own process. Funny that, don't you think? The same moment De Forest hit on his system."

Hoffner was glad to hear the edge in Vogt's voice. It gave the man a hint of spine. "So you're saying the American filched it?"

Vogt shrugged, then bent over to the desk's bottom drawer and pulled out a stack of papers. Halfway through he found a sheet and passed it to Hoffner.

It was a Berlin patent imprint, official stamps, a date—"February 7, 1919"—and signatures.

"The second paragraph," Vogt said. "Give it a read."

Hoffner obliged: " 'The "Tri-Ergon Process" relies on the use of a photoelectric cell to transduce mechanical sound vibrations into electrical waveforms and then convert the electrical waveforms into light waves. These light waves are then optically recorded onto the edge of the film through a photographic process to create a "Sound track." ' "

"I came up with that," Vogt cut in. " 'Sound track.' It's quite good. Neat. Precise. And less than three centimeters wide." He nodded for Hoffner to continue.

Hoffner glanced back at the page, but then stopped. Three centimeters, he thought. That's what it had been last night at Pimm's. He looked over at Vogt. "That's why it wouldn't fit."

Vogt shook his head. "Why what wouldn't fit?"

"Your film. Into a projector. The sound track. It's too wide."

Vogt understood and smiled. "It's not just a new recording mechanism. You have to have new projectors as well."

"How many did you produce?"

"Three. Why?"

Hoffner now wondered where the other two had been last night at The Trap.

Vogt nodded again at the page. "Keep reading, Herr Chief Inspector."

Again Hoffner read: " 'Another photoelectric cell is then used to transduce the waveform on the film into electrical waveform during projection.' "

"Sound familiar?" said Vogt.

Hoffner set the page on the desk. "So De Forest stole the blueprints but missed taking the little flywheel thing, and couldn't get it to work."

"Or maybe he did hit on it by himself. Who knows?" A bitterness crept in. "Leibniz and Newton managed to find calculus at the exact same moment. Maybe De Forest's another Newton. Or maybe he just didn't see the need for the flywheel."

Hoffner tossed the device back. "You seem rather cavalier about it."

"Phonofilm went bankrupt last year. I'm guessing Herr De Forest has other concerns right now."

"You're not very fond of the Americans, are you?"

"Are you?"

"They haven't stolen anything of mine, just yet."

"Give them time." Vogt finished the last of his drink and set the glass down.

Hoffner said, "This wasn't the first time they'd managed to take something of yours, was it?"

Vogt's face seemed to numb, the weight of the silence drawing his eyes farther off even as he spoke: "They're going to change the world later this year. October, I think. It's called *The Jazz Singer*. Mr. Al Jolson singing and dancing and talking and talking and talking. A talking picture, except—"

"Except it isn't," Hoffner cut in.

Vogt's gaze snapped into focus. "No. It isn't."

"Someone should tell Mr. Jolson."

Vogt tried another weak smile. "They think they've mastered it. They're not even using the right process."

"Something else of yours?"

"Pfff." Vogt shook his head dismissively. "Remember, this is all about synchronization, Herr Chief Inspector, not something the geniuses at Western Electric fully understand. They've managed to develop a completely meaningless technology—Vitaphone. Even the name is ridiculous. Somebody sneezes and the whole thing goes off kilter. But that's what the great minds at Warner Brothers wanted, so now they have it." Vogt saw Hoffner's confusion and began to spin his finger as if around an old wax cylinder. "*Jazz Singer* is sound-on-disc. The projector is connected to a recording disc that gets scraped by a needle, and then gets played back at the same time. Two completely separate components, so when the film slows down or speeds up, the disc doesn't, and synchronization goes out the window. Genius."

Hoffner was liking Vogt more and more. "Not that you're terribly bitter about all this," he said, "but what do you care? If it doesn't work, all the better for you."

"Oh, but they'll make it work. They're the Americans. And the infuriating thing is that it should have been ours. Tri-Ergon's. Sound-on-film. Had Ufa shown even the slightest bit of backbone, none of this—not Mr. Jolson, not your dead accountant—neither of them would have been an issue. But Ufa didn't. And that's that."

Hoffner heard the rawness in Vogt's frustration, and as much as he needed to see the connection between the studio and the accountant, he knew there was more to be found elsewhere. "So what was it the Americans took from you?"

Flickers of spite, self-pity, even hopelessness cut across Vogt's face, until all that was left was a kind of muted resignation. There might even have been a relief in it. "It's not as petty as that, Herr Chief Inspector."

"It never is."

Vogt sat silently staring across the desk. His eyes dipped to the floor for a moment. Then, without warning, he was on his feet. He reached across for Hoffner's glass. "Nineteen twenty-five," he said as he set the glass down. "That's when the first full-length talking picture was made, Herr Chief Inspector. Would you like to see it?"

THE STEPS TO THE CELLAR were worn through, the light from above a single bulb as Hoffner followed Vogt down into a storage basement. The smell of disinfectant and rat poison collided with something sweet as they reached the bottom.

"She grows tobacco," said Vogt, pushing aside a few mops, a saw-horse with a half-filled tin of paint teetering on its top. "Fräulein Edel-baum. Rolls it herself, although I can't understand how she manages to keep the plants alive down here. The whole thing's a bit bizarre, but people are buying it, so if she can make a little extra money, why not."

There was an opening in the back wall—less a doorway in the brick than the work of a sledgehammer—and Vogt led them through to a second room. The damp now outstripped the smells as Vogt felt along the wall. He flicked on another bulb to reveal a space wider than the first, its low ceiling forcing the two to hunch their way back. Standing alone against the far wall was a tall metal cabinet. Vogt pulled a set of keys from his pocket and opened it.

Less than five minutes later, Hoffner was seated in front of a small screen as Vogt continued to thread a reel into what Hoffner imagined was the second of the three newly developed projectors. Finished, Vogt stepped over, turned off the bulb, and made his way back through the darkness. There was a loud click, and the screen filled with light.

A girl stands on a street corner amidst the hustle and bustle of cars and traffic, the hum of pedestrians walking to and fro, cars honking.
"Buy some matches!"

Her voice rings out as the scene shifts, a Santa guiding a child through
a Christmas market. Somewhere, a hand organ plays—other sounds,
other voices—until the child begins to make her way across a snowy field
to a wooden statue of Mary and the crèche.

Hoffner felt his hand moving toward the screen as if to touch it, something unnerving in hearing the crunch of feet on snow, but Vogt's voice held him back.

"You think it's there, don't you? That somehow your fingers will feel the cold. Amazing how sound can do that."

The child reaches the statue, knocks gently on the wood—the raps
perfectly hollow—when an old woman appears. She speaks with the child
for what might be only seconds, but the passage of time is now irrelevant.
Other figures emerge, other conversations, entire scenes, but all there is
are the words, the sounds, the tremors of life, and it is impossible not to
ask, How can this be? In a sudden flash, the screen is white and black,
and then silent.

Hoffner sat in the darkness, certain he could still hear them. The bulb flicked on, and Vogt said, "It's the first reel. There are five others."

Hoffner was now acutely aware of the silence. "Yes" was all he could manage.

"What you just saw is a thousand times better than anything Mr. Jolson will be doing. He'll have a few songs on disc, maybe a line of dialogue here and there, but nothing like that, nothing continuous, unrelenting—sound in perfect combination."

Hoffner nodded, his eyes on the empty screen as his mind raced to process it all. Last night, the bouts at The Trap had been too short, the images too raw. The girl's screams had lingered, but nothing else. This, however, held a truth that, in its simplicity—maybe because of it—was something he could claim as his own. And it was that, and that alone, that gave it a power beyond the cries of even the anguished.

"Without sound," said Vogt, "all you have is shadow and light. Flat, soulless, barren. Sound is the third dimension. Sound is what gives it texture. Sound is what makes it real."

Hoffner finally turned to face him. "Then why wouldn't they want it? Why not take this?"

Vogt was removing the reel. "Because it made more sense to destroy it."

Hoffner hesitated. "But you have the film, this projector?"

"Not the thing itself. Not the technology." Vogt slipped the reel back into its canister. "The idea of it. That was enough." He snapped the top on and looked at Hoffner. "And that, Herr Chief Inspector, is what they took from me."

Hoffner tried to understand. "The idea?"

Vogt started to answer, but had trouble finding the words. Finally he said, "We were asked to make a film—a film for Ufa. They knew what we'd done in '19. They'd been at a screening we'd had in '22— a series of short sound films at the Alhambra dance hall downtown. Very big news. By '23 they wanted something bigger. Continuous sound, scene to scene, full-length. Naturally, we were desperate to do it, but they said we'd have to work under someone at Ufa—a man named Guido Bagier—chief music advisor, or something like that. Of course we didn't like it. We worked on our own. But then Guido turned out to be a real artist, the only one at Ufa who understood what we were trying to do. And he let us do anything we wanted. If we needed sound booths with absolute silence, he created them. New microphone instrumentation, he found the technicians. Film developers, they were there. All he wanted—all he ever said—was a few reels. A few perfect reels."

"And where's this Bagier now?"

Vogt ignored the question. "Guido became our great champion. Even when the idiots at the top pressured him, he always kept them away. You can't imagine how difficult that must have been. And by '25—October or early November, I don't remember which—we had it. Six reels. *The Little Match Girl*. Not brilliant with story or acting, but astounding with everything else. Of course we didn't know the whole thing was falling apart at the time."

Hoffner needed only to narrow his gaze for Vogt to explain. "Ufa," Vogt said. "We'd been kept in the dark the whole way through. They never bothered to tell us that the studio was on the verge of bank-ruptcy. Oh yes. No one knew it then—no one knows it now—but Ufa had been losing money for years, going so far over budget on films that entire months of bookkeeping had simply been thrown away. That, I imagine, is what you get when you try and compete with the Americans. Naturally we were going to be the ones to save them. Here we had it. Talking pictures. Ufa leading the way. Even the Americans would have to line up and pay."

"But the Americans knew that." It was the first moment of clarity Hoffner had experienced in the last half hour.

"Exactly."

"And they knew they didn't want to get in line."

"Of course—but they were cleverer than that. Ufa was about to be ruined. It needed money. Sound looked to be the answer, but elimi-nate that—eliminate even the idea—and where would Ufa have to go for help?"

This was where Vogt had been leading him all along. "The Americans."

"Exactly. It turns out the studio had been negotiating with Para-mount and Metro as far back as '25—millions of marks in loans—as long as Ufa signed over most of its distribution rights in Europe. They even came up with a little name for their agreement. Parufamet. Brilliant, don't you think? The Americans wanted three-quarters of the market for their own films, and Ufa kept holding them off, waiting to see if our experiment would save them. And it would have, had the whole thing not been sabotaged."

"You really don't like the Americans, do you?" When Vogt said nothing, Hoffner asked, "You're sure it was sabotage?"

Vogt's silence became disbelief. "No, I'm sitting here with you in a damp little cave, showing you something you still can't quite believe you saw, and yet maybe—just maybe—it didn't work. Of course we tested it. For days, weeks. And each time it ran perfectly. All six reels. All sound equipment. Everything. But then we get to Ufa—the great day in the Mozartsaal—and suddenly the storage batteries lose power. Suddenly the statophones start producing this dull roaring sound. Suddenly the potentiometer can't get out more than a squeak of sound even at its upper ranges. And had any of this—even *one* of these things—ever happened before? Never. And yet the audience is laughing, hissing, and the Ufa generals are slinking off in humiliation, and we're left to—" Even the memory was too much. "Four days later they signed their agreement with the Americans. Or at least that's when they announced it. Never even a thought to give us a second chance. My guess, the ink was already dry before we'd left the building." Vogt nodded his head. "Am I sure of it? Yes, Herr Chief Inspector, I'm sure."

Hoffner admired the sincerity. "So the Americans took a piece of Ufa and eliminated the competition for their sound-on-disc technology all at once."

"Very clever, these Americans. One day they'll save the world." Vogt had begun to fold up the projector. "Whether it needs saving or not."

"You know a great deal about all this for a man who was kept in the dark for so long."

Vogt slipped the projector into its case and slowly walked it over to the cabinet. "Yes. I do." He placed it on a shelf and headed for the screen.

Halfway through the rolling up, Hoffner said, "All right, you have my attention. Why?"

"If they'd stolen six years of your work, wouldn't you want to know why?"

"Wanting to know and knowing are two very different things. I'm guessing they didn't sit you down and explain why they were stealing from you."

"Well then, you'd be wrong." Vogt had the screen in a tight roll and stepped over to the top shelf. He slid it in.

Hoffner said, "As some sort of threat, or just to be cruel?"

"There was no need to threaten us. They knew we still wanted to work in film. An accusation would have put an end to that. I don't think they were clever enough to see the cruelty in it."

"Then why?"

"Because they didn't tell us—then." Vogt finished stacking the canisters. "Had they, I would have bought a pistol and shot every last one of them. And then I would have shot myself. I believe they knew that." He locked the cabinet. "No, they waited until three months ago, when Gerhard Thyssen—yes, that Gerhard Thyssen—came and asked us to create something even better for Ufa. Something to make the Americans pay. I believe Herr Thyssen is dead as well."

Hoffner needed a moment. "And that's why you didn't want the police."

"My partners are in Switzerland, Herr Chief Inspector. They told me I should go with them. They made a very strong case—the accountant dead last week, Thyssen yesterday, Fräulein Volker missing. It seems as if the Americans are playing a much more dangerous game this time round."

Something didn't fit. "How did you know about Thyssen and the girl?" It took Hoffner another moment to answer his own question. "Ragier."

"He's a good friend."

"Is he involved?"

"No. You have my word."

Again Hoffner needed to clarify. "So what did Thyssen say he wanted?"

"Something to make sound-on-disc look ridiculous."

"But you'd already done that in '25."

"Yes—we had. He said it wasn't enough."

Hoffner heard something in Vogt's voice. "Three months," said Hoffner. "That's not a long time to come up with something new."

"We'd never stopped working," said Vogt. "The gramophones were just a way to keep us afloat."

"So you needed the time to work out the kinks, perfect your new device."

Vogt hesitated before answering. "Yes. We did."

"And that led you to the sex films?"

This was the question Vogt had been hoping to avoid. He stared across at Hoffner. "You're expecting me to say it wasn't my idea. It wasn't, but that doesn't matter, does it?"

"No, it doesn't."

Vogt accepted the rebuke. "You have to understand how careful we had to be, protective, especially after the sabotage disaster in '25. Thyssen felt we needed something to cover us beyond the gramophones, something we could use to test the new technology without anyone wanting to take a look at it. Sex was ideal when it came to the Americans—they're so terribly afraid of it even when they're so desperate to see it. Give them a public whiff of pornography and they run screaming in the other direction. And Ufa—they were paying for the films. Thyssen needed to cover himself there as well. Funny how Ufa was willing to put money into sex films without batting an eye. And in typical Ufa fashion, they needed to see the books the whole way through. Hence your accountant. What they didn't know was that we were using the films to perfect the new instrumentation."

"But there's no market for sex films. Why would Ufa fund them?"

Clearly this was not something Vogt had ever really considered. "People want sex films." He was barely convincing himself.

"Not on this scale," said Hoffner. "And not this brutal. Where would they show them?"

His hesitation grew. "I—I don't know."

Neither did Hoffner. It was pointless, though, pressing Vogt for an answer. "So you had no trouble with the content?"

Vogt's eyes snapped back into focus. "Of course I had trouble with it. What do you want me to say? That I thought Thyssen was wrong to go down that route, that he might actually have had a real interest in these films? Fine. Yes. He found the people—I think he might even have made one with the girl—I don't know." Vogt's frustration peaked. "I wanted to get this right. I wanted to show them they had made a terrible mistake using us like that. I wanted the men at Ufa who had sold us out to look foolish. And I wanted the Americans to beg for my new work. Maybe that's why. Let it all come out. Ufa the sex peddlers. In the end I would have had my system—something so far beyond what you've just seen that I wouldn't have cared what kinds of films we were making."

Hoffner gave Vogt a moment to regain his composure. "And did you?"

"Did I what? Not care?" Vogt's eyes wandered to the floor. There was no point in answering.

"No—did you have your system?"

Vogt's eyes froze. Almost imperceptibly, he began to nod.

Hoffner said, "Thyssen had it."

Vogt looked over. He nodded again.

"Blueprints or actual device?"

Vogt's regret was palpable. "Both, of course. We were ready to show it. Thyssen said he needed everything together. I'm not a very clever man."

There was no need to make him feel any worse than he did. "You should be in Switzerland."

"As I said, I'm not a very clever man."

Hoffner got to his feet. "That depends on what your new device does."

Vogt let out a nervous laugh. "No worries there, Herr Chief Inspector."

"Would the girl know what to do with it?"

"Impossible."

"Anyone at Ufa?"

Vogt shook his head. "I just figured the thing out myself. Ufa isn't even thinking in these terms."

"It's that remarkable, is it?"

Vogt was holding the keys to the cabinet in his hand and began to swing them gently in his palm. Without warning, he hurled them to the far corner of the room. The metal slapped against the brick and the chain fell to the ground.

Vogt waited for the silence. "That," he said. Hoffner shook his head, and Vogt explained, "Sound has movement, Herr Chief Inspector. One place one moment, another the next. A train in the distance, a voice behind you. Even with sound-on-film, it's sedentary. Place the speaker by the screen, and there it sits. But find a way to capture sound in motion—then you have the fourth dimension. The passage of time through sound. There's no greater reality than that."

The man's certainty was almost enviable. "And you managed that?" Hoffner needed only to look at Vogt's eyes to have his answer. "You should get yourself to Switzerland, *mein Herr*."

"And you, Herr Chief Inspector, should get me my device."

OUTSIDE, HOFFNER LIT UP. For the first time in days, the sky seemed forgiving, if no less sterile.

Going through the last hour in his head, he wanted to believe that things had come clearer, but Vogt had only raised more questions. What exactly had been going on out at Ufa to prompt Thyssen to hide the research in the first place? Vogt had seemed certain that the Americans were involved again, but why? They had made their killing a year and a half ago with the loan agreement, and the Jolson film was about to place their sound process at the top. What was there to be gained by destroying a new component—remarkable as it might be— to a system no one was using anyway? And why had they been willing to put money into sex films when there was no market for them?

And yet, Thyssen was dead and the Volker girl was missing. And that left Hoffner right back where he started.

He took a pull on the cigarette. At least he had convinced Vogt to take the next train out of Berlin. He was also now in possession of a drawing of the device, the thing oddly similar in both look and dimensions to a kerosene lamp. Hoffner folded the sheet of paper and slid it into his pocket. It rubbed up against the ledger, and he pulled the two out. Slipping the sheet inside, he stopped for a moment.

It was the little book that focused him. He stared at it, following its path back—from Vogt, to the accountant, to The Trap—when he suddenly realized where he had let himself go wrong. It was the ledger that had brought him here, the ledger that had been left behind—and that made no sense. If Vogt was even remotely on track, no one would have been stupid enough to leave the thing simply lying around. It was too perfect a piece of bait to send someone off on the hunt.

And that meant Hoffner had to go back to Leni.

THE SPEAKER

RITTER WAS ONLY TOO HAPPY to lace in with a nice earful when Hoffner finally got through: something about important men having important things to do, far more important than wasting their time waiting for some inspector to show up. Ritter even managed to get in a little jab about Georg, his disappointment and surprise there as well. Hoffner took it all, tossing in that perhaps a double homicide in Prenzlauer Berg (no one had actually died in Prenzlauer Berg today) might just have taken precedence over the inconvenience of those very important men. Ritter's silence on the other end of the line gave Hoffner the opportunity to ask about Leni.

"A meeting with Herr Lang, Inspector?" Ritter said.

"Yes, *mein Herr*. Did the Fräulein say if she was meeting with him?"

"With Lang? I— Yes. I believe she did. Herr Lang is in town today. I can get you the address and telephone number."

Twenty minutes later Hoffner stood outside Lang's apartment building, a high-rise in the Wilmersdorf area of town, very expensive and very restricted. Just in case the streakless windows or porcelain white of the stone, or even the paperless gutters, failed to initiate the unsuspecting to affluent Berlin, the doormen along the street made it clear just how valuable those inside were. Broken noses, swollen knuckles, and necks of faded welts all pointed to years lost in the ring. Hoffner wondered how many of these boys he might have seen at a beer-and-sausage brawl up in Rixdorf, the chance at a prizefight with the likes of a Diener or a Walter Neusel, or maybe the new boy Schmeling tearing up the place: memories where the scent of blood and ammonia lingered in the nose. Hoffner had actually been at the Sportpalast the night Breitenstrater—Blond Hans—had shattered some Italian's jaw, August of '24, teeth and bone flying to the pock-pock-pock of flashbulbs and jeers. You could fill two dental surgeries now with the number of molars Berliners claimed to have smuggled off the canvas that night.

None of these, however, had ever made it to those ranks. They were sponge and muscle boys, big enough to keep the street clean, but little more. A badge was sufficient to render them harmless.

"And how can I help you today, Captain?" Lang's doorman spoke in a dull German, the tongue heavy from too many years failing to get his hands up.

"Herr Lang," Hoffner said. The man looked unconvinced, and Hoffner added, "I'm guessing the young lady's already gone up?" A moment of recognition, and Hoffner said, "For the film. I'm the one who's going to be bringing in the 'true-life' flavor, if you know what I mean."

The man nodded, even if he was still thinking things through. "She's been up there awhile."

Hoffner smiled. "Always takes them time to get to the real stuff. The fellow who's lived it. Still it's a few marks in my pocket. 'The reality beyond the truth.'" Hoffner raised his eyebrows, and the man nodded more eagerly. This he had heard before.

"Yah, yah," he said. "Herr Lang's come to me for some pointers, too." The hands rose up in a few leaden swings. "*Mabuse*. The bit in the casino. I was the one to show him that."

Hoffner laughed and headed for the elevator. "Which floor?"

"All the way at the top. Six."

Hoffner pressed the button and watched as the last few jabs disappeared behind the sliding door.

LANG'S VALET WAS LESS TRUSTING. Even so, the badge had the desired effect. Hoffner was escorted to the edge of a sunken living room with a derisive "A policeman, *mein Herr*."

Three heads turned at once—Lang's, Leni's, and a woman's Hoffner had never seen. She was seated on a sofa by the window, blond hair that was her own, and a face that seemed devoid of character. Everything was pale and round: even the eyes looked more suited to the man he had just finished with downstairs. It made the bite in her voice all the more unexpected.

"And this must be our Inspector Hoffner, sneaking up on us," she said as she lifted her cigarette in greeting. "Thea von Harbou. The second Frau Lang. He's kept me around a bit longer than the last one."

The place was a clutter of African art and modern sculpture, the furniture reminiscent of the same mindless angularity that had caged the Volker girl's flat, although here the self-conceit was kept off the walls and reserved for a long, narrow desk that ran the length of one side of the room. Lang was standing behind it, notebooks and drawings scattered across the top, its focal point a large sheet that had evidently just been pulled out for Leni's benefit. She was standing at his side, the look on her face relief, as if she had done all she could to weather the Langs' hospitality.

"The Herr Chief Inspector never sneaks up," Leni said, her eyes on him. "There are very few surprises there."

Von Harbou laughed as she leaned over and crushed out her cigarette. "Is she making fun of you, Herr Inspector?"

Hoffner pulled out a cigarette and stepped down. "She's an American. I imagine so."

Von Harbou smiled and sat back. "You've come to take a look at our bathtub?"

A certain callousness always rounded out this brand of intelligence, thought Hoffner, as if knowing more than everyone else permitted a bending of the rules. He had met it before, the malice reasoned away with a laugh or, in the face of genuine sensitivity, a disdain for feeling altogether. That a man was dead hardly mattered. After all, von Harbou had never really meant it.

"I managed one this morning, Madame," he said as he lit up. "But I'll keep the offer in mind, thank you."

Lang said, "She wants to know if you've figured it all out. That way she can steal it for her next script."

"*Our* next script," von Harbou said. "Drink, Inspector?"

Hoffner noticed a wooden mask propped up on one of the shelves. It was a dark brown with elongated Negro features. The nose was particularly flat. "Thank you, no."

"They don't really look like that in Africa," Lang said. "At least that's what I've been told. I've never been. I do remember the Negroes in New York looking a bit similar. Not quite so drawn out, but still, something like it."

"Either way," said von Harbou, standing, "not terribly attractive. Brandy, Inspector? Or is it whiskey?"

Hoffner stepped over to the desk. "No, nothing, thank you." She seemed almost disappointed.

Lang said, "I was showing Fräulein Coyle the drawings I made while I was there. Quite inspiring, New York."

The sheet was filled with charcoal renderings of skyscrapers, bridges, endless little dots at the bottom of the page.

"And these?" said Hoffner, pointing to them.

"The people," said Lang, sweeping an errant hair from the sheet.

"That's Fritz's idea of humanity, Inspector." Von Harbou was pouring herself another drink. "Specks to be flicked from a page. Rather sad, don't you think?"

Lang eyed the drawing with a healthy reverence. "This was where I found my *Metropolis*. Hopeless isolation amid all that vitality. The modern world destroying the inner man."

Hoffner let Lang linger a few moments longer before asking, "The girl hasn't been in touch, has she?"

Lang continued to stare at the drawing. "The girl . . . ?" He looked up. "Oh, the girl." Lang peered past Hoffner. "Has anyone called?" Von Harbou shook her head, and Lang said, "There you have it, Inspector. I gather you haven't figured it all out, then."

It was an odd response. Lang had needed to be reminded. "I thought Fräulein Coyle would have already asked."

Lang looked at Leni with a coy smile. "Are you a detective as well, Fräulein? I had no idea."

Leni was more than a match for him. "The Herr Chief Inspector gives me too much credit, *mein Herr*. I'm here simply to see if we can't steal you away from Ufa. Let Metro and a bit of money—"

"An obscene bit of money," said Lang.

"Yes," she said. "See if either might tempt you to make your next film with us. You're not being terribly receptive, are you?"

Lang shrugged with the careless indifference of a man desperate for adulation. Von Harbou said lazily, "How we all love our Fritz."

"It's just we've had a call from her," Hoffner said. "Very brief, anxious. Rang off before we could get much out of her. Probably realized a policeman wasn't the answer she was looking for." Hoffner enjoyed the shift in Leni's expression. "I thought she might have gone back to what she knows. Evidently not." He looked directly at Leni. "Herr Ritter, Fräulein. He was kind enough to tell me where

I might find you. I thought you'd want to know as soon as possible."

It was masterful the way she brought things to a close: a few laughs about nothing, the effortless finishing off of her cigarette, the sudden recollection of a meeting, one last honey-mouthed plea to von Harbou to let her husband venture west, inching to the door, her coat and wrap . . .

"Are you driving out that way, Herr Chief Inspector?" It was as if the thought had just occurred to her.

Hoffner let her twist for a moment before saying, "I suppose I could, Fräulein."

"And so gallant to boot," said von Harbou, back at the sofa. Her afternoon drunk had begun to strip her of what little charm she had: plain and clever held an allure; ordinary and tight was simply ugly. "If I end up in a tub, Herr Inspector, I'll make sure they send you to find me."

Lang was already at the door. He had learned over the years to keep his wife's audiences to a minimum. "You'll let me know when the girl turns up."

Hoffner followed Leni into the corridor, leaving Lang to sort through his own complications.

SHE HAD HER ARM THROUGH HIS the moment they stepped out onto the street.

"For the doorman's sake," Leni said as they moved along. "He's already looking at you in an entirely different light."

"You're that much of a prize?"

"Do you really want to go down that road?"

"A rather well-traveled one, I imagine."

She smiled. "Now you're just being cruel. I suppose that's the charm in the German art of seduction. Does it ever work?"

"I've no idea. I've never tried it."

"When did the girl call?"

Hoffner enjoyed how easily she got to it. "She didn't," he said, and felt the slightest tensing in her grip. "Who gave you the ledger?"

He half expected another instant of hesitation, but she was too good to give in to it. "Ritter," she said. "How did you know?"

"Why?"

She reached into her purse for a cigarette. "The same reason I gave it to you. Because he thought it would help me find the girl." She stopped and waited for a light.

Hoffner obliged and said, "So you knew about the films before last night." Leni let out a long stream of smoke but said nothing. "Quite a performance."

"Not really. I'd never seen them before."

"And that justifies it?"

"We should find a bar," she said, pocketing the cigarette case. "One that sells American whiskey. I'm getting tired of all this watered-down stuff." She turned to find a cab, but Hoffner held her arm.

"It's a little early for me," he said.

"That's not true."

"That doesn't seem to be at much of a premium right now, does it?"

She said coyly, "Don't tell me you're taking any of this personally? That would be a real disappointment."

"What do you want from the girl?"

Her eyes narrowed as though she were trying to locate the source of his confusion. "We've been through this. Metro wants—"

"No," he said evenly. "It doesn't." He was surprised to find himself still holding her arm. "Why would they want what they already have?"

She continued to search his eyes. "What was in that ledger?"

"Whatever I was supposed to find, I imagine." His grip remained firm. "Why do you want the girl?"

Uncertainty slipped into something less comfortable and she pulled away. It was the last thing he expected—vulnerability, defensiveness. It made her all the more unknowable. "You're baiting me," she said. "It's not terribly attractive."

"You have my apologies."

"Then try not to enjoy it quite so much." She dropped her cigarette and began to crush it into the pavement.

"You knew about Metro and Paramount," Hoffner said. "Parufamet." Leni stopped but refused to look at him. "Ufa was at their beck and call. All the Americans had to do was make a telephone call and the girl would have been on the next flight to Los Angeles. But they didn't do that, did they?"

"No—they didn't."

"So the rising starlet story doesn't really hold water, does it?"

She slowly looked up at him. "No. It doesn't."

"Then why are you looking for this girl?"

He could see her struggling for control. She reached into her purse for a cigarette.

"Why?" he repeated.

She found one and said, "The man—the *men* who sent me—they wanted this particular girl."

"Why?"

"Because she was Thyssen's. Because they wanted Thyssen's girl."

Hoffner knew the reason: Vogt had made that crystal clear. Even so, he needed to hear it from her. "And what had Herr Thyssen done to deserve this attention?"

She lit up. "Maybe he was tired of ponying up and decided to use the films as leverage."

"For what?"

"Distribution, another loan—I don't know. Hollywood's not exactly filled with the most savory types." She pinched at a piece of tobacco on her tongue and flicked it to the ground. "Remind them they control the most powerful business in the world and they'll think they can do whatever they want, to whomever they want. And they're always willing to pay."

Hoffner stopped himself from answering. She was taking them down the wrong path: this was sex—not sound—and that made no sense given how Vogt had dismissed the sex as nothing more than a distraction. "So why kill the golden goose?"

"Maybe Thyssen was getting greedy."

Or maybe he had another egg in the basket. The trouble was, why did Leni know nothing about that? "So Ritter was willing to give up the girl that easily?"

"He's a lawyer," she said. "I don't think they like dying any more than anyone else." She took a drag.

"And that was the message you were sent to bring him?" When she said nothing, Hoffner pressed, "And the girl, when and if you find her—I don't imagine there's anything terribly savory waiting for her."

"That doesn't really concern me."

"And here I'd heard Los Angeles was all sunshine and warmth."

"I do better in a cold climate."

"As I'm discovering, yes."

She stared at him. He said nothing and she began to shake her head. She then took a last pull—she had a knack for giving up on a cigarette too soon—and tossed it to the ground. "Everything laid out in front of you," she said, "and still you need me to say it. And you think *I'm* heartless." She looked up at him. "It was because they gave me no choice."

The banality of the phrase, read in too many bad novels, made her frailty no less a beacon to him. "You don't seem the type."

She continued to hold his gaze. Her face was suddenly soft, her eyes stripped of pretense. It was an honesty he had never imagined. "Neither do you," she said quietly. "But then you're no less worn down than I am. Makes us pretty easy prey, doesn't it?"

He said, "So what do they have on you?"

Her laugh was at once dismissive and pitiful. "Have on me. You make it sound like there's an envelope somewhere—daring pictures, a scribbled note, the deed to the family farm. You don't really think the world works that way?"

The resilience of women amazed Hoffner. She had gutted herself in front of him, and yet there were no signs of a scar, not even an incision. A man would have asked him to stare at the entrails, recognize the pain and self-loathing it had taken to bring them out. Men needed that sort of admiration for their powerlessness. She stood atop hers with a careless defiance.

"Then why not just let it go?" he said. "Tell them she disappeared and then disappear yourself."

"And do what?" Her disbelief bordered on contempt. "The girl in the bar—the one you so cleverly pointed out yesterday. The way out isn't any more complicated than the way back in. Trust me."

And there it was. Hoffner was struck by how effortlessly she had said it—and how stupid he had been to miss it. The way back in. Her year drying out in Los Angeles spent on her back. For her, it was always there, the permanent mark across her chest, written in bold scarlet letters, all of it so terribly American. At least this was a novel he had read.

"They won't care," he said.

"Then you don't know them."

She continued to stare up at him, and it was all he could do not to pull her in.

He finally said, "The booze you want is back east." He found a cigarette. "They haven't the stomach for it out here."

A cab appeared at the top of the street, and he raised his hand to hail it.

THEY DRANK FOR AN HOUR, talking about nothing, until he insisted he drop her off at her hotel. Luckily, she was too far gone to give him much of a fight. That had been half an hour ago.

Now Hoffner was in that sour-mouthed duskiness where the gray-black of the sky seems almost an illusion, as if the day might still be hiding somewhere behind it: if only he knew where it had gone. It was a long time since he had had this much to drink by six in the evening. His only way out was another drink. At least that way he could keep the smell of his own breath out of his nose.

Pimm was standing at the edge of a dock, the river beyond him. A gathering of his boys stood at the far end loading crates onto a barge. Pimm kept his hands in his coat pockets as he watched Hoffner work his way down the gangway.

"Twice in one week," said Pimm.

"Not even waiting for full-on dark." Hoffner was doing his best to keep his legs under him. "No shame at all."

"I pay enough not to have any. Someone spill a bottle of schnapps on you?"

"Long day."

The river spread out as a gray flatness, the far shore visible only in pockets of reflected light. Even then, the outline was deceptive. Only the smell of the Spree offered any kind of bearings this far east. Here, it was the scent of baking bread that rose off the water, the grain boats moored all the way up to the Oberbaum Bridge. The granary itself loomed in the distance, tall and dreary: even in daylight, its sooted walls kept it black and unforgiving. Now, at the edge of twilight, it was nothing more than a wide emptiness in a sinking sky.

"How far to the other side?" Hoffner asked.

"Why? You thinking a swim will clear your head?"

"Remind me—you use the barges for what, cocaine, black-market coal?"

Pimm shouted to one of his men: "There's two more trucks coming down. Pack them in tight." He took out a flask and handed it to Hoffner. "It's not for drinking. Sprinkle some on your face and coat. Do us all a favor."

Hoffner sniffed at the contents: lavender and talcum. That was twice today he had had to suffer through it. "Men actually wear this?"

"When they smell like you, yes. You can keep the flask."

There was a splash at the far end, and Pimm said, "Now what?" He was about to head over when a figure appeared from the shadows. Even in the half-light Hoffner recognized the lanky frame of Zenlo Radek. The man never seemed to age. The sharp features of his face remained preserved under a thin coating of skin, just enough to cover the bone. Somehow the eye sockets always looked to be in need of a bit more.

"It's nothing," Radek said. His accent was equally taut, eastern European, although Hoffner doubted if even Pimm knew its exact origin.

"Nothing?" said Pimm. "I don't pay them to lose—"

"The thing," said Radek with a quick glance at Hoffner. "What we talked about. How long until the next truck?"

Even with his head in knots, Hoffner laughed to himself. "I don't want to know what or who, do I?"

"Who," Pimm echoed. For a moment Hoffner thought he saw something else in the eyes. Pimm then echoed the laughter and said, "That's right. I'm going to dump a body this far downriver, especially with a winter current in the water? I'd do better delivering it straight to the Alex. You really don't think that much of me, do you?"

"The problem is, I think too much of you and manage to forget all this."

Pimm turned to Radek. "Fifteen minutes. Tell them to take a smoke."

Radek nodded and headed back.

"Nothing's in the works," said Pimm. He had promised to make a few calls: a crankman out at Luna Park, the projector operator up at Hugo Geller's Burlesque Emporium, and two London boys who ran a strip and squirt room in the attic of The Barrister's Bonn—originally slated as The Barrister's Bone (those clever English), but the boys had ordered the gas signs over the telephone and had failed to confirm the spelling. What a lawyer's imagining of a southern German town had to do with a self-gratification parlor remained a mystery to most. To those in the know, it made the place only more laughable. Still, they were the best in the city at getting people in front of a camera.

The last on Pimm's list was a chemist out in Treptow who, when not dispensing arthritis and bladder curatives to the dying poor, was known to be the top developer of nudie films in Berlin. None of them had heard a thing.

"What about Americans?" said Hoffner.

"What about them?" When Hoffner said nothing, Pimm added, "I don't do a lot of business in those circles."

"You disapprove?"

"No," Pimm said easily. "Not at all. How people do what they do—not for me to judge. Funny enough, they don't use as much muscle as everyone else. You'd think they would, but they don't. It's the French who like all that—knives and knuckles and kneecaps. Maybe it's because they think they actually won the war. Why should I be looking for Americans?"

"There's a girl—"

"Now that's where you'll find your muscle."

"A German," said Hoffner. "She's got hold of a piece of equipment some Americans might want."

"And she knows they want it?" Pimm nodded to himself. "That always makes for a bit of desperation. You're sure she's not dead?"

"I'm guessing they want her for more than just the equipment."

Pimm nodded again. "The sex films. Someone wants a new leading lady."

It was a remarkable mind, thought Hoffner. For a man who had spent the first ten years of his life killing stray dogs so as to eat, Pimm saw things with a clarity that denied his natural viciousness. Then again, maybe that was what had kept him alive.

"I'll see what I can find," Pimm said. "You need some bacon?" He peered out at the barge.

"Bacon?" said Hoffner.

"Danish bacon. Very nice this time of year."

Hoffner smiled. "No. No bacon. Thanks."

"Just wondering."

DARKNESS ALWAYS CAME as a reprieve to Wedding. Whatever decay lived on the streets during the day, nightfall brought at least temporary relief from the humiliation. True, the place had yet to succumb in the ways that Prenzlauer Berg and the Mitte districts had: workers here still carried their pride in little lunch pails and Sunday suits fit for bodies twenty years younger. Nonetheless, it was hard for a man to find his way through when all he could see was how much worse it would be for his sons, more so for their sons yet to come. Even the violence in the night struck out with a kind of depressed rage.

Hoffner took the subway steps two at a time and emerged to the leaden quiet of a deserted square: the locals knew to stay in on nights when the Pharus Hall opened its doors. The only sound was the trickling of water from a fountain, and Hoffner was suddenly reminded of how parched he was. He made his way over and scooped out a few handfuls. The water had the sour taste of stone and rust. Both seemed to bring some life back to his head.

Sadly, the surroundings were less inspiring. Brown stucco tenements stretched on from block to block with a silence that belied the life within. Sounds of squalor kept themselves hidden inside the courtyards, where the smell of boiled cabbage and water-rinsed clothing hung in the air like the unwashed breath of poverty. There was nothing to distinguish the buildings from one another except for the occasional weathered number on a porter's door.

Hoffner took the turn onto Müllerstrasse and heard the first rumblings of the crowd, raucous even by its usual standards. A bright light spilled out onto the street, and the figures moving to the door seemed to form out of the yellow haze of the streetlamps. Several open-back trucks were parked along the road, their drivers sitting in the cabins as Hoffner made his way over. He checked to see if these might be from the local precinct—always good to have the threat of a roundup in view—but they were commercial. Maybe the Rummelsberg and Erkner party members had decided on a little outing, a bit of support for their city brothers. Did Communists actually use the word "outing," Hoffner wondered. It still failed to explain why Sascha would be putting in an appearance.

A few shouts rang out and Hoffner joined the crowd. All he could think of was Georg and how completely ill equipped he was for tonight. Not that the Reds were always looking for a dustup: they were, but that hardly distinguished them from any number of Berlin's other bare-fisted bands of roving politicos. These simply needed to bore their would-be followers with hours and hours of impenetrable speeches. How a group of factory men and cobblers found inspiration in these endless rants always astounded Hoffner—long-hairs shipped in from far more reasonable parts of town, where discussions of economic inevitabilities and five-year plans tended to make more sense over a nice cup of black-currant tea and a sticky roll.

He scanned the faces for Georg, rough men with deep-set eyes carved out by drink and defeat. They came to each other in the vain hope of finding some untapped purpose. It would have been too much to call it inspiration, but for those young enough not to know any better, there still might have been a faith even in that.

A pamphlet was thrust into his hand, and Hoffner slipped it into his pocket as he moved into the auditorium. The sudden heat of sweat and tobacco stifled the air as a babbling of voices filled the room. People were either sitting or milling about all the way up to the stage, where a group of men stood on either side of a podium. One barked orders to an unseen figure in the audience; another flipped through pages of what looked to be a very long speech. The rest stared out at the crowd checking their watches with surprising consistency. There was something uncertain to the room, as if a single shattered glass might bring the whole thing crashing down, but Hoffner was now strangely unaware of it. Instead, he was staring at the second figure from the right. The face was a bit fuller, the chest broader, but the rest appeared as if time had forgotten the boy.

Sascha was a young twenty-four, still too thin, and still with a gaze that showed no hesitation in how it viewed the world. Even smiling, he looked incapable of pity.

Hoffner felt a quick push to his back. The crowd behind him was evidently not as taken with the sight of his son. He stepped to the side, found a place along the back wall, and continued to stare.

What made for the passing of eight years, he wondered. A minute ago, he might have been able to reconstruct it with a kind of coherence—maybe not a meaning, but at least something to approximate movement. Now all he had were flashes of time, and Sascha appeared in none of them. Even the sound of his voice was completely unknown—that perhaps oddest of all—watching his son speak in the distance, trying to make out the words, and hearing only a boy in his head.

"I can't believe it."

Hoffner turned and saw Georg moving through the crowd.

"You actually made it."

Georg drew up, and Hoffner reached over and hugged him. It was no different from what was happening in the rest of the hall: men embraced with fat slaps to the back, the exaggerated gestures of camaraderie. Here, however, it was foreign to both of them. Hoffner felt the solidness of his son in his arms and let go.

Georg's expression was a mixture of amusement and confusion as he stepped back. "Well, it's good to see you, too, Papi." He nodded up to the stage. "Have you seen him?"

Hoffner nodded quietly, his eyes fixed on Georg, and Georg suddenly understood what had just passed between them. He was no better for it, his smile too wide, the pat on his father's shoulder too emphatic to hide his inexperience with this kind of affection. Both knew there was nothing to trust in it.

"I told you he was doing well," said Georg. "He's the personal secretary—something like that—to the man who's speaking. We should go over."

"He looks busy," said Hoffner. "I don't want to get in the way."

"The fellow's notoriously late. Sascha said so. We've got time."

Georg slipped into the crowd, and Hoffner had no choice but to follow. The men around them seemed even more ragtag than Hoffner had thought outside. Communists usually put on a better face. This had the smell of a beer hall.

They neared the stage, and Sascha caught sight of Georg, a hand up, the same stifled smile. It was another second before he saw Hoffner.

There was an ease in the expression, stiff as it was, that dispelled any connection the two might still have had.

"Georgi," Sascha said as he came down the steps: Hoffner thought he was hearing his own voice. "And Nikolai Hoffner. So there is some courage in there, after all."

The phrase had the tone of being too well practiced, but Hoffner let it go. Eight years for a boy of twenty-four deserved the first cut.

"So, you've come up to Wedding" was all Hoffner could find to say. "Bit of a surprise."

"Right in their backyard," Sascha said. "But that's the whole point, isn't it?"

Hoffner nodded, not understanding what the boy meant, and not caring. "You look good, Alexander."

"The living continue living, Fath—" Sascha caught himself, his eyelids heavy for a moment. He found his recovery in another cut. "Doesn't look as if you've been doing much of that."

Hoffner bobbed his head in agreement. "The old get older."

There was an awkward silence, and Georg jumped in with too much energy. "Father's been working on something out at the studio, so I suppose the game's up there, but he's been pretty good about it."

"Not that keen he's out of school," said Hoffner, trying to match Georg's lightness. It was a poor attempt.

"You'll get over it," said Sascha.

The blows were coming more accurately now. Hoffner glanced beyond Sascha and found refuge in the movement up on stage. "So this is . . . ?"

"A meeting," said Sascha. "Like any other." Again, there was too much preparation in the tone. "The man I work with"—not for, but with, thought Hoffner—"he has some very powerful ideas. And he's not afraid to throw them back in the Reds' faces. Naturally, we're prepared for whatever they might have in mind tonight."

Evidently this was some sort of gauntlet being thrown down, out beyond the fringes of real politics. What else were a few broken bones and bloody faces good for? The local cops would come in, toss the worst of them in the clink for the night, and give the rest of the less committed a sense of martyred victory. And the next speech and meeting would begin with the names of the gallant few . . . It was a mindless game Berlin had been tolerating for too long.

"Kurtzman."

One of the men called down from the stage, and Sascha turned. Hoffner had done his best to forget this little tidbit. Taking his mother's maiden name had been Sascha's last act of defiance. Or perhaps it had been his first. Hoffner had never figured out which.

"He's here," the man barked, and headed for the wings.

Sascha turned back to Georg and said, "You'll want to meet him. He's very approachable." For the first time, he looked at his father with something other than disdain. "You can come, too, if you like."

Hoffner followed them up the stairs and into the backstage area. A man handed Sascha a clipboard and then led them toward a door at the far side. It opened out into an alleyway, where the sound of a car door slamming brought Sascha to full attention. He cleared his throat and waited.

A small man, early thirties and in a leather long coat, appeared in the doorframe. His fedora looked too large for his narrow face, although the nose did manage to keep pace with the brim. There was something of the little Jew to him, and Hoffner wondered how far afield Sascha had managed to go in just eight years.

The man spotted Sascha and raised his tiny hand. Hoffner now saw where the boy had learned his stiffness.

"Kurtzman," the man said as he walked over. He had a limp that everyone seemed careful not to notice. "Excellent. Have we had any trouble?"

"Police had the place barricaded until about twenty minutes ago." Sascha spoke with a newfound authority. "I'd say two-thirds of the crowd is Red. They've been waiting a good half hour."

"Then I'll need to go in through the front, won't I?"

"That might not be the best—"

The hand went up again, and the man smiled. "Open warfare. That's the whole point, isn't it? And this is . . . ?"

Sascha stepped back. "Oh yes. This is Georg Hoffner." The two shook hands. "And his father." Hoffner took the small hand, the fingers like slick bone. Still, it was a firm grip. "Herr Doktor Joseph Goebbels," Sascha continued. "Leader of district Berlin-Brandenburg." Hoffner noticed the little badge on his lapel, an open-winged eagle perched on a wreath, surrounded by leaves. It was not a war medallion he knew.

"You've seen the crowd, *mein Herr?*" Goebbels spoke to Hoffner as if the two had been friends for years. "On edge, are they?"

Hoffner said, "That would be an accurate way of describing it, *mein Herr*. Yes."

Goebbels's smile had all the subtlety of oil. "Then we mustn't disappoint them." He turned to Sascha. "Give me two minutes to get through the crowd out front, then have Daluege announce the opening of the meeting. That should get things flying." He put a hand on Sascha's shoulder. "Don't look so worried. Can't be worse than charging up a trench, and I've been through that." He added a playful slap on the boy's cheek and then headed for the door.

Hoffner waited until Goebbels was out of earshot. "He seems fond of you."

Sascha continued to watch Goebbels go. "Yes."

"That must be nice for you."

"Yes."

Hoffner had hoped for at least a glance from the boy, but Sascha kept his eyes on the little man: how much clearer to see oneself erased from a life. He said, "He doesn't exactly look like Freikorps material."

Sascha turned to his father with the same even gaze. "National Socialist. We still use old members of the Korps, but only when we need to show a bit of strength. It's a thinking man's party now."

Hoffner recalled something about these thinkers, somewhere in the south. Evidently they were setting their sights on bigger prey. "I see. He's surprisingly nimble, what with the—"

"Yes, he is," said Sascha. "One of the remarkable things about him. Took four bullets to the calf in the Somme. They said he wouldn't walk."

Hoffner now understood why he had been invited. Burgeoning hero worship always softened the sting of old betrayals: so much easier to extend the olive branch to those no longer with any claim. The boy, however, was still his to protect.

"That wasn't from a bullet," Hoffner said.

Sascha looked momentarily puzzled. Here he had made the effort, and here was his father finding a way to ruin even that. "You're right. It was four bullets."

"It wasn't any bullets." Hoffner gave up on the pretense. "The man never fought in the war, Sascha."

The boy stared at his father, a familiar coldness rising in his eyes. "Really?"

"The boot he wears. It's from before the war. The old leather and wood. Used to see them all the time. They've improved on them since then. Had to, really. Too many boys coming back without legs. I imagine Herr Goebbels was born with his leg that way."

The boy's tone, like his gaze, remained unchanged. "You really are a piece of work, aren't you?" Sascha waited on the silence and then said, "What is it that you do? Spend your life with murderers and thieves, tinker about trying to figure out why they do what they do, see things they can't see? And so arrogant that you even get your own wife killed." There was nothing but precision in the eyes, no loss, no venom, not even contempt. "But you saw they were going to do that, didn't you? You picked out that little detail that made sure you knew you were right. She's dead, boys without a mother, but you had it. And now you've noticed this. A boot. I won't even pretend to question your expert eye. Bravo."

Hoffner slapped Sascha across the face. The boy hardly flinched.

There was a sudden booing from the auditorium, followed by shouts of "Bloodhound!" "Murderer of the workers!" Sascha continued to stare at his father before checking his watch. He turned to a man by the curtain. "He's in the hall. Go out and announce him." He looked back at Hoffner. "You're welcome to stay for the speech, if you like. There are seats out front." He turned to Georg. "I've a place for you onstage. I was hoping you'd want to sit with me."

Georg nodded quietly. He was unable to look at his father.

From the stage, the man announced the meeting, and a single jeering cry rose up from somewhere in the hall, "The meeting will come to order!" Almost at once the entire crowd took up the chant, "The meeting will come to order! The meeting will come to order!"

Sascha, the first sign of concern in his eyes, moved to the edge of the stage. "It's time," he shouted to the man at the podium. "Send the boys out and get rid of the Reds."

Hoffner noticed Goebbels now onstage. His coat was disheveled and his hat was missing, but there was a glow in his face as if this was what he had been waiting for. A glass of beer flew up, the liquid catching Goebbels's face before it shattered behind him. The next moment, the entire place erupted.

"Georg!" Hoffner shouted over the noise. "This way." He motioned to the alleyway door.

Georg stared back, his eyes all but empty. He then turned and walked to his brother.

Hoffner imagined himself moving to him, but there was nothing in that. All he had now was the silence beyond the door, and the gray hope of distance between them.

HOURS LATER, a pair of elevator doors opened and Hoffner stood convinced he was smelling flowers—lilies or roses—although he might just have been tasting the whiskey in his throat.

He had found a bar somewhere near the hall, another closer into town, the last a dingy hole off Linienstrasse. Naturally, there had been a girl along the way, a few choice words with her rather fat man—the threat of something in an alley—and then a cab and a tram, the last half hour spent on his feet. Surprisingly, the walk had done him good.

Everything before that had grown dull—the purpose of it all, he imagined—so at least he had accomplished something tonight.

He drew up to the door and knocked. He waited, then knocked again. He heard footsteps.

"Yes?" The voice was hesitant.

"It's me," he said. "Nikolai."

The door opened, and Leni stood in a long dressing gown tied at the waist. The room behind her was lit by a single lamp.

"I've brought you some cigarettes," he said, patting at his coat for a pack.

"Have you? Looks like a coffee would have been a better bet."

"Yah," he said, then nodded slowly.

She continued to stare at him. "Not terribly romantic, is it?"

"Not really about romance."

She waited, then pulled back the door and invited him in.

CHAPTER THREE

PHOEBUS

LAMPLIGHT SKIRTED THE EDGE of the curtains, and Hoffner felt a soreness at the base of his neck. His back was damp from the goose-feather comforter around his waist, but the pillow remained cool. It was his breath that was giving the silk its particularly stale tang. He tried a swallow, but his throat had no room for it.

"There's a glass of water on the side table," Leni said. She was seated in an armchair at the end of the bed, her robe pulled to her neck, her knees cradled up to her chest. She blew into a cup of something hot.

"What time is it?" he asked.

"Five something. Why?"

"You don't like sleeping?"

"Never been very good at it."

Hoffner might have said the same—he was a notorious insomniac—but he could feel the heaviness in his legs and back. He had slept hard. "What time did I get here last night?"

"It might do to get yourself a watch."

"It might."

She sipped at the cup. "Around midnight. Somewhere in there."

He had managed a little more than four hours. He always liked to know the number. It gave him a sense of his limitations. Four gave him another fifteen By nine tonight, he would be useless. He sat up and took the glass.

"You're not at all what I imagined," she said.

He drank and tried a nod, but his neck strained against it. He was never terribly skilled with this: best to continue drinking.

"No interest at all?" she asked.

He set the glass down. "I'm very pleased you were surprised. Probably better if I don't know which way. That wouldn't be coffee, would it?"

"Hot water," she said. "The Chinese call it white tea. Very restorative."

"Do they? I didn't know."

"I don't sleep with everyone," she said. "Despite the published reports."

He saw his pants on the carpet by the bathroom door: no chance of getting to them anytime soon. "Well, I hardly sleep with anyone," he said, "so I suppose that puts us somewhere in the middle."

She smiled through another sip. "It's the politics that don't really fit, but I've never been a very good judge of that."

Hoffner ran through this last bit to make sure he had heard correctly. "What?"

"The Jew-baiting. Not my business. Not that I really care. But it just seems odd."

"The Jew . . . ?" He watched as she picked up a pamphlet from the armrest. It was the one from Sascha's meeting last night. She glanced at its back page and said, "Even in the dark it makes for some fascinating reading."

"It's not mine," he said as he swung his legs to the floor. He was relieved to find himself not completely naked. She reached down for his pants and tossed them over. She said, "Just to save you the asking."

"It's my son's, if that makes any difference." He began to slide his legs through. "Not the one out at Ufa. The one who blames me for his mother's death, although they both might be doing that now. Evidently, he also hates Jews. Do you have my cigarettes?"

Her smile reappeared above the cup. "They say they learn it at home."

"He's been away from home for a very long time." Hoffner was looking for his shirt.

She tossed over the pack. "So you're a great defender of the Jews?"

"I didn't know they needed defending." He lit up and spotted his shirt under her chair.

"There's a razor and cream in the bathroom. I had them send one up."

"But no coffee?"

"I didn't know when you'd be up."

It might have been nothing, but little acts of thoughtfulness always struck him. She had waited on the coffee so as not to have it go cold.

He went down on his knees and pulled out the shirt, only to find her staring at him. There was nothing plaintive in her gaze, no sudden warmth. For some reason he placed a hand on her cheek and drew his thumb across. It was enough for both of them, and he stood and headed into the bathroom.

"Aren't the Communists mostly Jews?" she said from her chair.

He stared at himself in the mirror. There was something soft to him now. With a woman like Maria, he had been able to dismiss it without a thought. Here, it made him feel raggedy. "Makes it worse for them," he said. "Being tied in with the Reds." He found the cream and turned on the faucet. "Most Jews are nice little burghers running their nice little businesses and trying not to get in anyone's way." He lathered up as she appeared in the doorway. "But if you couldn't trust them before . . ."

"So you actually take this seriously?"

"Not really."

"Then I'm very relieved."

He rinsed the blade and started in on his neck. "Well, I'd be careful there." He found a particularly rough patch under his chin and rubbed in a bit more cream. "Hating Jews is something we Germans never get too far from. We're addicted to it in the same way Americans are addicted to arrogance. The only difference, no one has ever been stupid enough to make arrogance a political ideology."

"You know you're in a very vulnerable position." She was standing next to him, watching the blade slide down his throat. "And if you think arrogance isn't an ideology—"

"Yah, but they haven't put it in a pamphlet just yet." He set the cigarette on the edge of the sink, scooped up a handful of water, and swirled some in his mouth. He then rinsed his face. She handed him a towel.

"So, are you going to find the girl?" she asked.

He reached past her for his shirt and felt the silk of her robe cross his back. "We shall see."

"You probably won't want my help now, but—"

"No—I won't." He tucked the shirt into his pants and stepped out into the room. There was still the jacket and coat and hat . . .

She remained in the doorway leaning against the jamb: she had kept her cigarette for longer than usual. "So you wanted me to be the helpless girl from the start. Honest but useless. I don't think that would have been as attractive."

"Oh, I don't think you were ever that helpless. And you're certainly not helpless now."

"You're sure of that?"

He picked up a blanket and discovered his coat. Pimm's flask was peeking out from the pocket.

She said, "That, by the way, is dreadful stuff. Unless you're planning on selling ladies' underwear. Then it's absolutely perfect."

He picked up both. "It's not mine."

"The theme of the day."

He found his jacket underneath and put it on. He said, "So what do you do now?"

She laughed quietly to herself. "Yes, I can tell you're very concerned." She stepped over and held open his coat as he slipped his arms through. "Why, I suppose I just wait in my room for you to call."

He turned to her. It was still early, he thought. Why was he already dressed?

She said, "You're not going to hold me desperately now, are you?" She was staring up at him, the fullness of her neck freed from the robe.

"I wasn't planning on it."

"No, I don't think you were."

He brought his hand to the small of her back and drew her up into him. Her lips tasted of powder and mint, and he let go.

She said, "I knew you were a liar."

His hat was on the rack by the door. Somehow it had managed to find its way to safety in all the stripping and tossing of clothes. "There's a new Aschinger's up on Friedrichstrasse," he said. "I usually stop in for a bite around one."

"Do you?"

He took his hat.

"Bit far from my room," she said.

Hoffner finished buttoning his coat. "Everything's a bit far from this."

He then pulled open the door and stepped out into the bright white of the hall.

. . .

THE MAN AT THE FRONT DESK dismissed him with a thin smile. The only kindness to be found in the lobby lay hidden behind the tired eyes of the doorman, a concern for anyone venturing out this early. Berlin before sunrise was infamous for its chill. Even in summer there was something unforgiving to that first slap of air, as if the night had a right to defend its solitude. By February the wind was downright spiteful.

Hoffner took it willingly enough, his eyes tearing up before he felt a sharp twinge in his mouth. There was nothing for it now except perhaps scalding coffee—he had always placed great faith in severe heat as an answer to pain—but aside from the kitchen at the Adlon, he knew he was unlikely to find a cup anytime soon. His stomach made booze an impossibility.

He stood on the street, alone, certain that a car or the sound of voices would find him, but everything remained unnervingly still. He had walked through silences like this before, deep in the west and the rarified air of Schöneberg or Charlottenburg. The sleeping rich, however, offered a kind of comfort in their dark houses and neat-cropped lawns. Murder and rape might appear more brutal in their midst—the novelty of it all, he imagined—but the quiet beyond the searching police lights and the parlor-room interrogations always dulled the terror and disbelief within. Tenement rooms in the east, on the other hand, had a tendency to kindle fear and self-loathing until, like a brushfire, they would leap unnoticed from one hovel to the next, erasing even the hope of breath.

There were no such distractions outside the Adlon. Comfort and despair waited on the distant fringes of the avenue, while here the line of leafless trees seemed to take life down to its very minimum. Everything was numbed except, of course, for the tooth, and Hoffner did what he could to soothe it with his tongue. By the time he found a cab, he was tasting blood.

The man behind the wheel was less than happy to be taking him east. The late-night sex clubs—at least those whose clients arrived by taxi—were back in the west, on the Kufu and Kleiststrasse. They were a hair more daring than The Trap and The Cozy Corner, but even then, every cabbie in town knew which tourists could stomach the downgrade. The transvestites strutted a bit more freely, the oral sex was more public—under a table or perhaps up on a banquette—but the prostitutes outside still flaunted their pigtails and leather strops with a disregard for taste and temperament. Any of them might turn out to be a man, but as they said, the prettiest girl on the street was invariably Conrad Veidt.

East was an entirely different matter. Charming visitors to the city never knew of the attic rooms on Fröbel and Moll Strassen. It had always seemed strange to Hoffner that the vilest acts in Berlin took place not in candlelit grottoes or dank basements but high above where their practitioners could gaze out at the city from behind gauze-thin curtains, as if to shower her with their own decay. Violence and narcoma, masquerading as pleasure and escape, invited the dead as much as the living, the morgue at the Alex never shy on room for one more used-up woman or rail-thin boy not much past the age of eleven. Bleeding or asphyxiation was usually the cause of death, the bodies placed in alleyways in the hope that someone might find enough humanity in the dead to get them underground.

The climb up at this hour was littered with empty vials and half-conscious faces. By seven, everything would be swept away by a landlord not all that far removed from his tenants. For now, though, the night still had a last half hour to work with: there was always the chance that some of these might not be making it back at all.

The last door on the hall showed a strip of light at its bottom, the sounds beyond a shuffling of feet under whispered, halting conversation. Choked laughter and groaned release rarely issued from these places: no one had the energy for them. The only link to something—anything—more tame was the crackling of a phonograph needle caged within the limits of its grooves.

Hoffner pushed open the door and was at once struck by the smell of formaldehyde, a common enough base among the low-grade narcotics. Along the far wall, loose, unclothed flesh—men or women, it was hard to say—lay propped up on couches and divans with a kind of pained drowsiness that seemed desperate to ward off sleep. Hoffner could only imagine the dreams awaiting them. Better to grasp at consciousness—dying as it was—than to surrender to the terror beyond. Still, it was the formaldehyde that stayed with him. These were closer to it than they knew.

He stepped inside and nearly kicked out the crutch of a man hunched against the wall. Hoffner had barely sensed him, let alone seen him. Shadeless lamps provided what light there was, the current strong enough only to inspire dim streaks of filament. For a moment, Hoffner expected the man to strike out or speak, but there was no movement save for the slow retreat of the rubber pad along the floor: evidently the crutch had a life all its own.

It was only when he peered more closely that Hoffner saw the single eye staring back at him. It took another moment to realize that the man was in fact asleep, his face the victim of grenade fragments. They had left him with only half a lid, enough to protect the eye but never hide it. Worse was the suturing of the mouth, now a gaping hole that curled to the upper reaches of the cheek and tucked itself under the gum in a stretching of lip and skin. The few lower teeth—chipped though remarkably preserved—added the last detail to the demonic stare, a cruel touch to make even pity seem disdained. There was no price to induce the girls on the Kufu to sleep with this.

The eye suddenly opened full and peered back at Hoffner. It was clear that the man had grown used to waking to such stares. He slowly raised the crutch and placed it on Hoffner's chest, then gently pushed him to the side. The man continued to look past him as he nodded his head twice before lowering the crutch. Hoffner followed the gaze and saw a trio of women seated on one of the couches along the wall. The tallest and thinnest—her ribs in plain view around small yet sagging breasts—stood and began to make her way over. She wore nothing but stockings to the thighs, although it was anyone's guess how she was managing to keep them up with barely any thickness in her legs. Her shoes had kept a deep blue—to match the bows in her braids—and though chipped at the toe, they still had enough height to give her back something of an arc.

As she drew up, the syphilitic dots on her face, along with the pin-pricks on her arms, came into focus, blue veins crisscrossed by an intermittent threading of skin. Hoffner guessed heroin. It was the easiest narcotic to come by, even in its most impure form, best to inject the stuff directly into the arm. He could still remember the none-too-distant advertisements for the lozenges and pastilles—heroin salts and elixir—the miracle cure for asthma, bronchitis, consumption. The great chemists at Bayer AG had promised no addictive quality to it. That had been the opium. Even the image on the packaging had stayed with him: a lion and a globe. This, they had said, would save the world. Hoffner wondered which of those men might be taking the woman now standing in front of him to his Nobel Prize gala.

She reached into the man's coat pocket and pulled out a few coins. He shook his head, and she dropped half of them back in. He shook his head again, and she held up a single coin. When he nodded, she tossed the rest into the pocket and reached into his trousers.

"We'll have a chat while he gets it going," she said to Hoffner. Her voice came as a complete shock, low and inviting. She might have been thirty. She might have been fifty. When she spoke again, her teeth seemed to be fighting against each other at odd angles. "He can't talk, no tongue, but he likes it when you do it as if he isn't there."

A low gurgling began to rise in the man's throat, and Hoffner did what he could to ignore it.

"I can do more than this, you know," she said. "Even the tools, if that's what you want. You look like you can pay."

This far at the edges, no one recognized a cop. No one questioned who might be walking through the door or what they might be in need of. Hoffner tried not to imagine what "the tools" entailed.

"He'll be wanting something more in a minute," she said. "And then he'll have to pay and I won't have time to chat so pretty with you, so what'll it be? You won't get much better in here. You wouldn't have a cigarette?"

Hoffner reached into his coat and held the pack out to her.

She looked at him as if he might be crazy. "Not the whole thing, idiot. You want to get me killed?" She snorted a laugh. "A girl with a whole pack. They'd rip my arms off if they knew. Just tear one in half and light it."

Hoffner did as she asked.

It was nearly gone in a single pull. "You didn't come to buy, did you?" Smoke streamed from the side of her mouth. "You like to look. That costs, too."

Hoffner again reached into his pocket, but this time her face turned to abject terror. "Not me," she whispered viciously, trying not to look at him. "Goddamned idiot. I'm done with you. Don't look at me again. Just move on."

Hoffner watched as she dug her face into the man's chest. Her hand continued to work, but it was as if she, too, had disappeared.

He stepped away. There was a hierarchy even here. Why should it have surprised him?

Across the room, a man had taken an interest: apparently, this was where the money went. Dressed in a weathered soldier's tunic, he was standing in a doorway that led off into the rest of the flat. He kept the top buttoned tight to the neck, his woolen pants tucked deep into a set of workman's boots. Again age was a mystery. The hair was cut short in the style of a young recruit, but the bulbous nose was too many years in a bottle to make them much of a match. At least from this distance he was still sporting all his vital parts.

Hoffner made his way over. The room beyond them was darker still.

"You're new," said the man. The grain in his voice had him long past forty. "I won't make you regret that. In the future, you come to me. We work things out. Girl, boy, pills, needles."

"I'm looking for someone."

"That's nice for you."

The man needed a little prodding. Hoffner reached into his pocket for his badge, but the man stopped him with a dismissive laugh. "And that's going to make a difference in here?" he said. He snorted something in his nose and spat to the side. "What are you—Kripo, Polpo? I've a director of yours who likes to beat a girl before he buggers her, every Tuesday. Means I have to have two or three girls in rotation, but better that than the commandant who makes me round up boys so he can have them beat him to a pulp. Twice they've almost killed him. Not the hands, though. Those he makes sure they never touch. He needs them in good working order for the boys he likes to fondle. Hairless boys. And you think you impress me?"

Hoffner drove his fist into the man's abdomen and watched as he doubled over, choking for breath. Leaning in, Hoffner said, "I'm not here to impress you. I'm here to find someone." He then tilted the head up and brought his fist across the chin. At once he felt a sharp pain in his hand. Hoffner had never been any good at this—all the more reason not to understand the sudden eruption—but all he could do was continue to land blow after blow. He saw the blood on his knuckles, his own confusion, when a sudden burning drove up through his lower back. The man had found a hidden reserve and was letting go into his ribs and kidneys with an equal abandon. For a few moments, Hoffner tried to ignore it, but too soon he felt his arms pulling in, his head lower, all of it too late as his legs were kicked out from under him, leaving only the cold scrape of the floor to dig into his cheek with each blow.

There was a sudden pause, and the scent of rancid breath hovered just above him: "Did you find your someone, Kripo?" Hoffner could smell the blood on the man's lips. "I'm betting no."

Hoffner tensed for the final barrage.

"Enough." A voice came from somewhere behind them. Hoffner tried to find it, but the room was too dark. "You've had your fun. Step off. He's come to see me."

A warm mixture of blood and spit landed near Hoffner's cheek before the legs retreated. Half a minute later, a second pair appeared in front of him.

"That was stupid, Nikolai." The man squatted. Hoffner lifted his head as best he could and saw the gaunt face of Zenlo Radek staring back at him. "You could have just asked."

Hoffner felt a hand under his arm. Radek was surprisingly strong for so thin a man. He brought Hoffner to one of the couches and sat down next to him. "You usually have to pay if you want a beating like that."

Hoffner was working his tongue around his mouth. At some point, the fists had taken on his face. He felt something dislodge at the back and he pulled out a tooth. He stared at it. At least now he could forget having to make that appointment. He tossed the tooth to the corner and sat back.

Radek said, "You're not a happy man, are you, Nikolai?"

"So you're a philosopher now."

"A Freudian. I like those Austrian Jews."

Hoffner checked to see if he had broken anything.

"What did you do to deserve it?" said Radek. "You knew he'd thump you."

The ribs would be sore, along with the lower back, but everything else seemed to be in working order. "Did I?"

"Subconsciously, Nikolai. Subconsciously. That's why I'm such a bad man. No one loved me."

A boy emerged from the back room. He was in tight shorts and nothing else. He lazed against the wall and stared at Radek, who ignored him. Hoffner said, "You seem to be doing all right by it now."

"That's not love, Nikolai. That's something far more useful."

Hoffner was never sure if Radek fully understood the words he chose. The clipped tone made them seem all the more unkind. "Pimm doesn't think much of it, does he?"

"No. He doesn't."

"But he turns a blind eye. That's love, isn't it?"

Radek laughed quietly. "You know, I could have let our soldier friend kill you."

"Yes—but then you would have had to kill him yourself, and that can be so messy."

"He's more resilient than you think."

"Pimps are pimps. They die as easily as anyone else."

Radek swept an inordinately long finger across the room, ticking off the bones and skin like so many entries on a page. "He saved all of these. Didn't save them for much, but he saved them."

"Then my apologies. He's quite the hero."

"Unhappy and bitter. It's not an attractive combination, Nikolai."

Hoffner leaned forward and spat a wad of blood onto the floor.

Radek said, "You've no idea who these are, do you?" Hoffner spat again. "Most of them—not all—but most were frontline whores. Maybe a kilometer from the shelling, nice little brothels, bombed-out houses, widows, young ones who got pregnant—or raped—then tossed out by families, even when the boys who'd gotten them there promised to make good on the deal. You didn't know that, Nikolai? I'm so surprised." Hoffner sat back and tried to swallow the taste of blood from his mouth. Radek continued, "The boys died, naturally—what else were they going to do out there—then the babies—"

"I remember the war."

"Do you? Not this one. These weren't your Berlin or Paris fucks. No glamour here. Not even your inflation girls, who had to lift their skirts to pay the rent. At least those had some class. These were country girls. Too fat, too thin, too stupid. And the boys they fucked were the ones who somehow didn't die—all those frontline hospitals to keep them alive. For what, no one knows. Maybe for this—to stand in the shadows so a girl could work through the wires and metal clasps crisscrossing their arms and legs and asses to give them a bit of pleasure. Your pimp brought them here. When the fighting stopped. They probably thought they'd be dead by then, but they weren't. Maybe that's why they seem to make pain so much a part of it."

Hoffner was hoping Radek had brought a drink. He hadn't. "So he makes his money off the living dead. I'm even more impressed."

Radek's jaw tensed. "That's across town, Nikolai. We both know that. Here they live on what they need."

"Or die on what they need."

For some reason Radek smiled. "We all do that." He ran a finger along the little dots running up his arm. "I've been waiting a long time on mine, but it never seems to come."

"There are easier ways."

"But none with such promise."

Years ago, Hoffner had found himself oddly comforted by Radek, a strange source, to say the least. It was just after Martha's death, so maybe Herr Freud had gotten something right after all. For Hoffner, it had simply been the distraction of a nihilist with hope.

This, however, was new. Radek had grown impatient. The attic rooms and the heroin were his way to accelerate the process.

"All that scum in the west." Radek was so easy with his venom. "They think we're all just racing up and up and up."

Hoffner bobbed his chin. Radek never needed more by way of encouragement.

"All their sudden freedoms and clubs and willingness to life—their chance to be corrupt with everyone cheering. But there isn't an ounce of genuine pain among them. And they'd all collapse in on themselves if they had to admit it." Radek gazed out. "They want to know where Berlin is going? Take a look and see this. Berlin isn't running toward anything—she never is. She's simply giving in to the weight of what's behind her."

Hoffner glanced over at the man on the crutch. His business done, he had made his way into a grouping with a bottle. Hoffner nodded in his direction. "He seems to be holding himself up."

Radek looked over. "You're a prick to find hope in that."

"I don't really believe it, but if he's willing to see it, isn't there something in that?"

Radek pulled a Luger pistol from his belt loop and pushed himself up. He walked over. He placed the gun on the man's forehead and cocked back the lock. The man simply stared at him.

For several seconds, nothing happened. The sounds of the place hardly shifted. Slowly Radek brought the gun down. He placed a few marks in the man's hand, then headed back to Hoffner and sat. "That was his moment of hope, Nikolai. Don't let yourself think it was anything else."

The first wave of stiffness drove up through Hoffner's hands and he did what he could to flex them. "That makes you even more of a bastard, doesn't it?"

Radek stared out silently. "Gives him something to think about." He took in a long breath. The lesson was over. "I never thought you'd put in an appearance here."

"I must have been missing all these uplifting little chats."

"You're better in a bar, Nikolai."

"A minute ago I would have said the same of you."

"What do you want?"

A woman laughed somewhere, a throaty, unnatural sound. Farther off, the phonograph needle found an old war song and a young voice began to crackle, *"There comes a call like thunder's peal . . ."*

Hoffner said, "The sex films."

Radek settled for another lazy laugh. "Pimm told you he'd found nothing."

"I know what Pimm told me. He also thinks the world is still an ordered place. You and I know it isn't."

"I'll tell him you said so."

Hoffner pulled a cigarette from his pocket. His hands were now in a good deal of pain. "He should be smarter than that, shouldn't he? And that worries you." He lit up. "Tossing things into the river for him, things he doesn't want to see. Not a good sign."

Radek's face hardened. "He'll always be cleverer than you think. Trust me."

Hoffner let go with a stream of smoke and said, "I think you wish you actually believed that."

Radek continued to stare straight ahead. "As I said, what do you want?"

Hoffner knew he had pushed far enough. "The films," he repeated. "It's studio money but not their talent. I need to know where they're getting their actors, cameramen, whatever else they're using."

"Any girl on the Kufu can spread her legs for a film."

"They're after a different kind of thing here. More desperate."

"Or more expendable," Radek said bitterly. He motioned over to the pimp. The man had been watching them and began to make his way over. Radek continued to speak to Hoffner. "There'd be no reason to put any of these on film, Nikolai. Who'd want to watch them?"

"Then somewhere between these and the girls on the Kufu. Pimm doesn't have access to that. Or at least he doesn't want to."

The man drew up. He had a cut over one eye and his lower lip had split. Aside from that, he looked fine. He said nothing.

Radek asked, "What have you heard about films, sex films?"

The man seemed just as ready to take another swipe at Hoffner as answer. "There's no real money in them," he said.

"Yah. What about the rough ones?"

This seemed to confuse him. He shot a glance at Hoffner. He was liking him less and less. "Cops having trouble with something like that?"

Radek said, "What have you heard?"

The man continued to stare until Hoffner raised his hands in mock surrender. "My apologies, *mein Herr*. It was my mistake. I evidently wanted the beating. You have my thanks."

This only added to the confusion.

"Shut up, Nikolai," said Radek. He kept his eyes on the man. "Studios are putting money into it. I know you. What have you heard?"

The man shrugged, and the tunic dug into the fleshy part of his neck. "There's been some noise, camera boys, and new money. Not Berlin money."

"Working through Ufa," Hoffner said impatiently. "Yes, I know." The man obviously had the information on who and where they were filming.

The man stared a moment, then shook his head slowly. "Ufa wouldn't do anything with this."

Hoffner sat back in frustration. "Then you're obviously not as well informed as you think."

It was clear the man had learned to contain his rage over the years; it seemed to deaden him completely. He looked at Radek. "If he knows so much, why does he need to ask?" Hoffner said nothing, and the man turned to him. "I'll throw you a bone, Kripo. For Herr Radek, here. Phoebus is fronting them. I don't know why, and I don't really care. They haven't done anything to my people, so none of my business. See what you can do with that." He nodded once to Radek and started to move off.

"You do know why," Hoffner said after him, not backing down.

The man stopped. He was staring across the room. He took a moment and said, "The sun's coming up. You'll want to see this."

Hoffner said, "And if they were doing things to your people?"

The man continued to gaze out. "Then I'd know a bit more." He waited before moving off.

Hoffner was ready to go after him when he felt Radek's hand on his arm. With barely any movement, Radek shook his head. "He's right. You'll want to see it, Nikolai."

"Why wouldn't he say?"

Radek spoke easily. "Because he doesn't know. And that worries him." He gazed past Hoffner. "It really is quite lovely." Without waiting, Radek stood and made his way over.

It was only then that Hoffner realized that the entire room was on its feet—or whatever else was propelling them along—moving toward the windows. They had emerged from the dark pockets like an unspeaking chorus, a single mass to fill the void brought in by the light. Hoffner stood and followed.

Pulling up at the back, he watched as the first lines of pink began to break through. There was nothing particularly stirring in it. Sunrise in Berlin came like anywhere else, with a reverent silence for the vanishing gray. Here, however, the colors that followed slid too quickly into the wash of faceless buildings and barren streets. As bright and unforgiving as the sun quickly became, its arrival brought a heaviness from which the night seemed oddly freed. The only word for it was joyless.

Even so, there was something to inspire in the grotesqueries of the half eyes and lips, the haggard folds of skin on the almost smiling faces. Nothing childlike or eager in them—no one would have been stupid enough to call it hope—but for a few moments each of them seemed to stake a claim to belonging, a worth, that quickly gave way to the thought that maybe today would see it all finally come to an end.

The boy in the shorts drew up and tucked himself in at Radek's side. Radek placed an arm around the boy's shoulders, and they stood and watched with the rest. Hoffner thought to say something, but he was as alien to this as he was to any other moments of kinship.

The phonograph needle slipped again into rootless scratching, and Hoffner turned and headed for the door.

THE HASENHEIDE

Y OU'RE SURE YOU DON'T WANT ICE, at least for the hands?"

The man behind the counter set down another pot of coffee, then took the coin by Hoffner's cup. Hoffner shook his head. "Won't do much good now, anyway."

The man nodded in the direction of the café's large front windows as he tossed the coin into a drawer. "I told you. Every morning. First one in."

Hoffner turned to see a young man—a boy, really, not much older than Sascha—moving down the street. He wore a dinner jacket with the tie undone and a long overcoat opened at the front.

"Same outfit. Same idiotic grin. For the last three weeks, give or take."

Hoffner forced down another half cup as he continued to watch.

"Nothing but weak tea and day-old rolls when he's in here. You'd think he'd order something a bit livelier—a glass of Sekt, maybe sardines. I think he dreams of being an accountant."

The man might have been surprised to hear what lives accountants were leading these days. "When do the rest show up?" said Hoffner.

"The artistic types? Not at all since Smiling Boy started putting in an appearance. Don't ask me why. Before then, around ten. In here for a coffee, schnapps, whatever else they could convince me I'd be tossing out, and then the mass migration over. A very skinny, very pretty herd of legs and eyes moving off."

"You're quite the poet."

"Yah. Now if only I could get some of those eyes and legs into bed with me I'd be happy to bring out the good rolls in the morning."

Hoffner picked up his hat and placed a few more coins on the counter. "I'll take a pass."

The man slid most of the money back. "It's too much."

Hoffner stood and swallowed the last of his coffee. "My contribution. To the big-game fund."

Outside, Friedrichstrasse was showing healthy signs of life. This far south, the avenue was a quick trip in from the suburbs. Senior clerks and dentists and minor bureaucrats could leave their middle-class homes well past seven and still make it here by eight, having already peeled through the *BZ* or the *Morgenpost* or, for those who fancied themselves serious businessmen, a few pages of the *Börsen-Courier*. These were the little worker bees who tried so hard to understand all the densest articles, conversations over lunch about trade agreements and currency revaluations, all of it gibberish. More likely it had been a tram ride in, rapt in the *BZ* and the lurid details of how some husband had finally beaten his wife to death, "the last act of the tragedy coming, one neighbor said, when 'he turned her gas off.'" Murder always kept the public reading. Then again it was Wednesday. The *Morgenpost* would be running its Regular Talk from Old Man Mudicke, who didn't like taking a few slaps at all those fat cats running things now.

It was something of a surprise, then, to come across the Phoebus Film Company in such staid surroundings, more so to find all its studios, costume shops, construction halls, and storage rooms crammed into the single six-story building at number 225. Twenty years ago, a few cameras and the same dozen costumes had been sufficient for the four or five films shooting on any given day. Things had grown more complex since then—Ufa had seen the future as far back as 1912, with its purchase of the Neubabelsberg land—but Phoebus had decided to keep its costs to a minimum. Not that anything it had ever put out warranted that kind of expansion. Fright films with a bit of skirt could be shot almost anywhere. Even so, there was an air of desperation or denial that hung over the place with the same dreary certainty of failure now etched into the unwashed stone of the façade.

Hoffner crossed the street and caught sight of his reflection in a window. His hat was helping to shade the bruising around his eyes, but there was nothing to mask the welt on his chin. Above, the cuts on his lips had grown into a railway track of dried blood leading up to the cheek. At least his gloves were hiding the swelling on his knuckles.

A woman in thick glasses emerged from one of the shops. As she passed, she stared at Hoffner a moment too long. Evidently today would be filled with explanations.

He reached Phoebus—the *P* and the *H* of the logo lost to a peeling of gold plate—and pressed the bell. He heard nothing and tried again. It was only then that he noticed the door resting off its latch. Hoffner slowly pushed forward and followed the handle in.

The place looked as if a stampede had run through it. It was a wide-open space, with thick wires sprouting from holes in the few walls that were still standing. Hoffner could see where the offices and studios had been, but they were all reduced to piles of chipped plaster and rubbled brick dotting the floor. The one solid piece remaining was the staircase on the near wall. Taking hold of the banister—it was surprisingly firm in his grip—Hoffner headed up.

The top floor, like the rest, had no internal walls to speak of, although here the windows were letting in a good deal of sun. Something large and white jutted out about halfway down, but it looked more like an abandoned set piece than anything of structural value. The only nod to an office was in the far corner, a desk, ten or so filing cabinets, two chairs and a couch, the last of which displayed Herr Dinner Jacket draped across in apparent sleep. Hoffner did his best to kick through several piles of plaster as he approached, but the tilt of the boy's head suggested that even a brass band might have had little effect. Hoffner settled for a quick shaking of the shoulder.

The boy's eyes blinked open. He seemed unsure where he was before squinting up and running a hand across his nose. "What the . . . You lot usually don't start in until ten. It's not ten, is it?"

"Gives you enough time for a nap?"

The boy brought his hand up to shade his eyes. "What?"

"You've been down for less than five minutes. Trust me, you're not all that groggy."

The boy pulled himself up and rubbed the back of his neck. "What time is it?"

Hoffner pulled out his badge. "Time to wake up." He moved to the desk and opened the top drawer. "So, who usually doesn't come in until ten?"

The last half minute replayed itself in the boy's eyes before he cleared his throat and stuck a hand out in Hoffner's direction. "Let me see that again."

Hoffner tossed the badge over and continued to sift through the collection of loose clips and half-smoked cigarettes. He pulled out two reams of advertising postcards, one for something called *Queen of Spades*, the other for an equally menacing *Ghost Train*. He placed them on the desk.

"Kripo," said the boy. For some reason he continued to stare at the badge.

Hoffner finished with the drawers. "So who are we waiting for?"

The boy looked over and tossed the badge back. "Waiting for . . . ? Oh. Construction. They're redoing the place. Usually get to it without bothering me."

"From what is obviously your very important work."

The boy tried a laugh, but something caught in his throat. He grimaced and swallowed.

Hoffner said, "It's been a rough three weeks, then, since the girls stopped showing up?"

The boy stretched as he looked over. "Very nice. Am I meant to be impressed?"

Ten years ago a boy like this would have pissed his pants at the sight of a Kripo badge. Now it was a yawn and a smart remark. "You've an admirer in the café across the street," said Hoffner. "What happened three weeks ago?"

The sudden laughter caught Hoffner by surprise. "I got the sack. At least now I've got my evenings to myself."

The wear on the dinner jacket made clear how eagerly the boy had taken to his recent freedom. "You might think about a good clean for that shirt."

"Why?" said the boy. "I won't be able to afford a club in a week's time, so why waste the money? No one notices, anyway."

Even elegance had grown dingy, thought Hoffner, and not for the excesses. It was simply a matter of effort, and boys like this had given up on that. What, then, was the point in a moral decline without a little panache to ease the fall? At least back east the half-dead had kept their bows clean and their stockings rolled tight to the thigh.

"So they sacked you the same time they started ripping up the place," said Hoffner. "What a coincidence."

"Not really." The boy stood and made his way over. "It won't be workable for another few months. Perfect time to toss out a few junior execs. Trim the fat and so forth."

"You don't seem terribly put out."

The boy shrugged. "I'm young. I'll latch on somewhere. Plus, this place is sinking." He picked up one of the advertising cards and shook his head. "*Ghost Train*. I'm sure you can't wait to see this beauty." He flipped the card back onto the desk. "They've done a few of the mountaintop flicks—the noble climber and skier up in the clouds— but there's nothing much to them. Me, I'm looking for something more serious. You know, the arty stuff—Murnau, Pabst. All these

SHADOW AND LIGHT

swinging tits and screaming ghouls don't really have a future, if you ask me." He looked over. "I mean unless you like that sort of thing. I suppose people do. They can be fun in a . . ." He was struggling to find the words.

"In a kind of dull-witted-heavy-handed-middle-class-Kripo-cop sort of way?" Hoffner let the boy dangle a moment longer before saying, "Screaming ghouls don't really do it for me, either. So why do they have you here?"

"No idea. Make sure nothing gets taken while they're shipping it out?"

"Storage?"

The boy shrugged again. "They don't keep me apprised."

"So they shut it all down. That's going to lose them some money."

"Can't really lose it when you're not making any to begin with."

For the first time Hoffner gave in to a quiet laugh. "I can't imagine why they sacked you."

"Yah. I'm a big supporter of the firm. So what is it the Phoebus Film Company can do for the Kripo?"

It was a question Hoffner had yet to answer. "Where are they sending everything?"

The boy went with what he knew: he shrugged. This time, though, the nonchalance seemed less convincing.

"So you haven't had to sign for anything?" said Hoffner.

The boy hesitated. "Is there someone I should be calling about this?"

"Ah," said Hoffner. "The sudden pangs of loyalty."

The boy laughed again. He was handling himself well beyond his years. Hoffner had to appreciate Phoebus's choice in sentries.

The boy said, "You obviously don't know the film world, do you, Inspector? I'd actually like to work again somewhere. So if certain information gets out, and if that information turns out to be a problem for Phoebus, and it happens to lead back to me . . . you see my concern."

The boy was wrong. Hoffner did know the world. Petty crooks and unwritten codes were the same no matter where, or how flush, the bank accounts. He reached into his pocket and pulled out his notebook. "What about Lang?"

The boy needed a moment. "What?"

"Lang. Fritz Lang. Is that serious enough for you?"

Again the boy waited. "Sure. Of course."

"Good. Hand me the telephone."

Hoffner dialed and then held the receiver up between them. A man's voice answered. "Hallo. Herr Lang's residence."

Hoffner recognized the icy charm of Lang's valet. He looked at the boy and said, "Yes. This is Chief Inspector Hoffner. Is Herr Lang available?"

"I'm afraid you've just missed him, Herr Chief Inspector."

Hoffner kept his eyes on the boy. "He asked me to get in touch today."

"Herr Lang will be at the theater all day, *mein Herr*. You can reach him through Herr Reinhardt's secretary. I have the number."

Half a minute later, Hoffner hung up the telephone.

"Is that enough of an incentive?" he said.

The boy was still piecing it together. "You can get me a meeting with Lang?"

"I can tell him to hire you if things go well." Both knew it was a lie, but Hoffner had come to recognize the vital role of exaggeration in this particular world.

The boy studied Hoffner's face—it was the first sign of his inexperience—and smiled. "The place is finished, anyway."

"Yes, you've said that."

Again he hesitated. "The Hasenheide. Everything's getting shipped out to an address in the Hasenheide."

"And the filing cabinets?"

The boy held out his hand. "I'll be needing a card and Lang's telephone number, I think."

Hoffner obliged, and the boy pulled a set of keys from his pocket. "All you'll find is a bunch of old contracts, but be my guest." He reached for his coat.

"Weak tea and a roll?" said Hoffner. The boy looked over and Hoffner added, "Order the sardines. You'll make a new friend."

The boy smiled. "I can give you an hour." He slipped on his coat and headed for the stairs. Halfway there, he stopped and turned around. "I'm trusting there's still an honest cop in Berlin. I shouldn't be concerned you've already had your face bashed in this morning, should I?"

Hoffner had almost forgotten the bruises. "I'll leave the keys on the desk."

The boy nodded and walked off. "Try not to bleed on anything."

FORTY MINUTES LATER, Hoffner had filled two pages of his notebook with what amounted to nothing. The boy had been right. The cabinets were stocked with contracts, shipping forms, release documents—the usual minutiae of German efficiency—some of it dating as far back as 1908. When he finally found the folder with the Hasenheide papers—mislabeled as CORRESPONDENCE: 1924—it proved to be much the same until he reached the last sheet. Reading the signature page, Hoffner felt a sudden need to sit down.

According to the first few pages, Phoebus had purchased two new long-term storage warehouses on the northern edge of the Hasen-

heide three months ago, but not without help. The co-signer had been
a limited partnership with the name of Ostara KG. Not that Hoffner
was terribly familiar with the legal jargon, but it appeared that the
Ostara Company had loaned Phoebus the money on an "extended
and non-terminable basis." In other words, there was no expectation
of the money coming back. There was also no indication that Phoebus had any intention of retrieving its equipment anytime soon.

The rest of the document was a short statement on what "all interested parties" could hope to gain from the new purchases, very vague
and even more jargon-laden. That was all interesting in itself, but
far more troubling were the signatures that followed. They read:
W. Lohmann, T. von Harbou, J. Goebbels, K. Daluege.

The first, Lohmann, was completely unknown to Hoffner. The
last three, however, were—as of yesterday—all too familiar: Thea
von Harbou was the current Frau Lang and the apparent link to Ufa;
Joseph Goebbels and Kurt Daluege had been at the Pharus Hall with
the new National Socialists; even the name Ostara struck a chord.

Moments like these usually brought some sort of satisfaction—
even if the why remained elusive—but this time none of it seemed to
matter. The inclusion of Goebbels and Daluege meant that Sascha
was somehow involved. Knowingly or not, the boy had stepped onto
a stage far beyond the confines of right-wing crank politics. Hoffner
felt the need either to protect or beat him senseless. Then again,
hadn't he started in on that last night?

He flipped the notebook shut and tossed the keys onto the desk.
With the file in his coat pocket, he headed for the stairs.

THE MORGUE AT THE ALEX is more of an examination room
than a full-scale facility, even if the last few years have seen the arrival
of various machines and storage trays to rival the city morgue across

town. Bodies are no longer stacked in tiers on wooden platforms inside the ice rooms; now everyone has his own private compartment. The only trouble, of course, is the smell. Traces of ammonia and sulfur have a tendency to trickle up through the stairwell. By the time the swinging doors at the end of the corridor come into view, the whole thing is at full stench. Granted, it could be worse. Up until a year ago, the attendants had been using some sort of chloride mixture when one of their own had lost a lung to a leak in two of the steel cabinets. The whole place had been contaminated for a week, sending several of the less pressing cases up to the third floor in makeshift tubs of ice. Naturally, a different kind of smell had followed. Hoffner was happy enough to suffer through the more familiar tang as he pushed through the doors.

Truth to tell, this was the last place he had expected to be twenty minutes ago. Then, he had been planning on a quick visit with Lang— a few questions about his rather surprising wife—when, half a block from the theater, Hoffner suddenly recalled the truth about legal documents: they were never about what was on the page; they were about what was missing from it. The name Gerhard Thyssen had been conspicuously absent from the Hasenheide file. It was now time to find out why.

A man in a patrolman's coat was seated behind the desk, his face buried in yesterday's motorcycle results. The sound of the hinge brought his eyes up. He quickly deposited the paper in a drawer and pulled out something official-looking. He began to scribble as Hoffner drew up.

"Burggaller manage to keep the bike under him this time?" said Hoffner as he waited for the eyes, but the man continued to write.

"Third in Essen," said the man. "Italians were one, two."

"Shame," said Hoffner. "If only they'd been able to shoot that well, who knows, we might have won the war."

The man finished and looked up. "So what is it we can do for the Kripo?"

No one ever requested a posting to the morgue. It gave those who ended up here a kind of freedom when it came to respect: they doled it out to no one. "Thyssen," said Hoffner. "Gerhard Thyssen. He came in two days ago. Apparent suicide."

The man opened another drawer, pulled out a clipboard, and flipped through the pages. "Number 11. Personal effects are in bin 6. What happened to your mouth?"

Hoffner stared at the vacant face. "It wouldn't have made more sense to put them in bin 11?"

"There is no bin 11."

Hoffner thought to answer, but the man had landed at this particular desk and was therefore grappling with his own incompetence. Why make him take on a whole department's?

A minute later, Hoffner was spilling the contents of a small bag onto a tray. The naked Thyssen had evidently been dressed at one point. A silver cigarette case and lighter, along with a Patek Philippe watch, scraped noisily across the metal.

"I didn't see a suit of clothes." Hoffner spoke loudly enough to be heard at the desk. "Where was all this?" He watched as the man grudgingly pulled himself away from his paper and retrieved yet one more clipboard from the drawer. This time, Hoffner couldn't help himself: "You don't think it might do to keep it all together?"

The man continued to flip through the pages. "Personal bits. Families like to take a look at the paperwork. Make sure nothing's gone missing. We don't want them seeing more than they need to. Make enough sense for you, Herr Kriminal-Kommissar?"

Hoffner stood obediently and waited for the answer.

"No suit," the man said as he read. "Most of it was lying about the office or in the desk. The rest they found in the pockets of a pair of trousers that were in a closet. The trousers are in bin 4."

Hoffner knew to let this one go. The man held out the pages as he went back to his paper. "You can take a read, if you want."

"No. That's fine."

The pages dropped to the desk and Hoffner turned back to his tray.

It was an odd assortment of business cards, receipts, a program from an exhibit that had been at the Cassirer Gallery in August of last year. There was Thyssen's university ring—he had studied at the Ludwig-Maximilians in Munich—a woman's earring, thirty marks or so in paper, but nothing to do with either Phoebus or Ostara. The dim logic in the choices made it clear that the Kriminal-Assistent who had put this all together was well on his way to a posting at the morgue.

Hoffner was slipping everything back into the bag when he noticed a pin caught inside the program. It was no bigger than a fingernail, and when he turned it over, he found himself staring at an open-winged eagle perched on a wreath. This time, however, the wreath was circling what looked to be two runic letters.

The first thought, of course, was of Herr Goebbels and his tiny badge, but there was something else here that Hoffner recognized. The trouble was, he had no idea what that might be. Instead, he continued to stare at the symbols.

It was nearly a minute before the voice at the desk interrupted: "You all right?"

Hoffner looked up. The man was peering over. "What?" said Hoffner.

"Your breathing. It's very loud. You having trouble or something? What happened to your face?"

Hoffner focused. "No. No trouble."

The man waited, then turned back to his paper.

It was the distraction that cleared the way. Staring again at the pin, Hoffner saw why the university ring had been in the bag, why the names had appeared in the file inside his coat pocket, and why he had been right to come looking for Herr Thyssen. He scanned the cabinets across the room and headed for number 11.

The chemically pale Thyssen slid out easily. It was not, however, his lifeless expression that held Hoffner's attention. Taking the left bicep, Hoffner slowly pulled the arm away from the torso. The body's stiffness made only a small gap possible, but it was enough to detect the outline of two symbols cut into the soft flesh at the upper reaches of the ribs. They were identical to the ones on the pin.

Hoffner felt the sharp pull of anticipation in his chest. He had seen these symbols before, studied them. The fact that they were locked away in a file somewhere up in his office only sent the acid deeper into his throat.

ROSA

IT WAS AS IF EIGHT YEARS had vanished in a matter of minutes.

Hoffner sat at his desk and wondered how he could ever have forgotten these drawings. The same lingering doubts, the same self-delusion that had claimed success then, now resurfaced with the appearance of the ten yellowed sheets lying in front of him.

He reached into his drawer and pulled out a bottle of brandy as he read:

Notes on meetings, December 4, 1918, through January 18, 1919, Thule Society, as recorded by Kriminal-Bezirkssekretär Stefan Meier, Kriminalpolizei, Munich:

December 4: Our first meeting outside the beer hall. We meet at the house of Anton Drexler, a locksmith in the employ of the railroad shops. Drexler is a small, sickly man who talks for over an hour about the "mongrelization" of the German people and the corruption of the socialist regime. He refers to members of the government as "the Jew Eisner and the Jew Scheidemann." There are nine of us. I believe we are only one of several cells of "initiates" meeting throughout the city tonight. Unlike Eckart, Drexler is a poor speaker. We are instructed to bring documented proof of our Aryan ancestry to the next meeting.

December 9: Again we meet at the house of Drexler. Only four of us are permitted to remain once our papers are examined. Two other members of the Society are present, but we are not told their names. One of them is a doctor. He takes a sample of blood from each of us. We are then given copies of two books written by Guido von List (The Invincible and The Secret of Runes), magazines published by Jorg Lanz von Liebenfels (Prana and Ostara), a directory of pan-Germanic and anti-Semitic groups by Philipp Stauff (The German Defense Book), and the manifesto of the Armanist Religious Revival from the organization known as the Walvater Teutonic Order of the Holy Grail, written by Hermann Pohl. An excerpt from Liebenfels's Ostara I, #69 makes clear the general thinking behind all of these writings: "The holy grail is an electrical symbol pertaining to the panpsychic powers of the pure-blooded Aryan race. The quest of the Templars for the grail was a metaphor for the strict eugenic practices of the Templar Knights designed to breed god-men."

December 13, 18, 24, 29: We meet at the house of the journalist Karl Harrer (founder of the Workers Political Circle and chairman of the German Workers Party [see below]). He is no better a speaker than Drexler and, over the four nights, takes us through the history of the Society (see below), the rituals of Rebirth and Order (see below), the Covenant of the pan-Germanic people (see below), and the hierarchy of the races (see below). We are each required to recite long passages from The Invincible and to exhibit physical stamina and strength by withstanding long periods of heavy objects being placed on our chests.

January 5: We are taken to a house on the outskirts of the city, where we are given our first initiation rites. This includes full disrobement, the cutting of two runic symbols into the underside of the left upper arm, and the laying on of hands by a man we are instructed to call Tarnhari. We are told that he is the reincarnation of the god-chieftain of the Wölsungen tribe of prehistoric Germany. We are now required to recite from memory passages from The Invincible and to pledge a vow to our racial purity.

January 9, 14, 15: The rituals continue at the house of Rudolf Freiherr von Seboottendorf, where we are joined by seven other initiates from around the city. Seboottendorf is a mystic trained in the art of Sufi meditation. Over the three nights he leads us in séance-like rituals meant to contact the Ancients from the lost island civilization of Thule. Seboottendorf is the only one of us to make contact.

January 18: We are brought to the lodge on Seitz Strasse and introduced to the members of the Thule Society. There are, by rough estimation, seventy men present. I am able to learn twenty or so of the names (see below).

The detective sergeant who had infiltrated the Thule Society and written the report in 1919 had been found dead in his apartment three days later, another apparent suicide. To this day, Hoffner's friends in the Munich Kripo remained skeptical—and with good reason. Hoffner closed the cover and ran his thumb across the label: Sewer Construction Applications—1906. Like the men at Phoebus, Hoffner had managed a little misdirection in filing of his own. Even now, the Rosa Luxemburg case was too raw to keep any of its papers properly filed. Red Rosa—the "Devil Jewess"—had last been seen bobbing in the Landwehr canal eight years ago, and while questions still remained about her disappearance, her death had brought the revolution of 1919 to a screeching halt.

All those weeks with soldiers spilling into Berlin like wastewater, pitched battles along the Siegesallee and the Schloss Bridge, armed workers determined to bring every stone down—and then two shots to the back of the head, and Rosa Luxemburg and Karl Liebknecht were dead. The leaders were gone. The Communists were finished.

And the bodies? Liebknecht's turned up the next morning—trampled, beaten, bloodied—an "unknown man" discovered in the fighting. But not Rosa. She was nowhere to be found. Two months slipped by, and everyone wondered where she had gone. Was she really dead? Had she escaped to the east, plotting her return with comrades Lenin and Trotsky? Could there still be reason to panic? And then, mercifully, the little corpse had floated up—swollen, disfigured. She had been there all along. That's what they told themselves. The city was safe again. There had never been a Luxemburg case. There had been no files, nothing for the Kripo and Polpo to deny. There had been only an angry mob and the justified killing of a fanatic. And Berliners quickly forgot that Rosa had ever troubled them at all.

And yet here was Hoffner with her file in his hands. The Thule Society document was frightening enough, but it was the story beyond the sergeant hanging from a rope that now troubled him—those eight weeks in 1919 while Berlin waited for Rosa's body to appear: the weblike intricacies that had connected the Thulians with a ritualistic killer set loose on Berlin; the deceptions that had plunged the city into a panic fueled by the fear of Bolshevism; Rosa's dead and preserved body, found that first night and ferreted away by the Polpo until they could use her to heighten the panic. All of this had been orchestrated by the Thulians with the sole aim of tearing down the then-fledgling government in the hope of replacing it with their own vision of purity and order: a mythic rebirth, forever seared into the flesh by those tiny runic symbols.

Sascha had been seduced by these men. Fichte had been betrayed by them. Martha had been killed by them. And now, these Thulians, who had used Rosa Luxemburg—and Hoffner himself—and whose failure had forced them to slip silently away eight years ago, were once again making themselves known in Berlin. Hoffner had been lucky in 1919, lucky to find enough in the tangled strands to threaten them with exposure. The price for that luck had been almost everything. Maybe that was why he had chosen to forget as well.

Hoffner poured himself another glass and picked up the telephone. The men of the Thule Society—once again hiding in the shadows— had evidently found a political outlet for their message. Why it had them venturing into the world of film and sound and sex was another question entirely.

"Yes," Hoffner said when the line engaged. "Kriminal-Kommissar Nikolai Hoffner here." The woman on the other end seemed to perk up at the mention of the title. "I need to speak with someone at your political desk. Someone familiar with parties, organizations . . . Berlin, Munich . . . Yes. Thank you."

Half an hour later, Hoffner underlined the date "1926, October" and said, "You've been very kind, Herr Wenkel . . . No, I won't be needing a complimentary subscription . . . Of course, if I'm working on anything of interest, the *Tageblatt* will be the first to know . . . Very good."

He placed the telephone in the cradle and stared down at his notes.

It all looked so straightforward when laid out on a page. Draw a few arrows between the dates, and it was a direct line from the back room of a Munich beer garden to the Pharus Hall:

1917: Workers Political Circle formed ➤

1918: members of WPC form German Workers Party ➤

1919–1920: GWP purchase of *Völkischer Beobachter* (newspaper edited by Dietrich Eckart) ➤

1920: new party leadership and addition of National Socialist to name ➤

1923, November: failed Munich Beer Hall Putsch (response to January occupation of Ruhr by French for unpaid reparations, former General Erich Ludendorff and unknown Corporal Adolf Hitler at helm) ➤

1923, December: Eckart dead (heart failure) ➤

1924, April through December: leaders of party in Landsberg prison (Ludendorff acquitted) ➤

1925: twelve seats won in Reichstag ➤

1926, October: Joseph Goebbels in Berlin

It was a nice bit of digging for a reporter who seemed eager to make his mark. Not that the man at the *Tageblatt* had any inkling of the connection between the Thule Society—the organizing force behind the Workers Political Circle—and the group now calling itself the National Socialist German Workers Party. Nor could he have known that the detective pressing him for information had spent a rather interesting evening in 1919 in one of those Munich swill holes listening to the drunken rantings of the late Thulian Herr Eckart. Given Hoffner's recollection of the man and his capacity for schnapps, heart failure seemed a kind assessment as the cause of death.

It was on the morning after that meeting that Hoffner had been handed the file now lying in front of him. With its lists of members and publications, it made clear just how much money the Thulians had been sitting on in 1919. And yet, according to the reporter at the *Tageblatt*, the new National Socialists were dirt poor. Evidently failed coups and prison terms tended to dry up the coffers. They also attracted a very different kind of following. Perhaps, then, it was no surprise to hear the latest Thulian incarnation calling itself a "thinking man's party"—an unemployed, pfennigless, marginalized, Jew-baiting, Communist-hating thinking man—but in large enough numbers to keep violence at the forefront without the help of old friends like the Freikorps.

Even so, the Thulians had somehow found enough money to bankroll Phoebus's purchase of the Hasenheide property. So, as it turned out, Hoffner's first instincts to see Lang this morning had been right, after all.

SOMEONE HAD WASHED the lobby carpets last night, leaving the smell of wet wool and lye as Hoffner's first impression of the Deutsches Theater. It might have been worse. There might have been singing coming from behind the wall of doors.

Instead, the theater was dark as Hoffner stepped through. The rows of seats looked like a legion of silent dwarfs readying for attack. The only thing keeping them from the stage was the presence of a bare-bulb lamp, whose glow was casting menacing shadows all the way down into the orchestra pit. The effect was a little sinister for merry widows and student princes, but maybe that was what lunch breaks were all about.

The security man out front had told him to head for the Kammer-spiele, the small theater where the real dramas rehearsed and per-formed. It was a quick march under the balcony overhang, past the left flank of dwarfs, and over to a door where a flight of stairs led down. Half a minute later, Hoffner heard the telltale sounds of acting.

He pulled back a door and found himself the focus of perhaps twenty pairs of eyes. With them came an instant silence. The stage was directly to his right and up half a meter. In front of him, fifteen rows of seats climbed to the shadows of the back wall. Most of the eyes were positioned in small clumps throughout the house. No one seemed to move until a man stood and said, "This is a closed rehearsal, *mein Herr*. I'm sorry, but I'm going to have to ask you to leave."

For the second time today, a voice from the darkness reached out for Hoffner. "My fault, Max." It was Lang. "It's up here, Nikolai." A bit of light caught the reflection of a cigarette case somewhere near the back, and Hoffner headed up.

This time, Lang was in the back row.

"Coward," said Hoffner.

Lang laughed a quiet, throaty laugh and offered Hoffner a cigarette. "That's films, Detective. This is the theater. The farther back, the better."

Hoffner took the cigarette and sat. "So what are we watching?"

"Actors."

"You don't sound all that keen."

"Just because I have to use them doesn't mean I have to like them."

"Actresses, on the other hand . . ."

"Very different, of course."

The three men onstage were back to whatever it was they were working through. One of them was perched on a ladder with a large bucket in his hands.

Lang said, "Do you like Brecht, Detective?"

"I don't go to the theater much."

"Most of the people who like him don't go to the theater much. The ones who've never been adore him."

Hoffner lit up. "Is the one with the bucket meant to be cleaning the ceiling?"

"I've no idea, and I've been watching him for over an hour. What is it I can do for you, Detective?"

Hoffner placed his hat on the seat between them. "You might be getting a telephone call from a young producer. He was just let go from Phoebus." Hoffner expected at least some recognition, but Lang continued to stare at the stage.

Lang said, "Word is that they're in a bit of trouble, though what do you expect with—"

"Yes," said Hoffner. "With all those swinging tits and screaming ghouls. I've heard."

Lang nodded and made a wincing face as the bucket clanged to the ground. "He does that every ten minutes or so. I think he's bored. Then again, it might be part of the thing. Who knows. So why will I be getting a call from this producer?"

"He was rather helpful."

"Introduced you to a young lady friend of his?"

"He let me see a few files I needed."

Lang's eyes followed the bucket back up the ladder. "That was very kind of him. And now you want me to hire this little rat. I'm glad I could be so useful." The man settled in again atop the ladder, and Lang said, "By the way, speaking of young ladies, have you found ours?"

Hoffner said, "Yours, not mine. Your wife's name was in one of the files."

Lang's gaze remained unchanged. "Has she written a script for them, Detective? That would be a breach of contract. Naughty, naughty."

Hoffner was done with the charming Lang. "She's loaned them some money. A great deal of money, I think. Would that be your money, Herr Lang?" Lang's face hardened, but he continued to stare ahead. Hoffner said, "I believe you're making some rather dangerous films."

"Am I?"

"And using some rather unfortunate women."

"I believe you have me at a loss, Herr Inspector."

"No, I don't believe I do."

For the first time Lang turned to Hoffner. The coldness in the gaze was to be expected. "Then you'd be wrong there." Genuine truth was not something that came easily to Lang. It made its appearance all the more surprising. Lang said, "What's happened to your mouth?"

"Lunch!"

The barked command rose from somewhere in the house, but the actors were already off the stage, one of them moving up the aisle toward Lang too quickly for his slender and awkward little body. "Fritz!" he called out as he began to slide himself down the row in front of them.

Before turning, Lang said under his breath, "You'll like this fellow, Detective. Remarkably talented, but don't let on you know." Lang turned, and the careless sheen of camaraderie swept across his face. "How nice of you to come and say hello."

"Have you been watching?"

"Of course. You have to tell Klaus to keep a better hold on that bucket."

The little man looked momentarily confused, and then gave in with a smile that seemed to squeeze his face into a mass of cheekbones. "Very funny. Yes, I'll tell him to keep hold."

Lang motioned to Hoffner. "This is a friend of mine, Nikolai Hoffner."

"You're not an actor, are you?" said the man.

"No," said Hoffner.

"Good. For a moment I thought Fritz was giving you my part. You won't be giving him my part, will you, Fritz?"

"I don't believe I've given *you* a part, so no worries there. Nikolai, this is Peter Lorre. Peter Lorre, Nikolai Hoffner."

The two shook, and Lorre said, "You could be an actor. You've a nice sort of look to you. Something beaten down that would work wonderfully."

"I'll take that as a compliment," said Hoffner.

"Don't," said Lang.

Hoffner asked, "So you're good with beaten down, Herr Lorre?"

"Oh no," Lorre said, smiling. "I'm an ugly little Jew. I make people laugh. What else is there for me to do?"

Lang said, "You could scare them, Peter. Jews are very good at that."

Lorre produced an impish smile. "But then I like playing against type. What excuse have you got, Fritz?"

Lang seemed surprised by his own laughter. "You find me that frightening?"

"You say you're only half a Jew," Lorre said, "so maybe not that scary, but I don't believe it. I think you're one hundred percent. It's Nikolai here who's the real half-breed. Aren't I right, Nikolai?" Hoffner's expression was enough to prod Lorre on. "You see, Fritz, that's what an actor does. He sees through it all." He looked again at Hoffner. "Your mother?"

Hoffner waited before answering. "Very good."

Lorre said, "It was the name. Hoffner. Not really Jewish."

"As opposed to Lorre," said Lang.

Lorre laughed. "Fair enough. Not likely to see a László Lowenstein up on a Fritz Lang poster anytime soon."

"Not likely to see a Peter Lorre up there, either," said Lang.

Lorre smiled again at Hoffner. "He tries to be cruel, but he's not very good at it." Lorre reached into his pocket and pulled out a folded piece of newspaper. "You've seen it, of course, Fritz?" Not waiting for an answer, Lorre opened the page and began to read: " 'Noteworthy is only the young comedian Peter Lorre for whom no part, not even the smallest and the silliest, is routine, but a chance for a grotesque human portrayal. This theatrical gift, perhaps the strongest and most original of the entire ensemble at the Kammerspiele, deserves the most attentive encouragement and cultivation.' "

"Did you write it yourself?" said Lang.

"I wouldn't have been so subtle," said Lorre. "You didn't see *Girls on the Couch*, did you?"

"Not in the theater," said Lang.

Someone down by the stage called out, and Lorre turned and waved a hand. "It's only half an hour for lunch," he said to Lang. "You'll be here when I get back?"

"Probably not."

"But you will have something for me soon?"

Lang said, "Think about fear, Peter. Think about what you could do with that."

Lorre tried another smile, but this one seemed less willing. "My own or someone else's?"

"There's a difference?" Lang removed his monocle and began to wipe it on his lapel. "So—you make people laugh. Good for you. It's just a flick between that and terrifying them."

Lorre's smile was all but gone. "You think I don't know this, Fritz?"

"Look at you," said Lang. "It's because they want to laugh when they see you. They *need* to laugh. And you let them do it because otherwise, you'd have to let them see what you're so frightened of."

Lorre shot a glance at Hoffner and let out an uncomfortable laugh. "Fritz knows me so well."

"You see," said Lang. "Even now it's too much for you." Lang

replaced his monocle and smiled. "And that's what makes you extraor-
dinary, Peter."

Lorre did his best to return the smile. It was an awkward moment
for all of them. He looked again at Hoffner. "Good to meet you,
Nikolai. Fritz." His return to the aisle was no less clumsy.

Lang said quietly, "He's going to change the way people watch
films. He just doesn't know it."

Hoffner finished his cigarette and crushed it into the seat's ashtray.
"So you're a Jew. That's something of a surprise."

Lang kept his eyes on Lorre. "I don't make a secret of it."

"You don't advertise it, either."

"The people who need me to be one, for good or bad, do the advertising. That's what it is to be a German." He turned to Hoffner. "And
it seems, by all rights, you're one as well."

"But not your wife."

Lang studied Hoffner before answering: "No. Not my wife."

Perhaps the Thulians had been willing to overlook Fräulein von
Harbou's indiscretion. Lang's direct involvement as a Jew, though, was
now not a possibility.

"Still," said Hoffner, "all that money. One wonders where she's getting it."

Hoffner expected another icy stare. Instead, Lang's expression
showed a precision unseen until this moment. "Think, Herr Inspector.
I'm not stupid. Whatever Thea has gotten herself involved in, it has
nothing to do with me, my companies, or any of my projects. Thea
might have made some money on the side from one of her books, but
there's very little money in books, and please don't think I don't know
exactly where every pfennig of it is. The truth is, Herr Inspector, this
is my reputation as well, and it's not something I take lightly. Which
means, from now on, I'm going to need to know how far things take

you. I suppose we'll both be keeping an eye on my wife for the time being." The sharpness in the gaze retreated, and Lang said easily, "Still, some very nice digging, Detective." He stood and called out, "Peter." Lorre was down at the stage. "Don't skulk off. You'll have lunch with me next week and I'll show you a script. Fair enough?"

Lorre forced a smile and then quickly ushered his friend through the door.

Lang continued to stare ahead. "It's what I said. The reality beyond the truth. That's where you're heading now." He looked down at Hoffner. "Very new ground for you, Herr Inspector. Very familiar to me."

METROPOLIS

SHE WAS AT ONE OF the window tables, with two cups, one of them placed in front of the empty seat.

"I got you a coffee," she said, refusing to look up at him.

Hoffner sat and placed a hand around his. It was ice cold. "Sorry I'm late."

Leni raised a hand, and a waiter stepped over. "We'll have two more. And menus."

The man took the cups, moved off, and Hoffner pulled out a cigarette. It was only then that she noticed his face. "My God. What happened to you?"

"I fell."

"How many times?"

He smiled. "You had a pleasant morning?"

She wasn't in the mood. "I had a pointless morning. Ritter called to find out if you'd made any progress."

"Really?" Hoffner lit up. "So who else does he have looking for her?" Not that Hoffner had considered the possibility until this moment, but it seemed logical enough.

"I have no idea."

That, on the other hand, did not.

The waiter arrived, and Leni scooped a healthy spoonful of sugar into her coffee. Hoffner said, "So you're letting Ritter run the show?"

She continued to stir. "And what's that supposed to mean?"

"The ledger. Thyssen's apartment." He looked at the waiter. "I'll take a roll and cheese." The man moved off, and Hoffner said, "You do what Ritter tells you to do, and he tells you nothing."

If he was trying to provoke her, he had succeeded. She looked up and said, "Having me last night gave you second thoughts, is that it?"

"I just wanted to make sure the wounded lady from this morning was gone. She wasn't much use."

She continued to stare at him. "The scabbing on your mouth, it's an improvement."

"Anything would have been an improvement."

"Now who's playing the wounded female?"

He smiled again and poured some cream into his cup.

She said, "Ritter doesn't want this to get out. He's playing it all very close to the chest. That's what Metro and Paramount told him to do."

"Better to be discreet than to find her."

"Exactly."

Just as casually, he said, "Then why involve the Berlin Kriminalpolizei?" Something in what Lang had said—something about the unfamiliar—had hit a nerve. Murder masked as suicide was such an old card to play. Ritter could easily have swept it all away that first morning—the body removed from the tub, a story about a failed romance, anything to make it seem mundane and plausible; Hoffner had dealt with the whitewash before—but instead, Ritter had left it all

too perfectly in place. He had known it would send Hoffner in search
of Lang. He had known it would send him after the Volker girl. And
he had known it would send him to Thyssen's, where he would find
Leni. How better to manipulate a man than to throw him into the
unknown, but with all the trappings of the known around him.

Leni said, "Thyssen was dead. Who else were they going to call?"

"You tell me. It's your business." He saw the now familiar calcula-
tion in her eyes before she answered. "You think I'm not telling you
something," she said.

"I think you're choosing not to see certain things. Your friends have
Thyssen killed—"

"That wasn't my friends." She spoke with such certainty that it
took Hoffner a moment to respond.

"How do you know that?" he said.

"Because they still have me looking for the girl."

And there it was, the most obvious point: and the one he had somehow, once again, missed. More important, he needed Leni to understand what exactly she was admitting. "And why would they have you
doing that?" he said.

She waited before answering. "What difference does it make?"

"Because you said the only reason they wanted Thyssen's girl was
to get to him. They're not going to have sent you all the way to Berlin
just to find some sex toy. It was about Thyssen. With him dead, why
keep you looking for her?"

This time her hesitation forced a momentary glance at her cup.
"That's not something I have to care about," she said. "They want me
to do it. I have no choice."

"And they've told you this?"

"Yes."

"You've spoken with them directly?"

"This is about discretion, Nikolai." She was almost aggressive.

"They talk to Ritter. Ritter talks to me." It was only saying it aloud that brought the first doubts to her eyes.

Hoffner let them take root before saying, "Very convenient, isn't it? Or at least convenient for Ritter." Hoffner knew where her mind was going. All he needed was to help it along. "If you're not doing what the Americans sent you here to do, where exactly does that leave you?"

Doubt turned to something darker. The waiter approached with the roll and cheese, but Leni was already on her feet, gathering up her coat.

GRAVEL KICKED UP into the housing, and Hoffner pulled the car into one of the spaces in front of the Grosse Halle.

She had said nothing on the trip out. Even now, Leni continued to stare through the window, her cigarette more ash than paper, until Hoffner said, "You're going to burn yourself," as he turned off the motor. She looked at her hand and then crushed the stub into the ashtray. With nothing more for him, she opened the door and headed up to the studio.

The elevator ride up was equally charming, the man at the lever smart enough to know when to keep his eyes locked on the arrow gliding along the numbered floors.

Ritter's anteroom was empty save for a too-blond secretary and a boy sitting on a chair with an envelope. Leni moved to the desk with a surprising warmth. "Good afternoon, Fräulein," she said. "What a delightful brooch."

The girl returned a less than inviting smile. "Yes. Thank you, Madame. Herr Ritter is unavailable. Can I take a message?"

Leni said easily, "He'll want to speak with me, Fräulein. Why don't you just put the call through."

The girl picked up her pen and pad. "What message may I leave, Madame?"

Leni's smile took on a nice chill. "Pick up the telephone, Fräulein, or my guess, you'll be in some sub-basement sorting through old costumes by this afternoon. Don't worry. Herr Ritter will still find the time to screw you. He just won't feel the need to give you such nice trinkets as his thanks."

Hoffner saw the slightest grin appear on the boy's face.

The girl waited a moment and then picked up the telephone. "Herr Ritter. Yes, there's a—"

"Fräulein Coyle," said Leni.

"Fräulein Coyle here to see you . . . Yes, sir."

The girl placed the telephone in the cradle, moved back her chair, and stood. She walked around the desk and opened the door to Ritter's office.

Moving past her, Leni said, "That's a good girl."

Hoffner did his best with an awkward nod.

Ritter was standing behind his desk. "Fräulein," he said affably. "And the Herr Chief Inspector. We didn't have an appointment, did we?"

Leni said, "You wanted to be told the instant we had anything on the girl. I hope this is all right?"

"Of course," said Ritter. "Please, have a seat." He sat.

"Tell me again," Leni said no less easily. "Why is it we're looking for this girl, Herr Ritter?"

Ritter showed only a moment's concern. "What is it you've found, Fräulein?"

"Maybe we should get Los Angeles on the telephone. Let them hear the news."

Again Ritter hesitated before glancing at his watch. He nodded slowly. "Nine hours. That makes it, what, a little before seven in the morning?" He looked up at her. "You're quite sure they get in this early, Fräulein?"

"They'll want to be woken for this."

"Will they?" He peered over at Hoffner. "Is there anyone you need to speak to in California, Herr Chief Inspector, or are you here just for show?"

Hoffner said nothing. Better to see where Leni was taking him.

She asked, "What is it you really want with the Volker girl?"

Ritter waited before saying, "Why don't you have a seat, Fräulein."

"Why don't I stand."

Ritter smiled casually. "You know, I usually have an actress or two rushing in here every day, always hysterical, and always better when they take a seat. Nothing, Fräulein, is ever as tragic as it seems."

"No one mentioned tragedy, Herr Ritter, just the truth."

Ritter remained unflappable. "There's nothing I want from the Volker girl. It's your friends in Los Angeles who can't seem to live without her."

"Thyssen's dead," she said. "They've gotten what they wanted."

Hoffner wondered if any of Ritter's actresses had ever stripped things down to such a cold reality. He had to admire Leni's recklessness.

Ritter glanced at Hoffner before answering. "Is that what they wanted? Then I was misinformed."

"You can stop all that, Ritter," she said. "He knows. He knew before I did." Half true, but Hoffner liked the way she was playing it. Make the cop seem smarter than he is. Lawyers always blanched at disheveled intelligence.

"She isn't even that pretty, is she?" Leni continued. "Whatever she was willing to do on film, my boys in Hollywood wouldn't have wasted the time on her once Thyssen was out of the picture."

What Hoffner had taken for sulking on the ride out had evidently been far more productive. Leni had put enough together to see beyond the sex. That she had no idea what that might be was no reason to make her play out the bluff.

Ritter said, "Maybe you're right, Fräulein. Maybe we should put that call in to Los Angeles." He reached for the telephone, and Hoffner said, "Do the Americans know about Herr Vogt, *mein Herr*, or is that something you're keeping from them?"

Ritter stopped. He then looked across at Hoffner. "No murders in Prenzlauer Berg to keep you busy this afternoon, Herr Chief Inspector?"

"None that needed my attention."

"None yesterday, either, I hear."

Hoffner let the obvious slap pass. "That must have been quite a shock to hear that the girl had gone missing, especially when Vogt was so close to completing the device. Thyssen must have been in quite a state when he told you."

Ritter took hold of his cigarette case. He pulled one out and lit it. His silence was no less affecting than his charm. Hoffner finally said, "Where else did you think the ledger would take me, *mein Herr*?"

Ritter reached for an ashtray. "Ah. The ledger." He nodded to himself. "Of course. That's why you're here." He began to curl the cigarette into the glass as he spoke. "I imagine you're very good at what you do, Herr Chief Inspector, but you might want to ask the Fräulein that question."

Leni had been trying to follow. Her confusion gave way to a less than convincing defiance. "He might not have given it to me exactly. What difference does it make?"

"Apparently none," said Ritter, still focused on the ashtray.

Leni continued to stare at Hoffner. "What device? What are you talking about?"

Hoffner had to remind himself that they had come to confront Ritter. How she had managed to get them here was of little importance. Hoffner said, "She's asked the perfect question, *mein Herr*, wouldn't you agree?" Ritter was too well practiced to show a reaction. Even so, Hoffner continued to stare at him. "Sound, Fräulein. We're talking about sound. Talking pictures."

It took her a moment to respond. "And you knew this last night?" Hoffner thought to answer, but knew there was nothing he could say. The silence hardened her. "That doesn't make any difference, either, does it?"

Hoffner asked Ritter, "So when did she go missing?"

"About two weeks ago," he said. "Give or take."

"And Thyssen told you she had the device and the blueprint?"

Leni said, "You're a real bastard, aren't you, Nikolai?"

Hoffner did his best to ignore her. "When did he tell you?"

Ritter let go of the cigarette. "He didn't need to tell me once the girl went missing."

Hoffner was beginning to see things more clearly. "The Americans. They called you. They wanted to know where she was."

"There was a new film of hers due. It never arrived. They were very fond of her, yes."

"But not for the same reasons you were."

"No, not for the same reasons."

"It was just the sex for them."

"Yes," Ritter said coolly. "Just the sex."

It was good to hear Ritter admit it. Hoffner said, "A bit risky, then, using Fräulein Coyle to hunt down the device for you once Thyssen was dead."

"The device?" Ritter was mocking him. "Fräulein Coyle was looking for sex, Herr Chief Inspector. You've just said so yourself. That's what the Volker girl was to the Americans. Why would Fräulein Coyle have seen her as anything other than that?"

"And if she had found the girl?"

"Then she would have brought her to me. Sex delivered. I can assure you that Ingrid Volker would never have mentioned anything about a sound device to an American."

"Unless she was planning on selling it to them."

Ritter dismissed the idea out of hand. "That, Herr Chief Inspector, is absurd."

"You really think the Americans had no idea what you were doing?"

A sourness crept in as Ritter spoke. "The Americans are trying to buy Ufa out from under us, Herr Chief Inspector. If they had any idea about Herr Vogt and his sound machine, we wouldn't be having this conversation. We wouldn't be here. The Americans would, having bought the studio before we could get the thing to work. And if I was very lucky—and they very forgiving—I would still have a job, trying to find Vogt's little device for them. Chances of that, though, would be slim."

The shock of what Ritter had just said took a moment to register. If not for the venom in the eyes, Hoffner might not have believed him. But Ritter wanted this crystal clear. The trouble was, it made no sense. Hoffner said, "The Americans already control the studio. The Parufamet agreement took care of that two years ago."

"Did it?" said Ritter. "Distribution's a very different thing from full ownership, Herr Chief Inspector. Significant, yes, but nowhere near what they've always had their eyes on."

"So why didn't they simply take what they wanted?"

"Because up until Herr Lang's monumentally brilliant *Metropolis*, we were managing. Struggling, but managing. The Americans were waiting to make their offer until we were desperate. And then Lang's masterpiece hit the theaters and the roof fell in."

Now Ritter was talking nonsense. "Struggling? *Metropolis* is bringing in money hand over fist."

"Is that what Lang told you?" There was no need for Hoffner to answer. "Of course he did. I think he actually believes it himself. Tell me, Herr Chief Inspector, have you seen the great work? It's incomprehensible. And dull. Deadly dull. And I'm being kind. That's a rare feat, to manage both, but Lang is really quite gifted."

It was all coming too fast now. "And the Americans knew that?"

"Knew it was crashing? Of course they did."

"So how much has it cost you?"

"Initially? I think it was about two million marks over budget. Now, it's closer to four."

Hoffner was amazed at how easily Ritter could toss around these figures. "And that would be enough to make you desperate?"

"Oh, well beyond desperate, Herr Chief Inspector."

That still didn't explain the sex. "So you're telling me your only recourse was pornography? That's ridiculous."

Ritter nodded easily. "I couldn't agree more." For the first time in minutes he turned to Leni. "Your friends in Hollywood have some rather peculiar tastes, don't they, Fräulein?"

It was all she could do to look at him. "Tastes you were happy to indulge."

"Was I?"

It was not the response she expected.

Ritter retrieved his cigarette and said, "These films, they revolt me as much as they do you."

"Really?" said Leni.

Ritter's tone grew colder. "As I recall, Fräulein, you were sent here to bring back a girl who was expected to do unspeakable things for these friends of yours in America, and you're accusing me of something? Please."

"Then why produce them in the first place?" she said.

"Because I didn't produce them." Ritter took a long drag and

Hoffner wondered if anything was ever going to remain clear for more than a moment.

"You'll have to explain that," said Hoffner.

Ritter took a last drag. "Will I?" He crushed out the cigarette. "All right. Let's make this very simple for you, Herr Chief Inspector. Up until about two months ago I was on the telephone probably two, three times a day with the Americans trying to convince them that their information about *Metropolis* was wrong, that we were in fact well beyond the worst of it. Of course, they knew it was only a matter of time. They were getting ready to make an offer, finish off what they had started two years ago with the distribution deal—following so far? Naturally, the bleaker the news on *Metropolis*, the lower the price. And down, down, down it went. I was on the verge of having to take it, when one day—just like that—I stopped getting buyout offers. Instead, the Americans were now calling to talk about future joint productions. They had a sudden new faith in the great Ufa. And I had no idea why."

Hoffner said, "And this happened the same time the films started being produced?"

"The exact same day, as it turns out."

"So Thyssen was doing this on his own?"

Ritter wiped the ash from his hands. "Evidently."

"And when did he decide to enlighten you?"

"Only when he needed more money."

Hoffner decided to take a little jab of his own. "And he told you what was in these films being shipped to the Americans?"

"He said he'd found a way to pull the rug out from under them without their knowing."

Again Hoffner asked, "Did he tell you what was in the films, Herr Ritter?"

Ritter waited before answering. "Yes."

"And you were appalled."

"Don't sound so smug, Herr Chief Inspector. Whatever had placated the Americans, it had given us more time. I couldn't concern myself with how we had gotten that time."

"So for a few despicable acts on film, these very savvy American businessmen were willing to forgo full control of Ufa and give the studio a second life? That's . . . remarkable."

Hoffner saw the first dip in Ritter's seamless arrogance. "They're Americans, Herr Chief Inspector. There's no explaining what they do. And they're rather peculiar when it comes to sex."

Hoffner was no less glib. "You just didn't care, did you? Whether it made sense or not."

"Oh, it made sense," said Ritter, once again in full control. "They were calling with specific requests—breast sizes, shapes of feet and asses, various positions. They weren't shy in asking for what they wanted."

Hoffner tried to forget that Leni was in the room. "As I said, you just didn't care."

"No," said Ritter. "I didn't."

"Even though you knew Herr Vogt was using the films to perfect his sound machine?"

Ritter paused. "But you see, I *didn't* know Herr Vogt was involved. I don't believe that was something Herr Thyssen thought I needed to know at the time."

Once again, Hoffner found himself trying to keep up. "What do you mean you didn't know?" When Ritter said nothing, Hoffner pressed: "You're telling me you had no idea about Vogt?"

Ritter shook his head. "Not then, no."

"Then when?"

"A few weeks later," Ritter said easily. "I found him the same way you did—when I came across the ledger. I'd seen enough of them. I knew where to look. And the moment I unearthed Tri-Ergon—and our old friends Vogt, Massolle, and Engl—it wasn't too difficult to understand what Thyssen was doing. One set of silent films for the Americans to sate their needs. And one set of sound ones for us—so we could figure the thing out and put Ufa back on track. Maybe Thyssen knew it was better to keep me in the dark. Obviously he was right. What he knew got him killed."

Hoffner took another moment before asking, "So how much money did he want?"

"More than we could give without making the Americans aware that something was up."

"Then where did he get it?"

Ritter smiled. "That's a very good question, Herr Chief Inspector. I have no idea."

As ever, the crucial questions were being left unanswered. Thyssen had been stringing everyone along. And if it wasn't the Americans who had killed him, that meant the Thulians and their Ostara Company were growing more interesting by the minute.

Leni had been standing patiently, waiting. She finally said, "Well, then it looks like the Americans are going to know something is up now, aren't they?"

Ritter turned to her. "Really? And why is that, Fräulein?" His gaze showed nothing. "You think you're the one who's going to tell them?" He shook his head. "You're completely expendable. That's why they sent you. You have a knack for this sort of thing. You know your way around the filth and the muck. Their words, not mine. My guess, if you were a bit younger they'd have expected you to perform whatever they had in mind for Fräulein Volker. But you're not." For just a moment, Ritter's face showed some pity. "Look at where you are, Fräulein. Are these really the men you want to help?"

Hoffner saw the sudden paleness in her face before Ritter managed a moment of remorse. "Find the Volker girl, Fräulein—find me that sound device—and I'll convince your friends in America to let you stay on with Ufa. They don't have to know why. They let you go, and we forget what brought you here."

Leni stood unmoving, her gaze distant.

Ritter said, "I'm going to have a swim." He stepped out from behind the desk and toward Hoffner. "Usually takes me about an hour." He glanced back at Leni and said, "You'll have her on the road by then, I imagine."

Ritter moved past him and out the door, taking with him what air there was in the room.

LENI BREATHED IN, her eyes lost on something beyond the window.

"One thing to know you're worth nothing," she finally said. "Another to hear someone say it." She turned with an unconvincing ease. "I'll take a cigarette." Hoffner reached into his coat, and she said, "No, one of his. Yours are . . . Just one of his. He left the case on the desk."

Hoffner stepped over, took two, and handed one to her. He lit it, then his own.

"Talking pictures," she said vacantly as she let go with a long stream of smoke. "And here I thought we'd already done that."

Hoffner laid the lighter on the desk. "You could always go to the Americans, tell them what Ritter's doing, use the leverage you have." He was barely convincing himself.

"You don't really believe that, do you?" She didn't wait for an answer. "It's horrible being weak, you know. Men seem to be drawn to it, though. Are you one of those, Nikolai?"

"Never really given it much thought."

"That's a lie, but at least it's an answer. The better one is 'No, of course not. And you're not weak, Leni dear. You're vibrant and cunning,' and on and on and on. It's all so pathetic standing in an empty office trying to decide who's going to save you."

Hoffner wondered why these moments always seemed to find him. The pity he had felt for women in the past was never the demeaning kind, but more a feeling of sadness, and not because they had ended up with him. That would have been too infantile. They made their choices: choosing him was not something to earn them his compassion. No, his pity was for their hope, and that had nothing to do with him. Still, it had been upsetting to watch them dig around knowing there was no depth to be found. Martha had been the worst. Maybe that was what came with children.

"You're probably one of those who felt sorry for his wife," she said. Hoffner's eyes snapped into focus. "What's worse, she probably thought it made her stronger."

Anywhere else, Hoffner would have struck back. Protecting the dead required no depth, just a bit of anger, and he could always find that. For some reason, though, he felt none of it. "Strength is what the hopeless have," he said. "All it requires is a little self-pity."

She gave up on the cigarette and crushed it out. "You thought that little of her?"

"You don't need to know what I thought of her. What are you going to do now?"

She let go of the cigarette. "Not something you really care about, is it?"

"It's easier for you that way?"

The bitterness in her smile told him to expect the worst. "You don't have to try and save me, Nikolai. We both know you're not terribly good at it. I suppose that's why your boys blame you."

Hoffner tasted the first acid in his throat. "So what are you going to do?"

"You've asked that."

"Yes, I have."

She waited. "Find the Volker girl."

"And why is that?"

"Because it's something you haven't done. I do what I was told to do, then at least I've done it."

Even grasped-at arrogance had a power. He said, "There doesn't seem to be much sense in that."

"No, there doesn't, but it hardly makes any difference." She started past him and he reached back for her arm. He held her there and felt the heat from her cheek. "Don't do this," she said, without looking at him.

He tried to let go. "My choice, isn't it?"

Had he been anyone else, Hoffner might have managed something caring. Instead, he slowly let go and followed her out.

FOUR-THIRTY ON A WEDNESDAY usually put Georg in some distant basement cataloguing film stock. This, however, was the second Wednesday of the month, which meant—according to his supervisor on the third floor—he was fencing at the Fechtschule Liechtenauer until seven o'clock. That the boy would be holding a saber in his hands the next time they met was only slightly more worrying than the thought of actually speaking with him.

The ride into town was little better than the ride out. Leni said nothing until they reached the outskirts of Wilmersdorf, and then only to point out the sudden brightness of the streetlamps. At quarter to six, Hoffner pulled up in front of the building and tried not to recall the distant tremors from his own lessons here a lifetime ago. He had hated the place then. He hated it now, even if, like his own father, he had brought his boys here every week until the age of fourteen so that they, too, could develop a talent they believed would somehow bring them closer to him. It was a failure of cross-generational proportions.

"You don't have to do this on my account," Leni said as she walked with him across the street.

"That's not why we're here."

The building was four stories tall, of once-gray stone, now black, which only made the pristine white of the front steps all the more glaring. They had grown uneven from two centuries of Prussian dedication, the place now more a club than a school. Passing through the front doors, Hoffner was at once struck by the stifling scent of military privilege. The sitting rooms off the main cathedral hall stunk of old leather and brandy, while the life-sized portraits of men in full regalia hung with a suitable disdain under the pale yellow glow of chandeliers. Off to the side, a few recent combatants from upstairs were strutting in their whites, helmets in one hand, glasses in the other. Two or three turned to peer out into the hall as one of their own called out to Hoffner.

"Yes, hello there," the voice shouted.

Hoffner stopped just before the grand staircase. He turned to find the man almost at his side.

"Nikolai Hoffner," Hoffner said as he forced a cordial smile. "I'm a member here, *mein Herr*."

The shape of the legs made the man cavalry. The cut of his mustache and age made him a colonel. "Of course. Herr Hoffner." It was clear the man had heard the name only in passing. "You're aware, then, of the rules." The colonel glanced at Leni with what looked to be a smile, although the mustache was too cleverly placed to make it a certainty.

Hoffner had never brought a woman here before. It had never even crossed his mind. He looked at her before saying, "It's Chief Inspector Hoffner, Herr Colonel, with the Kriminalpolizei. And yes. The rules. Of course. I'm simply here to meet my son Georg. Would it be all right if the Fräulein sat in the main hall while I go up and fetch him?"

Proximity to the police always brought a bristle to a career militarist. Hoffner had never been sure whether it was simple vanity—the defense of a nation's honor set side by side with the dirty business of public order—or humiliation at his own impotence during these endless spells of peace. The war had done something to shake the foundations, but nine years was a long time to expect self-recriminations to last. This one looked to be too certain in his place to feel anything other than self-importance. The loss of a few fingers might have added to the man's sense of entitlement, but the colonel was in possession of all his extremities. To his credit, he was managing to keep his sneer despite his wholeness.

"Certainly, Herr Chief Inspector. Your boy is . . . ?"

"Sixteen."

"Then probably up on the fourth floor."

"Yes, Colonel, I know." He looked at Leni. "I won't be more than a few minutes. I'm sure the colonel will make you comfortable."

The man motioned Leni toward one of the sitting rooms, and Hoffner headed up the stairs.

The smell grew distinctly more human as Hoffner neared the fourth floor, although the clink of steel on steel did give the last few steps a nice marched-to precision. Two large oak doors were opened to the corridor. Beyond them, pairs in full whites and helmets lunged and parried with various degrees of skill. It was impossible to pick Georgi out among them. One boy with particularly good form was along the far wall, but he was too tall. Another was showing tremendous flexibility with the wrist and elbow—*mano di ferro, braccio di gomma* (iron hand, rubber arm)—but the legs ruled him out. Hoffner's only choice was to walk to the middle of the hall and wait for Georgi to find him.

There was, of course, the possibility that the boy had already seen him. Given the way things had gone last night, Hoffner imagined this might be a rather long wait.

"Do you remember how to use one?"

Hoffner turned and saw the boy a few meters off, his helmet cupped under one arm. He looked as if he had been expecting him. As with most things to do with Georg, Hoffner had gotten it wrong. There was no reason to ask why.

The boy drew up and handed Hoffner the saber. It was a good weight, the distribution across the haft nice and even.

Georg said, "Just in case you thought I might use it."

Hoffner tried to find a hint of humor in the face, but there was none. He handed back the saber. "It's been a long time since I've used one."

"You're better with your hands now?"

The boy's quick appearance had been no reprieve, after all. This was a different kind of suffering, to be reprimanded by a sixteen-year-old son. "Yah," said Hoffner. "About that—"

"You're not going to start explaining yourself now, are you? That would be odd."

The boy was unlike anyone Hoffner had known when it came to moments like these. Even the disappointments at the age of six or eight or ten—the trivialities of a missed air show or a forgotten afternoon in the park—had been met with a candid understanding. Not that Georg had ever excused the mistreatment, or felt his sadness any less deeply, but he saw through to the heart of things. Why his father had acted as he had was not confirmation of a flawed man. It was simply what it was. To find resentment in it, or to wish it otherwise, would have been pointless. What probably struck them both was that Hoffner, at each new turn, should be so surprised by it.

"Still," Hoffner said, "bit thuggish on my part."

"Well then, at least you were in good company."

This was also not expected. "You stayed for a while longer?"

"Until the Schutzis got there. Sascha thought it might be best if we didn't get arrested this time."

"This time?" said Hoffner.

There was a break in the boy's stare. "Don't worry, Papi. I'm not much for the kind of hate they're pushing. You can't tell Sascha that. I don't think he's that keen on it either, but there's something there that's got him hooked."

How much older this boy was, thought Hoffner, than Sascha had been at this age—than he had been himself. But then, it had nothing to do with age. The boy was a better man at sixteen than either of them would ever be. It was the one constant Hoffner carried with him that came as near to pride as he could manage.

"I need to see Sascha," said Hoffner.

Georg waited before answering. "And that's why you're here."

"No," Hoffner said quickly. He continued to shake his head as he spoke. "Not really. I—" He looked at Georg. "I need to see him. I can't imagine he'd see me without you."

Georg said, "We could have dinner?"

"Good. Fine."

"No, tonight. Now. You and me."

There was always a price. What made Hoffner feel its sting all the more sharply was that he should have been eager to pay it. He nodded. "Good."

Georg said, "He knew you'd slap him. That's why he dug into you."

When Hoffner said nothing, Georg said, "I'll get my kit and change."

"I've got someone with me downstairs," said Hoffner. He did his best to hold the boy's gaze. "She'll join us. That would be all right, wouldn't it?"

Georg needed another moment before nodding. "Fine," he said: disappointment, when it did show itself, always came quietly with this one. "I'll meet you downstairs."

TWO AND A HALF HOURS LATER, Hoffner had had enough drink for all three of them. He was, however, feeling none of it as he walked, and not for the crispness in the night air. He was simply saddled with an unpleasant clarity.

Georg had been cordial, even charming, at the restaurant, somehow managing to bring Leni out of herself. They had laughed through the veal and potatoes while Hoffner had foraged through his plate hoping to find something not overcooked.

"I'm not sure how you managed to produce him," Leni said as she walked at his side. They had dropped Georg off at his flat half an hour ago. She had her arm through his, but it seemed unfair: she had stopped at half a glass of a very bad French wine.

Hoffner said, "He'd probably agree."

"No," she said. "He adores you. You don't even hear it, do you?"

"I doubt that."

"You're that much of a coward?"

Hoffner usually let these highly insightful probes into his dark and dreary self pass without a thought. What women chose to see—and what they felt the need to say—was something that always found the surface without any help from him. But the day had left him with a sourness in his throat. Not that he knew why. Maybe the drink had seeped in, after all.

He said, "Am I meant to run back to his flat now, tell him I understand everything? Is that the next little piece in the drama?"

He expected her arm to slip from his. Instead, she said, "It's infectious with you, isn't it?" The lightness had gone from her voice. "Everything snide and empty."

It was his own fault. He could have let it go, given her his silence and the victory. She might even have deserved it. But there was too much rattling around his head from this morning and afternoon to leave room for kindnesses.

"Tomorrow might not be such a good day," he said as they reached his building. The thought of Sascha was weighing on him.

"Really? And after today was such a charmer."

He tried to find the most painless way out. "You'll probably want to get a good night's sleep."

She stared up at him before laughing quietly to herself. "You have no idea what I want," she said. "What? Are you going to offer to find me a cab now? Do they even come through this part of town after dark?"

It was a fair point. The street was deserted. Two of the lamps at the far end had gone out. Best not to think what might be happening beyond them.

She said, "It's enough you're letting me come along tomorrow, isn't it? Pity as your act of contrition? But that would make it too easy for you."

All he wanted was a bit of sleep. Let the films, Ritter, Sascha, all of it sit idle for a few hours. It would be nearly impossible finding sleep alone, but the thought of her next to him was exhausting.

He took her arm and headed up the stairs, and knew the sun would never come quickly enough.

CHAPTER FOUR

HUGENBERG

BY 3:00 A.M., he had done what he could. Cases had a tendency to find their focus in dead-of-night quiet. This time, however, he had managed only flashes, some brighter than others, but none to give what he had a coherent picture. The prospect of seeing Sascha was no doubt clouding things, but knowing that hardly helped.

The heat from the bed stayed with him as Hoffner stepped out onto the street. At any hour, Prenzlauer Berg was ugly. That might have been unfair, but it was why he had chosen it. He could claim it was closer to the Alex, cheaper, a place where cops never lived—and why not be the only cop on the block?—but no one cared who or what he was, and that was perhaps more important than anything. Ugliness brought anonymity.

Somewhere near the Rosenthaler Platz, he realized the back of his shirt had gone damp through. He had made it to the edge of Berlin's nightlife. A boy bar called the Swaying Palm was still open across from the U-Bahn station. Its rival, the less daring Fat Gerda's, stood a few doors down and boasted girls of fourteen dressed in Eton jackets, monocles, and drawn-on mustaches. Gerda's was a bit passé—Paris had done the naughty-straight-girl-boy routine two years ago—but for a first-time tourist, it was dangerous enough. Both closed up shop around four, so it was always a lark to see the two groups colliding out on the street: those who truly enjoyed the goods dangling high on a thigh, and those who had yet to find the courage to take hold of them. Shouts of "Scaredy-cock" and "Nervous Willie" could be heard most nights. The current favorite was a verse from a cabaret song now popular among university-trained homosexuals:

> *What kind of feelings do you have, Moritz, Moritz, Moritz?*
> *Are they cool ones or muggy ones, Moritz, Moritz, Moritz?*
> *You don't say yes, you don't say no.*
> *You're so fine and yet so cruel!*

A group of four were well into the song as Hoffner moved along the square. He looked over as he walked, two of the boys holding up a champagne bottle in mock toast, the others tossing sugar cubes down the street at their would-be targets.

If he had thought about it, Hoffner might have been amazed to see how far things had come. Unrepentant homosexuals taunting their ersatz counterparts was something new even for Berlin. Evidently the crime was now of a different sort of pretense.

Ammunition gone, the boy farthest down the street was making his way back for more. There was an intensity to the sweating face that seemed oddly out of place. It became clear why when, a few seconds later, three of his recent victims appeared. Their jeers were anything but playful, the exchange brief, before the largest of the three snatched the champagne bottle and smashed it against the wall. Hoffner stopped under the awning of a shop and watched as the boys stood silently staring, all of them fully aware of how this would end.

For some reason, Hoffner was drawn to the pieces of sugar still resting on one of the recent arrivals' hats. Its brim was pulled down low, making the tiny bits of white seem like the remnants from a child's snow fight. One of the singing boys tried to run, but Herr Sugar Cubes quickly caught him and threw him against the wall. An arm flew up from the boy, but all it managed to do was knock the hat from its attacker's head. In an instant, the back of a hand slapped across the boy's face.

Hoffner might have felt the blow himself, for caught in the lamplight, and red from drink, was Sascha's face peering down into the eyes of the now cowering boy.

What followed came with hardly a sound. Hoffner's throat choked as Sascha landed blow after blow. His friends were having an equal go of it with their own homosexuals, but there was something in the way Sascha struck, measured and taut, that made his beating more brutal. With the boy propped up against the wall and Sascha heaving for breath, Hoffner thought the thing might finally be at an end, when Sascha suddenly gripped the boy's jaw and pulled him up close. The two stared at each other. Sascha then leaned in and, with what seemed an unimagined tenderness, kissed him.

The stillness lasted only moments before the kissing grew more frantic. Sascha began to drive himself onto the boy, one hand grabbing at the buttocks and thighs, the other cupping the testicles. He then slipped his hand into the boy's pants and began to move with an even greater need. The boy's pain gave way to a different kind of violence, his back and buttocks in spasms, his bloodied face lost to release. He fell back against the wall, and Sascha slowly wiped his hand across the boy's face. Sascha then pushed him to the ground, turned, and vomited.

Hoffner stared at the hunched-over figure of his son, a wire of saliva caught between lips and pavement. He knew he was meant to feel something, hear a thousand questions racing through his head, but all he found were the mundane and the obvious: How long had it been, how much did Georg know? Any thoughts for Sascha's turmoil or self-loathing, or even happiness, were beyond Hoffner's grasp. He had never tried to understand the boy's fears or triumphs before. Why should he do so with this?

Sascha suddenly straightened himself up and called over to his friends. The smaller of the two was pissing on the slumped body of his own victim. The other was having a smoke. Sascha found his hat and wiped the edges of his mouth with it. A lone sugar cube fell to the ground, and he picked it up and hurled it at the boy. A minute later, all three were gone.

Hoffner waited before stepping out. The wet in his shirt had chilled. He pulled his coat tighter around his chest and suffered through the momentary shock. It took him another minute to realize he needed to be walking.

That it was all happenstance hardly mattered. He had seen it. So what of that? Sascha was other, had always been other. Not that Hoffner could have known it stemmed from this—if, in fact, this was the reason at all—but the last ten minutes had changed nothing. It would have been so much easier pinning it all on some stifled perversion, but who ever had that kind of luck? All Hoffner knew was that they shared nothing, and that made Sascha somehow less terrifying. Perhaps, then, fate had simply been kind enough to remind him of that.

Hoffner stepped over the tram rails and heard the sounds of the boys getting up from behind him. There was no reason to turn. They would find their way home, patch each other up, and convince themselves that this was the way their lives were meant to be lived.

THE MARQUEE ALONG TORSTRASSE came as a surprise, then a relief. Hoffner was feeling a heaviness in his legs, and the city's only all-night Film Palast—a recent stroke of genius from the minds at Ufa—seemed his best bet. The last real theatergoers were always gone by two. Even the pianist was sent home after that, leaving the 4:00 a.m. showing sufficiently quiet for those in need of sleep. All that was required was a hat over the eyes to take care of the flashing light from the screen. That the place had become a plush seat in a warm room for Berlin's well-heeled vagrants—those who could afford the three pfennigs—was probably not lost on the studio sages. They were making their money while Berlin slept, even if they did have to spend a little extra on disinfectant.

Hoffner settled in about twenty rows back. As he brought his hat down, he caught sight of something familiar on the screen. It was that same mass of people, that same endless building, he had seen in the screening room out at Ufa.

So this was *Metropolis*, he thought. He watched for another few seconds, then pulled his hat over his face. At least now he could tell Lang he had truly seen it.

SOME THREE HOURS LATER he found himself waiting in line at the men's toilet, a particularly dapper *stromer* keeping them all waiting while he combed through his mustache. There was a trace of something well fitted in the suit and shoes, but the rip in the cloth just above the back of the knee and the laces tied only halfway up the tongue (couldn't the man find a few longer pieces of string?) made the hair seem a misplaced vanity. Hoffner rinsed his mouth, ran a bit of water over the back of his neck, and dried off with a towel already moist with infection. It was its smell of hair cream, though, that took him over the edge.

Outside, the glare was already at full pitch, though the novelty was wearing thin. It had begun to sour the streets. Folded newspapers had become extensions of every hat, held up to the forehead as if the morning commute were a game of pirate search, troves of buried gold as yet undetected in the distance. Others simply moved with their heads down, inviting any manner of shoves and bumps. It brought a meanness to walking.

The café was exactly where Georg had said it would be, a jaunty little place that kept two tables and a heating lamp outside for anyone stupid enough to think that charm had a chance against this sky. Hoffner saw the boy through the wall-front window. He was reading a paper at one of the back tables. A little bell jangled, and Hoffner stepped inside.

"Not getting much sleep these days?" said Georg as his father drew up. He slid the paper into his satchel. "The stubble's a nice touch, though."

Instinctively, Hoffner rubbed a hand across his cheek. He felt more scabbing than hair. The smell of the towel was still on him. "You got home all right?"

It was an odd question, and Georg moved past it with a hand for the waiter. "So, how do you want this to go, Papi? He'll be here any time now."

Hoffner placed his hat on an empty chair and sat. "Does he know I'll be here?"

"No."

"That was kind of you."

The waiter arrived, and Hoffner ordered them two coffees and a plate of sweet rolls. "You've been in touch with him?" said Hoffner. "On a regular basis, I imagine?" He found a stain on the table and began to wipe at it with his napkin.

Again Georg looked confused. "Yes. I suppose. You saw the letters."

"And he's satisfied with the way things are?" Hoffner continued to work through the last of the stain.

Georg was no less perplexed. "Between the two of you?"

Hoffner looked up. "Between . . . ? Oh no. That's . . ." He tried a smile. "Things are what they are there. I'm just wondering if he's—"

"Happy?" This was the most bizarre question yet. Georg waited for an answer, but his father looked to be no better equipped for the idea than he was. "It's Sascha, Papi. Things are either remarkable or devastating. I don't think he'd be much good with happy."

Hoffner nodded as if this made any sense to him. "No, you're right, of course."

"Is he in some kind of trouble?"

The bell jangled, and both looked over to see Sascha at the door. The brightness around him did nothing to soften the image Hoffner had witnessed earlier this morning. In fact, the light only made the boy's corruption more defined.

Sascha waited several seconds before closing the door and heading over. Hoffner imagined it was pride that had won out. Georg did his best to lighten the mood. "Am I the only one who's getting any sleep?" he said. "You look dreadful."

Sascha's smile showed a genuine feeling for his brother. "This is all very admirable of you, Georgi, but I'm sure Nikolai here would agree it's a little soggy on the sentiment." He looked at his father. "I had no idea you'd be here, either."

"It wasn't Georg," said Hoffner. "This was my idea."

Sascha took a moment. "Then I doubt it was sentiment."

"You're here," said Hoffner. "Why not have a seat?"

Sascha said, "I can see someone didn't take to your smacking them about as well as I did. Sometimes they fight back, don't they?"

Hoffner waited as the man arrived with the coffee and rolls. "I'm sure you were out late," said Hoffner. "Have something to eat, at least."

The awkwardness was pressing on Sascha. He looked at Georg and then turned to the waiter. "You'll bring me the bill for the young man when we're done here. Also another coffee and a plate of cheese." The man moved off, and Sascha sat. "I'll be paying for Georg's breakfast."

Hoffner nodded as if this somehow made the momentary détente possible. "You're doing all right, then?" he said. He pulled a flask from his coat pocket and poured a healthy splash into his cup.

"To buy a coffee and a roll for my brother?" said Sascha. "Yes, I'm doing just fine."

Hoffner took a drink. "I was impressed with your meeting."

"No, you weren't. You find things like that ridiculous. You always have."

"My shortcoming, I suppose."

"I won't argue."

"Then why invite me?"

Sascha looked at Georg. "We can all hope, can't we?"

Hoffner laughed quietly and took a second drink. "Another shortcoming."

Sascha's breakfast arrived. He placed a piece of cheese on the bread and lifted it to his mouth. Hoffner saw the slight hesitation. Imagined or not, the remnants from this morning registered in the boy's eyes. They made Hoffner feel Sascha's filth as if it were his own. Sascha stood and said, "I need to use the toilet." Sascha made his way to a back corridor, and Georg said, "He doesn't have the money for it, you know."

Hoffner took a bite of one of the sweet rolls and nodded. The raisins had gone hard.

Georg said, "Don't try and pay. He'd find that—"

"Yes," said Hoffner. "I know. Does he have a decent place to live?"

"Depends on what you mean by decent. He shares a flat with two of the fellows from the other night. Bit of a hole, but they don't seem to mind. Not sure Sascha likes them all that well."

"And why is that?" Hoffner knew the answer: one thing to take the occasional dip into the muck, another to live side by side with it.

Georg shrugged. "The time I met them, all they talked was politics. That can get tedious."

Hoffner finished his cup. "Not if it's all they have." He raised it in the direction of the waiter. "He hasn't encouraged you to join the great cause, has he?"

"At the beginning. Now he knows it's not my sort of thing."

The man arrived and set the pot on the table. Hoffner said, "Things might take a bit of a turn here, Georgi. I don't want you to be concerned about that—all right?"

The man moved off just as Sascha reappeared at the back and began to make his way over.

Georg said, "If he's in some kind of trouble, Papi—"

"Get the stink off your hands?" said Hoffner as Sascha drew up.

This time there was no hesitation. "A friend's car. It broke down on the way back from the Grunwald last night. Takes forever to get the smell of petrol out."

"You should try sugar cubes," said Hoffner. "Crush them up and rub them around. Old mechanic's trick. Good for all sorts of smells."

For a moment, Hoffner saw Sascha as a ten-year-old boy, the moment of discovery at some trivial offense caught in the eyes. Just as quickly, the boy's face hardened. This had been coincidence, nothing more. Hoffner knew to let him believe it.

"Really?" said Sascha as he sat. "I should give it a try, then."

Hoffner took out his wallet and placed a twenty-mark note on the table. Any good feeling between them quickly slipped away. "I said I would be paying," said Sascha.

"That's not for breakfast."

"I'm doing fine."

"Yes," said Hoffner, "I'm sure you are, working for a bunch of beer-hall hotheads without a pfennig between them. I hear they do their prison time very easily. That must make them seem quite noble. Take it."

Sascha had yet to develop a workable sneer. "You realize how ridiculous you look playing the caring father. Even the amount is ludicrous."

"So fifty would have been better?" Hoffner again pulled out his wallet, and Sascha said, "Please." The sneer had grown into amusement. "You're making it into bad Italian opera now. We both know you're not the least interested—unless you're planning on singing. That I'd stay for."

Hoffner appreciated the boy's arrogance. It made this less difficult. He said, "You won't convince me you don't need it, Sascha, but if you don't want it, that's fine." He placed the wallet back in his pocket. "Think of it as a donation to the great cause, if that makes it easier for you."

Sascha laughed to himself and then looked at Georg. "Did it look like we needed donations the other night, Georgi?" Georg knew not to involve himself. Sascha turned to his father. "We managed that on only four days' notice, and in the Reds' backyard. That doesn't just happen."

Hoffner did his best to sound uninterested. "Fair enough."

"You always know better, don't you?"

Hoffner poured himself another cup. "Look, I'm glad you've found yourself a little group, Sascha, but they are what they are, and I've seen too many of them to think otherwise."

It was impossible for Sascha not to take the bait. "How much do you think that cost? All told? How much?" He waited. "Hall, trucks, beer, newspaper boys . . . ? No? Well, I can tell you they don't just show up because they're interested in the speeches. You have to give them an incentive, and that takes a lot more than twenty marks on a café table."

Hoffner nodded as if conceding. "Yes. You're right. Far more." He looked at Georg. "You want another roll?"

"You have no idea, do you?" said Sascha. He waited until he had his father's attention. "How much?"

Hoffner knew this was wrong—using Sascha like this—or if not wrong, then at least symptomatic of a corruption no less damning than the boy's. The problem was, he had no other choice. "You've got some rich friends who like to waste their money," said Hoffner. "Fine. I'm very impressed. So does every other windbag group in Berlin. The Reds have the Jews, and those are some pretty deep pockets. I'd watch out there, Sascha." He looked again at Georg. "I'm getting another. You can share it with me if you want." Hoffner raised his hand for the waiter and felt Sascha's resentment growing.

To his credit, the boy had learned to stifle it. "They don't have who we have," he said coolly.

Hoffner knew it was too soon to ask. Instead, he signaled to the waiter. "I'm sure they don't." All three sat in silence until the man appeared. "Another of the rolls," said Hoffner.

"Anything else?" said the waiter. "While I'm here this time. I've got other tables, you know."

"Do you?" said Hoffner more aggressively. "Well, we wouldn't want to get in the way of that, would we? Just the roll, then." The waiter began to move off, and Hoffner said loudly enough to be heard, "You'll be sure to give him a little extra, Sascha. He seems to think he deserves it."

Hoffner might have been playing it a bit too coarsely, but it was having the right effect.

"You've really become quite absurd, haven't you?" said Sascha. "The money, the drink, calling out a waiter. And on top of it, the great authority on all things political. Your Reds are finished and you can't even see it."

This was something Sascha had always clung to. Hoffner was amazed to hear it trumpeted out again. But if it was what the boy wanted to hear, why not? "I don't give a rat's ass for the Reds, Sascha. I never have."

"That's right. Convince yourself of that. They'll be gone soon enough, anyway."

"But not your great benefactor," Hoffner said sourly. Had Sascha not been the target, Hoffner might have enjoyed playing the part.

The dressing-down of his father had lent the boy an authority dangerous in the hands of one ill equipped to handle it. He spoke with too much swagger. "We don't have to pay for all of the newspaper boys. Some of them come on their own. They're told to, really, by their boss. He'd be very disappointed if they didn't."

And here it was, thought Hoffner, right in front of him—all but for the asking. He pulled out a cigarette and said, "So it's a publisher. Very nice. Some Munich rag seller with big ideas, no doubt." He lit up. "Tell him he's going to be disappointed."

"Really?" Sascha said no less easily. "You think Alfred Hugenberg puts out rags? I'll tell him you said so. No doubt he'll be crushed to hear that a washed-out cop doesn't like the papers he's publishing."

Hoffner did what he could to keep his own shock in check. This was not a name he had expected to hear. Hugenberg was too much a Berliner, too powerful, and too looming a specter on the right-hand side of the aisle, to take even token interest in a ragtag pack of blowhards from the provinces. This was old Prussian money, and everyone knew just how much of it Hugenberg had been stockpiling for decades—those high times as head of the Krupp munitions conglomerate. But then the war had ended—coupled with some nasty little provisions out of Versailles—and suddenly guns, grenades, and bombs had become bad business. Luckily, the great Hugenberg had seen the future. Reinvesting his fortune—estimated at an almost unthinkable 30 million marks—he had turned his attention to another, equally toxic enterprise: Der Hugenberg Konzern, which now controlled two of the largest publishing empires in the world—Scherl House and Vera GmbH—with newspapers and magazines running into the hundreds. And just in case his ultranationalist voice wasn't coming through clearly enough, Herr Alfred had also bought the Telegraph Union, the third-largest news agency in Europe. Suffice it to say, anything printed in Germany had Hugenberg's fist marks all over it. Along with a seat on the Reichstag as a member of the National People's Party, he was making sure that traditional German values and proper business sense were being well tended to.

But what if that wasn't enough? The image of Herr Vogt's flywheel device suddenly came to Hoffner's mind. If Hugenberg was willing to fund these latter-day Thulians on the political stage, why not elsewhere? Why not give Thyssen the money to play with sound, propaganda in the form of talking newsreel films in every theater palace in the country? Pabst, Lang, Murnau—but first a little something on German purity. The question was, why wouldn't Hugenberg have gone directly to Vogt himself? Why not simply fund the technology? It left Hoffner no clearer as to what Hugenberg might possibly gain by an association with this "thinking man's" Freikorps.

Nonetheless, he knew to nod meekly—an act of contrition to please the boy. He reached for his cup and said, "Good for you."

"Yes," said Sascha. "It is good for us." He picked up the twenty and slid it into his pocket. "And now you can say that you and Herr Hugenberg share the same interests. His commitments might run a little deeper, but every little bit helps."

Hoffner was about to answer when he saw Leni standing directly behind Sascha. It was unclear how long she had been there. Somehow he had missed the bell this time.

"Hello there," she said. "Am I too late for breakfast?"

The boys turned, and all three stood at once. Georg pulled over a chair from another table.

"No, no," said Hoffner, trying again to mask his surprise. "I'm just on my second cup. This is my older boy, Alexander. You know Georg from last night."

Everyone managed the usual courtesies—nods, smiles, words with no meaning—until they were all seated again, except for Sascha.

"Unfortunately, Fräulein," he said as he picked up his hat, "I have a meeting to get to. A pleasure to have met you, if only briefly." He looked across at his brother. "Georg." He even tried a nod for his father. A few seconds later, the bell jangled his departure, and Leni said, "He's quite handsome. You didn't tell me."

"Yah," said Hoffner absently. "I didn't realize you'd be joining us."

"Oh." Her own surprise was less convincing. "Well, you did mention the place last night. I thought I'd give you a bit of time with your boys, but if I'm intruding . . . ." Graciousness was not her strong suit.

"No," said Hoffner. "I can't remember the last time I had dinner and breakfast with the same people. It'll make for a nice change."

Twenty minutes later, Leni headed to the toilet while Hoffner paid the bill.

"Don't worry, Georgi," he said as the waiter fished through his purse for the change. "Sascha's end of it is on me. You're covered." The man held out the coins, and Hoffner said, "That's for you, Herr Ober." It was nearly half as much as the meal had cost. The man looked mildly astonished, and Hoffner said, "I told you I'd take care of you."

When the waiter had gone, Georg said, "It was quite a performance." There was more disappointment than accusation in his voice.

"That obvious?"

"Evidently not for Sascha. Did you get the information you needed?"

Hoffner wondered where the boy had learned this, how far inside he could really see. That kind of empathy usually brought a softness, but not so with Georg. He had felt no need to protect his brother. What judgment he had, he reserved for his father, and there was nothing Hoffner could say to answer for himself.

"By the way," said Georg, "I've seen her before, at the studio."

"Who?"

"Fräulein Coyle."

Hoffner pulled a toothpick from his pocket. "I'm not surprised." Something had lodged in the newly vacated space at the back of his mouth. "She works with Ritter."

"No, I know that. She told me last night. It's just that she was one of the people I'd seen at those late-night meetings in Thyssen's office." He reached for his satchel. "But you probably knew that already."

Hoffner stopped with the pick. This was turning into a breakfast full of surprises. He did his best to show nothing as he watched Georg unclip the latch and pull out the paper. Georg then stood, and Hoffner continued to stare as the satchel slipped over the boy's head and onto his shoulder. Finally, Hoffner said, "No, of course— Yes." He stood and said offhandedly, "When was that, roughly?"

Georg was adjusting the strap. "I don't know. Around Christmas, maybe New Year's?"

Hoffner nodded as if remembering it himself. "That's right."

"Shall we?" said Leni as she reappeared at the table. Hoffner forced a smile. He then took her arm and followed Georg to the door.

. . .

HALF AN HOUR LATER he thought about apologizing for his office, but the question was where to begin. Instead, he cleared a space for her on a chair across from his desk, then tossed his hat onto the rack.

"It's very cheerful," she said. "The bare wall is particularly festive."

Hoffner sat. He leaned back and clasped his hands at his chest. "So," he said easily, "how many of these late-night meetings with Thyssen did you manage to make it to?"

She was remarkable at holding a stare. "Pardon?"

"The meetings. Out at Ufa. Thyssen was having them on a regular basis."

Her face remained impenetrable. "Georg's a clever boy."

"He's got a good memory."

"I knew there was a reason I didn't like police offices." She waited for a response. When none came, she said, "I don't know. Three or four. How else was I going to get the films?"

Hoffner nodded to himself. "So you were the courier. They weren't being sent directly to America."

"All much too sensitive. You knew that. Everything needed to be discreet."

"That's right. Now I remember. They're very big on discretion." And before she could answer, "So you've been in Berlin for what—the last six, eight weeks?"

"What are you trying to say, Nikolai?"

He shook his head casually. "Nothing. I just want to get things straight." His stare was no less penetrating. "You see, I had you here after the girl went missing. After your American friends discovered that she was gone. And long after Herr Vogt—that's our sound man—started working on his new device. But now you tell me you were here before that. That's very different, isn't it?"

She pulled out her cigarettes. "What does this have to do with any-thing? I don't believe I told you when I got to Berlin."

"No, you never did. I must have just been assuming." He watched as she lit up. "Who exactly was at those meetings?"

She shrugged as she let out a stream of smoke. "I don't know. I don't think it was studio people."

"No one's name you remember?"

"I never heard any names."

Again Hoffner nodded slowly. "Yah. That would have been too helpful, wouldn't it?"

She opted for a look of puzzlement. "Have I done something wrong, Nikolai? You're being very cagey."

"*I'm* being cagey." He smiled as he came forward and stood. "I can drive you back to your hotel now."

She waited. "I thought we were going to make some telephone calls?"

"No. We weren't."

As if on cue, puzzlement sank into self-reproach. "Nikolai, if there's something I've done—"

"You can stop that. It's not likely I'm going to believe it, whatever it is."

"You're being terribly unfair." She continued to stare up at him. "I don't even know what I've done. I wasn't at those meetings. I was told when to show up, I was handed the canisters, and I was told to ship them out. You have to believe me. I saw two or three of these people leaving once—once—and that was by accident. It was the last time I drove out. I must have gotten there twenty minutes earlier than usual. I don't know why. I didn't think it would make any difference. Thyssen was always alone. This time he wasn't, and he was furious. Three days later he was dead, and I panicked. I thought if I told you I'd been there . . . I don't know."

It was impossible to tell how genuine her vulnerability was. At each crucial turn, it came out with just the right touch of helplessness. The damnable thing was that it made sense.

"You don't know what?" he said. "That I would have thought you'd killed him? Please. You're much too clever for that."

"I don't deal with dead people every day, Nikolai."

"No, you just track the living to deliver them up to someone else who can take care of that."

It took a moment for the edge to return to her face. When it did, she looked as if she might say something. Instead, she stood.

The silence became too much for him, and he said, "What?"

Her cigarette was already in the ashtray. "I'll take that ride back to my hotel now."

Hoffner fought the urge to grab her by the arms, shake the strength out of her. As much as he hated her vulnerability, he felt lost without it. He stared a moment longer and said, "Fine," and wondered when this would finally break him.

OUR FRIENDS THE FRENCH

THE SMELL OF WET CARDBOARD and dust lingered in the room as Hoffner opened another of the volumes stacked on the table in front of him. The books were massive things, their leather bindings already cracking from the damp. What genius had decided to keep records in these conditions was anybody's guess. Not that the place was old. Berlin's Handelskammer—Chamber of Commerce—had been established less than twenty-five years ago, three vaulted floors in the Italian-palazzo style along Dorotheenstrasse. At least someone had had the good sense to build an equally grand marble fireplace just off the entrance doors to the reading room. No one had bothered to light it, but still, there was hope.

A man was seated at a desk in front of the floor-to-ceiling bookshelves, his gray mustache and spectacles giving him just the right touch of place. He wore a stiff wing-collar shirt, a swallowtail coat, and a tie tucked neatly into his striped vest. The costume hadn't changed in twenty years, and neither had his posture. He sat ramrod-straight, scribbling into a volume, with an occasional glance at the four or five men seated at the long-row tables. Two were young lawyers, from the look of their briefcases. They were here for the drudge work, although they were putting brave faces on it. Another had all the trappings of a much-too-eager academic deep at work on some dissertation, no doubt exploring the critical evolution of Berlin property codes between the years 1906 and 1911. Riveting stuff, to be sure.

Hoffner let the cover of his book drop just too loudly, so as to bring some life to the room. The man at the desk was evidently immune, the academic too engrossed to take any notice. Only the lawyers looked over, but that was more to indulge the distraction than anything else.

"That's the second time you've done that," Leni whispered. She was seated across from him, her own stack of books barely dented. "They're looking over every few minutes anyway."

An hour ago, the drive from the Alex to the Hotel Adlon had been another standoff in silence, until she had turned to him and slapped him across the face. Luckily, he had already been parked in front of the hotel, so no harm done. He had expected it to be the last dramatic gesture before her exit from the car, but she had just sat there staring ahead. And then she had laughed and said, "That was a little over the top, wasn't it?"

"No," he answered. "I was due for another beating. Once a day seems to be working just fine."

"You know you have to believe me."

Hoffner continued to stare out the windshield. "Do I?" There were any number of reasons he could have reached past her and opened her door. There was only one to keep him where he was. He turned on the car. "No more surprises," he said, and pulled out into traffic.

Now, another short ride and various volumes later, they were no closer to finding what they needed. He had given her the task of digging through any Letters of Incorporation from the last three months that included Alfred Hugenberg's name. According to the city records, Hugenberg had been busy. Thus far, she had come across four references to add to his three. None was promising in the slightest.

"This is going to take all day," she said as she ran a finger down the page, scanning for the name. "And you won't tell me why I'm doing this?"

"And ruin the excitement? It's police work. That should be reward enough."

"Very glamorous. So when do we start shooting at people?"

"Well, you could try the professor over there, although he looks quite fast. It might just be the twitch, though."

The man at the desk looked over and cleared his throat. It was enough to provoke a nod of apology from Hoffner.

Two hours later, he was onto his sixth volume and twelfth Hugenberg citing. It was as a board member for a firm called Mentor Bilanz. The names alongside were again of no help. Hoffner was about to move on when he noticed a small marking following the name of the firm. It looked to be part of the z until he bent forward and realized it was a tiny cross. Looking down to the bottom of the page, he noticed—crammed in just below the last line of text—the same cross followed by a string of almost indecipherable words. He brought his nose almost to the page and read *affiliate IvS, undersigned W. Canaris, W. Lohmann, Capts.*

Hoffner continued to stare. It took him another moment to reach for his notebook. He sat up and flipped to the pages with his notes on the files from the Phoebus Film Studio. Scanning through, he found the listing of the signatures that had appeared on the purchasing document for the warehouses out in the Hasenheide. Instantly, he knew he had been right to look here. There were check marks next to the first three names: *T. von Harbou, J. Goebbels, K. Daluege.*

Only the last had a question mark next to it: *W. Lohmann.*

The link to Hugenberg was growing more interesting by the minute.

Hoffner quietly pushed back his chair and walked over to the desk. The man shifted his glance, but nothing else. "I have the name of a second firm, *mein Herr*," said Hoffner. "I would like to cross-reference it with any other names."

Hoffner had tried this two and a half hours ago with the limited partnership Ostara KG, also named in the Hasenheide document, but it had come up empty. The man took the slip of paper and headed through a private door along the far wall. Ten minutes later he returned with four cards in hand.

He spoke in a dry whisper. "I remind you, Herr Kriminal-Oberkommissar, this is not information you may show to anyone outside the Polizei Presidium, unless they are listed on the cards themselves, or have a legal claim, which would require proper court papers as verification." He peered past Hoffner toward Leni and then back again.

"Yes," said Hoffner. "I remember you telling me the last time, *mein Herr*."

The man nodded and handed Hoffner the cards.

At the desk Hoffner spread them out and began to read.

The first was for the affiliate company IvS, now written longhand as Ingenieurkantoor voor Scheepsbouw, apparently a Dutch firm. His best bet was that this was an engineering office for some kind of shipbuilding enterprise, but he had no idea to what end. The card also listed offices in Cádiz, Spain, and Istanbul, Turkey. The second was for a firm named Caspar-Luftfahrt-Werke with aircraft design offices in Lindingö, Sweden. The third was simply called The LA Company. It listed no locations and no products. All three referenced Mentor Bilanz, but with no explanation of the link. The last, and only German, listing was for a privately supported bank, Berliner Bankverein, whose chairman was a Captain Walther Lohmann of the German Navy.

Dutch shipbuilders, Swedish aviation experts, and what seemed to be a very private California firm, and all fueled by German money. Apparently the film business was taking on all sorts of new partners. Hoffner wondered how much Leni's Hollywood friends had failed to tell her about their interests.

She peered over, and he quickly retrieved the cards.

"Something good?" she said.

He finished taking notes and picked up the cards. "We're done here."

At the desk, Hoffner noticed the professor watching Leni move to the door. It was only a moment, but time enough to see a little grin perk up the sallow, if longing, face.

THE ADDRESS FOR the Berliner Bankverein turned out to be somewhere in the middle of the Spree River. Hoffner had guessed as much. It was why Leni was now waiting in the car, and why he was sitting in an office on the fourth floor of Der Bendlerblock, a mammoth compound of white stone just south of the Tiergarten. Impos-ingly impotent, it housed the Ministry of Defense, General Staff Headquarters, and the Offices of Naval Personnel.

As ever, a police badge required several viewings from a string of ever-more-impressive ranks before a white-haired Fregattenkapitän finally agreed to see him.

"A condition of the heart, Herr Kriminal-Oberkommissar." The Fregattenkapitän was scanning the pages of a surprisingly thin dossier on his desk. "That is the reason why Herr Kapitän Lohmann took early pension in March of 1923."

"And before 1923?" asked Hoffner.

The man continued to flip through. "You say this is all routine, Herr Kriminal-Oberkommissar?"

Hoffner had sized up the Herr Fregattenkapitän the moment he had stepped into the office. The full display of ribbons on his chest and the weathered skin spoke of a life lived at sea. The appointment to Berlin had been the Navy's way of easing him out. To his credit, the Herr Fregattenkapitän was taking the slap with a dignified resent-ment.

Hoffner said, "The Kapitän's name came up as a witness in an old case. A burglary in 1921. The man finishes his sentence in a month, and we're obliged by the court to inform anyone involved. Unfortu-nately, our files were damaged. These things happen, as you well know. We had the Kapitän listed, but nothing else. As I said, all very routine."

"And his history in the Navy? This is routine, as well, Herr Kriminal-Oberkommissar?" The Herr Fregattenkapitän looked up for the first time in several minutes.

"Bureaucrats," said Hoffner with a knowing nod. "They get their hands into everything these days. I lose four hours' work so they can have all their forms and sheets properly filled out. Unfortunately, I don't make the rules, Herr Fregattenkapitän."

The man was back with the dossier. He, too, was nodding. "None of us do, Herr Kriminal-Oberkommissar. Some of these people seem to enjoy sitting behind a desk more than perhaps is necessary." He turned to the front page of the file and said, "So why don't we try and get you back to your work as quickly as possible."

The Herr Fregattenkapitän read through Lohmann's appointments: noncombat logistics specialist during the war; member of a subcommission in 1918–1919 to negotiate the disposition of the merchant fleet and to direct shipments of emergency food supplies to Germany; lead negotiator in 1919–1920 for the return of German prisoners of war; and finally commander of the Naval Transport Division in October of 1920.

He stopped for a moment when he read this. "Really?" This was more for himself than for Hoffner. "I wasn't aware of that." He looked across the desk. "I wasn't posted to Berlin until '24. It seems that your Herr Kapitän was a king among bureaucrats." He quickly raised a hand in apology. "Very important, of course. The Navy doesn't run without them. But not a sailor. My guess, the heart. You can't have that sort of thing on deck, can you?"

"The Transport Division?" said Hoffner. "I'm not familiar with that, Herr Fregattenkapitän."

The man nodded as if expecting the question. "No reason you should be, Herr Kriminal-Oberkommissar. It's relatively new." He continued to explain: "The division is a recent creation made necessary by the restrictions after Versailles. All those ships we weren't permitted to keep in the fleet. We had quite a few of them sitting idle once the treaty stripped us down to twelve destroyers, six battleships, and six cruisers." It was clear that these numbers were never far from the Herr Fregattenkapitän's thoughts. "And, of course, no submarines. Very generous of the English and French. The division is more of a commercial civilian enterprise than real Navy. You'd be surprised how many potatoes you can squeeze into an old troop frigate."

"At least the ships are being used."

"I suppose they are," he said as he went back to the dossier. Turning to the last page, he again seemed caught by something.

"Yes?" said Hoffner.

The man flipped the page over, clearly expecting more. When all he found was the back cover of the dossier, he let go with an unexpected "Hmm."

Hoffner waited until the Herr Fregattenkapitän looked up again. "Something wrong?"

The man closed the dossier and placed it inside the top drawer. "No, no. It's just there's usually a letter or form. It's nothing."

"A form?" said Hoffner with mock dread. "I'm not going to disappoint my clerks back at Alexanderplatz, am I?"

The Herr Fregattenkapitän tried a stiff smile. "A letter that details the officer's decommissioning. They go missing all the time."

Hoffner knew to return the smile. "So your clerks are as inefficient as ours are?"

The man's relief was all too clear. "Exactly, Herr Kriminal-Oberkommissar. The world is now run by eleven-year-olds. I can have someone try and find it for you."

"No reason," said Hoffner as he stood. "I have more than enough to get this off my desk. You've been very kind."

Downstairs, Hoffner asked a young Oberleutnant at the entrance kiosk for the location of the Naval Transport Division. The main office, he was told, was on the third floor. However, if the Herr Kriminal-Oberkommissar wanted the routing bureau, that was not in the building. Funnily enough, it turned out to be on the same street as the Berliner Bankverein, although Hoffner guessed that this time the address might just be above water.

LENI WAS WAITING in the passenger seat of the car, reading a newspaper, when Hoffner opened the door. He held two chocolate brioches in his hands.

"All those floors and guards just for a bakery?" she said as he slid in next to her. "And French pastry, to boot. Who'd have thought?" He handed her one, and she took a healthy bite.

"We take our sweets very seriously," he said as he lapped at a bit of chocolate on his lip.

"Don't you think they'd freeze in those little costumes?" She had the paper open to an advertisement for something coming up at the Palais der Friedrichstadt. " 'The Cassvan Ice-Dance Troupe,' " she read. " 'Four nights of high-culture skating ballet.' " She turned the picture toward him. Ten or so women were posing in a kick line, skates, silver scanties, and brassieres, and an odd sort of silky helmet on top. It was a nice collection of legs and cleavage. Leni said, "I'm guessing low culture means it's just the little hats. Any interest?"

Hoffner pressed the starter. "There's always interest."

She folded the newspaper and said, "So—the Handelskammer and Reichswehr headquarters. Either Thyssen was making some very dull films or things are moving in a bizarre direction."

He took the turn toward Potsdamer Platz and stuffed the last of the brioche in his mouth.

Leni said, "I thought it was ham in the early afternoon with Berliners. A nice little *brötchen*, pickles, maybe an onion or two?"

"You're hungry?"

"Whatever gave you that idea?"

He took them past the Haus Vaterland dome at the center of the square, the statuettes above always reminding him of a kitsch St. Peter's, crosses and faith tossed aside in favor of a robust cup of coffee and a few steins of bad beer. The swarms of people between the Kaffee Kempinski and the U-Bahn entrance were still thick from the lunch rush. There was no point in pulling over.

"We'll see what we can do," he said as he darted the car in front of a tram just turning for the center of town.

DAS MARINETRANSPORT-ABTEILUNG Wegewahl-büro—Naval Transport Division Routing Bureau—lacked any of the grandeur of the Bendlerblock. In fact, it looked more like a second-rate business office: a few modern floors in an otherwise soulless heap of glass and steel tucked in among the rest of the buildings along the street. A silver plaque, with the single word "Routing," nested among the row that listed Roepke Insurance, Bieberback Tailoring, and Ebbinghaus Travel Publishing. Such was the Navy's fate in a post-Versailles Germany. At least they had garnered the top floors.

"Is Hugenberg doing travel brochures now?" Leni said as she glanced at the plaques.

"I'm thinking of a new suit," said Hoffner.

"Really? I'm very good at picking out suits."

He reached into his pocket for a few coins. "There was a place about a block back. Looked nice enough. Not too crowded." He held the coins out to her. "I'll take a plate of noodles with some sausage. White sausage. And a beer, not too cold." When she continued to stare at him, he said, "You said you were hungry."

"While you get yourself a suit?" she said flatly.

"Something like that."

She took the coins. "You know you're coming due for another slap."

"Then let's hope it can wait another ten, fifteen minutes." She gave in to a half-smile and he said, "Staying at Ufa when this is done. That wouldn't be so bad, would it?"

He had caught her unawares, himself as well. Still, it felt right asking.

When she had recovered sufficiently to answer, she said, "Are you saying you want me to stay?"

He imagined that was exactly what he was saying, but why muddy things with what he wanted. "What do you really have to go back to?"

"This morning you were ready to leave me at my hotel."

"Three days ago I didn't know who you were."

He thought she might take his arm. Instead, it was just an instant in the eyes before she slipped the coins into her purse. "White sausage and a beer," she said. "I'll try the ham. More traditional."

"Good to hear."

Without a thought, she brought her hand gently to his cheek. There was no reason for anything else before she headed off.

HE EXPECTED TO BE TOLD there was no one of that name in the office: Lohmann—no. Mentor Bilanz—no. Berliner Bankverein—no. Remarkably, Hoffner never got to the company names. Instead, he was ushered down a narrow corridor, with little offices on either side, and told to wait in the single chair outside the last room in the row. Herr Captain Lohmann would be with him presently. For a man who no longer existed according to Naval Personnel, Lohmann was proving quite accommodating.

Three minutes later, a woman appeared from one of the offices. She moved quickly down the corridor, knocked once on Lohmann's door, and then turned the handle. She stepped back and motioned Hoffner in.

"The Herr Captain will see you now, Herr Chief Inspector."

Hoffner thought he might just as well have been at the dentist's. He stood, nodded to the woman, and pushed through the door.

Lohmann was seated behind a desk, trying to find a place for an overlarge inventory volume amid the endless stacks strewn across the carpets, chairs, and shelving. There was a second door squeezed in between two of the shelves. Hoffner felt oddly at home.

"Herr Chief Inspector," Lohmann said as he finally decided on a not terribly steady pile. He stood and extended his hand. "Captain Walther Lohmann. The place is an absolute disaster. You'll forgive me." Lohmann was dressed in Navy uniform, although his coat was hanging on a rack in the corner and his shirt sleeves were rolled to the elbows. "Can we get you something to drink?"

Hoffner took Lohmann's hand and said, "I've caught you at a bad time, Herr Captain. I should be the one apologizing."

"No, no. Not at all." Lohmann spoke affably and pointed to the only chair that was even remotely empty. "What is it I can do for the Kripo, Herr Chief Inspector?"

Hoffner removed a ream of paper and sat. "The Navy has you on pension, Herr Captain. You're aware of that?"

"Pension?" Lohmann spoke with surprised amusement. "Then I suppose I should be receiving double pay each month, shouldn't I? Not that either could really keep me afloat." He raised a hand and laughed. "Old Navy joke. My apologies."

"Personnel has you retired in March of 1923."

Lohmann's eyes bulged wide, and Hoffner wondered if this was, perhaps, the most animated figure the Navy had ever produced. "How very odd," said Lohmann. He pressed a button on his desk. "Fräulein Zeck. Could you get in touch with Naval Personnel and inquire as to the status of my retirement? Thank you." Lohmann released before she could answer. "But I can't imagine that's why the Kripo is here, Herr Chief Inspector."

"Just some routine questions about a file that came across my desk."

"Really? Routine? And they led you here, even though apparently I don't exist according to the Navy? Is that right?"

Evidently Lohmann was going to be more of a challenge than the boys at the Bendlerblock. "Perhaps a little more than routine, Herr Captain." Hoffner pulled out his notebook: that and a little silence always helped to focus the mood.

Hoffner flipped as he spoke. "It's a company called Mentor Bilanz. Funded by . . . where is it . . . yes, the Berliner Bankverein." He looked across at Lohmann. "Do those sound familiar, Herr Captain?"

Lohmann answered without hesitation. "I'm the chairman of the Bankverein. The other—I'm sure what you have is correct. I'd have to check my files. What kind of business is it?"

The Herr Captain was proving full of surprises. Hoffner hadn't expected the candor. "Shipping, I think."

"Little too broad."

Hoffner hesitated. "Dutch or Swedish?"

Lohmann stood and began to scan the ledgers on one of the shelves by his desk. Hoffner said, "You wouldn't know why the address for the Bankverein is somewhere in the middle of the Spree, would you, Herr Captain?"

Lohmann was busy running a finger over various spines. "It should be this address, Herr Chief Inspector," he said distractedly. "The same as the routing office." He pulled a book out and immediately put it back. "I seem to be the victim of some very poor clerking all around town."

"Yes," said Hoffner. There was no point pressing it. "And why is a naval captain the chairman of a banking concern?"

Lohmann nodded in agreement as he continued to scan the books. "That's a very good question, Herr Chief Inspector." He angled his head so as to read something on one of the bottom shelves. "As you can see, not a great deal about this office screams Navy." He crouched down. "In fact, not a great deal about the German Navy itself screams Navy anymore, except, of course, for those sweet old men and little boys who stumble around the Bendlerblock entering incorrect information in their files." Lohmann turned and swept a hand around the office. "We're in the world of business now. Germany is trying to become the Continent's leading transporter of goods." He went back to his search. "Ships, rail, air. We'll never match the English—that would upset them too much, and given the reparations and our current troubles with our friends the French, upsetting the English isn't exactly something we want to do." Again he pulled out a book. This time, he managed to get as far as the first page before shaking his head and slotting it back in. "The air command was under Navy jurisdiction during the war, so we still technically decide where the aeroplanes go. Rail is another matter entirely, and thank God this office doesn't have to deal with that. The Russians—" He raised a hand. "Pardon me, the *Soviets*—think they'll be running the rails across Europe, but that's ridiculous given the infrastructure of their system. Still, no reason to make the Bolsheviks see reality." He stepped over two piles and knelt to look at a collection of files stacked loosely by the door.

Hoffner had underestimated Lohmann: the man might just be the most animated figure in the world of German commerce. "So, the bank, Herr Captain?"

"The bank," Lohmann repeated with another nod as he continued to peel through the files. "If we're moving into private business, Herr

Chief Inspector, we also have to have our hands in private finance. The government can't be held responsible for any failed venture we happen to get ourselves into. It's a safety measure." He looked back at Hoffner. "Simply put, we the Navy are trying to make a silk purse out of a sow's ear." He set the stack to the side and pulled out a thin volume that had been hiding behind it. "England, France, Russia—they still have their navies intact. To the winner go the spoils, and so forth. But that means their ships are still being used for military purposes." He began to flip through the book. "We have—or rather had—a significant number of ships sitting in dry dock waiting to be scuttled once the Versailles restrictions went into effect. And then someone had the brilliant idea of turning that loss into a gain. Refit the ships and put them to work moving lace from Belgium, potatoes from Ukraine, and suddenly Germany is where Europe looks to move its goods."

"And that someone was you."

"I suppose it was." Lohmann closed the book. "No luck, I'm afraid." He slid it back in and took a last scan of the shelves. "You haven't told me the reason why I'm looking for this company, have you, Herr Chief Inspector?"

"No. I haven't."

Lohmann nodded with a smile. "Silly question, I suppose." He looked over. "Any other names I could try?"

Hoffner knew it would be pointless. He shook his head and said, "And business is good, Herr Captain?"

"The *idea* is good, Herr Chief Inspector. Business takes a little longer to catch up."

"You know you're listed in the official records as an undersigner with the company. With Mentor Bilanz."

"I'm sure I am." Lohmann made his way back to his chair. "I've probably signed close to fifty contracts in the last half-year. We're venturing in any number of directions, including and beyond shipping."

As Lohmann settled in behind the desk, Hoffner noticed for the first time how the books and ledgers were interspersed with small model ships, framed advertising pages out of various newspapers and magazines, and even a few award placards for business production. They were displayed with the same haphazard enthusiasm as the files and volumes. This, evidently, was the way the new business spirit flourished.

"Is there ever any outside help with the funding?" Hoffner asked. It was too much to hope to hear the name Hugenberg, but still, he had to try.

Lohmann leaned back. "On occasion."

"Any of them to do with film?"

Lohmann thought a moment. "Not off the top of my head, no, but—" Lohmann stopped himself. "Is there something wrong, Herr Chief Inspector?"

Hoffner was staring at one of the framed advertisements above Lohmann's head. He had run by it at first. Now he couldn't take his eyes off it. It was written in English:

LEAVE DANEPAK BEHIND AND MOVE TO DANEBRAND . . .
SLICES OF REAL FLAVOUR!

"Chief Inspector?"

Hoffner spoke almost to himself. "Bacon."

Lohmann cocked his head to see behind him. He smiled. "Oh yes. That's one of our ventures. I know it quite well. There's real hope in that one."

Hoffner looked at the framed page, the perfectly white packaging, the bright blue label, below it a plate with eggs and a few healthy strips laid out. A woman's hands seemed to be serving it.

"It's the Berliner Bacon Company," Lohmann said rather proudly.

"We started it last year. Do you know who eats the most bacon in the world? The English. And for some reason, they love Danish bacon. The Danes can't seem to produce enough of it, so we've been buying it up by the shipload just to put a squeeze on the market. But here's the best part. We've been at work on a bacon of our own, cured in an entirely new way just for the English palate. I don't like it much, but the English who've tried it say it's perfect. We're calling it Danebrand. No harm in taking advantage of the name."

Hoffner had been listening with only half an ear. Danish bacon was what Pimm had been moving two days ago on the docks. Hoffner nodded and said, "No harm at all, Herr Captain."

What was becoming patently obvious was that Lohmann was nothing more than a signature on a page. His business tactics were like the strafing of a tommy gun: fire enough shots and eventually something hits. Hoffner wondered if the man even knew of the Hugenberg connection to Phoebus.

Pimm, on the other hand, played at a much savvier game. The bacon, though, was hardly enough to place him at the center of any of this. In fact, Hoffner might not even have recognized the connection at all if not for something far more recent—something he had taken in the completely wrong direction—and that now put Pimm's name directly in front of him.

The LA Company.

The card at the Handelskammer this morning had had nothing to do with Hollywood or Leni or any of her friends in California. Of course there was no location for the company. Of course there were no products. Anyone in the syndicates would have known instantly what LA stood for: Little Alderman.

And the Little Alderman Company meant Alby Pimm.

Hoffner was on his feet before Lohmann had a chance to respond.

"You've been very helpful, Herr Captain. I don't want to take up any more of your time."

Lohmann was momentarily at a loss. "Are you sure—" He cut himself off and stood. He extended his hand. "Very good, then. I hope I've been helpful."

Hoffner took his hand. "Best of luck with the bacon."

BAGIER

L ENI WAS SEATED AT THE BAR. There were plenty of tables in the all-but-empty café, but for some reason she seemed to need a higher perch. He saw her saying something to the barman, who moved off as Hoffner stepped through the door.

"He's been keeping it warm for you in the oven," she said. "You can—"

"You have two pfennigs?" he asked. "I gave you all my change."

Without asking, she reached into her purse and pulled out the coins.

Hoffner started for the back. "Tell him to keep it where it is. I'm making a telephone call."

The smells of ammonia and stale cigarettes were familiar enough near the toilet, but there was no telephone box. Hoffner headed back to the bar. The man was already standing behind it, a plate waiting in front of him, along with a telephone.

Hoffner reached into his pocket for his badge, but the man shook him off. "The Fräulein's told me. Call whom you like." He stepped away and added, "Oh—and lunch is on me." Hoffner picked up the receiver and put the call through to the Alex. Two minutes later he had a detective-in-training on the line.

". . . Yes . . . Yes . . . Look," Hoffner said, shutting the boy up. "Your detective-sergeant will understand. Now get up to my office and call me on the number I just gave you . . . Yes, I'll be sure to mention you in my report." Hoffner hung up and took a forkful of the noodles. "They're making them more unbearable every day. I think this one might be twenty, if I'm lucky." He looked over at the barman. "You have any salt?" The man brought over a shaker. "And I'll take an Engelhardt, and one for the lady. Don't worry. Those I'll pay for." The man made no protest as he poured out the beers. Leni was being uncharacteristically patient. Both took a sip, and the telephone rang. Hoffner picked up. "Yes . . . Catch your breath, Detective . . . Yes, you can sit on a chair." Hoffner brought the receiver to his chest. "I have a real idiot here." He heard the boy's voice and brought the phone up. "What? . . . Yes, it's where I told you, in my filing cabinet . . . No . . . No . . . Yes. Immertreu. Under *I*. It should be rather thick . . . Good, now there should be a separate folder for Alban Pimm . . . You have it. Excellent. Look for a tab that says something like 'Schedule' or 'Appointments' or . . . Yes. 'Weekly Calendar.' Now look at the listing for Thursdays." He covered the mouthpiece. "Our idiot's making progress." The boy came back. ". . . Yes . . . Excellent. And after two o'clock? . . . What?" Hoffner's face sunk. "Damn. Of course . . . No, no, not you, Detective. The Grunwald. I should have remembered." Hoffner thought a moment. "What about after seven? . . . One of the upstairs rooms at the . . . Yes, I'm well aware of where it is . . . What?" Hoffner's expression now darkened. "Say again? . . . What do you mean on my desk? How many of them?"

The boy did his best to sound assertive. "Four, Herr Chief Inspector. Received by the switchboard operator and brought up to your office."

"And every one of these messages is from my son?"

"From a Georg Hoffner, Herr Chief Inspector. One each hour, on the hour, according to the time notation on each page."

"What do they say?"

The sound of shuffling papers filled the line before the boy's voice came back. " 'Get in touch,' " he read. "Nothing else, Herr Chief Inspector. Except for the time notation . . . which I mentioned before."

Hoffner checked his watch. It was four minutes to three, which meant that, if Georg was true to form, he would be calling any minute. "All right," said Hoffner. "Listen to me, Detective. I need you to wait at my desk until the next telephone call comes through . . . Yes. It should be any time now, and it should be from my son . . ." Hoffner's frustration was growing. "Yes, Detective. From a Georg Hoffner. I need you to tell him to call the number I gave you so that he can get in touch with me here. Do you understand? . . . No. No, you're not to mention anything to do with Herr Pimm or any calendars . . . That's right . . . Yes . . . Yes . . ." Hoffner's pitch rose ever so slightly. "Just hang up the telephone, Detective." Hoffner rang off and took a healthy swig of his beer.

Leni's sandwich remained half-eaten on her plate. She waited until he had finished drinking. "Is something wrong?"

Hoffner picked up his fork and scooped up more of the noodles. "No." He brought them to his mouth. "Maybe. I don't know. We'll see in a few minutes." He barely chewed before swallowing.

"And the Grunwald?" She picked up her glass and took a sip.

"The man I was trying to find—"

"Pimm," she said. "You keep a file on his whereabouts. Not a nice man, I gather."

Hoffner swirled another forkful. "Nice enough. He goes shooting in the Grunwald every Thursday afternoon. I should have remembered." He took a bite.

"For sport?"

"For boar. He's been doing it since he's a boy. Then it was to eat. Now—"

"He just likes to kill."

Hoffner had never thought about it that way. Then again, he had never thought about a lot of things with Alby. "Something like that," he said.

"And he'll be back in town after seven?"

Hoffner ripped a piece of bread from the loaf and dipped it in the sauce. Popping it in his mouth, he nodded.

Leni tried some more of her sandwich. They sat in silence until she wiped the corners of her mouth with a napkin and said, "So this Pimm. He knows where the Volker girl is?"

It was said so casually, as if any of this should make sense. Hoffner took another drink, swallowed, and set his glass down.

She said, "That's not something you'd like to believe, is it?"

He continued to fork silently through the noodles.

"So," she said, "I suppose we've got nothing to do until seven. I wonder if the skaters have a four o'clock showing."

Hoffner finally took a stab at the sausage. He brought one up to his mouth and looked at it. "These aren't going to be terribly good, are they?"

"He warned me they might be dry."

Hoffner took a bite. "He was right." He swallowed and stabbed at another.

"I told him you'd insisted on the white ones."

"My mistake." The telephone rang, and Hoffner picked up. "Yes?"

"Papi?" It was Georg. The boy sounded calm, safe. Hoffner swallowed.

"What's going on, Georgi?"

"I'm fine."

"Fine but persistent," said Hoffner.

"Are you alone?"

He heard the first strain in Georg's voice. "No."

"Is Fräulein Coyle with you?"

Hoffner did everything he could not to look at her. "That's right."

Hoffner waited through the silence until Georg said, "Then probably best if I do the talking. All right?"

Hoffner scooped up the last of the noodles. "Good, good. That should be fine."

"This morning at breakfast," Georg said. "You didn't know she'd been here since before Christmas, did you?"

The boy was really quite remarkable, thought Hoffner. He glanced at Leni, and she raised her eyebrows as if to ask. He shook his head with a smile and said into the telephone, "You're in the wrong line of work, Georgi."

"I suppose I'm meant to take that as a compliment."

"Yes, you are."

Georg said, "I decided to do a little poking around."

"That might have been foolish."

"I wonder where I learned that."

Hoffner set the fork down. "I'm all ears, Georgi."

"The visitors' lists," the boy began. "They're meticulous about them out here. No one gets on or off the lot without signing in. Including your American friend."

Hoffner had scribbled his name on enough of these sheets in the last few days not to need reminding.

Georg continued, "It's the same with the individual departments. Each one has its own separate sheet. I told them I was looking for an actress. A request from Herr Ritter's office. Naturally, they just handed the books over. I've been through most of them dating back to November."

"In a film-processing booth?" said Hoffner. "That's inventive, Georgi."

There was a long silence before Georg said, "What?"

"No, I understand that, Georgi. It's just, do you have any of the names? That might be of help." Again Leni leaned in, and Hoffner cupped the mouthpiece loosely in his hand, making sure Georg could still hear him. "It's a girl," Hoffner whispered to Leni. "Something to do with the two of them being where they weren't meant to be. I'm sure Ritter can straighten it out." He brought the receiver back up to his ear. "So yes, go ahead."

Georg said, "That was the best you could come up with? A girl? You're making me sound pathetic. Thank you very much."

"No trouble at all," said Hoffner. "Now, do you have any of the names?"

Again Georg needed a moment. "The names of the people she met with?"

"Yes, yes. That's exactly right. And I can't imagine they'd dismiss you over this, especially if the girl was pretty. She was pretty, wasn't she, Georgi?"

Hoffner heard Georg flipping through several notebook pages. Hoffner laughed for no reason, and Georg said, "December 9, she met with Teicher in accounting. December 10, Sterne in public relations. December 10 again, Pieck in research. December 11, Bagier in music. December 13, Krause in design—"

Hoffner cut in. "Really?" He was doing everything he could to keep his voice steady and his eyes on his plate. Bagier had been Vogt's link to Ufa, the man behind the sound. "That should be it, then."

"Krause?" said Georg.

Hoffner kept his breath as even as possible. "No, no. Maybe it would be better if I did come out. Make things easier."

"Bagier?" said Georg.

"That's it. You'll just wait for me, then. No reason to do anything until I get there, all right?"

Georg said, "You want me to meet you at the music department, is that it?"

"Excellent." Hoffner looked at Leni and nodded, with a smile, the kind only a father manages when mopping up a child's misstep. "And really," he said. "Do nothing, Georg. You understand?"

"I'll see you there, Papi."

Georg rang off, and Hoffner said, "Excellent. Bye-bye."

Hoffner had, in fact, never been called upon to mop up either of his boys' infractions. That would have required some sort of genuine connection. His look of knowing affection had been as foreign to him as had the phrase "bye-bye." Nonetheless, Leni seemed convinced.

She said, "You're showing a bit of courage, after all, aren't you?"

Hoffner did his best with a nod.

"I told you he adores you. He wouldn't have called otherwise."

Again Hoffner nodded.

"So," she said. "Lucky we have until seven. That should be plenty of time to get us there and back if the traffic's good."

Hoffner was struggling to wrap his mind around this latest tidbit. She had seen Bagier over two months ago, and as much as he wanted to throw it back in her face, he knew he hadn't the stamina to weather another explanation or accusation or self-recrimination. Worse, he knew he would hear only what he wanted to hear, and that, above all, was driving the blade deeper in than any betrayal ever could.

"He sounded embarrassed," Hoffner said. "Getting caught with a girl like that. He doesn't play the fool very often."

"You see? You know him better than you think you do."

"Maybe . . . Look." He tried his hand again at fatherly concern. "I'm just wondering. If he's in a spot—I mean, if he's feeling foolish—"

She nodded. "Then my coming along might embarrass him even more?" The nod became a smile, and she took her purse. "You might actually be getting the hang of this, after all." She leaned in and kissed him on the cheek. "I'll be at the hotel. Just pick me up when you get back."

If he'd had the will to stop himself from watching her go, he might have, but there was little chance of that. He called to the barman.

"You have a razor?"

The man nodded.

"And some decent soap?"

The man shook his head.

Hoffner stood and said, "Fair enough," and headed back to the toilet.

THE AIR WAS HEAVY with the smell of petrol and tree sap as Hoffner took the turnoff for the studio. If the sky had looked any less chalky, he might have expected rain. Even the dust was kicking up without much interest.

The guard at the gate looked equally bored. Hoffner signed the sheet and followed the man's directions to a remote area of the lot. It was a good ten minutes before he saw Georg waiting outside one more indistinguishable building. All that set this one apart was its virtual isolation, except for the three large warehouses that stood a few hundred meters behind it. Beyond them was nothing but empty fields.

"You can leave the car here," Georg said as his father pulled up. "No one's going to care this far out."

Hoffner stepped down and walked with the boy along a dirt path toward the door.

"Bit desolate out here," Hoffner said, his eyes in front of him.

"I suppose so."

"I take it you didn't care that much for the Fräulein. Going to all these lengths."

Georg stared ahead as well. "Not that many lengths to go to, Papi. And not really her I was concerned with."

It was hardly adoration, but Hoffner felt its pull no less strongly. He wanted to say something but found his voice unwilling. Instead, he brought a hand up to Georg's shoulder and squeezed. The boy said nothing, and the hand quickly retreated.

They walked in silence until they reached the building's waiting room, where the smell of fresh paint was overpowering.

"The whole area's new," said Georg. He pointed to a gap in the ceiling. "They still haven't put in all the fixtures."

The reception desk was behind a glass partition, and empty. Georg pressed a button and a bell rang somewhere beyond the wall. He waited, pressed again, and the door at the back opened. A young man in a bow tie quickly made his way over.

"Guido Bagier," said Hoffner. "Tell him Hans Vogt is here to see him."

There was something birdlike to the young man. His head twitched as he glanced first at Georg, then at Hoffner. He said, "Herr Bagier is at the sound stage, *mein Herr*. He's not to be disturbed."

If Hoffner had understood what this meant, he might have had a response. Instead, he pulled out his badge and held it up at eye level. The young man glanced at it and said, "You're not Hans Vogt."

"No," Georg cut in. "He's not. Stop wasting our time. Which stage?"

The young man hesitated. "One, but—"

"You'll show us," said Georg.

The head was now at full twitch. "I can't leave my desk—"

"You weren't at your desk when we got here," said Georg with just the right touch of annoyance. "There's no one in the building. We both know it. You sit in the back reading your magazines all day. I don't know why you can't do it out here at the desk, but that's your choice. And if you'd read the entire badge and not just the name, you'd have seen that this is the Kripo. A Kriminal-Oberkommissar with the Kripo. So you'll now step outside, take us along the path to sound stage number one, and then you can come back and do all the reading you like. Are we clear?"

Outside, the young man kept himself a few meters in front of Hoffner and Georg as he led them through the grass and up toward the largest of the buildings. His gait brought to mind an angry stork.

Under his breath Hoffner said, "That was nicely done."

"Thanks," Georg said. "You just have to imagine you're in one of those early Fritz Lang films. I think he actually thought I was going to slap him around."

Hoffner said, "He was in the toilet. Probably does some of his best reading there, but most of the magazines were on a chair behind the desk."

"Damn," said Georg with a smile. "That would have made it more fun."

The Schall-Stadium Eins was a massive box, four stories high and perhaps twice that in length. It might have been any other warehouse except for the look of the front wall, which was covered by an enormous piece of metal sheeting. It was as if the entire thing had been welded together without a single seam. Only one part of the wall was separated from this unbroken unit: it was a wide, movable door at the far end that rose two stories to accommodate set pieces and the like. Even when closed, though, it was slotted into the rest with only the slightest trace of a crack. A very clever piece of engineering, thought Hoffner.

The young man led them to a small access door within the larger door and opened it, and it was here that Hoffner saw how they had managed to keep everything so snug. A long strip of embedded rubber ran the entire way around the inside of the frame. Opening the small door had produced a sucking sound.

The young man remained in the grass. "Herr Bagier will be in the sound control booth," he said. "It stretches along the back of the top level. There's a stairwell. I'm sure you'll have no trouble finding it. I have to get back now."

"Don't worry," said Georg as he followed his father in. "We won't tell him it was you."

The door squeezed shut behind them, and they moved through to a cavernous hall. Its only light was coming from some twenty meters above, where a glassed-in booth ran the length of one of the far walls. It cast enough light to show a series of black wires strung like spiderwebs across the ceiling. Theatrical lights also hung from long poles, but within a few meters, everything faded to gray. At ground level, the space was nothing more than a collection of amorphous shapes. It would have been impossible to navigate through them if not for a single bulb that was affixed to a staircase at one of the far corners. Even then, Hoffner and Georg kept themselves close to the walls as they made their way first to one corner, then the next, and finally to the steps. Remarkably, there seemed to be no echo coming from their footfalls.

The last few stairs brought them through a trapdoor and onto a series of metal catwalks. Here the sound picked up again. At first, Hoffner thought it was the buzzing of electrical machinery. A few steps on, he realized it was the sound of a man humming. Hoffner followed it to a doorway, where both volume and light grew stronger. He stepped through.

A tallish figure was stooped over a tabletop console that housed endless rows of dials and gauges. Boxed amplifying speakers sat below and above. Beyond was the glass and the limitless backdrop of gray.

"Herr Bagier?" said Hoffner.

The man nearly jumped. He looked into the reflection and turned. His confusion quickly gave way to hostility. "Who are you? What do you want?"

Hoffner lifted a reassuring hand. "I'm with the Kripo, *mein Herr*. Hans Vogt suggested I get in touch with you."

The receding hairline and black-rimmed glasses only accentuated Bagier's mistrust. "I have a weapon."

Hoffner held out his badge. "Then you have me at a disadvantage, *mein Herr*."

Bagier took it and, without looking up, said, "Who's he?"

Hoffner glanced back for a moment and then said, "My son. He works here at the studio. In . . ." Hoffner realized he had no idea what the boy did.

"Script research," said Georg.

Bagier nodded as if this meant something to him. It didn't. "Hoffner. I was wondering when you were going to pay me a visit." He handed back the badge. "The device isn't here, if that's what you were thinking."

"I wasn't. But thanks. Why the gun?"

"That's a rather stupid question, don't you think?"

"Depends on who's asking."

The two stared at one another until Bagier said, "This isn't exactly the sort of thing I involve myself in, Chief Inspector. You'll forgive me. It's not been a good week."

"I'm sorry to hear that."

Hoffner's concern was of little solace. Bagier motioned to a chair and watched as Hoffner pulled it over. "I only have the two," said Bagier. "My apologies again." He sat. "We just haven't had the time. They probably should have kept us in the old digs until everything was sorted out, but they're so panicked about *Jazz Singer*, and so desperate to get it up and running, that they've got us out here in the middle of nowhere." He seemed to find comfort in the sound of his own voice. "I'd offer you some water, but . . ." He shook his head in mild disgust. "Even so, we should be ready to go by the end of the year."

"Ready to go where?" said Hoffner.

Bagier's confusion returned. "Into full sound production, Chief Inspector. That's why you're here, isn't it?"

It was a logical question, just not the one Hoffner had an answer for. "Not exactly, *mein Herr*." He pulled out a cigarette. "May I? It's not a problem in here?"

For the first time, Bagier seemed to relax. "It's electrical equipment, Chief Inspector, not explosives. Be my guest."

"There was a woman," said Hoffner as he lit up. "About two months ago. She came out to meet you. An American."

"Fräulein Coyle," said Bagier. He saw Hoffner's reaction and said, "I'm not likely to have forgotten her, now, am I, Chief Inspector?" He glanced at Georg. "So it's not just script research the boy is good at."

Hoffner said, "I'm assuming, then, you'll remember what she wanted."

"Naturally. She came to see how far we were in our sound development. Studios, equipment, that sort of thing. What does this have to do with Hans?"

"And you were happy to show her all of that?"

Bagier realized he was here to answer questions, not ask them. "Some of it, yes."

"But not all."

"No. Not all."

"That was very kind of you to show an American from Metro the back rooms at Ufa."

Bagier reached into his pocket and pulled out a pipe and pouch. He stuffed the pipe with a nice wad. "The Americans have people here all

the time, Chief Inspector. They like to keep an eye on their investment." He tamped down the tobacco and lit it. "So if I'm anything but
charming with the charming Fräulein, they begin to look a little
harder. I wasn't about to have that happen, knowing what Hans was
working on, now, was I?" Again he glanced at Georg. "You're sure you
don't want the boy to wait outside?"

"Trust me," Hoffner said, "he's far better at this than I am. So you
knew what Vogt was working on?"

"More or less."

"And you knew about Thyssen?"

"Of course."

"And the films?"

Bagier nodded.

Hoffner said, "I should have come to you from the start. It would
have made things much easier."

"No, it wouldn't. The device would still be missing, and you'd be
no closer to finding out why Thyssen is dead. I'm not sure I'm following why this has anything to do with the Fräulein?"

It was an odd question given the obvious answer. Hoffner said,
"The Americans must be as keen to find this thing as we are. Maybe
more so. You don't think that raises questions about the Fräulein?"

"No," said Bagier with absolute certainty. "I don't."

"And why is that?"

"Because, like all the Americans, she had no idea it existed."

Hoffner had heard this before, from both Vogt and Ritter. "You're
sure of that?"

Bagier took a long suck on the pipe. "She wanted to know how
many sound stages we were planning—the other two weren't up yet.
She wanted to know how much we thought it might cost for the
soundproofing, the cylinder cases, the floor dampeners, the microphones, the secondary booths, and on and on and on. It was typical

American penny-pinching. Besides, even now the Americans have no idea what Hans was working on. So how could they want what they don't know exists?"

Georg said, "Was she ever alone in your office, *mein Herr*?"

Both Hoffner and Bagier looked over. Bagier waited before saying, "Scripts and police work. That's quite a combination." He turned to Hoffner. "Training him for the future, Chief Inspector?"

Hoffner tapped out his cigarette. "So—was she ever alone in your office?"

Bagier thought, then shook his head. "No. I don't believe so."

"You don't believe so," said Hoffner. "But you're not certain."

"It was two months ago, Chief Inspector. No, I'm not certain, but even if she had been, what was there for her to find?"

"You had nothing that might have linked you to Vogt?"

"No."

"No letters, or addresses, or memoranda about the design—"

"No. No. No. Honestly, you're the first person who's come to talk to me about this, Chief Inspector. There must be a reason for that, don't you think? Maybe because there was nothing to connect me to Hans?"

Georg said, "Or because there was nothing else you could help them with."

Hoffner shot Georg a quick glance. Not that the boy hadn't said exactly what he was thinking himself, but Hoffner doubted Bagier was finding these interruptions quite so impressive. At the moment, the man was having trouble enough defending himself to himself.

"There's nothing she could have found," Bagier insisted.

"And yet here you sit with your gun," said Hoffner. Bagier remained silent, and Hoffner let it pass. "Was she ever in here?" he asked. "In this booth?"

"Yes," Bagier admitted.

"How much of the equipment was here at the time?"

Bagier shook his head again. "This wasn't someone who knew the electronics, Chief Inspector. She was a woman from the accounting department—"

"That's what she told you?"

"Yes. As I said, they're here all the time."

Hoffner repeated, "How much of the equipment?"

Again Bagier hesitated. "Most of it."

"And ready for the device?" Bagier looked momentarily lost, and Hoffner said, "The booth. Was it designed with Vogt's device in mind? Could you install it in here?"

Bagier stared. It was clear he was trying to find an answer. Finally he said, "No one knew that but me. No one."

"So it was designed that way?"

"Yes," he said, needing to explain himself. "But the brilliance in Hans's design was that all it required was a small modification to the input equalizer. Attach a line to the ampere exciter lamps in the camera, run it through the converter, up to the booth, plug it into the device here"—he pointed to a hollow space under the table where a few loose wires were waiting—"and that's it. No one would have noticed even if they'd come across it, and that's for someone who knows these things inside and out. That wasn't your Fräulein, Chief Inspector, accountant or not." And then, more flippantly: "Of course you'd need a little thing called a sound stage, as well, to make it work. A few thousand square meters. Look, the woman was in here for maybe three minutes. I was with her the entire time. The same in my office. It still doesn't make any sense if no one *knew* about the device. And that I can tell you with certainty was the case."

Hoffner nodded slowly to himself. He then said, "Except for Thyssen. He knew."

Bagier waited. "Yes. You're right." He became more defiant. "Absolutely, Chief Inspector. Herr Thyssen knew. And you're telling me he would have told this woman about it?"

Hoffner no longer knew what he was telling him. Leni had been looking into God-knows-what as far back as November, and fobbing herself off as some kind of accounting underling. It was impossible to know what she had uncovered. More troubling was why. Maybe she really had been sent here to do the books. Maybe when the girl went missing the men at Metro recognized they already had someone in Berlin to take care of the dirty work. Maybe it was as simple as that. Maybe, maybe, maybe.

Or maybe Hoffner was hearing Leni's voice in his head rather than his own. Bagier was doing nothing to quiet those concerns.

Hoffner said, "No, I don't imagine Herr Thyssen would have done that, *mein Herr.*"

Bagier looked pleased with himself at the victory. "Then your young lady seems to be a dead end," he said.

There was nothing else to learn here. Hoffner said, "I'm sure you're right." He stood. "I can send a patrolman out if you want. Let you keep your gun at home."

"And draw attention to myself?" said Bagier. "We might not have enough chairs or drinking water, Chief Inspector, but it's very comfortable being at the edge of the world. People tend to forget about you. No, you come and find me when all of this is behind us." He nodded his head in Georg's direction and smiled. "I'd be more concerned with the detective-in-training here." He pulled a long lever under the console, and the entire space beyond and below the glass filled with light. What had seemed unnavigable twenty minutes ago was now just an odd assortment of standing lights, broken chairs, microphones, and a few dozen coils of wiring. All of it was dwarfed by the size of the place.

Bagier said, "I wouldn't want you stumbling around down there."

Hoffner nodded. No amount of light, though, was going to help with that now.

GEORG POINTED to one of the studio buildings, and Hoffner pulled the car over.

"So," said Hoffner. "We'll have that dinner soon. Just you and me."

Georg nodded. "Good."

"This was very helpful, Georg. Thank you."

The boy nodded again and opened the door. "I'm glad." There was an uncomfortable silence, and Georg said, "So—what do you do with her now?"

They had managed not to talk about it. The boy's empathy evidently had its limits. "Not much I can do, is there?" said Hoffner.

"Or not much you want to do."

This caught Hoffner unawares. "Pardon?"

"Bagier might not want to see it, Papi, but this Fräulein isn't someone to trust, is she?"

"That's not really the point, Georg."

"That seems to be the entire point."

Hoffner wanted so desperately not to ruin this. "Georgi, look—you did beautifully. Really. Finding what you did, the questions with Bagier. Brilliant even. But this is a little subtler than that."

"Is it?" The boy's tone was taking them to the edge.

"Yes." Hoffner said it as much to convince himself. "If she's involved, and I let on, then she knows. And if she knows, I can't control what happens. My only link disappears. And if she isn't involved—"

"And that's what this is really about, isn't it?"

Hoffner could feel it slipping away. "Is there something I'm missing, Georgi?"

The boy said nothing.

"What?" said Hoffner.

"You're going to do nothing, aren't you?"

Hoffner tried not to provoke him. "Yes."

"So there was no point in coming out here at all, was there?"

"I came, Georgi, because you called me. Because you were concerned."

A girl emerged from the building, and Georg watched as she walked down the path. He said quietly, "Are you listening to yourself, Papi?"

Martha had used silences like this. It was uncanny that a boy of sixteen—who had lost her at half that age—could so readily conjure them. It made Hoffner want him to understand all the more. He said, "There has to be room for hope, doesn't there?" He bit at the words: absurd to hear them coming from his own mouth when they had no business being his.

The girl walked by the car, and Georg bobbed her a smile as she passed. When she was gone, his smile faded and he said, "Depends on who you want to put your hope in." He waited and then stepped out. Closing the door, Georg bent over and peered back through the window. He tried another smile, but he had none. Instead, he stood, rapped a hand on the roof, and headed off. The silence became oppressive, and Hoffner pulled out.

WISSMANNSTRASSE 46

H E CALLED HER FROM THE LOBBY and told himself he had no reason to go up to the room again. "Five minutes," she said over the telephone. She had sounded tired.

She looked the same when she finally stepped from the elevator.

"Bad traffic?" she asked.

Hoffner nodded and took her arm. He could smell the booze on her breath. Nothing much, but still, he knew this was taking its toll on her.

"I thought you were abandoning me," she said.

"Not just yet."

Leni smiled. "How was he?"

"Fine." There was nothing in his voice. "He could have managed without me."

They stepped into the revolving door, and the silence seemed to amplify in the space. Outside, the doorman called over a cab, and Leni asked, "We're not taking your car?"

Hoffner waited for the cab to pull up. "I'm tired. It could be a long night." The man opened the door, and Hoffner followed her into the back. "The Double Cup," he said through the glass. "Off the Kufu." The driver flipped the lever on the meter and took them out into traffic.

An hour alone parked in his car had done little to settle Hoffner's mind: his isolation had never felt so raw; it was a numbness without any kind of refuge. The batterings he had taken in the past—even the discovery of his Martha lying faceup, lifeless, the weight of that unbearable guilt—had always come and gone through pain: acute, unrelenting, but ultimately fleeting. And then nothing. This was something else. This was a sense of loss, for the boy, for Leni, even for Pimm. Hoffner had tried to understand it on the road back. He had even been willing to give himself over to the pain, but it had never come. And then he had seen her in the lobby, and he had known: it was the chance to make things right—to sweep away the imagined deceit and save them all—that was stifling him. This was the burden of hope, and all it did was make him feel pitiful.

"I talked to Ritter," she said. "His offer's still good."

Hoffner said nothing.

She tried again: "If you think he's someone to trust?"

Hoffner continued to stare out the window, and Leni knew enough to leave him to himself. She turned and watched as the city raced past.

The west never comforted under lamplight. The pale-boned smoothness of its walls and the trimmed precision of its branches came across as sleights of hand. Even the garish smiles on the advertising posters—that white, white light, lit from below—looked less inviting than anywhere else in town. It was as if the place took offense at those who strayed in, fearing what they might find if they peered too closely. Hoffner was one of the very few who knew exactly what was there.

He leaned forward. "Take the next right," he said to the driver as they sped away from the Tiergarten. "Just after Bellevue. You'll avoid the traffic on the Kufu."

"Can't do it, *mein Herr*," said the man, angling his voice over his shoulder. "One way now. Since January."

Was it? thought Hoffner. He waited and then leaned back. "That's right," he said quietly. "My mistake." He watched as the road disappeared. He then shut his eyes. Nothing for it now but to let it all slip by without him.

TEN MINUTES ON, the cabin filled with light and Hoffner opened his eyes to find the cab pulling up under the DC's wide awning. It was all potted palms and music-hall bulbs, a thousand little orbs in an enormous rectangle above that gave off more heat than the sun had managed in over a week. The door opened, and Hoffner followed Leni out. He took her arm and headed up the stairs and into the casino's main hall.

For some reason, the place always smelled French to him. Not that he knew what made this a particularly French smell—too much cologne, or the trace of garlic coming off the perspiration of the gambling rich—but whatever it was, Hoffner attributed it to his own special distaste for everything and everyone inside. He was suddenly reminded of the great hall at the Château Russe, his mother and all those desperate lives waiting for extinction, except here everything glittered as it was meant to: the chandeliers above at full glow; the tuxedoed and tunic-clad men huddling greasily around playing tables; cigarettes colliding with champagne, medals with women. The sound of laughter hovered above it all like the *click-click-clack* of the roulette wheels and made any thought of kindness even more remote here than it would have been across town.

Hoffner kept his badge in his pocket. His suit and hat had announced him well before the first tables.

A man approached. "Trouble tonight, *mein Herr*?" The man looked as if he were sliding on ice. "Did someone call?"

"No," said Hoffner. "No trouble. I'm here to see Pimm."

"Is he expecting you?"

"Tell him it's Nikolai Hoffner. I've come for my bacon. I'll wait." The man disappeared, and Hoffner said to Leni, "You should give one of these a try." He nodded toward a table. "I imagine you know your way around."

She shook her head. "Not really. It's such a beggar's chance of winning, and even if you do, you always stick around too long to enjoy it. What's the point?"

"I was talking about the roulette."

She curled a smile and said, "What exactly happened to you out at the studio?"

A woman squealed, and Hoffner turned to see a chip rolling his way. The woman, somewhere past fifty though painted to look anything but, pointed a fat little finger after her recent escapee. Her cleavage jingled in accompaniment as a man half her age darted out to retrieve it. Hoffner bent down to pick it up and the man said, "That's very good of you." He held out his hand and Hoffner handed it back.

"A two-mark chip," said Hoffner. "We wouldn't want that to go missing, would we?"

"Is it?" said the man. The part in his hair looked as if it had been seared into his scalp. "I though it might be a thousand. No difference, really." He turned and headed back, the prize held high, the woman reaching out toward him, applauding his efforts.

Leni said, "That's another reason to avoid these places. Little ticks like that. I punched one of them once—dead on the nose. I think he cried."

Hoffner continued to watch the hero's return: the coy giggles from the bevy of fleshy throats, the raised glasses from the rest of the well-oiled escorts. "Was it worth it?" he said.

"My hand was sore," she said. "But he bled. Someone paid for the drinks, I think. Someone always paid."

The woman eased the chip into her bosom, and a man's voice behind Hoffner said, "Enjoying the show?"

He turned to see Zenlo Radek looming in a tuxedo. Evidently even bow ties could look gaunt. Hoffner said, "I thought this part of town was all scum to you."

"It's easy money," said Radek. "And I look so good in an evening suit."

"You don't."

"No," Radek said with a smile. "I don't. Not sure what you told him, but he's eager to see you." He turned to Leni. "And the Fräulein, as well."

Leni extended a hand. "Nice to meet you. Helen Coyle."

Radek looked at the hand, then at her face, still with that unnerving smile. "Yes. I know." He turned again to Hoffner. "He actually has a few boys out looking for you—at the Alex, that place of yours on Göhrener Strasse. You could do better than that, you know. And then here you are. How lucky is that?" Without waiting for a response, Radek motioned to the steps at the far end of the room. "Please." Leni hesitated before Hoffner nodded her on. She led them through the crowd and Radek said, "You should have kept the chip, Nikolai. What was he going to do? Piss his pants on you?"

PIMM WAS AT A CARD TABLE near the back, six or seven others around it, chips at the center. Poker, thought Hoffner. Not a game he was terribly familiar with.

Pimm was staring across at a woman whose stack was nearly twice that of anyone else's in the game, except of course for Pimm's. They were the only two with cards in front of them.

"You have nines," said Pimm to the woman as Hoffner, Radek, and Leni drew up. "I beat nines."

The woman, dressed in a tuxedo, and with short black hair around very red lips, pursed them and threw another handful of chips into the pot. "Then you beat me," she said.

Pimm continued to stare at her. "She has more than nines, Nikolai. A straight, maybe even the flush."

Hoffner said, "I don't know the game."

"You don't need to know it," said Pimm. "You need to know her. Does she have more than nines?"

Hoffner was about to answer when Leni said, "It's the straight, and you have the flush. So put all your chips in and see what she does."

Pimm slowly looked up at Leni and smiled. "You've ruined my fun, Fräulein."

"No, I've only added to it," said Leni. "Look at her face." Leni was staring at Pimm. "She knows it now, but she still wants to give you all her chips. Why is that?"

Pimm stared a moment longer and then looked back at the woman. He picked up only half a dozen chips or so and threw them in. Instantly, the woman pushed everything she had to the center of the table.

Pimm's smile grew. "I call."

The woman flipped over her cards and showed the flush. Pimm arched his eyebrows, then flipped over his, showing four eights. He said, "The Fräulein was wrong, *gnädige Frau*. You did have the flush."

The woman stared at the cards for several seconds. She then pulled back her chair and stood. She glanced at Leni before turning to go.

Pimm waited until the woman was gone to say, "There's an open chair now, Fräulein."

Leni said, "I didn't think Germans liked American games."

"Is it American?" said Pimm as he began to pull in the pot. "Who knew? So many things these days that have come over, you never know which is which."

"And you don't like them?" she said.

"Oh, on the contrary, Fräulein. I like them all. Jazz, talent agents, Marlboro cigarettes—although I think they were originally English. Great Marlborough Street comes to mind. I could be wrong, but they're so American now, aren't they? Once they get that American touch—well, they're just American."

Pimm pulled back from the table and stood. He buttoned his tuxedo and said, "Shall we?" There was a dining alcove off the main room, curtain, discreet lamps. Pimm motioned Leni toward it.

"Why don't you play a few hands?" Hoffner said to her. "I'm sure

Alby would stake you." Hoffner glanced at Pimm, who seemed to lose his grin for just a moment. "She won't cost you that much, Alby. I think you can afford it."

"It's never the money, Nikolai," said Pimm. "It's the company. No, I insist. You'll join us, Fräulein, and Nikolai will just have to suffer through it." He turned to Radek. "Bring us some drinks," he said as he followed Leni and Hoffner to the alcove. "American whiskey, I think. That would be all right, wouldn't it, Fräulein?"

"I'm not much of a drinker," she said.

"Yes. I'm sure you're not. You'll be all right with whiskey, Nikolai, won't you? That kind of night, I think."

Pimm drew the curtain closed and joined them at the table. He pulled a cigarette case from his jacket and offered them around. They were Rothmans.

Hoffner said, "I would have thought you'd be smoking Danish, Alby. I'm a little disappointed."

They all lit up, and Pimm smiled as he placed the case back in his pocket. "Are we going to lose the Fräulein here?" he said.

"I'm afraid so," said Hoffner.

"Don't worry," Leni said. "I'm used to it with him."

The whiskey arrived, and Pimm said easily, "You're thinking I know where the girl and the sound device are, aren't you, Nikolai? Because of some merchandise I'm moving for the Navy." He took a drink and enjoyed Hoffner's reaction. "Truth is, I might. Isn't that funny?" He took another drink and set the glass on the table. "I could have them bring up some steaks if you'd like. Or fish. They do a very nice trout here. Fräulein?" Pimm waited on the silence and then said, "Look, I could let you take me through all the clever detective work you've done, listen as you paint me into a corner, all your accusations and so forth, or we could just get down to it and have a nice meal. You'd be wrong, by the way, with the accusations, but I'm not going to convince you of that, so why bother. Does it really matter, Nikolai, if you can get your hands on the thing?"

Hoffner finished his drink and said, "You could have saved me a lot of trouble and told me this four days ago."

"Actually, no, I couldn't have," said Pimm. "But that's not going to make any difference." He looked at Leni. "Steak or trout, Fräulein?"

She was enjoying him. "Trout."

Pimm looked over his shoulder at Radek. "The same for me. I'm guessing meat for you, Nikolai. A nice rare piece with some potatoes. You look as if you could use it."

Hoffner said, "Radek here tells me you were trying to track me down. Why?"

Pimm stared across at Hoffner. "We're all very chatty these days, aren't we?" There might have been something in the tone, but Hoffner chose not to hear it. Pimm said, "I was looking because I have access to people who aren't likely to talk to you. They talked to me, and here we are."

Hoffner was hardly convinced. "Very kind of you—to do all this on my behalf."

"No trouble at all."

"And this business with Mentor Bilanz—"

Pimm raised a quick if calm hand. "Nikolai." Even so, his expression was now fully focused. "It's my information we're here for tonight. Tomorrow you and I can talk about all of that. Fair enough?"

Hoffner knew there was no arguing. "And what do you get in return for this information?"

Pimm smiled. "What an unkind thing to say."

"Yes," said Hoffner. "You have my sincerest apologies."

"No, just your eternal thanks. Trust me on this one." He turned again to Radek. "Make it three trout. Our friend's a little too edgy for the steak tonight. And something green. I don't care what it is." He turned back as Radek slipped out through the curtain. Pimm waited before saying, "You're still close with him, with Radek?"

Hoffner poured himself another drink.

Pimm said, "He's very good at what he does. Odd, but very good. You know, I have no idea where he's actually from. He just appeared one day—1907, '08. I never remember which. Just before they closed that shooting club. You remember—that place with the dog fights in the cellar, and the girl who had the big chest and the one arm shorter than the other."

"Finelli's," said Hoffner, "1907."

"That's right. Radek couldn't have been more than twelve. Quick learner, though. Fantastic with everything, and then, one day he's gone. A little note. Off to the war. No idea which side he went to fight for. No one else was stupid enough to go, but off he went. And a few days after the armistice he shows up again as if he'd never left. That's odd, don't you think?" Hoffner said nothing. "Make a good film, though, Fräulein, wouldn't it?"

Leni poured herself another. "Depends. Was there a girl?"

Pimm laughed to himself and then looked at Hoffner. "Was there a girl, Nikolai?"

Hoffner tossed back the last of his drink and said, "So where am I going with your information?"

"It's been a rough few days," said Pimm. "Have something to eat first."

"You've been keeping that close an eye on me?"

Pimm finished his cigarette. "I can see it in your face. The both of you. Fish is very good for that."

If he'd wanted to lose a few fingers, Hoffner might have boxed Pimm in the ear. Instead, he stood. "Not that keen on fish. I thought you knew that." Leni understood enough to stand as well.

For the first time Pimm's gaze hollowed: it seemed to perch the small alcove on the edge of violence. Hoffner felt it at once in Leni's breath and wondered if she had ever been so close to this kind of power. Its menace made men like Ritter and their world seem utterly meaningless by comparison.

"That's right," Pimm said coolly. "I always forget. No fish." He leaned slowly to his side and pulled a card from his jacket pocket. He placed it on the table. "It's a beach villa in Wannsee. A recent purchase. By the Langs. Fritz for his Thea. You'll pass on my regards."

Hoffner took the card. He then said, "And tomorrow we talk—"

"Yes," said Pimm, standing. It seemed incomprehensible that he should come up only to her shoulders. "Good night, Fräulein. You'll show yourselves out." Pimm pulled back the curtain. He then reached for the bottle and poured himself another drink.

ON THE STAIRS DOWN, Leni said, "A real gangster." She was trying too hard not to show her nerves. "And a helpful one at that."

"You think so?" said Hoffner. "He made that a little too easy, don't you think?"

Radek appeared at the bottom of the steps with a waiter and tray trailing behind him. "You're not staying?" he said.

"He wants to eat alone," said Hoffner.

"I doubt that."

Hoffner turned to Leni. "I left my gloves up there." They both knew he hadn't. "Why don't you get the doorman to call us a cab. I'll be right down."

Leni might not have liked the brush-off, but she was happy enough to keep moving. Hoffner waited until she was out of earshot to say, "How long has he been keeping an eye on me?"

Radek sent the waiter up the stairs. "You're not so special, Nikolai. He has eyes everywhere."

"Very poetic." Hoffner pulled out his cigarettes. "You've never liked being kept in the dark, Zenlo. Where's he looking?"

"Zenlo?" said Radek as he took one of Hoffner's and lit up. "Calling me by my Christian name. You must really be desperate."

"Yes, I must. Puts us in the same boat, I think."

Radek took a long pull. "What is it exactly you think I'm so concerned with?"

Hoffner lit his own. "You're waiting to die. You have been for years. Telling me might just get you there."

Radek stared a moment and then laughed quietly. "Is that it?" The skin on his cheeks seemed to stretch to its limits. "I could have done that years ago."

"He's in over his head and you know it. Playing with the film studios is one thing. Playing with the Navy and Hugenberg—very different. Even Alby doesn't go up against that and come out clean. None of you do."

Odd to see the eyes empty even as Radek's smile remained.

Hoffner said, "He's telling me to head out to Wannsee. To a beach villa. Is that where I want to be going?"

The eyes tightened.

Hoffner said, "It's always a risk saving someone despite themselves."

Radek dropped his cigarette to the carpet. "Now who's being poetic?" He watched as his foot crushed it out. "They don't like it when you do this here. Makes it cheap, they say. They have no idea." He looked up. "So you think he needs saving."

"So do you. Sons and fathers are like that."

"Oh, is that what this is?" said Radek. "And here I thought I was the one who liked all those Austrian Jews, Nikolai, not you."

"If you've got an idea of someplace else I should be going—and it turns out you're wrong—then I'm a little late getting out to Wannsee.

But if you're right, he'll thank us both, eventually." He held Radek's gaze. "Or kill us. But then, you'd get what you've always wanted, anyway."

Radek continued to hold the stare. "No one's ever that lucky, Nikolai." The silence stood between them like parched heat. Finally Radek said, "It won't make any difference."

"It might."

The instant of betrayal is always just that, an instant: a single flick to make everything before and after unrecognizable. Only the weak try to justify it and Radek was not one of those. "Two warehouses," he said. The words were almost mechanical. "No idea what he's got in them, but he's keeping a close watch. One man in the day, one at night. He doesn't think I know, and that's what makes this troubling. You understand?"

"You've seen them?"

Radek nodded.

"Where?"

Radek took in a long breath. "Middle of nowhere," he said. "The Hasenheide. I have the address." He saw Hoffner's reaction and said, "What?" He continued to stare. "Don't tell me you knew that?"

Hoffner shook his head even as he tried to focus. The Hasenheide—where Phoebus had gone for storage. And if this was taking him back to Phoebus, then it was taking him to Ostara and Lohmann and the Navy and von Harbou and Goebbels, and on and on and on. It was all flooding in on him, and still he had no idea why they would be keeping the device there—

Until he saw it, like the flash in a dream when a piece of truth floats to the surface. Hoffner looked directly at Radek and said, "You've seen them, these buildings?"

Radek's concern grew. "You've asked that, Nikolai."

"There's something odd to them." Hoffner spoke with an intensity.

"The front. It's smooth like you've never seen before. Not so much as a crack."

"How do you know that?"

Hoffner suddenly heard Bagier's voice in his head: " 'You'd need a little thing called a sound stage . . . A few thousand square meters . . .' "

Hoffner pulled his gloves from his pocket. "You were right." He looked at Radek. "He doesn't like to eat alone. And he'll be wondering where you are."

"SOUTH," SAID HOFFNER as the man took the cab out from under the awning and lights. His mind was still racing. "Shoot toward Kreuzberg and then down."

The man glanced in the mirror. "How far down are we talking, *mein Herr*?" South of Kreuzberg was not a stop on the DC crowd's usual itinerary.

Hoffner held his badge up to the glass. "North of the airfields. Just drive."

The cab accelerated, and Hoffner sat back and looked out the window.

Leni asked, "I thought we were heading out to Wannsee?" When Hoffner said nothing, she pressed, "Why aren't we going out to Wannsee, Nikolai?" He could hear the tension in her voice. "Why aren't we doing what we were told to do?"

Whether it was the last ten minutes, the past four days, or the need to shut out a mind that was nothing but accusation, Hoffner suddenly turned to her and said viciously, "And what exactly was that?" He grabbed her by the arms and held them roughly. "What were we told to do? Head out to Ufa for a tour of the music department? A little accounting for everyone back home?" He needed to see the shame in her eyes, but of course there was none. "It's always been something else, hasn't it? And I'm the boy who's made it all possible, the one who's handed it right to you. My God, that must please you no end."

She continued to stare at him blankly. "Let go of my arms."

"Why?" He needed to keep hold of his anger. "Tell me why."

"Let go."

He could feel himself squeezing into the cloth, the flesh below it, the bone, and still he grasped at her. Her eyes winced, but she said nothing. Finally, he released her and let himself fall back against the seat. His eyes locked with the cabbie's, a vacant, unforgiving stare in the mirror. The man quickly turned to the road.

If Hoffner had wanted shame, here it was, witnessed and totted up, and with ample regret for everyone involved. There wasn't room enough in Berlin for any of them to feel adequately removed from this.

She spoke quietly, staring out the window. "I'm exactly what you need me to be. And there's nothing I can say that's going to convince you otherwise. Good for you."

It had been a momentary lapse—that self-deluding need in him to see things as they are and not as they might be—rearing up to shatter even this. Why not give in to something beyond himself just once?

He reached for her, and she said, "Don't. You actually hurt me just then." It was gone, and Hoffner let his hand drop to the seat, the feel of her arm still clasped within it.

It might have been ten minutes later, but he had been staring out the window without a thought to the time. The cabbie again eyed him in the mirror.

"What?" Hoffner said impatiently.

"I said we've got company."

It took Hoffner a moment to understand. "What?"

"A black Buick," the man said. "The last five minutes."

Hoffner looked back through the glass and caught sight of the headlights some twenty meters behind them. "You're sure?"

"I've hooked around three times. He keeps showing up."

The road was empty save for the bobbing lights. Hoffner eased himself to the side even as he continued to stare back through the window. "Then put some gas into it."

The man shook his head. "That's not going to make any difference with a Buick, Detective."

"Just do it," said Hoffner.

The man reluctantly downshifted, and the cab grunted at the sudden acceleration. The grind of the engine and wheels deafened the cabin.

Hoffner watched as the Buick kept pace. "Why the hell is he keeping back? He knows we've seen him." He then understood. "Radek," Hoffner said to himself.

Leni had been looking back as well. "What?" she said.

Perfect, thought Hoffner. Radek had lost his nerve. He had told Pimm. This would all be pointless now. He shook his head distractedly and said, "Nothing." He turned to the cabbie. "How close are we?"

"What?"

"Time," shouted Hoffner. "How close?"

"Three minutes."

Leni finished her cigarette and tossed it out the window. "Are you sure he's following us?"

Hoffner barked, "Take a quick right here."

The man shook his head, but did as he was told, and Hoffner watched as the car behind took the turn with them. For the first time, the Buick began to gain.

"The next left."

"He's coming up," the man shouted. "You're done, Detective."

"Just drive the goddamned cab!"

The man took the car to its limits, and Hoffner and Leni held on to the straps as the cab tore through the empty streets. At each new turn, though, and with every stretch of open road, the car behind continued to reel them in. The cabin became a haze of lights as the Buick finally pulled to within a few meters. Hoffner raised his hands to try to see through it, but with a sudden hitch, the light disappeared and the car pulled up alongside them, edging closer and closer until it was forcing them from the road. Both cars swerved, and Hoffner tried to grab for Leni, but they were now being thrown from side to side. There was a sudden thud, and they careened to the far door, Leni's back pressing into him as he flailed for the strap.

"Jesus!" the cabbie screamed. "He hit me!" His eyes again darted to the mirror. "He fucking hit me!" He began to shake his head in panic. "I'm done here! I'm done!" The gears ground down and the engine howled as the cab suddenly began to slow. Hoffner did what he could to keep his arm in front of Leni as everything screeched to a dead stop. The man was breathing heavily, his head darting from side to side. With a sudden burst of energy, he leaped from the car and began to run down the street.

Everything else remained unnervingly still. The Buick was now angled directly in front of them—dark, silent—as Hoffner tried to steady his own breath. He waited for the doors to open, but the car simply stood there.

Seconds passed, and Hoffner tried to find his focus. If this was Pimm, what the hell was he playing at? And if not . . .

Hoffner reached for the door handle just as two men emerged from the Buick. Nothing about them—from the sculpted features of their faces to the perfect cut of their suits—spoke of Pimm or the syndicates. These might have been thugs, but they were of a different breed, and with too much taste to come from the streets. They slowly began to make their way over.

Hoffner's mind was racing for an answer. He turned to Leni, but she seemed frozen to her seat, the lamplight from outside cutting across her face. He needed something from her now, but all she could give was a momentary flash of remorse.

So this was how fear finally played itself out in her eyes. Perfect.

Both doors opened at once. The men peered in, and Hoffner— tapping into some imagined courage—saw himself barreling through them, saving Leni, when he suddenly understood who they were.

Hugenberg, he thought. Hugenberg had sent these men. This was the kind of muscle Hugenberg could afford.

Empty heroics be damned, Hoffner shot his arm across Leni and leaned forward. "She has nothing to do with this," he said. "We take this outside, *meine Herren*. The lady is not involved."

The man nearest Hoffner looked momentarily confused before turning to Leni. "You all right, Miss Coyle?" he said in English.

Had an iron pipe been cracked across his face, Hoffner might have felt the pain less acutely. It brought a ringing to his ears as he tried to convince himself he had misheard or misunderstood. A sudden wave of heat rushed to his face, and it was only then that he realized Leni was looking directly at him.

"I'm fine," she said in English.

Hoffner continued to gaze into her eyes as the man droned on: "Didn't think the streets would be so empty, Miss Coyle. Made us a lit- tle obvious. Sorry about that. Once you threw the cigarette, we knew we had to keep you close."

Hoffner's head was suddenly light, not as if he might faint—that would have been too easy—but somehow suspended over everything, witnessing the entire scene while perched high above it. There was something comical to the picture: the two wide men wedged into the doors, Leni gazing at him, his own witless face. And then a smile. For some incomprehensible reason, Hoffner was smiling.

"You're from Metro," he finally said. Hoffner's accent was thick, but it was still English. The men continued to look at her as she continued to look at him. "Of course." He needed another moment before he sat back. Staring into nothing, he said quietly, "There's a word." He turned to her and realized she had never looked so gentle, even harmless. She was young and untried and his. What a ridiculous thing to think, and yet here it was—betrayal as a kindness, and all he wanted to do was thank her for it. "Sap," he said. His eyes wandered from hers. "That's it. That's the word. Like something from a tree. I've never understood why. I suppose it makes sense."

Leni said, "This was the only way. I'm sorry for that."

His eyes settled on an advertising placard that was wedged into the glass partition. It was for tooth cream.

"It wasn't," he said. "And you're not, but best to keep to the script." He looked at the two men. They really were surprisingly large. "You two gentlemen have had an interesting few days. I'm sorry I couldn't have been quicker in getting you here, but I only just figured it out myself."

Leni took his hand. It was an absurd gesture, but for some reason he let her. "This part of the thing ends tonight," she said. "Not the rest. You have to believe me."

He bobbed a nod and managed to say, "Of course." There was no bitterness in his voice, although he did feel badly for the Metro boys. He could sense their discomfort, hardly their fault to have stepped in so late to the drama. Not that seeing it from the start would have made this moment any less awkward, but still, who wants to be witness to the last little strains of a gallant humiliation?

Even so, Hoffner decided to play it out. He let go of her hand and said, "You knew about it from the start—the device. You were always just after the device." He waited for her to say something, but knew she wouldn't. Still, if he was meant to play the part—

And then the last piece clicked into place. It was hardly anything, but damn him if it didn't make him want her all the more. He said, "There's no one in Los Angeles who's paying for sex films, is there?" Leni didn't need to say a thing. "Clever," he said. "That bit actually made sense—which of course you knew, so well done on all fronts."

"If it makes it easier," she said, "Ritter has no idea, and he's been involved much longer than you have."

"Yes," said Hoffner. "That makes it much, much easier. Quite a performance at his office."

"I'm trying to help you here, Nikolai."

What was all the more desolating was that he believed her.

She said, "They were using the films to refine the device, get it right. The sex—that was Thyssen on his own. We had no idea why, but it turned out to be the perfect way in."

"Of course it did," he said: things were coming clearer by the minute. "Thyssen thinks he's playing you, and you let him believe what he wants to believe." This one caught in his throat. "We're very good at that here in Berlin." Leni said nothing, and Hoffner glanced at the two men. "So which one of you two did she send to kill him?"

He could feel her body tense next to him. When he looked back, her eyes seemed to moisten. Odder still was the anger in her voice. "That wasn't us," she said. "That actually made things more difficult. Why do you always—" She shook it off and dug into her purse. "I don't have time to explain." She pulled out an envelope and set it on his lap. She stared directly at him, and her eyes filled again. It seemed to throw her. She shook her head, breathed in, and then looked at one of the men. "I need a minute here."

The man seemed unsure, and Hoffner said, "She means I'm harmless, Metro. You don't have to worry."

The man took another moment and then nodded to his friend. They both edged away from the car.

When he looked back, Hoffner found his hand again in hers. She was staring down at it as she drew her thumb across his knuckles. "One week," she said. "That's all I'm asking. And then I'll be back." Hoffner said nothing, and she looked up. "That's not so hard, is it?" Hoffner waited and then quietly shook his head, and she snorted, "You think there's something so wonderfully noble in letting this go. And over nothing. The device means *nothing*."

He watched her face as her eyes searched his. Did she actually see something worth her anger beyond them? Had he misjudged her even in that? He said, "I suppose it doesn't."

She moved closer and tenderly kissed him, again the taste of mint on his lips as she pulled away. He watched as she stepped over to the door. She then turned back. "Which building is it?"

It would have been so easy to say nothing. "You're just going to walk in?"

"Something like that."

He knew not to make this any harder for her. "Forty-six. Wissmannstrasse 46. The two warehouses. The device looks something like a—"

"I know what it looks like." The pain he had wanted for himself now fixed in her eyes. "One week, Nikolai. You have to give me that." She stared at him through the silence and then stepped out.

A moment later, the man reappeared at the door and pointed to the seat next to Hoffner. "You mind?" he said. "We're gonna be here awhile." Hoffner barely heard a word as the man settled in. "Oh," the man added. "And your gun. I'm gonna need that."

Hoffner managed to find his focus. "That's your American detectives," he said as he spread his coat wide. "We don't carry them here."

The man patted him down anyway. Finding nothing, he sat back and pulled a folded magazine from his coat pocket. It was a Hollywood rag with Jolson's blackened face on the cover. Hoffner glanced at it for a moment and then looked over at the woman and her toothbrush. She, too, was all smiles.

Hoffner shut his eyes, breathed in, and waited for the sound of Leni's voice to drain out of him.

TWO HOURS LATER, the man prodded him awake.

"She'll be in the air in about half an hour," he said. "We can drop you off then." The man's smile dwarfed his face. "No hard feelings? It's just the job."

Hoffner blinked the sleep from his eyes. His mouth was stale. He reached into his pocket and pulled out his cigarettes. The man already had a pack of Luckys in front of him. "Go ahead," he said. "Better than any of the crap you've got in this country." Hoffner pulled out one of his own and lit it. The man shrugged and said, "You gonna open that?" He nodded at the envelope, which was still in Hoffner's lap. Hoffner took a pull and then picked it up. There was nothing written on it except for the Hotel Adlon emblem. He tucked it into his jacket pocket and stretched his legs.

Hoffner said, "She's flying back to California tonight?"

"Yup," said the man. "Lisbon, New York, then out to the coast. We've had a guy waiting with a plane for the past three days. You gotta hope he's gotten some sleep."

"Yeah," said Hoffner. "You gotta." He regretted not having taken the Lucky. "You haven't killed anyone while you're here, have you?"

The man laughed. "Not yet."

Hoffner held out his hand. "I'll take a look at your magazine."

The man reached down to the floor and gave it to him. "They usually have some nice shots. Thighs and tits. Not this one. Pretty disappointing."

Hoffner nodded as he flipped through. Jolson in blackface filled almost every page, the caption below always the same: *Hurray for Sound!*

Now who could argue with that?

FORTY MINUTES LATER, the Metro boys pulled up to Wissmannstrasse and Hoffner stepped out onto the deserted street.

"You're never going to find a cab back," the man said. He looked only slightly ridiculous with his chiseled face and crisp suit behind the wheel. "She's gone, buddy. Life moves on. We were planning on buying you a drink, anyway."

Hoffner said, "What if I'd tried to run?"

The man smiled. "You weren't going to do that. She told us." And to soften the blow: "She said you were too smart for that. What do you say? Hop in the back, we have a few drinks. Take your licks and greet the dawn."

Hoffner wondered if everyone in Los Angeles lived on these pithy little chestnuts. With as much sincerity as he could, Hoffner said, "Gotta make sure the guy who gave me the tip-off was on the up-and-up."

The big face looked slightly confused. "Tip-off?" said the man.

Obviously Hoffner wasn't as good at this as he'd thought. "About where I could find the sound machine," he said. "The guy who told me it would be out here." Hoffner wondered if Radek had ever been referred to as "the guy."

"Oh," said the man, even though this was clearly beyond him. "So how you gonna do that when Miss Coyle's already got the thing with her on a plane heading for Spain?"

Hoffner was glad to hear that the Portuguese had finally ceded Lisbon to the Spanish. "All depends on if you know what you're looking for," he said. "Plus it's the only way I can clear the guy."

This finally made some sense: the bonds of loyalty. The man nodded. "A pal to the end. That I can understand." He slapped his hand against the outside of the door and raised two fingers in a salute. "For a cop, you're all right by me." Half a minute later, the cab was gone.

THE SWEET SMELL OF MANURE—packed deep in the earth—followed Hoffner as he walked. Twenty years ago this had been farmland. The few buildings he could see were ratty little boxes that looked more like sheds than anything else. That half of them were too far off the street to merit a number hardly mattered. Now, with a single streetlamp arching above them, the buildings could claim their place in the new Berlin. Numbers made them real. Numbers gave them purpose. Numbers meant their future.

He had told his chiseled friend that he was here to clear Radek—to make sure that the tip-off had been legit—but that really made no sense. Hoffner knew that, without the device in hand, Radek would have no way to explain his betrayal to Pimm. And since the thing was in an aeroplane heading for Lisbon, that seemed highly unlikely.

Instead, Hoffner convinced himself he had come for the loose ends: for Hugenberg and Thyssen, for Lohmann and the Langs. Even for Sascha. But if he were being honest, Hoffner would have admitted it was for her. What he needed now was to see the place: see it so he would always know—whether she was back in a week or a month or tomorrow or never—that this was where it had finished. The echoes of Bagier and Georg, even of Leni herself in the cab, would never be enough. They would fade. He would find himself explaining them away. No, he needed the physical certainty of it, the image of a few torn wires dangling in a hollow space to lock the memory in place.

Two buildings loomed up ahead, and he listened for any signs of life. There were none, and he moved onto the grass and made his way up toward the first of them. Even under the streetlamp light, the sound-stage design was unmistakable.

By his estimation, she had been here some two hours ago. Whatever she had done to get in, find the device, and get herself out had no doubt brought Pimm's man into the open. Hoffner imagined a scuffle, one of the big American boys making quick work of it. From the absolute stillness of things, he also guessed that Pimm's man was either out cold somewhere or on his way back into town to break the bad news.

Hoffner was halfway up the field when he saw a faint light bouncing along the grass beyond the far wall. A moment later, the muffled sound of voices broke through and he quickly dropped to the grass. The light and voices grew stronger, and two men appeared from around the side of the building. Both held flashlights.

"It's half an hour," one of them said. He was limping badly, his free hand holding the top of his thigh. "Jesus, stop your whining."

"There's always meant to be at least four of us out here," the other said. He was large, large enough to have given the Americans a run for their money. "Two's bad enough—but just me?"

"You'll be fine."

"We both know you've had worse. You can hold on a few more hours. They won't like this."

"And they'll like it if I bleed out?" Two Daimler saloons were parked in the grass and now appeared in the flashlight beams. "You think I'm happy about this? Look, I get to a telephone and have them send someone out. I'm telling you, half an hour—".

"It won't be half an hour," the other barked.

"What the hell is wrong with you?" They reached the cars. "I don't remember you ever shitting your pants sitting in a trench, and now you start crying? No one's coming over the top, Hermann. I'm bleeding here, and you're worried about sitting in the middle of nowhere for an hour—"

"See?" the other jumped in. "An hour. You said it yourself."

The limping man opened the car door. "Oh my fucking God. I *should* leave you out here for an hour. For two." He got himself behind the wheel and pulled the door closed. "You stick to the drill. Two walk-around patrols every fifteen minutes, both buildings. We clear on this?"

The other grunted something and then said, "Fine."

The man started the car. "Oh, and if I do happen to bleed out, Hermann, just try to hold on until dawn. That way they won't think you did it and ran off."

"Fuck you, Gunther."

"No, no," the other said as he began to pull out. "Fuck you."

The car bounced along the grass until it lurched onto the road. It then accelerated, and the sound of kicked-up gravel faded as the headlights turned and dipped out of sight.

Hoffner remained low as he watched the boy step over to the other car and open the door. For just a moment, Hoffner hoped young Hermann might be abandoning his post, but the boy reemerged with a flask. He glanced around, opened it, and took a few swigs.

Hoffner got to a crouch and quickly moved to the building. The boy was still drinking as Hoffner disappeared around the side and flattened himself against the wall. Not that he knew what he was doing, but better to have his back against something hard than to be lying facedown in the middle of a field. Either way, there was no chance of slipping away unnoticed now.

Without the streetlamp light, everything sank into a deep darkness. Hoffner waited for his eyes to adjust. He was also trying to understand who might be playing sentry on behalf of the Phoebus Film Company. Once again, these were clearly not Pimm's men. The spoken German also ruled out more Americans. What was most troubling, though, was the word "patrol." Things were taking a decidedly unpleasant turn.

Hoffner realized he might do well to find himself a weapon. He scanned the area around his feet, but as far as he could tell, it was grass all the way up to the wall, without so much as a stone lying about. His eyes began to clear, and he peered out across the field. Five, maybe ten meters in front of him he thought he saw a shape. The more he looked, the more it became a mound of earth, except it wasn't: it was too perfectly square to be soil. He then noticed what looked to be a series of long poles propped up against it.

Hoffner listened to the silence and then darted out. There was a tarp of sorts draped across the mound, but it was the poles he was interested in. He took hold of one and felt the wood in his hands. Reaching farther down, he found the curve of an iron blade. This was a trowel. For a moment, he thought it might work, until he wondered what exactly he was meant to do with it: wave it around wildly and hope Hermann might oblige by placing his head in its path? More than that, the boy would have a gun. Hoffner set it back down. The trowel was useless.

It was only then that he realized what was under the tarp. Of course—they were building here; the whole place was a work in progress. He pulled up the flap and found exactly what he needed: row after row of bricks. He realized he would have to get close enough to the boy in order to inflict some damage, but at least now he had something that packed a punch.

The sound of movement in the grass caught him by surprise, and

Hoffner quickly turned to see a beam of light edging its way beyond the side of the building. He grabbed one of the bricks and raced back to his perch by the wall. The light suddenly widened and turned, and the boy stepped around the corner.

"Hermann," barked Hoffner. "What the fuck are you doing?"

The boy was even bigger up close. He stood, momentarily stunned. "Who the—"

Hoffner ran at him, the brick held high. Hermann looked confused until, dropping his flashlight, he quickly reached inside his coat. Hoffner now leaped forward, landing with all his weight on the boy's chest and arm. It was enough to bring them both down, Hermann's free hand reaching up for Hoffner's throat even as Hoffner landed blow after blow of the brick onto the boy's head. The grip on his throat was unimaginable, as if his windpipe might snap, but Hoffner could feel the blood in his own hand, the brick growing tackier with each thrust. Finally he smashed it onto the boy's nose and the grip released. There was a long burst of air as the head fell back. A moment later the boy's body went limp.

Hoffner rolled off. He lay on his back, his chest heaving as his throat continued to choke for air. Minutes passed, and still he stared up, waiting for the throbbing in his head to subside. The brick finally fell from his hand, and Hoffner brought himself up. He thought he might vomit. Instead, he spat. He could hear the boy's halting breath: at least Hermann was alive. Behind them a flat pancake of light spread out across the grass. Hoffner got to his feet and picked up the flashlight. He then headed for the sound-stage door.

A hastily rigged padlock and chain hung across its handle. More offputting were the bullet holes strafed along the wall. Hoffner followed their path to the grass, where a few drops of blood caught in the light. He knelt down. They were dry. Evidently this was where Herr Gunther had taken it in the leg.

Hoffner stood and tried his luck with the chain. Two minutes later he returned with Hermann's gun and fired a single shot into the padlock. The sound echoed as the bolt jolted back, and Hoffner slid it from the chain. He tried the handle, but that, too, was locked. A second shot left a gash in the jamb, and Hoffner pushed open the door.

The flashlight was no match for the pitch black inside. It managed to bring out only a few darkened shapes, but there was no hope of defining them. Instead, he slipped the gun into his belt and aimed the flashlight at the wall nearest him. He began to scan for a switch that might connect with the overhead lights—he was hoping that Herr Bagier's control booth lever might not be the only way to bring one of these places to life.

Ten meters in, he found a box with a set of metal tubes sprouting out and up toward the ceiling. Hoffner pulled it open and flipped the switch. The place instantly filled with a white light, and he was forced to bring his hand up to his eyes. It was almost a minute before the pain receded and he was able to squint out.

What he saw at first confused him. He tried blinking, but nothing changed. He then peered up, but that, too, made no sense. There were no wires hanging from high above, no theatrical lights. And there was no sound booth peering out to monitor it all.

Instead, set out in perfect rows were what looked to be tanks—far bigger than anything he had seen during the war, but tanks nonetheless. For a moment, he imagined them to be set pieces for some futuristic epic, but it was impossible to think that anyone had managed to paint all this with such unerring detail. The metal casings around the wheel tracks had a weight that made them look impenetrable. The turrets seemed thicker still. And the guns—massive things—cast endless shadows across the floor.

Hoffner stepped over, hoping to see a line of wooden props behind them, but there was none. He rapped a knuckle against the side of the tank nearest him—again hoping for wood—but the dull clang of iron echoed in his ears. Still unwilling to admit what this was, he grabbed hold of one of the side rungs and climbed up to the turret. Pulling up the hatch, he peered in: endless levers and dials filled the inside of the cockpit. For some reason, he felt the need to lean in and sweep a hand along them. There was nothing but steel and metal across his palm.

As he stood upright, Hoffner took in the enormity of what lay beyond him. It was row after row of tanks, a silent legion undeterred by the blazing light from above. There was a precision to them that seemed to defy their lumbering weight, a power in the black symmetry of every gun, every wheel, every casing set out in perfect order. The absolute stillness only compounded their menace. He glanced beyond the last row, and his mind went cold. Hanging along the entire length of the far wall were more wheel casings, more axles, more tracks. Below them stood what he could only imagine to be other engine parts, laid out in clumps along the floor, with the half-formed bodies of still more tanks nestled in and among them. These he had no need to touch. These he knew were real. All of it was real.

He had no time to think, as a machine gun–like battering suddenly filled the hall. Hoffner leaped to the ground and instinctively pulled Hermann's gun from his belt as he raced to the lighting box. The sound was all around him. He flipped the switch and everything went black. Inching his way to the door, he peered out.

He felt it at first on his face, then his hands—wet, cold, and raw. He then saw it in the streetlamp light. Torrents of rain were heaving down. Everything else was perfectly still as he stepped out and let it pour through him.

The sky had finally given in.

CHAPTER FIVE

TOMORROW

I N THE WINTER OF 1889—in the wake of the last incident of White Sky—a Professor Doktor Ludwig Klingman of the Kaiser Wilhelm Institute for Physical Chemistry and Electrochemistry published an article in *Das Journal der meteorologischen Phänomene und des Grundes* titled *"Weisserhimmel und die Methoden für das Sichern gegen seine Nachmahd,"* detailing how best the city's residents might return to normal life in the aftermath of the phenomenon. Hoffner, a student at Heidelberg at the time, had read the piece with great enthusiasm and had even sent a copy of his own paper on Klingman's work to the great man himself. The Herr Professor Doktor had been kind enough to respond with a letter, which, if not quite as enthusiastic, had at least been civil in tone. Klingman pointed out that Hoffner might be confusing a deductive relationship between mineral crystallization and eye irritation—most notably in the ciliary muscle and the suspensory ligament—with an inductive relationship, thus making for some rather odd observations. In fact, it was Klingman who had suggested that Hoffner focus his attention on something that might take advantage of his more deductive inclinations. The kind of science

Klingman was engaged in had little place for that kind of reasoning. He had also advised Hoffner to continue wearing protective eyewear or gauze covering if he should return to Berlin before Lake Havel had risen at least four centimeters (4 cm) from a "cleansing rain." Until then, Berlin would still be recovering.

Hoffner took the last turn onto Göhrener Strasse and tried to ignore the freezing damp that seemed to be in every fold of his suit. He imagined the relief of the late Herr Professor Doktor Klingman on hearing of the torrential downpour: thus far for Hoffner, though, it had managed to produce only a dull pain in his lower back, thus making the driving all the more uncomfortable. Young Hermann had been kind enough to leave the keys to the Daimler on the seat. Hoffner guessed the boy might not be needing them for quite some time.

Sifting through the last hour in his head—and its myriad implications—Hoffner had come to the bold conclusion that he needed a hot bath. Anything beyond that was a muddle: films, sound, sex, tanks—it was all too much to make sense of. There was also the matter of a change of clothes—it had been days on that—and he suspected that distractions like these were good for him. He had no idea why, but what was the point in worrying about that?

He took the steps up to his flat and reckoned it to be somewhere past one in the morning: Schiller, his landlord, usually kept the phonograph running until after midnight, but the place was silent. Hoffner fumbled with his keys—his hand had gone stiff from the brick and the chill—but he finally managed to get the door open. Almost at once, the smell of spoiled meat wafted out. He couldn't remember whether he had tossed out the last of Maria's meal before heading off the other night. It was all a blur now, but the thought of opening a window to air the place out was just too much. Instead, he dropped his coat and jacket on the floor and headed for the bathroom.

Flicking on the light, Hoffner stared at himself in the mirror. The scabbing around his mouth had risen in nice red blotches from the cold, but at least the cheek was beginning to lose its color. He peered in to take a closer look and caught sight of something else in the reflection. It was the edge of the bathtub. It looked as though there was water in it.

Hoffner turned and saw Leni's lifeless face staring back at him. Her head lay propped up against the far wall, her breasts hovering above the water. A single bullet hole nestled just below her chest.

Hoffner found himself on his knees, vomiting. Leaning over on his hands, he waited for the second wave, but it never came. He spat and waited again. When his legs finally began to give out, he slumped down and leaned against the wall of the tub. Leni's hand hung loosely over the edge, the white of her fingers now streaked a pale blue. Hoffner stared at them: it was as much of her as he could bring himself to look at.

The door to the bathroom slowly inched forward, and Alby Pimm appeared above him. Pimm stared down at Hoffner—an oddly consoling look on his face—and said quietly, "What the hell have you done, Nikolai?"

HOFFNER SAT AT THE KITCHEN TABLE in his robe as Pimm hung the last of the wet clothes over a chair. Hoffner had no idea how he had gotten here.

"Drink it, Nikolai," said Pimm as he pulled over another chair and sat. He nodded at a glass of whiskey on the table. It was only then that Hoffner noticed it. He cupped his hand around the glass for nearly half a minute before bringing it to his lips and tossing it back. He winced at the sudden heat in his throat. Pimm pushed over a second, but Hoffner shook his head.

"When was the last time you ate?" Pimm said.

Hoffner continued to stare at the floor. "You're very concerned with that tonight, aren't you—my eating?"

Pimm reached for an empty glass on the shelf. "Why couldn't you just do what I asked you to do, Nikolai?"

"Asked or told, Alby?"

Pimm uncorked the bottle. "That's who you are, isn't it?" Pimm was beyond accusations: he was simply stating the truth.

Hoffner nudged the empty glass across the table. He saw Leni's envelope lying at the far side.

Pimm said, "It was in your coat."

Hoffner pulled the robe tighter around his chest. The booze was helping to clear his head. "When did you get here?"

"About half an hour before you did."

"And she was here?"

Pimm nodded as he poured himself a glass.

"You just sat in the dark?"

"I did." Pimm took a sip.

"Best to let me find her myself, is that it?"

"Something like that."

Hoffner turned to the window and pulled back the shade. He noticed a cat sleeping on one of the stoops. It might have been a pile of rags. He couldn't tell. "She played it well," he said.

"Obviously not."

"And according to you, that's my fault." He let go of the shade.

A bit of whiskey had spilled on the table, and Pimm set his glass down in the small pool. "Tell me, did you have the slightest idea what she was doing?" He began to spin the edge in the liquid. "I'm just wondering, given that she's dead in your tub."

Hoffner hadn't the energy for rage. It sat in his jaw like coiled rope. "To hell with you, Alby."

Inexplicably Pimm managed a grin. "That's not even an issue anymore." He let go of the glass. "I'd always hoped you wouldn't be join-ing me. Who knows, maybe you'll be fine. Stupidity might just be the way to salvation." Hoffner raised a weak fist to strike him, but Pimm caught the wrist and held it there. His grip was remarkably firm. "Are we done crying for ourselves, Nikolai, or are you going to find another way to muck this up?"

Hoffner caught sight of the red and blue on his own knuckles—remnants from his recent spate of beatings—and realized how stupid he must have looked. Pimm was being kind: he was actually taking this seriously. Hoffner unclenched his hand, and Pimm released. For some reason, Hoffner noticed a burn mark on the table. He began to run his thumb across it. It was old and soft—softer than he imagined. "She said she'd be back in a week."

Pimm finished his glass. "Then I imagine she would have been. She might even have stayed."

Hoffner's nail now scraped across the burned wood, digging into it until his thumb began to ache. His throat tightened. "I've got nothing now," he said. "For the first time, absolutely nothing."

"Please." Pimm shook his head even as he looked away. "Don't tell me we're going down this road—the sad cop who's lost the girl."

"Shut up, Alby." Hoffner looked over. "The case. I'm talking about the case. I can't see it and I don't know why."

Pimm brought out his cigarettes. "You do know why, Nikolai. It's lying in your tub."

Hoffner was finding his rage. "Don't."

Pimm lit up. "You haven't even thought to ask why they brought her here."

"I said don't." When Pimm smiled and shook his head, Hoffner said, "Who?"

"Who what?" Pimm was done coddling. "Who brought her here? Jesus, Nikolai, what have you been doing for the past four days?"

Hoffner's head was clear, and Pimm looked so small sitting across from him. "You tell me."

Pimm let go with a frustrated laugh. "You don't even know why she was in Berlin, do you?"

Hoffner stood and grabbed Pimm by the collar, hoisting him off the ground. He could hear himself grunting at the strain of it as he slammed Pimm into the bathroom door, and yet he felt nothing: Pimm was weightless, limp. Hoffner tossed him onto the tile— something shattered behind them—and his head filled with the sound of his own labored breath. "The device," Hoffner finally said, struggling for air. He wasn't sure if Pimm had punched him in the gut or if his lungs had given out on their own. Either way, he bent over with his hands on his knees. "It was for the device," he said. "For the Americans." He waited and then spat. "No reason other than that." Hoffner sucked in and waited for Pimm to have done with him.

Instead, Pimm sat quietly. He spat out something of his own: it was blood. Hoffner turned to see him sticking out his tongue. It was oddly pink. Hoffner had never noticed that before.

"You're a son of a bitch, Nikolai." Pimm's finger began to make the rounds inside his mouth. "And you've got me bleeding. How the fuck did you do that?" He winced somewhere along the lower gum and said, "Jesus." He pulled the finger out and spat again.

Hoffner got himself to the toilet. He sat and propped his elbows on his knees. He then dropped his head to his hands. His neck was throbbing. "We need to cover her," he said.

Pimm was slumped against the tub. "That's your biggest concern, is it?"

"At the moment, yes." Hoffner pulled two towels from the rack. They were damp and stale. He sat up, then stood. Stepping over to the tub, he laid the first across her torso, impossible not to notice the smoothness of her skin, her eyes mercifully shut. He saw the marks on her arms where he had grabbed her, a string of red welts amid the gray. He thought to reach for them—it was the last time he had held her. Instead, he opened the second towel and draped it across her face.

Pimm spat again. "Better?" he said.

Hoffner turned to him and said, "Did you break a glass?"

Pimm looked up and reached out his hand. "I think that might have been you. Help me up." Hoffner pulled him to his feet, and Pimm stepped over to the mirror. Again Hoffner sat on the toilet and watched as Pimm opened his mouth wide to resume his search.

"I hate dentists, you know," Pimm said. He began to pull at his lip to get a better view: it garbled his words. "I hate that you lie there. Not so much for the teeth. It's that your balls are exposed, lying back, that little tray over your chest. And you can't even put your hands on them or they'll think there's something funny with you." He spat again and looked at Hoffner in the mirror. "Don't do that again, Niko-lai, all right?" Pimm ran the water, rinsed his mouth, and took a towel. "She was supposed to destroy the device. Find it, the blueprints, and destroy them both, and then take what was left back to the Ameri-cans. And we were doing everything we could to make sure that happened. That's why she was here."

Hoffner was done trying to piece it together. When Pimm contin-ued to rub the towel along his gums, Hoffner said, "You actually have it, don't you? Out in Wannsee."

Pimm flashed his teeth in the mirror. They were remarkably straight and white. "Something you didn't believe earlier tonight. Do you know how much a porcelain crown costs these days?"

"I'm sure you'll let me know how much I owe."

Pimm glanced at him in the mirror and laughed. "You think I pay for it?" He slipped the towel onto the rack and said, "You need to get dressed."

"I'll call your tailor."

Pimm turned. "No, you need to get up and get dressed now."

Hoffner found a pack of cigarettes in the pocket of his robe. He pulled it out, but it was empty. "Otherwise I end up in a tub someplace?"

Pimm said easily, "I'd do that one myself." Hoffner tossed the pack into the trash, and Pimm said, "Who do you think put her here?"

Hoffner imagined he might want to figure that one out sometime soon. Right now, though, it felt better just to sit. "Oh, I don't know," he said. "Fritz Lang, his wife, the great Al Jolson. They're all at the top of my list."

"You've mucked this one up nicely, Nikolai, so now you're going to help me fix it. You need to get dressed."

Hoffner said, "From where I'm sitting, Alby, it looks like you managed that pretty well on your own."

"Really? And how's that?"

"I've no idea," Hoffner said flatly. "I can't tell you why she was meant to destroy it—thanks, by the way, for that little piece of information—or why you've clearly had the thing the whole time, or who this 'we' is you like to refer to. I could probably put in a guess, but I just don't have the energy. The only thing I do know is that you decided to keep all of it to yourself until now. So that makes it your mess, not mine. You want to string me along, fine, but don't blame me when the string breaks."

Pimm might have shown a moment of remorse before saying, "She needed to destroy it, Nikolai, because the Americans needed it that way. They don't see it destroyed for themselves, they don't buy Ufa. And if they don't buy Ufa, someone else does. Making enough sense for you?"

It took Hoffner another few seconds to see through this: He shook his head in disgust.

Pimm nodded over at the tub. "Who do you think did that?"

Hoffner hated Pimm for drawing him back in. "That isn't what Hugenberg does, Alby."

"You're right. It isn't. That's why he has friends—those new political ones he's been bankrolling. Who do you think was standing guard outside the warehouses tonight?"

The image of Sascha and his comrades pissing on the university boys this morning filled Hoffner's head. He pushed it from his mind and said, "So this is about who gets Ufa? She's dead because someone wants another notch in his belt?"

"It's not as simple as that. We need to get you dressed."

Pimm started for the door, but Hoffner said, "Seems pretty simple." Stifled rage had a tendency to quiet his voice. "Another case of the Americans trying to buy up German industry, and you're working with the Americans. Well done."

Pimm waited before saying, "You don't want to go through this, Nikolai."

"No, I think I do."

Again Pimm waited. "Get dressed." When Hoffner refused to move, Pimm said, "It's not going to help." Hoffner continued to wait, and Pimm finally said, "Fine. You want to know?" He shook his head as he sat on the edge of the sink; he needed them beyond this. "The company," he said. "Mentor Bilanz. The one you were so eager to talk about tonight. I have no idea what it does except I get paid very well to ship various things across Europe. Right now it's bacon."

"We've been through this." Hoffner's voice remained quiet. "What does that have to do with her?"

"As a token of his thanks," Pimm said, ignoring the question, "Herr Alfred put me on the board. It was a joke to him, of course, but his cronies liked having a gangster as a silent partner. Made them feel somehow more dangerous. Made no difference to me. I was still making my money. Of course I could never attend the meetings—that would have been too ridiculous—but the mysterious LA Company went onto the letterhead, and they all had a good laugh."

"I never pegged you as someone who liked being the butt of a joke, Alby. I'll have to remember that."

"Yes, you do that," Pimm said coolly. "And I'll leave you to figure this out on your own, shall I? Given that you've been so brilliant up to this point." Hoffner said nothing, and Pimm continued. "A few months ago, a memorandum came my way. It wasn't meant to. Some clerk decided to send it to everyone on the letterhead. Rather clever finding an address for me. It came to the club, delivered on one of those silver trays. Very nice. It was a proposition from Hugenberg. He wanted to buy Ufa. Even I knew that made no sense. The company was bleeding money. Only a matter of time before the Americans were going to swallow the industry whole. But Herr Alfred said he'd gotten wind of something Ufa was developing. Something that could revolutionize sound production—and cripple the Americans all at the same time. What could be better than that? Of course he knew his board would need proof. So he promised to show them this miracle device before asking them to invest."

"And that's when you decided to help the Americans? That seems a little thin, Alby."

"You're right," said Pimm. "It wouldn't have been nearly enough had the whole business with Phoebus not fallen in my lap."

"I don't follow."

There was a single knock at the front door, followed by three more short raps, and Pimm made his way out into the kitchen. Hoffner heard a hushed conversation before two of Pimm's men stepped into the bathroom. They each nodded over at him and then gently lifted Leni out of the tub. Hoffner followed them back into the kitchen, where a carpet had been laid out. They set her down and, with four quick turns, rolled her up tight. Pimm said, "I'm guessing the Kripo will have a few detectives here in the next hour or so. An anonymous call implicating one of their inspectors in his own case." They hoisted her up, and Pimm nodded his men to the door. "Better for you if she isn't here, I think."

The boys maneuvered her out into the corridor and then pulled the door shut behind them. Hoffner listened as the footsteps receded. He then moved to the door. Only its silence convinced him she was gone.

THERE WAS STILL THE SECOND GLASS of whiskey on the table, and Hoffner now tossed it back. "You were telling me about Phoebus."

"She'll be sent back to the States," said Pimm. "That's the right thing to do, I think."

Hoffner refilled his glass and said, "Yah." He drank.

"You mind pouring me one of those?"

Hoffner spilled out two more, and Pimm said, "Your friends at Phoebus. They had something else Hugenberg needed shipped. Film stock. It was getting produced at their studio and then processed in Switzerland."

Hoffner saw where this was going. He handed Pimm his glass and said, "So the charade at your club. The projector that couldn't run the film—all of that was just to send me in search of Herr Vogt's sound device."

Pimm said, "The Fräulein needed a guide. We figured the Americans would believe a Kripo detective leading her to it."

Hoffner brought his glass to his lips. The whiskey had lost its smell. He set it down. "For fuck's sake, Alby, you should have told me."

"And expect you to help the Americans? Please. I know you better than that. She had to think she was playing you. That doesn't happen if you know."

Hoffner was losing what little strength he had. "Not my fault alone, then, is it?" Pimm said nothing, and Hoffner suddenly felt ridiculous standing in his robe. There might have been other reasons for it, but he chose to focus on the robe. "Why not just destroy the device yourself?"

Pimm was growing impatient. "Think, Nikolai. The Americans knew Ufa was after sound. They knew Ufa had come up with something that could revolutionize the way films are produced. The Americans find that out, and they know they need to stop it. The problem is, if the Americans don't destroy Vogt's sound device themselves, they don't make an offer. We couldn't just tell them, 'Hello there—we've gotten rid of the thing. Now come and buy the company.' They wouldn't have believed us. They couldn't risk making an offer and then having Ufa make fools of them by trotting out the device. We needed Fräulein Coyle to find it—with some help from you—so that the Americans would be certain that Ufa was completely vulnerable."

Hoffner shook his head. "That still doesn't explain why the Americans would want to destroy the thing in the first place. Why not ship it back to the States, use it—and then buy out Ufa?"

"Because they can't use it," said Pimm, growing more frustrated. "They're committed to sound on disc. This is sound on film. It would cost them too much to change horses now."

"You're quite the expert."

"No, I know the same as you—just without the distractions."

Hoffner ran both his hands across his face. There was too much spinning through his head. He needed to simplify. "So why help the Americans? Why not Hugenberg?"

Pimm had yet to take a drink. He stared into his whiskey, then took a sip. "I might not be much of a believer, Nikolai," he said. "But when some lunatic's grand plan includes my elimination, I tend to take notice." He finished the glass and set it down.

"What?"

"Hugenberg's friends. The thugs at the warehouses. They're a charming bunch. I believe you've met them."

Hoffner always managed to forget this little piece to Pimm: the criminal Jew. Still, it hardly made sense. "They're fringe, Alby. They'll be gone in a year."

"Really? When was the last time Hugenberg stepped out onto the fringe? If this is who he's getting into bed with, then, yes—I'll take the Americans every time."

"And that's it?" Hoffner said, unconvinced. "Hugenberg throws some money at a bunch of Jew-baiters and you decide he shouldn't get his paws into Ufa? Not that I question your noble streak, Alby—"

"Don't push it, Nikolai."

"But I also know you better than that. You've had a man at the Phoebus warehouses for weeks—watching, waiting. That's how you knew to come here." Hoffner held Pimm's gaze: it was only then that he began to see it. "You have no idea what's inside them, do you?"

Pimm's stare was no less firm. "I'm guessing you do, though."

"And that's the reason you're here—aside, of course, from coming to my rescue with the Kripo. Very gallant of you." For the first time in hours, Hoffner felt his strength returning. "You couldn't find your way inside the warehouses, could you?"

Pimm looked mildly amused by the question. "Of course I could have gotten inside. What do they have—two men on the perimeter of each building? Walk-arounds every twenty minutes? It's a Luger for each of them, except for the little one who likes a rifle. I've been told he fires it into the sky when he drinks too much. Everything in six-hour shifts. Very exact. Very precise. It would have taken us ten minutes—at most—to get in."

"Then why didn't you?"

"Because the only person in Berlin who could do that, Nikolai—

aside from you and your friends in the Kripo—is me. And Hugenberg knows that. I take those warehouses and I've started a war, and I'm not sure that's what I want just now. Besides, everything else was moving so smoothly, why take the risk?"

Hoffner said with mock sincerity, "Yes, you're so unwilling to take risks."

"She doesn't know her limits anymore, Nikolai." Pimm spoke with a distant anger. "She doesn't know when to say, 'Enough.' "

Hoffner had no idea what Pimm was talking about. "Who doesn't?"

"Berlin," Pimm said. He sat back against the edge of the table and let his eyes drift to the floor. He stayed like that for nearly half a minute before saying, "Used to be, things would get a little wild, a new craze, and she'd find a way to rein herself back in. She doesn't seem to know how to do that anymore."

"And that's Hugenberg's fault?"

Pimm looked up. "Things run best when everyone has their own bit. I like the five districts and down to the wharves. Gröbnitz has the slaughterhouses, north through Wedding. The Sass brothers work west and south of the Hallesches Gate. And for some reason Frimmel loves the west. I don't know how he makes any money with it, but it's not my concern."

"I know how the syndicates work, Alby."

"Do you? Then you know how Berlin works. How we all watch each other. Hugenberg doesn't. He wants to have all the newspapers? Fine. The telegraphs as well? All right—I suppose that makes sense. And now he wants the films? And maybe that wouldn't be a problem, except the sort of thing he's got going down at those warehouses smells a lot like what I would be doing down there. Truck deliveries in the middle of the night. Trucks with the old Krupp factory insignia painted over." He pulled out a cigarette and tongued the tobacco. "I don't know what it is. Maybe he's running guns, black-market munitions—we've all been trying to get a hand in since Versailles clamped down. It's good money if you know what you're doing. But all of that is how I run my interests. It's not the way he's meant to run his, with his factories and his letterheads and his boards of directors. So I'm just wondering if Hugenberg is stepping out. Add to that these new friends of his—and that's no small concern for me, Nikolai. These people stink of a corruption to their very core. Just look at the films they make. You can't have things running that way. And if I don't make that clear to him now, then maybe Hugenberg thinks he can take it all. And then Berlin ceases to exist."

"Your Berlin, Alby."

"No, Nikolai." Pimm was now staring directly at him. "Our Berlin. You need it this way as much as I do." He finally lit up. "It's already slipping away. That's why you've lost your footing on this one." He exhaled a stream of smoke and said, "Now what does he have in those warehouses?"

The ring of the telephone startled them both. Hoffner waited for the second ring, then the third, before stepping over and picking up. It was the desk sergeant at the Alex. "Yes?"

"There's been an incident, Herr Chief Inspector."

Inexplicably Hoffner's mind raced to Georg. "An incident—where?"

"Your office, Herr Chief Inspector."

It took him a moment to answer. "What are you saying?"

"Two men. They tried to—"

"When?" said Hoffner.

"I—I don't know, Herr Chief Inspector. Maybe twenty minutes ago."

"Did they take anything?"

There was a pause. "Take . . . I don't think so."

"What do you mean you don't think so?" Hoffner stared across at Pimm.

"It's not clear at this time, Herr Chief Inspector. They did, however—well, they've left something."

The man was getting more irritating by the minute. "And what was that?"

There was another pause. "Best if you come down and see it, Herr Chief Inspector."

Hoffner let out a frustrated breath. "And you have them?"

The last pause was almost too much. "Unfortunately, we weren't able to—"

"Jesus Christ." Hoffner tried to think. "Post a man at my office, Herr Sergeant. I'll be there in half an hour. And try to keep track of anyone leaving the building—if that's not too much trouble for you."

TWENTY MINUTES LATER Pimm shut the car door behind them and yelled to his man: "Alexanderplatz." The driver pulled out, and Pimm said, "You're sure it's tanks?"

Even the short run across the street had soaked them both. Hoffner shook out his hat. "Well, it could have been a new type of tram, Alby. The big guns would certainly clear traffic quickly." Hoffner set his hat on the seat. "Yes. Tanks. Not exactly what you were expecting, was it?"

Hoffner braced for another outburst, but Pimm just sat there, nodding absently. It became unnerving, and Hoffner said, "You're telling me you had no idea? Even with the Navy connection—none of it?" Pimm remained lost in thought, and Hoffner said, "I should have checked the other building. That was stupid. Who knows what he's got in there."

Pimm suddenly found his focus and barked at his man, "Stop with the turns, idiot. Just straight down. What traffic are we avoiding at two in the morning?"

"That's right," said Hoffner. "Blame your boy. After all, he was the one keeping watch on those warehouses, wasn't he?"

Pimm snorted. "Shut up, Nikolai." He began to shake his head. "What the hell is he doing building tanks?"

"Oh, I don't know," Hoffner said as he pulled a soggy cigarette from his pocket. "An old monarchist with more money and power than he knows what to do with—and he wonders where it all went wrong." He tried to light it. "His Berlin's gone, too, Alby, and crying about it in his newspapers and the Reichstag obviously isn't getting the job done. My guess, he's found another way to get it back."

"By putting tanks on the street? Please."

"Would you put it past him?" Hoffner made one last effort before tossing the cigarette to the floor. "Jolson changes the world, and Herr Hugenberg gets all the sound stages he wants—to build whatever he wants. I'd call that being a very clever man."

"I've met him," said Pimm. "He's not that clever."

"Really? All of this, Alby—the films, the sound, the sex—Hugenberg doesn't care about any of that. He might put a few talking newsreels in a theater, let the novelty of that distract everyone while he gets his message out, but he's after much bigger things. All of this was so he could build his tanks. That's why he needs Ufa. And his new political friends—doing exactly what he tells them to do—they just make that easier for him."

"He gets nothing without that device." Pimm's arrogance was losing its edge. "She wouldn't have told them, would she?"

Hoffner rummaged for another cigarette. "Who?"

"The American—your friend. She wouldn't have said anything to Hugenberg's boys?"

"About what?" Hoffner gave up the search.

"About Wannsee, Nikolai. About Lang." Pimm was getting tired of pulling him along. "What else would I be talking about?"

The thought of Leni's last few minutes only now crossed Hoffner's mind. She had looked so peaceful in the tub. Cling to that, he thought.

Again Pimm barked at his man: "Take the next left. We're heading out to Wannsee. Scher—"

"No," said Hoffner with a newfound focus. "It's forty minutes to get there, even at this hour. You call Lang from the Alex. Either he answers or he doesn't, and we take it from there." He leaned forward. "We're going straight on."

POLICE HEADQUARTERS were surprisingly lively for almost half past two. Two Schutzis were posted at the entrance. Neither looked as if he had held a gun—let alone fired one—in the last thirty years, but at least they were upright. The desk sergeant also had company: two junior detectives were looking very busy while doing absolutely nothing.

"You have men at the back doors?" Hoffner said as he walked up. The two detectives looked at each other, then at the sergeant.

"Well, Sergeant?" one of them said. "The chief inspector has asked—"

Hoffner broke in. "He heard me, Detective. Get men in the alleys. Not that it'll make any difference now." Hoffner checked the clock above the desk and signed himself in. He began to move off when one of the detectives said, "Herr Chief Inspector." Hoffner stopped. The boy was looking at Pimm. "That's—" The detective leaned into Hoffner and whispered, "That's Alban Pimm."

"Really?" said Hoffner in full voice. "Then I've been terribly misinformed. He told me he was Charlie Chaplin. You'll stay down here, Detective, just in case the rest of his crew shows up dressed as the Tiller Girls."

Upstairs, a large guard was posted outside Hoffner's office. This one looked menacing enough. If not for the closed eyes he might actually have served as a deterrent.

"You're relieved, Sergeant," said Hoffner. The man's eyes bolted open as he tried to focus. "Get us some coffees. Black."

The man managed a clipped nod before darting off down the hall. Hoffner stepped into his office with Pimm behind him.

There was almost nothing to indicate anyone had been here. The books stood at their usual odd angles on the shelves, as did the stacks of papers across the floor. The only glaring difference was on the blank wall, which Pimm was now staring at as he picked up the telephone. "That's charming," he said, the words WONDER WHO WE'LL BE CALLING ON NEXT? written in a thick black ink. For some reason the word "calling" was underlined in red. "And so well thought out," said Pimm.

Hoffner was checking the rest of the office. "You'd think they would have put the emphasis on 'next.'" A small jar with two bones in formaldehyde lay knocked on its side. Hoffner stood it upright. "Obviously we're not dealing with geniuses here. Still, it makes its point."

The operator came on, and Pimm said, "I need you to connect me with Wannsee 772 . . . Well, I don't recognize your voice either, Fräulein . . . Yes, I know it's late . . ." Pimm thrust the receiver at Hoffner, who was kneeling at the filing cabinets. Hoffner took the telephone and said, "This is Chief Inspector Hoffner. You'll be good enough to connect the line." The numbers began to click through, and Hoffner handed the telephone back.

Pimm again stared at the wall as he waited. "And that's it?" he said. "They break in to send this terribly threatening message."

Hoffner was down to the last of the drawers. "They didn't break in, Alby. Incompetent as those Schutzis may be, no one breaks into the Alex. No one's that stupid." Hoffner slid the drawer closed: nothing was out of place. "The boys who did this were already inside. They just happened to get caught in the act." He stood and stepped around to the desk.

"Bad cops?" said Pimm.

Hoffner started in on the next set of drawers. "What a surprise that would be. Not that you've had any experience with those." Hoffner opened the bottom drawer: even the whiskey bottle and glass were untouched. "These cops aren't the types you deal with, anyway. They aren't in it for the bribes." He shut the drawer and scanned the office again. "My guess, these boys are young." The mirror on the far shelf was off-center: chances are it had been that way for months. "Young, impatient, and with a taste for politics. They were probably at the Pharus Hall the other night."

"That's comforting to hear."

"Yah."

"It's still ringing."

Hoffner peered around the edge of the desk. "Telephones tend to do that at three in the morning." There was something there.

"It's only quarter to."

"You be sure to explain that to Lang when he picks up." Hoffner dropped down and angled his body around to get a better look. He saw it almost at once. Had he been thinking clearly, this was where he should have looked first.

Of the four piles of film canisters stacked on the floor three nights ago only two remained. The young politicos had evidently spent too

much of their time on the artwork and not enough on what they had
been sent to steal.

"It's here," said Hoffner. He began to set the canisters on the desk.
"There's a ledger," he said to Pimm, "at the back of the third drawer
in the cabinet. I need you to get it."

Pimm kept the telephone to his ear as he opened the drawer
and began to dig through. "Yes, Fräulein," he said into the receiver.
"Yes, I know." He pulled out the book. "Just let it ring." He tossed
the ledger onto the desk and cupped the mouthpiece. "No one's
answering."

Hoffner stacked the last of them and stood. He opened the ledger
to the page with Leni's list and said, "I need you to read the names on
the canisters, see which ones they've taken." Pimm said nothing, and
Hoffner said, "You can put the telephone down, Alby. Obviously no
one's going to answer."

Pimm seemed unwilling to move. "You do understand that no
answer means—"

"Means what?" Hoffner said evenly. "That the Langs are heavy
sleepers? That they're both dead and your device is gone? Not much
we can do about either from here." He began to sift through the top
drawer for a pen. "If you think it'll make any difference, call your
boys. Let them take a drive out to Wannsee."

Pimm's stare hardened. "I'm not sure you've been paying attention,
Nikolai. That device is—"

"Is what?" Hoffner looked up. He was tired, wet, and the booze
was beginning to abandon him. "Don't insult us both by trying to play
at detective now, Alby. This is what they came to get. This is what they
thought was worth rummaging through an office in the Alex for. So
this is what we focus on."

"Really? And if Lang and the device are gone?"

"Then Hugenberg's beaten you before you begin. This is what his boys came for. We need to know why."

The large sergeant had somehow reappeared at the door and was doing what he could with an awkward cough. He held a mug of coffee in each hand. He said, "I can get some cream if you like, Herr Chief Inspector." His voice was thinner than his large body deserved. "Or sugar?"

Hoffner looked past Pimm and said, "You didn't happen to see any of them, did you, Sergeant?"

The boy was either at a loss or exhausted. Whichever it was, he was useless. "See who, Herr Chief Inspector?"

"The men who were in my— Never mind. Just set the coffees on the desk." Hoffner started in on the second drawer in search of a pen.

The boy moved past Pimm, and his eyes widened. He nearly bumped into the desk as he leaned over to Hoffner. "Herr Chief Inspector," he whispered, nodding his head back over his shoulder. "You know that's Alban—"

"Yes, Sergeant, I know." Hoffner felt something promising wedged in at the back. "I've finally caught him. We'll have a big party tomorrow. Now just put the coffees down."

The sergeant nodded awkwardly and did as he was told. Hoffner yanked on the pen, and a nice stream of coffee spilled over the edge and onto the desk.

"Oh no," said the sergeant. "Oh God, no."

Hoffner looked at the desk. Luckily the coffee had missed the canisters. The liquid was pooling around various scraps of paper. "It's all right, Sergeant," said Hoffner. "You're fine. Not your fault. Just go get us a—"

"Yes," said the boy frantically. "A rag. Right away, Herr Chief Inspector." He quickly dashed past Pimm, and Hoffner found himself holding on to a thin steel pipe. Where the hell was a pen?

He set it down and began to lift the papers out of the coffee. He glanced through them to make sure he wasn't throwing anything vital away. These were the switchboard messages from Georg this afternoon. He might have tossed them out en masse, except he recalled that each had consisted of the single line "Get in touch." This one had more on it. He checked the time signature: 7:45 p.m. Apparently it had come in after the meeting with Bagier. Hoffner placed the note on the desk and spread it out, doing what he could to wipe away the liquid with the back of his hand. The ink was smeared, but he managed to make it out:

HAVE LINKS TO THYSSEN MEETINGS. KURT DALUEGE, LUDWIG RICHTER, RUDOLF HESS. WILL GET IN TOUCH. TOMORROW.

As always, there was the caller's name:

GEORG HOFFNER

The boy had gone back to dig up more. Hoffner wondered if he had done it to clear Leni or to damn her—either way, it made no difference now: Pimm had already told him who had been making the films back at the flat. Granted, Hoffner might not have recognized the names Richter and Hess, but Daluege was Goebbels's man. His signature had been prominently displayed on the Ostara Company documents.

Hoffner was about to toss it with the rest when he stopped. There was a sudden stillness in the room; in fact, everything around him seemed to stop as he stared at the paper.

This one had been on top of the pile for anyone to see. KURT DALUEGE, LUDWIG RICHTER, RUDOLF HESS. And below them, GEORG HOFFNER.

Hoffner continued to stare at his son's name.

It was impossible to think that Hugenberg's boys would have

missed this, not with their own compatriots' names gazing up at them. Hoffner suddenly glanced up at the wall and again saw the red streak under the word "calling."

A panic crept into the stillness. There had been no mistake in emphasis. The artwork hadn't been meant for him. It had been meant for Georg—for the caller.

Hoffner's head went numb. They would go after the boy now. They would find him, just as they had found Martha eight years ago: another message for his own recklessness.

"We need to take these," he said as he began to stuff as many of the canisters as possible into his coat pockets.

Pimm was still on the telephone. His confusion gave way to concern. "So we *are* heading out to Wannsee?"

Hoffner scanned the floor. He saw a large leather bag filled with God-knows-what and quickly stepped over. Dumping it out, he slid the rest of the canisters and the ledger in and, without another word, bolted by Pimm. The sergeant was halfway down the hall, saying something, but Hoffner heard none of it. He pushed past him and began to run.

THE MYSTERY SOLVED

THE RAIN HAD TURNED TO SNOW, swirls of it like moths circling the lamps out in the square. It might have been the cold, or the shock of the whiteness all around him, but Hoffner only now realized he had no way of getting to Georg: no trams, no cabs. He was still struggling for breath as he pulled at his coat collar, the snow already thick on the wet wool. Turning back to the Alex, he nearly bumped into a wheezing Pimm.

"That was clever," Pimm said, his hand in the air for his car. "Leaving me unescorted. I think your big sergeant thought he was going to arrest me. What the hell is going on?"

The car pulled up, and Hoffner leaned into the driver's window. "Cranachstrasse," he said. He got in and barked, "Now." Pimm was barely inside before the car lurched away. Even so, Pimm knew enough to keep things calm. "So we're heading south," he said. "And why is that?"

Hoffner was still clutching at the leather bag. He dropped it to the floor and leaned forward insistently. "Can we take this any faster—put some weight behind it?"

Pimm caught sight of his man's eyes in the mirror and nodded. He then grabbed on to the seat strap as the car began to swerve with its newfound speed.

Pimm said quietly, "Roads are a bit dicey, Nikolai. Might be an idea to get there in one piece."

"My son," said Hoffner. "Georg. He left a note." Hearing it aloud only drove the knife in deeper. "I think they know he's involved."

The car careened around a turn, and Pimm called out, "Alive, Heinrich." The car slowed, and Pimm said, "And is he?"

Hoffner felt everything folding in on him, the weight of his own arrogance like a vise pressing down on his head. He alone was responsible for this. I've killed him, he thought. I've killed them both. There was no escaping Leni now. And for what? He knew there could be no answer—there would never *be* an answer. This was a self-damning too brutal to see beyond, and not for the pain of it—familiar and thus comforting—but for the absolute silence it would bring. And that terrified him.

Pimm said, "They lock up the Gymnasiums pretty tight at night, Nikolai." He was showing a surprising compassion. "Not likely they'd find their way in."

Hoffner snapped his head up. He had completely forgotten this: the boy wasn't at the Gymnasium; he hadn't been for months. The momentary reprieve filled his lungs, and Hoffner held on to it like a drowning man who believes in that single breath beyond his last.

CRANACHSTRASSE WAS EMPTY: better still, there were no tire tracks in the snow. The place was all lifeless trees, iron lamps, and powdered stoops. Hoffner pointed the driver to the building and leaped out before the car had come to a stop. He took the stairs two at a time and pressed the bell, glancing up, hoping to see a light. Everything remained unbearably still.

He pressed the bell again, and Pimm suddenly appeared at his side, pulling something from his coat pocket.

"A gift from the boys," said Pimm: it was a picklock, gold, with the initials *AP* etched into the gilt. " 'A little alderman for the Little Alderman.' I've never actually used it." He flipped out the two claws and within seconds had the door open. "Nice to see you never lose your touch."

Hoffner raced in and up the stairs. By the time he heard the sound of shuffling feet beyond Georg's door, Pimm was just making it to the fourth-floor landing.

"Yes?" said a tired voice.

Hoffner whispered, "It's Nikolai. Nikolai Hoffner. Open up."

The door slid back, and Georg stood there in his robe, bleary-eyed. Instantly Hoffner pulled him in tight. They had no precedent for this, at least not without sufficient booze to let it seem something other than it was. Hoffner grasped at the boy's back, the ribs and shoulder blades now padded by muscle and weight. For Hoffner, though, he felt something else, something long gone—the tiny-boned back, the chest concave, the cheek smooth against his own. He kissed the boy on the neck and whispered, "You're all right, then," and let go.

Georg stared at his father, his fatigue matched only by his confusion. He looked at Pimm and—with nothing better to offer—said, "Hello there."

Pimm smiled awkwardly. "I'll take a pass on the embrace."

Georg blinked some life into his eyes. "Fair enough." He stepped back and said, "I'm guessing you want to come in."

Hoffner followed the boy inside. His mind was fighting to find its focus. "You need to get your things. We need to go."

Georg was at the sofa, tossing various bits of clothing and paper onto the floor. "It's not that much of a sty, is it?" He sat.

"We need to go."

"Yes, you've said that."

"Look—Georgi"—Hoffner chafed at the word—"I'm trying to protect you here."

Georg swept something off the sofa's arm. "That'd be a first."

"I need you to listen to me."

Georg looked at his father. "And that would be part of the protecting, would it?"

The relief at seeing his son alive was losing its pull. "I never said I was any good at it."

"No," said Georg. "You never did." He dug his hands into the pockets of his robe. "So—what is it you're protecting me from?"

Hoffner felt suddenly parched. "You wouldn't have any water, would you?" Georg nodded to the sink, and Hoffner stepped over to fill a glass. He said, "Your flatmate should probably come as well."

"He's not here," said Georg. "He has a girl. She sneaks him in."

"I bet she does," said Pimm.

Hoffner shot a glance at Pimm. "This is Alby. He's a criminal." Georg and Pimm exchanged nods, and Hoffner said, "You were right. She was after something else." When Georg yawned, Hoffner said, "She's dead, by the way." Hoffner drank.

Georg did his best to show nothing. "Then I'm sure Albert will be disappointed. He was rather fond of her." When Hoffner stared vacantly, Georg said, "Albert . . . My flatmate . . . His girl." This didn't seem to help. "A joke."

Hoffner threw his glass against the wall, and the water and glass splattered on Georg's head. Instantly Georg leaped up and shouted, "What the hell are you doing?"

"Since we're making jokes," Hoffner said, "I thought I'd give it a try. Yours was funnier, I imagine."

Georg was still in shock as he shook the water from his hair. He pulled something off his robe and flicked it to the ground. "That was glass," he said.

"Are you bleeding?" Hoffner said coldly.

Georg was no kinder. "No."

"Then you should probably change. You're sopping wet. We'll wait."

"Look," Georg said, "I'm sorry your American friend is dead. I'm sorry you didn't manage to protect her as well as you clearly seem intent on protecting me"—the word sounded so cruel in his mouth— "but I think you missed your chance. On both of us."

"Georg. Listen. Please." A desperation began to creep in. "You're involved with this. The message you left at the Alex tonight—it connects you."

"The message?" Georg looked only slightly more concerned. "Fine. So you and the operator know I've done some poking around." He looked at Pimm. "And this fellow here. I'm not sure why that—"

"The people who killed her think you know far more than you do. Please, Georgi." It had come to begging, thought Hoffner: How much more self-contempt could he take? "Do what I'm asking you to do."

The boy's resolve showed a moment's hesitation. "Just like that?"

Hoffner spoke almost in a whisper. "Yes. Just like that. Please."

Georg heard the fear in his father's voice. He looked at Pimm, who remained perfectly still; in fact, the man barely seemed to breathe. Georg finally turned back and said, "We're done throwing glasses for the night?" Hoffner said nothing, and Georg stood silently. "Fine," he said. "I'll change."

Hoffner watched as the boy disappeared into the bedroom. He then turned on the tap and filled another glass. Pimm said, "I've got a few places he can stay. Send some of my boys—"

"No," said Hoffner. "I have a place." He drank. "Don't worry. It's on the way out to Wannsee."

THE GRAVEL YARD and garden looked almost cheery under the snow. It was a lie. The windows in the building above—blackened by soot and decay—deflected whatever charm there might have been in the untouched white. The snow that streaked the gray stone disappeared instantly, as if the walls themselves had lost the will to sustain even such tiny flecks of life as these. Hoffner pressed the bell.

Upstairs, it rang in a dream—as a train whistle that seemed to be drawing closer and closer—until her eyes opened and she saw the outline of the small table at her feet, the bed beyond it where Frau Rudzinsky lay with her silk pillowcases and her heavy breathing. Somewhere farther on—almost to the window—a body stirred, but Rokel Hoffner knew that most of these would hear nothing. The bell could ring for hours and never pierce their aging silence. She thought to get up, but reckoned that Herr Läbsohn would do that: handyman, night watchman, so pathetic in the way he took pleasure in making her feel older than she was. It was always that way with the bald, so ashamed of their own deformity, taking it out on the sick and the old and the not so old. Läbsohn was a dreadful little man, and she was pleased to know he would be dragging himself out of bed for this.

The bell rang again, and a light flicked on somewhere down the hallway. A thin crease of it edged its way through her half-opened door. A moment later the ringing stopped, and its absence filled her ears until she heard a group of voices rising on the stairway. They were muffled at first.

"Go back to bed, Herr Sluparov," Läbsohn whispered in an appalling Russian. "This doesn't concern you."

Rokel Hoffner lay back down and, seconds later, sensed the door to her room pushing open behind her. She recognized the footfall even before she felt the hand on her shoulder.

"Mama?" Hoffner whispered. She continued to pretend sleep. He shook her again and said, "Mama—you need to wake up."

Without turning she said, "Is it Monday?" She waited and then looked up at him. "What time is it?"

"You're awake."

"What time is it?"

"A little past four."

"Really?" She could smell the liquor on his clothes. "Well, if you'd waited another half hour or so you would have found me downstairs." She peered past him and saw Läbsohn's outline at the door. There was another figure standing with him, but she didn't recognize it. "Yes, Läbsohn, it's my plate of cheese you always complain about finding in the morning. There's the mystery solved." She looked back at Hoffner. "And then I come up here until they wake us. What a treat that always is. This, I imagine, is better."

Hoffner nodded as if he had been listening. "Yes, very clever. I need a favor."

"Who's the other one with you?"

Hoffner said, "We'll wait outside for you to dress. Then we'll go downstairs."

"They're all deaf, Nikolai. And I wouldn't care if you woke them. Who's at the door?"

Hoffner hesitated before saying, "We'll be outside."

She flung back the blanket and edged her legs over the side. "It's a robe, Nikolai." She sat up and reached across to her chair. "And house shoes. Very elegant." She looked past him again as she slipped her arms through the sleeves. "We're done with you, Läbsohn. You can go now. At least someone's managed to get you up on time for a change." She stood, steadying herself before flicking her free hand in Läbsohn's direction. "I said push off, Läbsohn. Put some coal in those stoves, and maybe we'll have a cup of hot coffee this morning." She looked at Hoffner. "Honestly, Nikolai, I'm not coming if he's still here."

Hoffner turned, but Läbsohn already had his hands up in retreat. "Not to worry, *gnädige Frau*," Läbsohn said. "All is in order. Good night."

"And put a hat on that head," she said as Läbsohn disappeared into the hall. "It's disgusting to look at." She took hold of Hoffner's arm and slipped her feet into her shoes. She then walked with him to the door. Out in the hall she asked, "Who's this?" She had barely looked at the boy.

"Georg," Hoffner said. "Your grandson."

Rokel Hoffner slowed, then stopped. She refused to look over.

Georg finally said, "Hello, Oma. You look well."

She continued to stare ahead. "Do I?" Her sense of betrayal seemed even more impressive than usual. Hoffner felt the grip on his arm tighten. Even at eighty she still had the stamina to induce physical pain. "Why is he here, Nikolai?"

Hoffner said, "I thought you said you wanted to see him?"

She waited for her shoulders to find their usual tautness before turning to the boy. "You thought I was dead, didn't you?" When Georg said nothing, she prodded, "Well?"

Georg said, "I hadn't really thought about it, one way or the other. I gather you're alive."

There had always been something clever and disarming with this one. She did her best to ignore it. "You're tall," she said. "You'll be taller than him. He was small at your age. What are you, twenty, twenty-two?"

"You know how old I am, Oma."

"Yes, I'm sure I do." She began to walk. "What did he tell you?"

"Not much."

"He's very good at that, isn't he?" They reached the stairs and slowly began to make their way down. "Did he mention this is a place for Jews—for old Russian Jews?" Georg was a step behind, but Hoffner felt the boy's gaze even without turning. "Bit of a shocker, that," she continued. "Granny a Jew, which makes Papi a Jew, which makes— well, only a quarter Jew, Georgi. That's not so bad." They came to the second-floor landing and continued their way around.

Hoffner said, "Georg needs to stay with you for a few hours. He'll keep you company."

"I don't like company."

"You'll like it today. You can tell him all the horrible things I've done."

They began the last flight down. Hoffner felt more of her weight on his arm as they moved in silence: this time she needed all of her focus for the stairs. When they finally reached the bottom she said, "Only a few hours, Nikolai? That hardly seems enough time for all the horrible things." The corridor to the kitchen was off the main hall. She flicked on the light and led them through.

Hoffner said, "You'll manage to squeeze in enough, I think."

They stepped through to the kitchen, and she turned on the overhead light. "I'll certainly try."

Industrial stoves and sinks stood along the far wall, cabinets everywhere, with a long wooden table planted at the center. There was a smell of ammonia and garlic rising off the tile floor. She pulled back one of the stiff-backed chairs and said, "Sit down, Georg. You'll want something to eat."

She headed to the icebox, and Hoffner leaned into the boy. "She's frightened enough," he whispered. "She doesn't need to know why you're here."

Georg had his hands tucked under his thighs. "I'm a little unclear on that myself," he said. "Do you smell bacon? Why would Jews—"

"Nikolai," she called over, "I can't find it. The cheese. Läbsohn's probably hidden it in the back."

Hoffner walked over and began to rummage through the shelves. She said quietly, "You're all right, then?" It was the first hint of concern she allowed herself.

"I will be."

"And the boy?"

"Just keep him here."

He pulled out the plate, and she took his arm, not for support, only to hold it. He stood there, and she said more quietly, "You could stay. Just for a while. Make him feel better."

Even comfort came with a price with her. What made it worse was that she was right. He waited before stepping over to the table. "We'll have a proper visit when I get back," he said as he set the plate down. He thought to look at her, but why see the disappointment when he could feel it like one more sodden layer of wool on his back? He tried a pat on Georg's shoulder, but that, too, felt pointless. Moving to the door, he said, "It'll give me a chance to defend myself." And, daring a look—she was already at a cabinet, having forgotten him—Hoffner wondered if any of them believed that was possible anymore.

"Be safe, Papi," said Georg.

Hoffner looked at the boy and tried to imagine where he had learned his kindness.

PIMM WAS WAITING in the backseat of the car. Läbsohn had been good enough to let him use the telephone. The boys were on their way out to Wannsee.

Pimm said, "I've circled the ones that are missing." He handed Hoffner the ledger as the car pulled out. "Everything all right in there?"

Hoffner scanned the page. Not that any of these helped: first names, with only an initial for the last, hardly made the films a threat to the men who had produced them. Even so, they had broken into his office to get them. There had to be some leverage in that.

Pimm asked again, "So the boy'll be all right with her?"

Hoffner nodded absently.

Pimm said, "I had no idea she was still alive. What other secrets are you keeping from me?"

Hoffner began to glance through the uncircled names. "It's the last place they'd look," he said. "The last place they'd ever step foot inside—a home for old Jews. Even the boy didn't know."

"He'll thank you later, I'm sure."

Hoffner continued to scan the pages. "You met her once, I think?"

Pimm watched as Hoffner read. "I had that pleasure. At Martha's funeral. She told me I had good hair."

"She likes her hair."

"We had a conversation about Sascha and how he would lose his one day. She said that would upset her."

"I imagine it would."

"And has he?"

Hoffner stopped at one of the entries. It caught him momentarily off guard. "Did you see this?" he said.

Pimm was grinning as Hoffner looked up. Pimm said, "I wondered how long it would take you to find it."

"And there's a reel?"

Pimm nodded.

"You've looked at it?"

"It's not bad," Pimm said. "Considering she's close to forty. Not that there's much to see from a few frames held up in this light."

"But you managed."

"I had to make sure, didn't I? She has surprisingly large hands."

"You could tell that in a few frames?"

"Unless everything else in the film was especially small." He saw Hoffner's expression and said, "Fruit, Nikolai. She's naked and eating fruit. I'm sure it gets more involved after that."

"Yes, I'm sure it does. Does he know?"

"Who?"

"Lang."

Pimm shrugged. "I doubt it. She writes well. That's all Fritz cares about."

"It's a charming marriage, isn't it? Did he know about the films?"

Pimm shook his head. "It was all about the device for Fritz. How they were testing it really didn't concern him."

"If he's a fruit lover, he might be sorry he didn't take more of an interest." Hoffner closed the ledger and tossed it into the bag. "But you knew she was involved."

"I had my suspicions. Thyssen floating in a tub flew a little too close to home. Such an obvious threat."

"So Lang must have known as well."

"Even if he did . . ." Pimm didn't bother to finish the thought. "As I said, she writes well. I'm sure that makes Fritz very forgiving."

The car hit a rough patch of road, and the two bounced along. Pimm grabbed on to the seat strap and said, "He's not the only one with family links to these people, though, is he?"

Hoffner had taken hold of his own strap. He let the leather dig into the flesh of his palm. "No," he said, as if confessing a crime. "He's not."

"At least Sascha made it easy on you by using another name."

The car bounced up again, and Hoffner said, "Yah—that's a great comfort."

"You can't blame yourself for it."

"Can't I?" The road leveled out, and Hoffner said, "So—how long have you known?"

"Same as you," said Pimm. "The Pharus Hall. I hear it was a rather tender reunion."

"Radek was right. You really do have eyes everywhere." Hoffner realized too late what he had said: no point, though, in trying to hide it. "And speaking of sons," he said.

Pimm chuckled. It was completely unexpected. "Wouldn't it be nice to see him in that light? Give what I do a human touch."

"Radek seems to look at it that way."

"Does he?" Pimm actually had to think about this. "How very Greek of him. Maybe that's where he's from. I should probably gouge out his eyes or—" He shook his head. "Isn't that the price for betrayal?"

"He wasn't betraying you. He was trying to save you."

"Was he?"

"All right, I was trying to save you."

"Then I should probably start by gouging out something of yours."

Hoffner had expected the more ruthless Pimm. This seemed

almost playful. Hoffner said, "So Radek gets a pass on this one. I'm glad to hear it."

Again Pimm chuckled. "You're that concerned, Nikolai? That's what makes you the father, and me not." Hoffner felt an odd pleasure at hearing himself described as such, even if it was guilt alone that redeemed him. Pimm said, "Of course I do nothing to Radek, and not for the reasons you think." He hesitated and then bobbed a nod at Hoffner's crotch. "He's got nothing down there." He spoke with a quiet intensity. "I saw it once. Horrible. Just a tube to piss through. From the war. Not sure what he does with his heroin boys at night. At least he doesn't know I've seen it. So, yes, he gets a pass. He wants to think it's something else, let him."

Hoffner might have explained how much crueler it was to leave Radek living like that; or maybe it was just another twinge of that untried fatherly instinct, limited as it was. Either way, Hoffner knew to move on. "The other night," he said. "At the wharves. Radek was taking care of something. Tossing something in. What was it?"

Pimm shrugged as if he didn't remember. "Nothing to do with this." He turned to the window.

"Come on, Alby. What was Radek tossing in?"

Pimm continued to stare out. Finally he said, "A body, Nikolai. What else do you throw in a river?"

K.

TWO OF PIMM'S CARS were parked in the driveway, with one of his men poised on a running board. He held a tommy gun at his side and was finishing a cigarette as Pimm and Hoffner pulled up.

"Anything?" said Pimm through the window.

The man shook his head. "He was asleep when we got inside. Earplugs. Says he never hears the telephone. Little Franz and Tomas are doing the walk-arounds. Kurt has the back."

"Who's inside?"

Again the man shook his head. "He said he was fine. He was pretty clear on that."

Pimm looked as if he might tear into the man; instead, he took in a long breath and nodded. "Fine. He's a son of a bitch. I don't blame you."

The driver pulled up to the door, and half a minute later, Hoffner pressed the bell.

Pimm said, "He's going to make us wait. He thinks he's above all this. I should probably let him get shot just to teach him a lesson." The door opened, and Pimm was suddenly all smiles. "Fritz," he said, his arms opened wide for a hug. Hoffner had never seen Pimm so much as shake a hand before. "You must be furious."

Lang was standing in a long silk robe, his hair perfectly greased, the monocle at its usual perch. Only the stubble on his cheeks suggested anything was amiss. "Get inside, you little prick." His tone might have been another hint. Lang turned and headed in. Pimm and Hoffner followed.

"Hello, Detective," Lang said, not bothering to look around. "Thank you for all your brilliant work on this. I actually had faith in you, which makes me a rather stupid man."

They stepped through to a large living room. It had a vaulted ceiling with a balcony that stretched along all four sides. Medieval tapestries and framed film posters filled the walls, with a few more African trinkets thrown in to shake things up. Lang stopped by a side table that sported two enormous black wooden breasts engulfing a half-filled decanter of whiskey. "Drink, gentlemen?" he said as he poured himself a tall one and headed for a sofa by the piano. "I imagine you can get it yourselves." He sat on an angle and crossed his legs, the knee peeking out through the silk of the robe. Lang slowly adjusted the monocle and cocked his head back, just so.

Hoffner stepped over and poured himself a glass. "Does that actually work with actors?" he said. He pulled on one of the nipples and found the ice. "I mean, I think it's terribly intimidating—especially the way you rest your hand on your thigh—but I'm just wondering if it sets your actors and producers all atremble." Hoffner dropped two cubes into the glass. "It's certainly got me shaking in my pants." He took a drink.

Lang remained perfectly posed. "I know the woman's dead, Detective, so I can understand why you feel so inadequate—the need to posture in front of me. The motivation is obvious, if a little over the top."

Hoffner said, "And what's your excuse for it?"

"Enough," said Pimm. He tossed his hat onto a table and sat in the only chair that looked remotely comfortable. It wasn't. "We all know Nikolai's mucked this up, and we both know you and I had a hand in that. Where is it?"

Lang sat a moment longer before leaning forward and placing his glass on the table. "You'll need to move that hat, Alby. She hates water stains on the wood."

"Where is it?" Pimm repeated as he reached over and tossed his hat onto a chair.

"It's safe," said Lang. "No worries." He looked at Hoffner. "The young ones, Inspector. They tremble at anything. And the ones desperate to please."

A woman's voice cut in from the balcony: "So that would make you either a terrible judge of age, Fritz, or a terrible judge of character— or both—at least when it comes to the detective here." Hoffner looked up and saw Thea von Harbou standing by a spiral staircase. She was in a silk robe as well, and looked surprisingly more attractive than the last time he had seen her. She began to make her way down. "The question is," she continued, "how do you manage to survive as a director if you can't get either of those right?" She stopped on the last step and said, "Good evening, Detective—Alby. A pleasure to see you both."

Hoffner's surprise left him with only one response: "I'm afraid I can't say the same, Madame."

She laughed. "Oh, be a sport, Detective. If Fritz can forgive me, you certainly can. Or have I misjudged your character, too?" .

Hoffner looked at Lang, who put up a reassuring hand. "She's drunk, Inspector. Very drunk. Par for the course, given what she's been through tonight. She just happens to be exceptionally good at it." He looked over at her. "Wake up Marget, dear. You always like doing that. Tell her we want something to eat. Eggs, I think."

Von Harbou thought a moment. "What a good idea," she said, and headed for the hall. There was nothing in her speech or gait to give her away.

Hoffner waited until she was through the archway to say, "How far gone is she?"

"Not so far that she won't remember everything," said Lang. "It's just the pain she's putting off. And the humiliation. Telling her that I've had the device the whole time—stringing her along with everyone else—I've got one up on her now. That's going to kill her tomorrow."

Pimm said, "I could take care of that tonight, if you want."

Lang smiled. "No," he said. "She'll find a way to put it in a script, and that's ultimately good for me. Dead she wouldn't write quite so well."

"And speaking of the dead," said Hoffner, "you wouldn't happen to have the Volker girl lying around here somewhere, would you?"

"The Volker girl?" said Lang. "She's far from dead, Inspector."

"Then lurking about?"

"With Thea in the house? God, no. We shipped her off to Oslo ten days ago. She was a rather brave little thing, delivering the device and the blueprints. I promised her a role in something, but I think she's clever enough to stay where she is."

Pimm said, "Does Thea have any idea the device is here?"

Lang shook his head. "That was meant to be a surprise. See her reaction when the Coyle woman destroyed it right in front of her."

Pimm said, "You've an interesting marriage, Fritz."

Lang laughed to himself. "I'm not completely heartless, Alby. Thea would also have seen the inspector's face the moment he figured it all out. That would have been fun for her."

Hoffner said, "She did try to frame you for murder."

Lang looked over. "You mean that Thyssen-in-the-tub business, Inspector?" He nodded. "Thea's a clever girl with a flair for the dramatic. I won't deny it. Bit of a shock, but I think it was more a scare tactic than anything else. Make sure that I knew that they knew that I knew—so forth and so on." Lang retrieved his glass. "Come to think of it, I might actually have deserved it." He stared into the whiskey. "After all, I was the one to tell the Americans about Herr Vogt and his device in the first place." He looked up at Hoffner. "You did see that, Inspector, didn't you?" Lang drank.

A day ago Hoffner might have cared. Now Lang's confession just seemed irritating. "So you're afraid of Hugenberg as well?" he said.

Lang set the glass down. "Isn't everyone? Not that I think Alfred would be such a terrible head of Ufa. In fact, he might actually get us out of the red."

"Then why?"

"Does there always have to be a single reason, Inspector?"

"It helps with people like me."

Lang laughed quietly. "You're very good. You'll make a wonderful character for Thea to play with. I'm sure you can guess who I have in mind for Alby here— No? You've met him."

Hoffner took a few seconds before answering, "The little one. At the theater. Lorre." He looked at Pimm. "Sorry, Alby."

Lang said, "Excellent, Inspector." He looked at Pimm. "Oh, come on, Alby. You won't be disappointed. The fellow's remarkable. I've got something else in mind for him before he does you, but you'll meet him and like him. And let's face it, you are small."

Pimm said, "Are we done?"

Hoffner said, "I'm still waiting on my single reason."

"Lubitsch," Pimm said impatiently. "That's why, Nikolai. Can we get on with this?"

Lang let go with a long laugh. "Jealousy is hardly going to be enough of a reason for the inspector, Alby." He looked at Hoffner. "Alby thinks it's because I want to make films in America, and I can't say it doesn't burn a little that my dear old friend Lubitsch is now the toast of Hollywood—even if he is churning out meaningless little comedies. But Hollywood means money and prestige and distribution. I suppose you could see Fräulein Coyle's offer as a bit of quid pro quo. I tell them about the device, and they bring me over to make some real films. Naturally she had no idea I *had* the device—I couldn't have just given it to them—but she knew I was the one to tell her friends all about it. She finds it, and off I go to America."

Hoffner said, "So it all comes down to ego. How—obvious."

Lang laughed again and said, "Fair enough. If you believe Alby."

"And, of course, I shouldn't."

"Well," Lang said, standing, "not entirely." He moved across the room to a poster of his *Siegfried*: two lovers sat holding hands in a garden, dressed in medieval garb. Except for the man's oddly large hands, Hoffner might have taken them for two women. "Did you see it?" Lang asked.

"I can't say I did."

"Shame. It's very good. When we were allowed to make serious films." Lang pulled back the frame and revealed a large safe. He spun the dial, opened it, and pulled out what looked to be an oversized lantern. "You know what this is?"

"I can take a guess," said Hoffner.

"Well, you might not be entirely right on that one, either."

"I'm not going to need another drink, am I?"

Lang pulled out his monocle and slid it into the pocket of his robe. "No. You won't." He tossed the device over. Remarkably Hoffner caught it, and Lang said, "Not all that impressive, is it—Herr Vogt's sound and movement machine. You can be the one to take the sledge-hammer to it, Inspector. Makes no difference to me."

It was lighter than Hoffner expected, and far less involved. Behind the glass, eight or ten wires passed through various tubes and boxes, the real genius evidently tucked away somewhere inside. "And the blueprints?" said Hoffner.

"Burned," said Lang. "I can get you the ashes if you like?"

Hoffner shook his head. "So why wouldn't I be entirely right?"

Lang pulled a cigarette case from his pocket. "What you've got in your hands there is the end of film as we know it—that's why." He tapped one out and lit it.

Hoffner shot Pimm a glance. "I think I preferred the other reason."

Lang smiled. "I'm sure you did. Don't get me wrong, Inspector. Sound will innovate. The masses will flock to it. But machines like this will shatter whatever inner life we've managed to put up on a screen. Joy, madness, despair—see these in shadowed light and silence and they're universal. You can touch them, feel them as your own. Add sound to that—and I don't mean music; music has its own universal mystery—but add an actor or an actress—or the sound of some train racing by—and it all becomes pedestrian, the echoes of a single voice, and far too particular to have any real meaning. Remove your own projections from what it is to moan or to shriek or to cry out with longing and you steal the very soul from a film."

Hoffner said to Pimm, "And here I thought you were the one with the noble cause, Alby. Jew-haters and the like. You never knew it was art you were protecting."

Lang said, "Better that than ego."

Hoffner said, "They're one and the same, aren't they?" Lang let out a long stream of smoke, and Hoffner added, "Your actors, by the way, might disagree with you."

"Destroying it stops nothing, of course," said Lang. "I know that. No matter how much of a disaster Jolson is, Pandora's box is open. But if doing this had let the Americans take over Ufa, and the Americans had been forced to see how real films are made, then maybe just a little bit of German art would have found its way into American films. And we'd have managed to protect something real."

"Thank goodness for that," said Hoffner.

Lang ignored the comment and crushed out his cigarette. "In return, we would have learned a little something from them. The freedom they give to their artists. Chaplin, Hawks, Griffith. These are great men, Inspector, with great vision. Nothing ever compromises what they do. We might have learned the value of that."

"And back we go to ego," said Hoffner: he was done with the smug Lang. "What's the matter, Fritz? Those horrible Ufa executives didn't allow *Metropolis* to be quite the masterpiece it should have been? A few people dead—a few more forced to perform unspeakable acts on film—but that hardly matters as long as Fritz Lang can give a tutorial on the making of film?" Hoffner enjoyed the turn in Lang's gaze. "Luckily for you, Fritz, there's more at stake here. Luckily for Alby, as well." Hoffner continued to watch Lang. "Tell him, Alby. Tell him

he was actually trying to do something worthwhile despite himself."
When Pimm said nothing, Hoffner added, "Hugenberg wants Ufa for
a different kind of German art. All those sound stages he'll be building—courtesy of Mr. Jolson and your masses—those aren't just for his
talking newsreels and propaganda. They're for his tanks and his aeroplanes and his submarines, and whatever else he thinks he might need.
Surprised, Fritz? Chances are, Herr Alfred's planning on teaching the
Americans a thing or two of his own."

FIFTEEN MINUTES LATER, Lang was back on the sofa, finishing
off his third drink, as Thea von Harbou stepped into the room. She
was followed by a shortish woman who was pushing a tray on wheels.

"Mushroom omelet," said von Harbou. "Doesn't it smell wonderful?"

"Sit down, Thea," Lang said coolly. "You can go, Marget." The
woman needed no other encouragement. She was gone before von
Harbou could answer. Lang repeated, "I said sit down."

Von Harbou flashed a mystified smile and started toward the sofa.

"The other chair," said Lang. "By the sound device. The one Alfred
wants so desperately."

Her smile was all but gone as she caught sight of the metal box on
the table. Pimm was already behind her. She glanced over her shoulder and said, "Hello, Alby. Quite menacing when you choose to be.
I've always wanted to see it."

Lang said, "I wouldn't test him."

Von Harbou ignored her husband and walked to the chair. She sat.
"I'll take a drink."

"Not just yet," said Lang. "Go ahead. You can hold it. Tell Alfred
what it was like the next time you see him."

She remained perfectly still. "I think you're missing a few pages of script, dear. You've jumped ahead, and you're getting it all wrong."

"Am I?" said Lang. "New warehouses for Phoebus, a little man with a limp, something called the Ostara Company—the inspector's been showing me those pages. You seem to be on every one."

"What a remarkable coincidence," she said. Hoffner had taken a fork to the eggs, and von Harbou looked over. "They're good, aren't they?" she said. "Marget sautés the mushrooms with garlic before adding them. Makes all the difference."

"Very nice," said Hoffner. He took another forkful. "Are you sleeping with Hugenberg, Frau Lang, or is it something else?" He swallowed and looked over.

"I beg your pardon?" she said.

"No, I know it's crass to ask," said Hoffner. "But you don't seem the type for political thugs—unless it's the sexual deviance you like." He looked at Lang. "Is that the sort of thing that excites her, Fritz? Otherwise I'm at a complete loss as to why she's tied up in this." Hoffner suddenly laughed to himself and looked at Pimm. "Tied up. I didn't even mean to say it."

The room remained uncomfortably quiet until Lang said, "What the hell are you getting at, Inspector?"

Hoffner dug through the eggs for a few more mushrooms. "These new friends of yours, Madame. They're a brutal bunch, aren't they? And they like seeing their brutality."

She was becoming less attractive by the moment. "I'm afraid I don't know what you're talking about."

"No, no, of course you don't." Hoffner now spoke with a controlled venom: "What's a few bodies, girls raped." He speared two more and ate them. "Actually Hugenberg's less a concern for me at this particular moment. Easy enough to expose what he's got in those warehouses, but again you know nothing about that."

"I'd like that drink," she said.

"Little less charming right about now, isn't it?" Hoffner said coldly. He looked at Pimm. "I think we can give her a drink, Alby." He turned to Lang. "All right with you, Fritz? Be a sport?" No one moved. "No?" Hoffner stepped over, poured out the whiskey, and brought it to her. "It's your dogs I want called off. You can give them a telephone call. Tell them they've killed enough people and I'd like them to stop."

She took the glass, then slowly set it on the side table. "I'm a little tired, Fritz," she said. "I'm sure you can destroy the thing without me. I imagine that's what you have in mind. I'll call Alfred in the morning and make sure he's not too disappointed." She looked up at Hoffner. "Unfortunately, I can't speak for those dogs, Inspector, since I don't know them. I suspect you'll just have to let them tire themselves out."

She started to get up, and Hoffner stood directly in front of her. She sat back. "They didn't quite get all the films tonight," he said. "Only about half of them." Hoffner stared down at her, but she refused to look at him. "You have a projector somewhere, Fritz? We could all take a look."

Lang waited for his wife to say something. When she didn't, he turned to Pimm. "What films? What is he talking about, Alby?"

Hoffner said, "I think Hugenberg might find that piece of information a little more disappointing, Madame."

It was a cold, unflappable stare that now peered back at Hoffner. "You think so?" she said. "I don't think Alfred gives a fig about those films, Inspector, though I'm sure he wouldn't mind having them for himself—a bit of leverage. You can never have enough of that, can you?"

Hoffner was no less contemptuous. "Still, a little uncomfortable if they were to come out."

Lang prodded. "What is he talking about, Thea?"

"Uncomfortable for whom?" she said. "For these people I don't know?"

"There's a particular one," Hoffner said. "Alby's seen it. He says it's quite entertaining—in a desperate, middle-aged sort of way. You might recognize it."

No amount of booze could have hidden the ugliness now on von Harbou's face. It was there only a moment, but long enough to make the sudden shift to the brave, wronged woman all the more transparent. She peered up at him. "Well, then you know I'm as much a victim here as anyone, Inspector."

Hoffner marveled at how the guilty never managed to see beyond the limits of a lie. "Of course you are," he said. All the emotion had drained out of him. "I'm just trying to protect you, Madame, seeing that you had no idea what you were signing, or what the money was for—or that there might have been hidden cameras in the walls."

"That's very kind of you," she said with a remarkable facility.

"So I'm sure you'll want to do whatever you can to make things rough for these people."

She finally looked past Hoffner to Lang. "But they terrify me, Inspector. I don't think I'm strong enough to put myself in that sort of position. You can understand that, can't you?"

Lang said, "What the hell is everyone talking about?"

Von Harbou said, "Sex films, dear. I'm not proud of myself. It seemed like a lark. Alfred suggested it." The lie had taken on a life all its own. "You knew he and I were close. But things got out of hand. Obviously the inspector has a copy. I'm mortified, as you can tell."

Lang was doing all he could to keep up. "Is that true, Inspector?"

Hoffner continued to look at von Harbou. It would have been so easy to slap his fist across her face. "No need to be terrified, Madame. The Kripo can protect you."

Von Harbou said, "I appreciate the offer—"

She suddenly stopped. Pimm was at her side. He had taken her hand and was bending her wrist ever so slightly.

Von Harbou managed to say, "You're hurting me, Alby."

"Yes," said Pimm. "I know."

Lang stood. "Alby—"

"Quiet, Fritz," said Pimm. He applied more pressure, and von Harbou tensed in the chair. "It's very simple to break a bone, Thea," he said. "Especially a woman's bone. If you squirm too much, you might do it to yourself." Pimm looked across at Hoffner. "What is it you need Thea to do, Nikolai?"

Hoffner hadn't expected this. Then again, Alby had known him too long not to sense Hoffner's need for it. "Call them," he said quietly. "Call them and tell them I have the films. Tell them to let this go."

Von Harbou was managing to keep herself perfectly still. "I can't," she said through gritted teeth. Pimm twisted a bit more, and she yelled out, "I can't! It was always through Alfred. I wouldn't know how to find them."

Lang said, "Enough, Alby. Please."

Pimm looked over at Hoffner, and Hoffner nodded. Pimm released. Von Harbou instantly began rubbing her wrist as Hoffner said, "Then I need names, Madame. Full names. You're going to help me get these people out from under their rock."

TWENTY MINUTES ON, Hoffner was running through the final group of uncircled entries in the ledger. Von Harbou had managed to give last names to about half of them, the rest still insulated by the anonymity of an initial.

"That would be Streicher," she said. "Julius Streicher. Dreadful man. He and Goebbels detest each other. He doesn't strike me as the filmmaking sort. No wonder they left his canister behind."

She was recovering from her bout of torture with a bag of ice for her wrist. Hoffner continued to read.

"No," she said. "No . . . No . . . Yes—that one . . . Huus   or Haas. I'm not quite sure."

Hoffner scribbled something and moved on: "Ernst R.?"

"Oh God," she said. "Roehm. A homosexual. I think a good many of them are homosexual. I was never part of any of that."

Lang was back on the sofa. He had given up on his whiskey ten minutes ago. "This is . . ." It was as much as he could get out.

"Yes," said Hoffner. "It is." He read the next: "Alexander K."

Von Harbou thought a moment and then said, "Goebbels's little friend. Kurtzman. Alexander Kurtzman. Another homosexual, I think."

Hoffner looked up from the ledger. He saw Pimm staring across at him. Without a thought, Hoffner reached into the bag and dug through for the canister. Luckily, Lang and von Harbou were too preoccupied with themselves to notice the momentary break.

Hoffner found it and pulled it out. He stared at the name for several seconds before twisting off the top and pulling out the reel.

Pimm said, "What's the point, Nikolai? There's no reason to look at it."

Hoffner held the film up to the light. Thirty or so frames in he recognized Sascha's profile. He quickly rewound the film and slotted it back into the casing. He then slipped it into his pocket.

Pimm said, "That's not going to help him, Nikolai."

Hoffner looked over. If he had done it to help the boy, it only now occurred to him. Funny how instinct could make even kindness seem unintended. He turned to Lang and said, "I need to use your telephone."

Lang looked over. He was barely focusing. "What?"

"The telephone," Hoffner repeated.

"Oh," said Lang. "Yes. The hallway. Be my guest."

Hoffner stood and headed for the doorway. Pimm waited until Hoffner was out of the room. "I'll take the device now, Fritz."

Lang was focused on his wife. "This stretches things, even for us, doesn't it?"

Von Harbou reached for a cigarette. "We'll survive. We've been through worse."

"Have we?" said Lang. There was an unwilling sincerity in his voice.

She lit up. Her wrist was still bothering her. "It's who we are," she said. "There's no crime in it if you can't help yourself." Something struck her. "The script for Lorre. I'll finish a draft. That should get us through."

Pimm took hold of the device and said, "Your little actor—will he be talking in the next film?"

Lang looked over. The question seemed to bring him out of himself. "I imagine so."

"Would he have broken her wrist?"

Lang thought a moment. "Yes. I believe he would have."

"Good," said Pimm. "Then maybe there's hope for the future of film, after all."

THE ROADS HAD ICED UP, making the drive into town something of an adventure. Pimm had stayed behind. He had wanted to make sure Frau Lang was kept clear of the telephone—not knowing whom she might decide to surprise with an early-morning wake-up call. Pimm had also kept the canisters, all but Sascha's. In return, Hoffner had been given a car and the crushed remains of

Vogt's sound device. What he intended to do with them was any-body's guess.

It was nearly seven when he pulled up to the building. Except for an hour or two at the all-night movie palace, Hoffner had been up for nearly twenty-eight hours. There was a chance, then, that he had gar-bled the address Georg had given him over the telephone, but the street looked grotty enough, the four-floor tenement with just the right touch of decay to make it a safe bet: the absence of a latch on the door—it opened with a nice shove of his shoulder—gave Hoffner even greater hope.

He knocked on the third-floor door and waited. He knocked again, then pounded, before a half-woken voice said, "You get your money tomorrow, Drecker. Now go away and leave us in peace."

Hoffner continued to pound until he heard the sound of heavy footsteps, followed by some not-so-quiet cursing, heading his way. "I'm telling you, Drecker—"

The door opened and a slim, not overly tall boy stood in his under-wear and socks looking slightly confused. Hoffner recognized him from yesterday morning. He had been the one to relieve himself on the beaten boys.

"What the fuck you want?" he said in an accent that had him from somewhere in the south—the long, drawn-out, swallowed vowels of slow thinking. He might even have been Austrian. "You have any idea what time it is?"

"I'm looking for Kurtzman," said Hoffner.

"Yah? So?"

Hoffner pulled out his badge. The boy looked at it, then turned back to the room, leaving the door wide enough open to show the di-saster inside. What light there was spilled in through two drapeless windows. A mattress without sheets lay across the bare floor, with a bowl of yellow liquid at its side. At least the boy could have had the sense to place his piss at the foot of his bed.

"Alex!" he yelled. "Kripo's here." He went back to his mattress and looked instantly asleep.

There was a distinct smell of egg and vomit coming from down the hall, which made the piss something of a relief as Hoffner stepped farther in. Sascha appeared from a back room. He was dressed in pants, no shirt, and suspenders.

"Fuck," he said to himself the moment he saw his father. He stayed by the door to his room. "What do you want?"

"Georg said it was decent enough. Looks like you're living well."

"You've come to decorate, then? We could use some curtains."

"I'll put it on my list." Hoffner looked for a chair; the walk up had taken more out of him than he wanted to admit. There was none. "I need to talk to you."

"Yah. You've needed that quite a lot recently."

"You run in very interesting circles, Sascha. You're a man of influence."

"You can get out. You can also fuck yourself."

Sascha turned to go, and Hoffner said, "Georg's in trouble. You can help him." Hoffner watched the back of the boy's head, its stiffness giving way to a few short shakes before Sascha turned again and said, "I don't believe you." It wasn't true, but he had to say it.

"There's snow on the ground," said Hoffner. "It's nice. We could walk." Anything to get them out of this place.

"What kind of trouble?"

"You have a coat?"

Sascha's gaze was all the more unforgiving for its emptiness. He shook his head again and snorted, "Yah. I might even have a pair of boots somewhere."

· · ·

THEY STEPPED OUT onto the stoop, and Sascha pulled up his collar. "You're moving up in the world," he said, nodding at the car as the two took the stairs down. "A little something on the side? I've heard that happens at the end of a career."

"I've got a little ways to go yet."

Sascha ran his hand along the hood as they walked past. "Still hot. You've been driving awhile."

"You would have made a good cop."

"And how nice that would have been for you. Or not. Might have forced you to take an interest, and we couldn't have that."

Hoffner said, "Life was so cruel to you, Sascha—I know. You're so very brave to be where you are now."

A milk truck passed, and Sascha laughed quietly. "I think what bothers you is that I don't even think about it anymore. You actually believe your failures shaped me somehow—made me 'the man I am.' What a force of nature you must be in your own mind. You don't realize how easily dismissed you are."

Hoffner heard the sound of metal on metal coming from a tinker's stand somewhere up ahead: someone was getting their knives sharpened. "Your friends with the pamphlets," he said as they continued to walk. "They were sloppy last night. I've got the full names of what they left behind. You need to tell them it's over."

Sascha tried to pretend he understood, but he was too long in answering to be convincing. "And why should I do that?"

"If you knew what I was talking about, that's not the question you'd ask." A woman appeared in a window a few buildings down and dumped a bucket of something out onto the street. It splashed a dull brown, and Hoffner said, "It doesn't matter. You'll do this anyway. I know what's been going on. I was there yesterday morning."

Again Sascha tried too hard. "You managed to get yourself a pretty one, this time. Bit old for you, though, isn't she?"

"She's dead," said Hoffner: chilling how easily he could say it. He stopped and waited for Sascha to turn. "Something else your friends managed."

Sascha hesitated before answering: "I'm sure you'd like to believe that."

"I'm not talking about the café," said Hoffner. "Nice spot, Fat Gerda's. Your friend on the mattress might want to know that pissing in public's a criminal offense." When Sascha continued to stare at him, Hoffner said, "Did the sugar cubes get the smell out?"

Even in this cold, the boy's color had gone from his cheeks. To his credit his voice remained strong. "Odd place to be in the middle of the night," said Sascha. "Unless it's where you're spending your time these days."

"It wasn't the location that was disturbing."

"Really?" Sascha was holding his own.

"You think your being homosexual matters to me in the slightest?"

Sascha's gaze narrowed. "What?"

"Come on, Sascha. Berlin thrives on it now. It's part of the tourist trade. Telephone one of the bus companies next time you decide to put on a show and they'll have a group waiting outside. No, what's disturbing is where it's taking you—and whom it's taking you to. You choose to lead this life"—Hoffner was trying to give the boy something—"Fine. I don't really care. But you don't have to find it with them. We both know it's not their politics that's drawing you in."

When Sascha spoke, it was as if he were staring directly through his father. "You think I'm homosexual?"

Hoffner heard it first, then saw it, the utter disbelief. It seemed inconceivable that Sascha could ask the question, and yet here it was, and Hoffner wondered if this degree of self-loathing was possible at only twenty-four.

Yes or no, it was a mountain Hoffner hadn't the strength to climb; he barely had the strength to get them back to Georg. "Your friends," he said. He was finding it difficult to look at the boy. "They think Georg is involved with something—"

"It's the party," Sascha said with a quiet hatred. "Not my friends. Not something else. Not what you need it to be." Hoffner continued to search the horizon; he knew there was no going back now. "Yesterday?" said Sascha. "That was a lark. Nothing else. We thrash a few of these people and move on. It's the bond we share, the commitment to something beyond ourselves. That's what gives us the freedom to do it. And for those who've never had it—who never *will* have that purpose—they feel the need to demean it, make it perverse, when it's their own perversions that distort what they see. What is it you think you saw, Nikolai?"

A coal truck took the turn onto the street. It drove slowly, with a soot-faced man hanging off the tail strap. His eyes were red from too much drink or too little sleep, or both. Still, he managed a smile as he passed.

Hoffner looked at Sascha: yesterday morning had evidently been about freedom and commitments and purpose, and nothing so meaningless as the raping of a boy. Sascha was right. There was no way to see beyond the distortion.

"I have the films," Hoffner said. "With the names attached. Roehm, Streicher. Other members of your—party. You need to tell your little limping friend it's time to go back and play thug in the south. And to forget about Georg. Your brother has no idea what this is about. He never did. Otherwise those names and films start finding their way onto screens all over Berlin." Sascha might not have known about last night's escapade at headquarters, but he knew about this. He said nothing.

Hoffner spoke quietly. "Why, Sascha?" There was something almost plaintive in the tone. "Why make these films at all?"

Even an unintentioned compassion was too much for the boy. The color rose in his cheeks. "And you have the right to judge?" he said with a newfound venom. "They weren't meant for the likes of you."

"Thank God for that," said Hoffner.

"What—you think it was anything more than a game? That any of it was real? You sicken me. Hiding behind some pathetic morality, but only when it suits your purpose."

Hoffner expected to find his own rage, a need to strike the boy, but there was no hint of the familiar here. Instead, he said, "And I thought I was the one without purpose." Hoffner slowly reached into his pocket and pulled out the reel.

Sascha looked at it and instantly knew what it was. "Perfect," he said with even more disdain. "And now you threaten me. You think I need to be threatened to help my own brother?"

Hoffner felt the chill in him now, his shoes soaked through from the snow. All those years believing he had let this one go—this unknown boy—only to find himself gutted by a meaningless defiance. Why was it, he thought, that the discarded always managed to inflict the deepest kind of pain?

"No threat, Sascha," said Hoffner. He held out the canister. "Take it. Do with it what you want." He saw the boy's confusion: there was no place for such gestures in his world. Another half minute and Sascha pocketed the canister with a grudging nod.

Hoffner said, "I'll be outside the Scherl building. After nine. If you're there, I'll know you've done this. Why or why not is up to you."

Hoffner turned and headed for the car. He tucked his hands inside his pockets and drew his coat closer in around himself. Even so, there was no hope of holding the cold at bay now.

THREE RIFLES, A SLINGSHOT,
AND A TUGBOAT

S OMEWHERE a church bell chimed the last of the quarter hour, and Hoffner mounted the steps.

He had put in an appearance at the Alex over an hour ago—a change of shoes, a shave, the use of his telephone—but there was no helping the haggard look on his face. Luckily no one had asked about the paper bag he was carrying filled with odd pieces of metal, shards of glass, and tubing. In fact, no one had paid him any attention. The wall in his office was once again a dull white, only a few drips of paint here and there to give any reminder of last night. For the boys at the Alex, the episode was all but forgotten.

It had been five days, he thought. Five days. It seemed an eternity. Someone should have at least taken notice of him.

Now Hoffner pushed through the doors to the Scherl building and was at once swept up in the clamor of newsmaking. Not that any of these people had access to influence. That was upstairs where the writers and editors and moneymen determined how Berlin should see itself. The boys in the lobby were nothing more than messengers and coffee retrievers—lackeys with grand dreams of the future. Hoffner marveled at how even they could move with such a sense of world-shattering importance. Life and death might be colliding elsewhere— in hospitals, prisons, on the street—but this was the news, judged, packaged, or simply created. It trumped them all.

He wove his way through the darting figures and over to the last of the elevators. There were two stanchions in front of it, with a velvet rope hanging between them. An elevator boy stood behind, his hands clasped firmly at his back.

"Private elevator, *mein Herr*," he said with a surprising friendliness.

He extended a gracious hand toward the others. "One will be along any moment to take you up."

Hoffner said, "I've an appointment with Herr Direktor Hugenberg."

The boy's smile became more strained. "I'm afraid I wasn't told of this, *mein Herr.*"

"Neither was he," said Hoffner as he pulled out his badge. "Chief Inspector Nikolai Hoffner. I'll wait while you telephone up to tell them I'm coming."

Ten minutes later Hoffner stepped out onto the eighth floor. He had expected more, something white and sleek, with black moldings and glass everywhere—or at least a sense of entitlement etched across the face of the woman behind the desk. Instead, everything was shades of brown in a faint yellow light, and small. Two chairs sat a few meters from the desk, a low table between them, bare except for an overturned glass and pitcher: the water inside looked as if no one had dared a sip in quite some time. The smell was also stale—wood and oil—with that mustiness that lives in old men's closets. The woman was pretty enough, but perhaps only by comparison. Hoffner made his way over, and the floor creaked.

"Herr Chief Inspector," she said, standing. She was barely taller than her chair. "The Herr Direktor is expecting you. May I offer you a glass of water?"

"Thank you, no."

Stepping out from behind the desk, she said, "This way, please," and, motioning to the door, led the way. After years of practice, she had learned to keep the creaking in check. She knocked once and opened it. There was some sort of nodded exchange between them before Hoffner stepped through, and the door closed behind him.

Here, at last, was the real light. The entire office—easily half the floor—was surrounded by floor-to-ceiling windows on three sides. A conference table stood about halfway in—neat, pristine—and de-signed in that thin-grained wood the Danes seemed to be shipping in by the cartload these days. The chairs were all metal, with high-angled backs that made comfort an impossibility. The only one with a bit of cushioning stood at the end. It was larger than the rest.

"Just put it on the table, Chief Inspector."

Hugenberg sat behind a desk below one of the distant windows. He was still too far off for Hoffner to make out any real details, save for the shock of peppery hair that seemed to rise from the top of his head like clipped stalks of corn. He was on the telephone.

"Yes, of course that makes sense," Hugenberg said into the re-ceiver. Hoffner was surprised by the easy cadence in the voice. The man sounded almost genial. "No, no, no, we won't bother with that . . . That's right." He laughed. "Very good. You'll send it over this afternoon. I'm delighted." Hoffner made his way past the table and now watched as Hugenberg tried to get a word in. "Yes . . . yes . . . Wonderful." Hugenberg motioned for Hoffner to take a seat in one of the chairs in front of the desk. "All right, then . . . Yes, this after-noon . . . Excellent. *Wiedersehen*." Hugenberg hung up and retrieved a large cigar from his ashtray. Again he motioned to the chair. "Please." Hoffner remained standing, and Hugenberg said, "Do you smoke a cigar?" He pushed a box across the desk and opened its lid. "I find them very relaxing."

Hugenberg was more bull-like than Hoffner expected. There were pictures, of course, but the man was famous for keeping his dis-tance—always poorly lit in the back row, or off to the side, or in pro-file. There had even been a competition for a full-on photo a few years back, but no one had had the courage to send anything in: Why bother when it had been a Hugenberg-owned paper that had run the contest?

It was the knuckles, though, that caught Hoffner's eye. They were thick and a deep red, the kind usually found in a butcher's shop. They matched the ears perfectly. Only the little round glasses and broad white mustache lent the face anything patrician. Hoffner closed the lid.

"So," Hugenberg said. "Here we are." He smiled and nodded at the bag. "I assume that's the device."

"It is."

"Fully destroyed?"

Hoffner nodded.

"Not even the blueprints?" said Hugenberg.

"Not even the blueprints." Hoffner placed the bag on the desk. All he had wanted was to see the expression on Hugenberg's face. Even that was a disappointment.

Hugenberg brought his hand to his ear and pinched at the lobe. It was almost playful. "I'll have a hell of a time convincing my board to buy out Ufa, now, won't I?" He let go of the ear and said easily, "Films are the next logical move, though. I'm sure I'll find a way to convince them."

Hoffner was feeling the heat in the room. He was also fighting back the first wave of nausea from exhaustion. He needed to get out of here. "I'm sure you will." He swallowed. "You've always got your tanks as a nice sideline, though—in the meantime. We'll all just have to wait and read about that in the papers, won't we?" Again no reaction. "Enjoy your device, *mein Herr*."

Hoffner turned to go, and Hugenberg said, "Tanks, Chief Inspector?" Hugenberg had kept his smile. "Oh, you must mean the ones you told Kurd Wenkel about at the *Tageblatt*. You telephoned him, what—an hour ago?" Hoffner turned back, and Hugenberg said, "I own the *Tageblatt*, Chief Inspector. I was the first one Wenkel called."

In his current state, Hoffner couldn't be sure if he had just been threatened or laughed at. Either way, it felt like defeat. He steadied himself and said, "So the story never runs."

For a moment Hugenberg looked concerned. "Are you all right, Chief Inspector?"

Hoffner felt his legs beginning to go. What could be better—a final show of weakness at Hugenberg's feet. There was no point in trying to deny it. "I'd take a glass of water if you have it."

Hugenberg poured one from the pitcher on his desk and slid it across to Hoffner. Hoffner took it and sat. His head was getting light as he drank.

Hugenberg said, "I can have the Fräulein bring in something to eat?"

Hoffner had missed it entirely. There had been no threat, no laughter. This kind of certainty took years to perfect. Hugenberg had reached the point where intimidation had no meaning. "No," said Hoffner. "You're very kind, *mein Herr*. The water will do." Hoffner finished the glass.

Hugenberg said, "By the way, we will be running the story. You did such nice work, you should have your name in the papers."

Hoffner set the glass on the desk. "Thanks, but I'll take a pass."

"Shame. You deserve it."

"A regular hero."

Hugenberg tapped out his cigar. He had yet to take a puff. "The warehouses might not have exactly what you thought they had—tanks sound so ominous—but I'm sure they'll find something there when Wenkel opens them up. A few submarine propellers, aeroplane wings. What do you think? That should be enough to make it front-page news."

Everything was unraveling. "So the tanks are gone."

"Tell me, Chief Inspector, what exactly did you think you were accomplishing? Except for putting a lot of people in danger. I was sorry to hear about the American woman."

Hoffner said, "I thought I was investigating a murder."

"I'm sure the Thyssen matter will prove to be suicide, don't you?"

Such perfect and complete certainty, thought Hoffner. "And the American?" he said. He had nothing to lose now. "These new political friends of yours. They're not so easily controlled, are they?"

Hugenberg placed the cigar in the ashtray. "It's a pity, you know," he said as he sat back. "Captain Lohmann's a good man. Clever. Perhaps a bit too clever—all that misdirection and false resignation papers. Your little visit caught him by surprise. Luckily, he's a very good actor when he needs to be, although maybe not quite good enough. But he's doing wonders for German business. This will be a blow to the Navy, having his name raked across every headline. My guess, someone in the cabinet will have to step down as well."

"You're really going to protect these people, aren't you?"

It was as if Hugenberg had been waiting for the question. "There are always growing pains, Chief Inspector. A group like—" He hesitated. "A group like these new political friends—they have the right idea, but they're just too eager. They think revolutions actually take place in the streets. Things are a little subtler now. Not for me to say, but that might be the reason Herr Thyssen ended up in that tub."

Hoffner's head was clearing. He poured himself a second glass. "Because of his lack of subtlety."

"It's not that hard to follow, Chief Inspector, is it?" Hugenberg retrieved his cigar and Hoffner drank. "Feeling better?"

Hoffner bobbed a nod. "Much. Thanks."

Hugenberg said, "Let's just suppose—you and I—that Thyssen had been given the chance to develop a sound device, and that somewhere in the process he'd used that chance to make some films of his own without consulting anyone else." This seemed to stick in Hugenberg's throat. "Say, with a group of young men primarily from old Freikorps units—Thyssen being Freikorps himself. Now suppose again that these units are somewhat infamous for their sexual appetites, and that it's those sorts of things that end up on film. Just as a lark, you understand. Very private showings. No one the wiser." Hugenberg's voice sharpened momentarily. "Foolishly kept hidden behind a single locked door."

"Sounds like a Thea von Harbou script," said Hoffner.

"Does it? I've never seen one of her films."

"You prefer the live show." Hoffner took another drink.

Hugenberg continued: "Now imagine that Thyssen's personal escapades had somehow gotten the Americans nosing around. That would have been a case of overeagerness getting the better of him, don't you think? And if pressure had been brought to bear to stop these films, and Thyssen had ignored those warnings—and then somehow misplaced the device and its blueprints—well then, the strain of the thing might have made a man like that take his own life."

Hoffner set the glass down on the desk. "Or have his death point the finger at Fritz Lang, the one man responsible for getting the Americans involved in the first place."

Hugenberg studied Hoffner's face and said, "Imagine that." He waited before saying, "Either way, Chief Inspector, it sends a message back to Thyssen's party. Time to do some housecleaning. Weed out the mavericks and undesirables. And everyone comes out ahead."

Hoffner nodded to himself and said, "Except for the American, and a little accountant somewhere."

"As I said, growing pains. I'd leave mention of the Freikorps and the films out of your report. The American is up to you, but I always think strain is reason enough with these sorts of things."

No threats, no intimidation. Hoffner wondered how many others over the years had sat here and been privy to Herr Hugenberg's good counsel. It made taking a jab at the man seem almost worthwhile. "Gums up the works for your secret war, though," said Hoffner. "No Ufa sound stages—no tank factories."

"Secret war?" For the first time Hugenberg seemed surprised. "You're not that naïve, are you, Chief Inspector? We haven't finished with the last one yet." He waited and then said, "You think signing a few pieces of paper in a railway carriage put an end to that?" He shook his head slowly. "Not on the terms we were given. Trust me, the French are waiting. The English as well. They think they're safe across the water, but they're getting ready all the same. And the Americans—they've already begun to take Germany, getting their hands into our businesses, bringing everything that smacks of America over here so that we're sure to welcome them with open arms— more jazz, please, more films—when they finally march through the Brandenburg Gate. If I were a cynical man—and, of course, I'm not— I'd say the Americans did all this just to make sure they'd have a rea- son to come back."

Hugenberg was aching for the question, and Hoffner hadn't the reserves to deny him: "And if you *were* a cynical man?"

"Well, I might wonder why the Americans took so long to get into the war in the first place. Why, in fact, they got in at all. You see, we'd managed to get ourselves into a nice little stalemate by '17. Something we Europeans have been very good at for the last five hundred years or so. The usual course has always been a treaty, the announcement of joint mea culpas, little bits of this and that being divided up—"

"The burying of the dead," said Hoffner.

Hugenberg showed only a moment's hesitation. "The Americans came in and changed all that. Suddenly the English fleet that had been building up since 1910—and that had been allowed to squeeze the life out of good German trade—was forgotten. France and Belgium suck- ing up what remained of Africa and leaving us none of it, that was simply sour grapes. Lo and behold, there had been no reason for us to attack in 1914. It was all our fault. And now we would have to pay—for everything. And the Americans? They went home to congratulate themselves. The great heroes making the world safe for democracy. But what about the mess they left behind? Inflation, starvation, reparations? They had vanquished the demon. Now it was time for the demon to take care of himself, just as long as the Americans were an ocean away."

Hoffner said, "And that's what your tanks are for?"

"What these National Socialists have right, Chief Inspector, is that Germany comes first. Versailles allows the English and the French and the Americans to prepare themselves for the moment when they're ready to finish the job. We can't be so blind or so reckless as to not see it coming, or to forget how to defend ourselves. And we certainly won't manage that on three rifles, a slingshot, and a tugboat." Hugenberg reached for the pitcher and poured himself a glass. "If you think about it," he added, "I should be thanking you. This business with Phoebus—it's out now. What everyone's been expecting us to do all along. So we'll run the stories, condemn Captain Lohmann and the Navy, and show genuine remorse. And they'll all wave a finger at us and think it's done." He drank.

"Until you find a way to take Ufa."

Hugenberg's smile returned as he set down the glass. "You see, even you have faith, Chief Inspector." He sat back. "And just think of the possibilities. Tanks in one studio, propaganda films in another. What better way to convince a country to go back to war than through a few patriotic films. Maybe even some newsreels. Much more effective than what I tell them to think in my newspapers. I could be wrong, but this Goebbels fellow looks to have a knack for that sort of thing."

"And the rest of them?" said Hoffner.

Hugenberg stared across the desk. "They really trouble you, don't they?" He waited before saying, "One might think you have something personal vested in it."

Hoffner was too worn down to know if Hugenberg had just given up Sascha. This, though, had all the trappings of a genuine threat. Hoffner said, "I've dealt with them before, yes."

"Really?" Hugenberg continued to show nothing. "What are the chances of that, do you think?" Again he waited before saying, "As I see it, we seem to be in a position to help each other. I want to make sure you don't look foolish when you talk to the papers about this, and you want me to clamp down on my new friends. Fair enough. So here's what we'll do. I'll convince Herr Goebbels to ratchet things up—beat up some Jews in the street and so forth. He'll jump at the chance, and then I propose to the Reichstag that we place a ban on any National Socialist organizing, say for a year. Coming from me, it'll pass in a heartbeat. My young friends get taught a lesson for their recent mistakes, and you don't say anything you might regret. Does that sound reasonable?"

It was the only false step Hugenberg had taken—making this moment seem spontaneous. Hoffner wondered if the ban was already in the works. Whatever the reason, he knew it was all that was left to him.

"So I'm the hero, after all," said Hoffner.

"There are no heroes, Chief Inspector." Hugenberg returned his cigar to the ashtray. "There are no villains. That's not the way things work. They just move on and the world takes care of itself. And someone like you never really has a part in that." He glanced at the clock. "Unfortunately, I suspect I have several impatient young men waiting outside my door. You'll be good enough to tell the Fräulein to send them in. Thank you for the device." He glanced at it for a moment. "Odd sort of memento." Hugenberg picked up the telephone and dialed. Evidently this was the way every meeting began and ended.

With nothing else left him, Hoffner pushed himself up and turned to go. Looking to the door, he realized how much farther the way out now seemed.

SASCHA WAS STANDING across the street, smoking a cigarette and stamping his feet for warmth, when Hoffner emerged from the building. Hoffner waited for a tram to pass and then darted across. Luckily, the cold air was already bringing some life back to his head. He was even feeling hungry.

"You're late," said Sascha.

"Your friend Hugenberg likes to talk."

The morning had taken too much out of the boy for him to hide his surprise. "How did you get in to see Herr Hugenberg?"

"You talked to your friends about Georg?"

The boy's gaze hardened: he should have known better than to try and engage his father. "They'll leave it alone."

"They know he's your brother?"

Sascha's face grew more sour. "That would open up a great many things, wouldn't it? No, your films managed that."

"My films?" said Hoffner. "That's a neat trick, Sascha, if you can believe it." To feel that much hatred peering through him and to have none to give back: it left Hoffner sad for the boy, sadder for himself. "You don't have to play this out," he said. It sounded so hollow coming from a place of such self-pity. "You don't have to be this for them."

A weariness unfair in a twenty-four-year-old settled on the boy's face, and for a moment, it gave Hoffner hope.

"You're young enough," said Hoffner. "It's not to the point where you have to believe what the world tells you you are or, worse, accept it so you can live with yourself." In the end this was all he had for his son: a chance at redemption through a father's self-loathing. "You still have the choice."

It was, of course, nowhere near enough. "You actually think I'm that weak, don't you?" Sascha's eyes sharpened. "Of course you do. And that's why you and I are so very, very different."

It had been foolish to think there was anything here to be saved—for himself or for the boy. Salvation was never meant for the likes of them. Hoffner waited and then said, "It's the last time we'll see each other, I imagine."

Sascha shrugged, with too much effort. "The last time I'll be the one to protect you." He saw his father's confusion and said, "You don't think they'd let this go so easily, do you? I told them you're not worth it. A stumbler who got lucky. It won't matter in the long run."

It was all empty posturing, but why not give the boy this much, at least. Sascha looked so cold and frail and defiant, and never more piti-less, and for the first time Hoffner understood the true menace that lay within. It left nothing between them.

They stood silently for a few moments before Sascha stepped past him and out into the street. Hoffner listened to the crunch of boots on snow—farther and farther off—until the sound disappeared, leaving him with only the noise of the morning as comfort.

LATER—AN HOUR, MAYBE TWO—Hoffner found himself alone, peering from a bridge into the canal. It had been so easy just to walk.

The water below ran quickly from the snow, a few pieces of ice still clinging to the banks as if they could hold off the onrush indefinitely. Everywhere else was white, the haze from above having come down to cover Berlin whole. It made the city unknowable.

Hoffner rummaged through his pockets for a cigarette and found Leni's envelope still sealed and tucked away. He hesitated, then pulled it out. It was rough in his hands, the lettering for the hotel distorted from the drying, all of it streaked in razor-thin lines of gray. The top corners had curled in, making it look like a weathered claw without the strength to grasp: weightless, powerless, weak.

He stared at it and wondered why it had come now—to taunt, to relieve—although neither would have been of much help. It seemed impossible to compress everything into this, and yet, why not? What lay inside had no meaning; it would change nothing. To everything and everyone beyond this bridge, the world of a week ago, or of next week, looked no different from this moment, and Hoffner knew he would have to find a way to believe that. The prospect brought a new kind of exhaustion, and one with no hope of relief.

He raised the envelope to his nose and breathed in, telling himself he could still smell the mint on it. He then held it out and, for a moment, let the light play on the creases before letting go. He watched until the water swallowed it and, moving off, knew it had as much chance of finding its way through Berlin now as he did.

One month later, Hugenberg did manage to buy Ufa with the help of Deutsche Bank and I.G. Farben. His 4.5 million mark investment gave his preferred shares a twelvefold voting right, and thus ensured that his was the controlling interest in the studio. According to an internal report from Scherl GmbH at the time, the holdings were "distributed in such a way that we will definitely achieve a majority in any voting, which shows that economic control of the company rests entirely in the hands of our group." Hugenberg immediately renegotiated the Parufamet agreement, paying off the loan and creating a producer-unit system of production identical to the one in Hollywood. After that he began to build for sound production.

Captain Walther Lohmann was held responsible for what became known as the Phoebus Affair, first reported by Kurd Wenkel in the *Berliner Tageblatt* in March of 1927. The article focused on the Navy's attempt to strengthen right-wing elements in Germany, but only mentioned in passing anything to do with rearmament. The Berliner Bankverein connection was barely touched on. There was no mention of Alfred Hugenberg. Much of the information about Lohmann's clandestine doings remained hazy, until a 1993 CIA report was released which detailed his "black funds" operations with the German Navy from 1923 through 1927. As it turned out, the Berliner Bacon Company was one of his most successful (if reviled) ventures, and acted as a front for submarine construction, which continued in Cádiz and Istanbul even after Lohmann's resignation. Defense Minister Otto Gessler and Navy Commander Hans Zenker were also forced to resign.

Within a few weeks of the exposé, the then-fledgling Nazi Party was banned from organizing in Berlin for a period of one year after several incidences of Jew-baiting and beatings in the streets. Hugenberg, however, was not the member of the Reichstag to propose the ban.

Fritz Lang needed a bit of time to recover from the catastrophic failure of *Metropolis*, but resurrected his career with what many have called his greatest masterpiece, *M*. It starred a brilliant Peter Lorre as a child-murderer. Lorre then went on to a famous, later infamous, career in Hollywood (Lorre's continued bouts with drugs and alcohol eventually left him playing a parody of the deeply disturbed character he had first created in Germany). In 1933, then Propaganda Minister Joseph Goebbels approached Lang to transform German film into Nazi cinema as its leading director. Lang politely refused and shortly thereafter immigrated to the United States, where he went on to direct the classics *Fury*, *Cloak and Dagger*, and *The Big Heat*.

His wife, Thea von Harbou, did not join him. They divorced in 1934, and von Harbou became an ever-more-devoted member of the Nazi Party (she had joined in 1932), going on to pen scripts and books for the great cause. She was detained briefly after the war by the British, and then released to do unskilled labor, before eventually finding herself working with sound synchronization and dime novels.

On June 30, 1934, the party finally got rid of its more "undesirable" elements. During the "Night of the Long Knives," Hitler purged the SA—his Brownshirts—which had grown out of those earlier Freikorps units. There had been rumors that the SA was a bastion of homosexual activity, even going so far as to imply a onetime relationship between Hitler and the SA's leader, Ernst Roehm. Thereafter, Hitler made homosexuality a prime target for eradication.

Eventually, Hugenberg was forced to sell Ufa to the Nazis. He was briefly a member of Hitler's cabinet but, like many other conservatives at the time, got himself into trouble by underestimating the Nazis. In perhaps his most famous line, Hugenberg boasted in 1933, "We'll box Hitler in . . . In two months we'll have pushed [him] so far into a corner that he'll squeal." Hugenberg was lucky compared to many of his friends who did not survive the year. He was allowed to remain a member of the Reichstag until 1945, but with no influence whatsoever. After the war, he also spent time with the British before dying in 1951 near Rinteln, West Germany.

As for the propaganda minister, his early interests in film gave way to a far more powerful medium. It was something new, something with a potential that film—talking or otherwise—could never achieve: the chance to step inside every German home. It was the radio.

(The song that appears in Chapter 4—*"Was hast Du für Gefühle, Moritz?"*—was written by Fritz Löhner-Beda and Richard Fall, and was made famous by the cabaret singer Paul O'Montis. Surround-Sound technology did not enter the marketplace until the late 1970s, a product of Dolby Laboratories.)

ACKNOWLEDGMENTS

This book might not have been possible save for the generous encouragement of David McCullough, and for that I am truly grateful. He set me on the path to Mort Janklow, who brings an insight and integrity to the art of agenting that is all too rare; it is a privilege to work with him. Mort brought the earliest pages of the manuscript to Sarah Crichton, and it was with Sarah that I discovered what old-school editing is all about. The discussions we had were always just that—a give-and-take that challenged, focused, and inspired. I cannot imagine a better editor.

I also want to thank Professor David Clay Large for his kind guidance in helping me to discover and imagine the world hidden beneath Weimar Germany.

I owe a debt of gratitude to Peter Spiegler, who was there at every stage of the manuscript. All writers should have such keen readers. Everyone should have such friends.

As ever, my parents were wonderfully enthusiastic, and, in no small measure, made the day-to-day writing of the book a reality. For the home away from home, I thank them.

And finally, for my wife, Andra, and my children, Emilia and Benjamin—they bring a light to my world that makes all shadows disappear.

Read on for an excerpt from
Jonathan Rabb's new novel

The Second Son

Available February 2011 in hardcover
from Farrar, Straus and Giroux

CHAPTER ONE

BARCELONA

THERE WAS NOTHING but heat and sun. And, from time to time, the young man forced himself to arch his neck just so as to feel the lines of sweat dripping down his back.

What had he expected, a German in Spain? It was his job to sweat, and look sickly doing it. His cheeks had gone a nice pasty red, even through three days' growth of beard. He wasn't smelling all that good either, but then neither were any of the others in the row, staring across the plaza, cameras at the ready, cigarettes hanging limply from the line of parched lips.

The young man had thought about keeping the beard, but he knew his wife would tell him to shave it off the moment he got back to Berlin. It would probably scare the boy anyway—"Where's my Papi! Where's my Papi!" ringing down the hall, screams and tears before all the presents came tumbling out of the suitcase. Presents were always good with a boy of four, even from a father he didn't quite recognize.

It hadn't been that long, he thought. Not this time—had it?

The young man kept his right arm on the crank of the movie camera, his eye through the viewfinder, and, with his left hand, he tried to grope for the can of water he had set down somewhere on the cobbled pavement.

He must have looked ridiculous doing it because a voice down the line blurted out, "You do juggling tricks, as well, Hoffner, or is it just the balancing act?"

The words were Spanish, but it was a thick eastern European accent that muddied the sound.

Georg Hoffner pulled himself back from the camera. He brought his long body upright, blinked the sweat from his eyes, and stared down to a fat Bulgarian with a handheld Leica strung across his chest. The camera looked twenty years old, cutting-edge for a Bulgarian.

"Why?" said Hoffner. "You have some balls that need juggling?"

There were a few laughs, those dry uncomfortable laughs that come with heat and sweat, but almost at once the line fell silent. Across the plaza, the doors to a vast building opened. Hoffner quickly repositioned himself behind the camera and peered through the viewfinder. He focused on the banner hanging above, hastily painted but still impressive:

PEOPLE'S OLYMPICS, 19–26 JULY, 1936, BARCELONA FOR THE PEOPLE, FOR THE WORKERS.

Young men and women began to pour out the doors, all dressed as workers, with red neckerchiefs and berets to signify their exalted station in life. To be a worker in Barcelona these days—to be a member of the proletariat—that was the stuff of dreams. To be a worker athlete—well, that was pure legend.

The fat Bulgarian snapped his shots as he tried to squeeze past the line of Guardia Civil, patent leather hats, patent leather boots—patent leather men with patent leather souls. How these soldiers were managing to stay upright in the heat was anybody's guess. Still, Bulgarians were never much good when it came to large Spaniards and cudgels.

The Bulgarian pushed once too often and his camera went crashing to the pavement.

Hoffner heard the moans from down the line, but it wasn't enough to draw his attention from the smart set of Germans striding across his lens. Hoffner cranked as they walked, his arm remarkably steady as he followed them along the plaza. There was something almost Soviet to the way these boys moved, triumphant and bedraggled all at once, their nobility protruding from the angle of their heads and the broadness of their chests. He recognized them from this morning's press conference outside the Olympic stadium. It had been a hell of a time getting the cameras into the funicular and up the mountain, where the smell of wheat and cow manure and maybe beets—he hadn't been able to place it—followed the tram all the way up.

It had been the German contingent on the podium this morning. The place of honor. After all, they were the ones protesting their own Olympic games—the Führer's chance to show the world the best of Nazi Germany. The Führer, however, would have to wait another ten days before parading out his Aryan ideals in Berlin. Until then, it was the worker athletes here in Barcelona—Germans, Swedes, Russians, English, on and on—who would remind the world that sport was pure and not meant to be used as a tool of politics. The Barcelona Protest Games. Hoffner suspected it was a logic only the Left could follow.

Truth be known, most of these boys hadn't seen Germany in years. They were Jews and communists and socialists—exiles living in France or England—but still, they had come to compete as Germans. Proletariat Germans. Protesting Germans. Take that, you fascist bastards.

The boys reached the buses parked at the edge of the plaza. They turned and waved to no one in particular, and then got on. Hoffner stopped the crank and stood upright. The Bulgarian was still yelling at the Guardia. The buses began to move and the Guardia, no less bored, headed off in various directions. The Bulgarian was left to shout into the emptying plaza.

"Come and have a drink," Hoffner said as he began to fold up the legs on his camera. "We'll let Pathe Gazette pay for it—what do you say?—and maybe we'll find you a camera lying around somewhere."

The Bulgarian stopped squawking. He picked up the cracked pieces of his own camera and headed over. His smell preceded him by a good ten meters.

THE BAR WAS DOWN in the Raval section of town, near the water and the docks, a good place for pimps and drunks and journalists. At two in the morning there was little chance of telling them apart; now, at four in the afternoon, it was primarily journalists. And one or two whores. They were big girls, with big chests, dark black hair like dripping tar, and tight skirts that hugged the thighs like two thick columns of flesh. The skirts were a kind of a protective measure for men too eager to get a passing hand up and inside.

"The games are a joke," the Bulgarian said to Hoffner. Two others were sitting with them, all four drinking what passed for whiskey. "You'd think if they're going to protest, they'd have someone who actually cares that they're protesting."

Hoffner was reading through one of the letters he had gotten from his wife. He liked reading them over and over, especially when he was sitting at a table with Bulgarians and Poles and—he couldn't remember what the dozing fourth one was. Russian or Czech. What did it matter? These types all got drunk the same way, spoke the same kind of broken Spanish, and tried to get the girls for cheap. But they all liked that Pathe Gazette picked up the bill for the first few rounds. Hoffner liked it, as well. He would have to remember to put in for it.

The Bulgarian said, "You think Hitler cares that a few communists decide to run the long jump? Or a socialist can throw a hammer?" The Bulgarian was fat and small, a winning combination. "I interviewed one of them. He's here for the chess. Can you imagine it? Chess—as Olympic sport? This one was terribly impressive after he cleaned his glasses and patted down his bald head. Now that's an athlete."

Hoffner continued to scan the letter. "My son's been reading the front page of the *Tageblatt* all by himself," he said. "Every word."

The Pole was pouring out his third glass. "He likes the news?"

"Let's hope not."

"How long has he been reading?"

"The last few months. He's four and a bit."

"I've been reading much longer than that. Are you impressed?"

"Only if you read better than you write."

The Pole smiled and drank.

The Bulgarian was leaning back in his chair and staring at one of the girls at the bar. She was staring back with just the right kind of indifference. The Bulgarian turned his head to the table. "She wouldn't go for less than ten *pesetas*, you think?"

"She wouldn't go for it when you asked her last night," said the Pole. "Or the night before. But don't let that stop you from asking."

The Bulgarian peered over at Hoffner. "Must be nice to have a wife who writes letters. And a little boy."

"Must be," Hoffner said distractedly.

"I have one somewhere. A wife. Not the writing type." He leaned forward. "Tell me, why is it that Pathe Gazette has a German working for them? It's an English newsreel. Shouldn't you be with Ufa-Tonwoche, or Phoebus? One of the German studios?"

Hoffner folded the letter and placed it in his pocket. "Phoebus never did newsreel."

"So why not Ufa?"

Hoffner took hold of the bottle. "Not too many Jews working out at Ufa these days." He poured himself a glass. "I'd say none, but then there's always one or two who've managed to slip through the cracks. Too good at what they do to have some government statute force them out. I wasn't that good in the first place." He drank.

"I'm a Jew," said the Pole.

Hoffner poured himself another. "Good for you."

The Bulgarian said, "And Pathe Gazette just happened to have an office in Berlin? How nice. I'm thinking they haven't had time to set one up in Sofia just yet."

"Don't sound so bitter," Hoffner said with a smile. "The girl'll think you don't really want her."

The Bulgarian shot a glance back at the bar. The girl was chatting up the barman.

The Pole pushed back his chair. "I have an interview with the Swedish fencing team," he said. "We're very keen on fencing in Warsaw." He stood. "Anyone interested?"

"Are there women on the team?" said the Bulgarian.

"I imagine so."

"My God. Swedish women in those outfits. And socialists to boot." The Bulgarian was on his feet. He piped his voice toward the girl at the bar. "No more negotiating, capitalist. I'm off to the Revolution."

The girl glanced over. She smiled and winked and went back to her barman.

"And yet she knows I'm a capitalist at heart. How it kills me." The Bulgarian picked up his rucksack from the floor. It was holding a new Zeiss Ikon, courtesy of the English Pathe Gazette Company. The Bulgarian had promised to get the camera back in one piece. Hoffner wasn't holding his breath.

"Fifteen *pesetas* for an hour," said the Bulgarian as he hoisted the strap over his shoulder. "It's a crime."

"Enjoy the Swedes," said Hoffner. He picked up his own bag.

The dozing Czech or Russian opened his eyes. Hoffner stood. He left a few coins on the table and headed for the door.

HIS ROOM SMELLED of wood polish and garlic, and looked out at the vast expanse that was the Plaza Catalunya. His hotel, the Colón, stretched the length of one side of the square and seemed to be perpetually in direct sunlight. Eight in the morning, nine at night, there was no escaping the glare. Hoffner thought it must have been some sort of architectural coup, but all it did was make the room unbearably steamy.

He had worked his way through descriptions of the square, the view of Barcelona, the taste of the food—a letter each day required topics to fill it. Lotte had written back with things far more compelling: their four-year-old, Mendy, had remembered to flush the toilet twice in the last three days; Elena, their cook, had experimented with Spanish rice (a gesture of solidarity for an absent father—not a success); Sascha, his brother, had inexplicably come calling—it was three years since they had last spoken. Lotte reminded Georg that she had never been fond of his brother. And finally Nikolai, Hoffner's father, had insulted the gardener. Something to do with the placement of a ladder. Lotte hadn't been terribly clear on the details but, save for the appearance of his brother, Hoffner was glad to hear that things were moving along at their usual pace. He would be home soon enough. Until then, he would continue to live for her letters. He started to write.

> My love,
>
> Have I mentioned it's hot? Very hot, and they seem to think
> that water makes you less of a man. I wouldn't mind it so

much, but I get thirsty from time to time and they offer wine or whiskey, and I find myself no less thirsty. Can you imagine it? (I hope you're laughing. I need to know I'm still wonderfully funny and charming to you.)

I smell awful. There's no reason to bathe (see water reference above). And yet, among the other journalists, I'm one of the few I can actually bear the smell of. There's a nice Frenchman who I think has an unlimited stash of women's perfume, and I'm coming close to asking him for some, but several Czechs have asked him to dance, so I think I'll hold off on that for as long as I can.

I ate bull's tail yesterday. Thick brown sauce. A little like brisket but stringier. And then apples, I think, in the same sauce. Not quite as effective. The whiskey was a help there.

I miss you—terribly. I'm amazed I've waited this long to say it. And Mendy. I try not to think about that. I suppose he's still trying to be very brave, but I do hope there have been some tears. Selfish of me, I know, but at least that way I can think I'm not forgotten (yes, there are always a few lines of self-pity in here, so you'll just have to bear with me—you always do).

Still, I am finding it fascinating here. All these idealists pretending to be athletes. I suppose it makes some sort of point. They're all very kind to me when they find out I'm a German. Brave German, they say. That'll show Hitler. Of course I don't tell them I work for an English company, or that I'm a Jew. I think it would deflate me a little in their estimation, and you always get a better reel of film and interview when they think more of you than they should.

As for being a Jew, no one cares here. It's almost as if I'd forgotten what that was like. You say you're a Jew, and they say, Oh, and then move on as if you've asked for the salt. There are the few who realize I'm a German, and the pieces start to click together, but for the most part, there's nothing more to it.

Can you remember what life was like when that was true? Can you imagine raising a son without having to explain that? They manage it here quite wonderfully, even with their aversion to water. Excuses aside, your father and I will have to sit down and have that talk when I get back. It can't go on. Is he still thinking the racial laws will be recalled? Is he still trying to stay as quiet as he can? Does he still shake at night?

I'm sorry. I don't mean to be so shrill about your father, but you and I both know the time has come.

Did I mention it's hot? And that I miss you—desperately. It is desperation. I love you beyond all measure. I'm a fool to go away as often as I do. So let's all go away.

I've been told I'm trying *suquet* tonight. No idea what it is. Maybe fish or potatoes. Think of me when you eat.

Your Georgi

He folded the letter and placed a wrapped piece of chocolate inside for Mendy. He would post it on his way up to the park. He checked his watch. He had time for a nap.